Prince Of Deception

A Myths of Airren Novel

Jenny Hickman

Midnight Tide
PUBLISHING

Published by Midnight Tide Publishing.

www.midnighttidepublishing.com

Book Title / Jenny Hickman- 1st ed.

Paperback ISBN: 978-1-953238-95-5

Hardcover ISBN: 978-1-953238-96-2

Cover design by Cover Dungeon

Character art by Lauren Richelieu

Pronunciation Guide

Gancanagh-(*gan•cawn•ah*)

Padraig- (*pa•drec*)

Tadhg- (*tie•g*)

Rían- (*ree•un*)

Fiadh- (*fee•ah*)

Ruairi- (*ror•ee*)

Áine- (*awn•ya*)

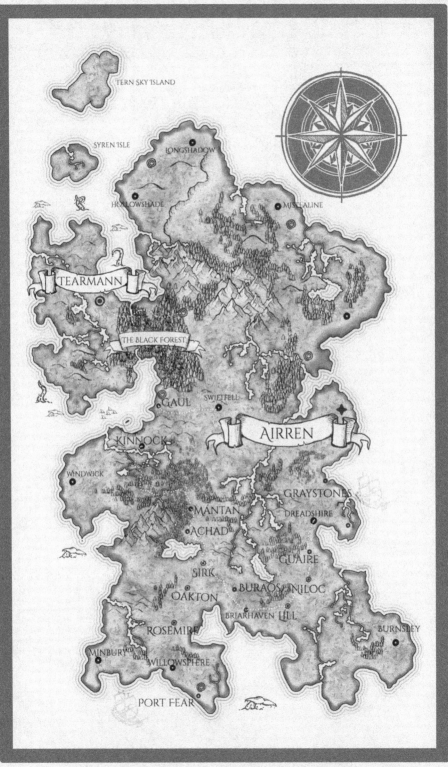

For those of us
who love the
wicked ones

PROLOGUE

Hearts can't be stolen.

At least that's what I used to think.

Until I met her.

By "her," I meant the woman lying next to me, with hair of fire spilling across the snowy white pillowcase, tickling my collarbone. Lashes fluttering like a butterfly's wings. Pink lips curved into the perfect bow. I held my breath, waiting for the moment Leesha's mossy green eyes would open and find mine.

If her father discovered us together, he'd have my head. The threat of a lowly human farmer wielding a garden hoe was nothing compared to what would happen if my mother found out about the two of us.

"You're meant for greatness, Rían. I've seen it."

Witches and their "sight." The Phantom Queen could keep her greatness. All I wanted was the angel sleeping next to me.

Sunlight leaked from beneath the closed door, glimmering like an iridescent bubble when it met the ward I'd created last night. My soundproof tost kept our even breaths and mingling heartbeats silent from passersby, ensuring no one would disturb us in our world of sheets and skin.

Leesha turned, raising her arms toward the headboard in a

slow, languid stretch. Her shy smile left my heart ramming against my ribcage. If she wanted the world, I would give it to her. All she needed to do was ask.

"Happy birthday, Rían," she said in a voice thick with sleep, her accent more lilting than humans from Airren's eastern coast. Was it any wonder? Her family lived so close to the Tearmann border you could practically spit on the Forest from her front stoop.

Leesha's short nail needled my side. "Did you hear me? I said happy birthday."

Nineteen years in the face of eternity wasn't anything to boast about. Still, if Leesha wished to celebrate the occasion, I'd start with nuzzling her neck and tasting the way her pulse hummed against my lips. "Thank you."

The heat from her sigh ruffled my undoubtedly disheveled hair. The mahogany strands could do with a cut. A task that could wait until later. First, I had a woman to ravish.

"I need to get up," Leesha murmured even as one long leg hitched around my hips, pressing me closer.

"Do you, now?"

"Mmmm hmmm. If I don't help Mother with breakfast, I'll be expected to help with dinner. And seeing as I have plans with a certain suitor . . ." Her weak protest melted into a soft moan the moment I shifted my hips in line with hers.

"Should I be jealous of this suitor?" I managed, already so hard I was fit to burst.

"He is quite handsome."

"How handsome?"

Fingers threaded through my hair, tugging me forward. "The most handsome man I've ever met."

"*And?*"

"And he has a heart of gold."

I huffed a laugh. My heart was more likely to be made of soot than gold, but if she wanted to see the best in me, who was I to set her straight? "*And?*"

"And he is a prince."

"A prince, you say? How can I ever hope to compete?"

She giggled, blinking up at me through hooded eyes. "Don't worry. He's also young and foolish."

"Not as young as he was yesterday."

"Rían . . ." She drew me closer, grinding her soft center against me. "We can't . . ."

"No?" I urged my hips forward, answering her call.

"Mmmm . . . I really should get up." The room around us went hazy when she guided me into her heat. If the world ended right now, I'd go to my death with a smile on my face.

"Off first, my love. Then up."

Despite all the books I'd read on physical intimacy, I'd been grossly unprepared for my first time with Leesha. Seeing as it was her first time as well, we'd found our way together. Six months later, we were getting pretty good at it, if I said so myself. I had to think about other things to keep from losing control too quickly. Didn't always work. Like right now. Counting the knots on her wooden headboard each time I thrust wasn't dulling the sensations as it had last night.

Her throaty moans weren't helping either.

Leesha unhooked my hand from its death-grip on the sheets, pushing it down past her navel. "Touch me."

I slowed my movements, forcing myself to focus on something besides the tension ratcheting up my spine. "Show me where."

She guided my hand to a spot just above where we joined. "Like this," she whispered.

I couldn't tell if I was pressing too hard or not hard enough. And with me focusing on that one spot, my hips had lost all sense of rhythm. "Is this . . . is this right?"

A smile played on her lips. "Yes."

"Should I go faster?" I felt like I should go faster.

"It's perfect."

The way her back arched gave me the opportunity to lather some attention on her breasts. I heard the change in her breathing. Felt the tightening of her body around mine. Watched the haze of pleasure wash over her features. "Did you—"

"Yes."

Oh, thank feck. It took about ten seconds to chase my own ending, leaving me shuddering and collapsing onto the bed next to her, our chests heaving in sync.

She brushed the hair out of my eyes. "We're getting really good at that."

"I don't know. I think we could use some more practice."

Her laughter was like sparks of sunlight.

Far too quickly, she kicked away the covers, rolled off the mattress, and cleaned the evidence of our lovemaking from her creamy white thighs using a linen towel. I watched her flit between the dresser and bed, my senses slowly returning, until I, too, got up and dragged on my own clothes with leaden limbs.

With no mirror in the cramped space, I had to rely on Leesha to get my cravat tied correctly. I'd offered to buy her a mirror before, but she'd refused. Maybe I'd give her one as a birthday gift when she turned twenty-one in two months.

Dressed in a simple lavender linen dress and white smock, Leesha wrapped her arms around my neck, pressing her head to my chest. "I'll see you tonight, yeah?"

I held her close, wishing I didn't have to say goodbye. "I already can't wait." But we didn't have a choice. Not yet, at least. When Leesha's sister was old enough to take over her duties on the farm, we would escape this island and never look back. "My brother will meet you at half seven. Don't be late."

"I love you, Rían."

The taste of her truth tingled on the back of my tongue. "Not as much as I love you," I whispered, pressing a kiss to her temple before disbanding the ward and evanescing back to the pit I called home.

Raging waves pummeled the cliffs below the onyx castle, the place hope and dreams came to die. I made my way along the path, trying to keep dirt from dusting over the tops of my black boots lest I be forced to spend my afternoon polishing them. Before I reached the high black gates, I withdrew the ceremonial dagger my father had given me. The locks and wards required blood to enter, a fun little treat every time I arrived home.

I cut my palm, watching deep red well from the wound—the only bit of color in this hell—and letting it drip onto the lock. The wards tickled against my skin, letting me slip past without additional bloodshed.

Two guards stood like statues on either side of the arched door facing the wasteland known as our front garden. Not even their eyes peeked from behind their black masks, making me wonder if they were actually people or some hideous monsters my mother had spelled to do her bidding.

My shoulders tightened when I crossed the threshold into the white marble foyer. *Princes don't slouch.* Never mind my brother slouched and slumped like a beggar, and his mother, my aunt Bronagh, hadn't given out to him once.

Tadhg could do no wrong.

I, on the other hand, could do no right.

"Where have you been?" a voice called.

I bit back my groan, turning toward the parlor to find the Queen sitting in one of the two wingback chairs in front of a barren fireplace, her spine never touching the cushion at her back. Heaven forbid she find comfort in her own home. Today, her mahogany hair had been plaited, draped over one shoulder to fall down the front of her—*surprise, surprise*—black dress.

"Good morning, Mother."

Her nose wrinkled as she scanned me from head to toe. Black veins protruded from the backs of her hands where she tapped the chair's arm. "Your cravat is crooked."

I straightened it as best I could while she continued looking on in disapproval. My hands dropped to my sides as I waited for her dismissal, doing my best not to fidget with the gold buttons on my waistcoat.

Inky black eyes returned to mine. "Who is she?"

"To whom are you referring?" I asked.

"The woman you've been rutting with."

Silence was my shield against this sort of interrogation. A lie would be punished. But so would the truth.

The Queen shoved to her feet, meeting my gaze head-on. "Come with me."

I waited to roll my eyes until she'd swept past, lest she take them as she'd threatened to for years. The two shadow guards now waited in the barren courtyard, a bound man kneeling between them, a burlap sack over his head.

Brilliant. Murder for breakfast. *Happy birthday to me.*

"This human was caught over the northern border," my mother announced, eyes never wavering from where I stood.

Grinding my teeth together, I withdrew my dagger. Humans knew better than to breach the wasteland separating Airren from Tearmann without my mother's permission or a sacrifice. They knew better, and yet they did it anyway.

"Did you cross the border?" I asked, struggling to match my mother's detached, indifferent tone. This was someone's son. Maybe someone's brother. Maybe someone's father.

The man's head lifted inside the burlap sack. "I did."

I inhaled the terrible yet familiar air laced with the smell of death, searching for the sweet tang of a lie but tasting only truth.

I adjusted my grip on the dagger's hilt, focusing on the gleaming silver blade reflecting the gray clouds overhead. Before I could do what was expected of me, my mother clicked her fingers. One of the guards yanked on the hood, revealing a man with thinning gray hair and eyes the color of a stormy sea.

The countless other times I'd been forced to do this, my mother had never removed the hood. Why now? Why today, of all days, did I have to see the life and defiance in this stranger's eyes? Both of which I was about to claim as payment for the death tax.

Knowing the consequences of balking at my duty would be far worse than getting on with it, I caught the man's forehead and drew the blade across his throat. His heavy body slumped onto the black earth, a final gurgling breath escaping before he fell as still as the cursed black trees beyond the gate. Another *click* of my mother's fingers sent the guard bending forward with a golden chalice to catch the old man's blood.

My tongue tingled when he held it toward me.

And I hated it.

The Queen descended from a long line of Abartach, ancient witches who drew additional power from blood. Although my father was fae, I'd inherited too many of my mother's traits. Probably had something to do with being stuck here with her three weeks out of every month. Since meeting Leesha, I'd abstained. I couldn't stop the killing. But this—I could keep myself from doing this.

When I didn't reach for the chalice, my mother ripped it from the guard's gloved hand, watching me through narrowed eyes as she drank deeply before shifting it away, freeing her hand so she could press it to the dead man's back. As she slowly inhaled, some of the more pronounced wrinkles across her brow smoothed. Considering his age, the human wouldn't have enough life force to erase her crow's feet.

I shifted a handkerchief to clean my blade, careful to keep the blood from dripping on my boots. "Is that all you needed?"

"For now. I expect you at dinner tonight."

"I have plans."

"Cancel them."

I didn't want to cancel them. Still, I nodded. "I'll have to tell Tadhg."

She gave a dismissive wave, stepping over the dead man's crusty boots and sauntering back toward the castle with the feathers of her skirt fluttering across the dirt-crusted ground.

Of all the days for her to insist on sharing a meal together, why did it have to be today? I'd been looking forward to celebrating at my father's castle, with Tadhg and Leesha. With the harvest coming in, there was no telling when Leesha would have another evening free.

With a curse, I stomped through the warded gates to evanesce. My mother was so feckin' paranoid someone would try and break into her fortress that she continually strengthened the feckin' things. No one was foolish enough to challenge her for her throne. And who would want it, anyway? Having to live in this cursed place, being responsible for guarding the Forest morning, noon, and night. It sounded like hell to me.

Not that my opinion mattered. As the Queen's only offspring, inheriting this vile place was my birthright. One I hoped to never claim.

With a burst of magic, I found myself standing amid emerald-green fields, the salty perfume of a summer's breeze replacing rancid death. Sea birds cawed above, dancing to the sound of the waves beyond.

The gray stones of my father Prince Midir's castle stood like a fortress against the backdrop of a crystal-clear sky. I marched toward the gates, the tightness in my chest loosening with each step. None of the people leaving waved at me. In the courtyard, two women with children tugging at their skirts stopped their conversation to whisper as I passed. The only person who smiled was the merrow sunning herself on the edge of the fountain, the scales of her green tail glittering. I made my way around the back, past the gardens and the dungeon entrance to a small stone staircase.

The kitchens always smelled like fresh pastries and sugar. The very same as the plump woman with curly gray hair springing from beneath a white mop cap, bobbling from the stove to the fireplace. When she heard me, she whirled. Her dark blue skirts were dusted with floury handprints. "Little Rían. Yer early!" Eava flicked her wrist, replacing the half-iced chocolate cake on the table with a suspiciously upturned wooden crate. "How's my birthday boy?"

"Miserable."

She evanesced to my side, catching my face in between her hands. "What's wrong?"

Sighing, I sank onto one of the high stools. "Besides being the spawn of a murderous witch?"

"What'd she do now?" Eava sighed.

"Doesn't matter." What was the point in dwelling on it when I couldn't change it? "Where's Tadhg?"

"He and Ruairi are around here somewhere."

Ruairi was Tadhg's new best mate. Ever since he'd come along, he'd stolen all of Tadhg's attention. I didn't see what was so great about him. He was just a feckin' pooka. Sure, he could shapeshift into different animals, but so could I, and Tadhg had never been impressed.

"Don't you worry." Eava gave my shoulder a pat, cursing and cleaning the flour she'd left behind. "Tadhg will be here as soon as he smells what I've baked. Not that he'll be getting any before yer party."

"I'm afraid there won't be a party. Mother has requested I dine with her this evening."

Eava's wispy gray eyebrows slammed down over her black eyes. "That selfish old crow. I really ought to—"

I used my magic to catch her next words before she could say them. There was no telling which servants in this castle had ties to the Queen. While everyone on either side of the border feared her, many of the Danú revered her as some sort of goddess, keeping them safe from the terrible, terrible humans.

Sure, some of the humans were terrible, but some of them were good too. Like Leesha and her family, guardians of the border portal near the Forest.

Tadhg appeared in the doorway, nose lifted toward the beamed ceiling, his unkempt dark hair curling around his pointed ears. "Do I smell cake?" A fork appeared in his hand.

"'Tis fer yer brother." Eava whapped him on the knuckles, stealing the shifted fork.

Tadhg evanesced around her, removing the crate concealing my cake with a flourish.

Eava shifted a wooden spoon and lifted it above her head. "Don't you dare—"

Tadhg's green eyes glittered when he grinned at me. "Rían doesn't mind, do you, Rían?" Eava paused mid-swipe, looking to me for confirmation. "This is considered dessert, is it not?"

Why the hell had I thought it was a good idea to bet my brother I could best him in a race to the shore? My foolishness had cost me my portion of dessert for six months.

"It's fine, Eava."

Another fork appeared in Tadhg's hand, and he threw himself onto the stool next to me. My heart sank as I watched that fork sink into the three layers of cake and frosting before disappearing into my brother's gawping mouth.

Eava's spoon rattled on the table. She glowered at Tadhg until he sighed.

A white plate appeared next to him, and he slopped a bit onto the plate before pushing it toward me. "Here. Don't say I never gave you anything for your birthday."

Feck it anyway. I didn't want to dine with my mother. I wanted to stay here with Leesha and Tadhg and Eava. I checked the time on Eava's clock beside a basket of dirty potatoes. "Can you collect her early?" I asked, determined to salvage a bit of this day. If Tadhg retrieved Leesha now, we could have a bit of a party before I had to return to the Forest.

"Why?" Tadhg asked around a bite of cake, crumbs spilling all over the table.

Eava smacked him in the side of the head.

"Ugh. Fine." He rubbed his temple. "Don't touch this. It's mine." The idiot created a ward around the cake, kissed Eava on the cheek, and started for the door.

I spent the next two minutes trying to break the ward. Eava smirked, flicked her wrist, and the entire thing dissolved. Laughing, I piled more cake onto my plate. Tadhg appeared a moment later, stealing the plate right out of my hands. "She said no."

My mother had said no? She never said no. "Why?"

Tadhg shrugged and resumed eating. "I asked if I could bring a human into and out of the Forest, and she said not today."

"Did you tell Leesha?"

"Went straight away afterwards," he mumbled around a mouthful. "She was not impressed. Said she had a surprise for you."

By the time I left, I felt a little less miserable. But that didn't last for long because the moment I cut my hand and crossed the wards, the Queen appeared on the steps. "Where have you been?"

None of your business. "Eava made me a cake."

Her dark brows arched toward the black crown she'd added to her ensemble from this morning. "Whatever for?"

"My birthday."

"Oh, is that today?" A smile appeared on her lips that left my stomach sinking. My mother's smiles only meant one thing. "Well, then it is a coincidence that I have a lovely present for you." She snapped her fingers at one of the guards, who quickly disappeared behind the castle doors.

The last time my mother had given me a present was for my fifth birthday. A long-haired kitten I'd named Sir Fluffy Paws. I'd loved that little runt even though he pissed on the rug constantly. On my sixth birthday, she'd thrown Sir Fluffy Paws off the cliff.

"Attachments lead to weakness," she'd announced over my wailing sobs as the waves claimed my tiny companion. "And a prince cannot afford to be weak."

The guard returned, towing something behind him.

Not something.

Someone.

A girl with red hair and moss-green eyes, gagged and bound and thrown at my feet like she was nothing.

I tried to swallow, but there was a boulder in my throat.

"I caught this human crossing the Forest without permission," my mother crooned. "She says she was going to the castle."

By some miracle, I kept my face an impassive mask despite a cold sweat breaking out across my brow, leaving me trembling in my boots. Leesha knew to wait for me or Tadhg. I'd warned her time and again what would happen if she went into the Forest on her own. What had she been thinking?

"I've seen her there," I said. "She's been meeting with Tadhg." Not a lie, but a careful truth. She had been meeting with Tadhg . . . until I arrived.

"One of your brother's many simpering fans, is she?" My mother pursed her lips, scowling at Leesha as tears tumbled down my beloved's freckled cheekbones and a choked sob escaped from behind the gag.

I could only nod. In truth, Leesha thought Tadhg arrogant and conceited. Not many people could see through his false smiles, but she had. I'd let myself fall in love with her that day, the day I knew she wouldn't leave me for him.

"You know the rule for crossing the Forest without my permission, girl?" my mother said in a soft voice, kneeling beside Leesha to untie the gag. "One life." She shushed Leesha as she sobbed, using her thumb to wipe the tears from her cheeks.

I wanted to scream. To rail. To feckin' beg. I stood there on trembling legs, unable to draw air into my lungs.

My mother's eyes met mine. "Well? What are you waiting for?" She appeared at my back, whispering in my ear, "Do it."

I withdrew my dagger from its sheath, my clammy hands making it impossible to get a decent grip.

Sharp nails bit into my forearm. *"Do it."*

My dagger clattered to the ground. "No."

"She's not Tadhg's at all, is she?" the Queen said. "She's yours." She shifted the dagger, plunging the blade into my abdomen. Pain exploded through my body, but I didn't dare cry out, not when Leesha screamed loud enough for the both of us. "You are nothing more than a weak, pathetic fool." The Queen twisted the blade, blood running like tiny rivers down her pale hands. "Your human broke the rules and must suffer the consequences. *Do it.*" She withdrew the dagger, forcing it into my palm. "Do it!"

"Mother, please," I choked. Heat from my magic knitted together my torn flesh. "I will do anything you wish. Anything, I swear it. Just let her go."

She sighed as if this was the heaviest burden to bear, when I knew—I feckin' *knew*—that deep down, she rejoiced at having found my weakness.

"Don't harm her. Please. *Please.*" An invisible force tightened around my torso, binding my arms to my sides. My knees finally unlocked, and I tried to rush forward and throw myself at her mercy. More magic cinched my legs together, sending me face-first into the blood-splattered dust. My mother knelt beside Leesha, her soulless eyes fixed on me as she whispered a spell that haunted my dreams, drawing from the endless well of dark magic that had consumed her long ago.

The fingers on her right hand began to glow like a branding iron. With a malicious smile, she flayed the skin at Leesha's breast, the sound of my love's screams ripping me apart.

I twisted. Writhed. The bonds tightened. I couldn't get free. Couldn't get to Leesha. Couldn't save her.

With the bloody cross drawn, the Queen pressed her fingertips into Leesha's wound and tore her still-beating heart from her chest. Blood oozed down her wrist, chasing the black veins to her elbow.

Leesha slumped, her green eyes open to the clouds above.

My bonds vanished just as a desperate cry left my throat. The Queen pressed a hand to my love's shoulder and inhaled.

"*No . . . no no no no no.*" I crawled forward, my breeches snagging on ancient bones, slicing my skin. The pain was nothing compared to the unending ache in my chest.

"Take mine too," I choked. "Take it! *Take it!*" Our hearts were one and the same. A life without Leesha wasn't a life worth living.

My mother turned to me.

Smiled.

And stole my heart.

I awoke on a settee in the parlor, my breaths the only sound in the silent room. I rolled upright, rubbing at my sore head, aching like the time Tadhg had convinced me to drink an entire bottle of wine and made me look like a fool in front of Ruairi. They'd laughed and laughed as I heaved my dinner into the blackberry bushes along the cliff walk.

I checked my reflection in the gilt-framed mirror leaning against the wall. My stark white shirt gaped at the neck, the corner of a scar peeking from between the open buttons. I pressed the heel of my palm to my chest only to find more silence.

The Queen appeared at my back, onyx crown reflecting the dull sunlight.

I remembered the nightmare. My finger traced the scar. *Not a nightmare.*

"Come with me," she ordered.

As if I'd follow her anywhere after what she'd done.

She flicked her wrist. In the reflection, I watched as blackness invaded my eyes. I had no control over my feet as she crooked her finger, forcing me to follow her through the marble hallway, down the staircase, and out into the gray light of morning to where a young woman with strawberry-blond curls sat cross-legged on the steps. A young woman I knew.

Leesha's sister.

I waited for the pain to come, but all I felt was hollow, like the Queen had scooped out my innards, leaving an empty vessel for darkness.

"She was caught crossing the Forest," said the Queen.

I could taste the truth in the witch's words. Still, I had to ask, "Did you cross?"

"Yes," the young woman sniffled, "but only to find my sister. She's missing since last night and—"

I cut off the girl's useless excuse with a swipe of my blade, taking her life as payment for the Queen's tax, vowing one day to do the same to the witch who had destroyed my world.

1

SHE DIDN'T KNOW MY REAL NAME.

She'd never seen my real face.

And she wanted me to fuck her in a shed.

Those three things summed up my "relationship" with Eithne O'Meara.

I stepped around the bench and table in the blacksmith's old tool shed, careful not to disturb the layer of dust covering everything. Sneezing and sniffling and watery eyes weren't exactly a recipe for seduction. I'd offered to meet Eithne in her husband's mansion overlooking the seaside. Unfortunately, she preferred our dalliances more . . . What had she called it?

Ah, yes. Seedy.

I was a prince in my world, not beloved like my brother but certainly feared and respected. In this world, I may as well have been the dirt on this disgusting wooden floor.

The soft sigh of misty rain kissed the shed's slate roof. Quick footsteps from the humans outside darted this way and that in a pointless attempt to avoid getting wet. The steady *clip clop* of horse's hooves grew louder as they approached Graystone's market square.

Eithne would want to hurry it on. I had things to do.

Thinking of her made my stomach revolt. I wouldn't have touched the woman if it wasn't absolutely necessary. I put duty above everything else, knowing all too well what would happen if I didn't.

I shifted my pocket watch to check the time. A gift left to me by my father when he passed.

Passed.

A polite way of saying "gutted in his sleep by a cursed dagger." The old fae prince had had no more fondness for me than I did Eithne. He'd only left me his watch and cufflinks out of guilt for abandoning me in the Forest.

I needed to be in Rosemire by half past if I wanted to make the trial. *Trial.* A polite way of saying "pre-execution."

I would have left without seeing Eithne, except I needed to know when more soldiers were to arrive from Vellana. Something was brewing, I could feel it in my gut. And Eithne was my key to learning what it was.

Her husband, and Graystones' magistrate, served as the Vellanian king's eyes and ears on the East Coast. His wife had a loose tongue. A tongue she jammed into my mouth as if she wanted to make sure my tonsils were still there.

A year ago, mass executions had been few and far between. Now, they were more common than not. I'd tried explaining my concerns to my brother. As usual, Tadhg either had his head buried in a bottle or his cock buried in a woman. The man blamed his curse for his uselessness.

We were all cursed. Every last one of us.

Drinking himself delirious wasn't going to fix it. Not that I could tell him that when he was in one of his moods. *His moods.* That's what Ruairi and Eava called his month-long binges. All Tadhg had to do was find a woman to love his drunk arse and he'd be free.

Some of us didn't have that luxury.

The door opened. There was a flash of light. A flurry of skirts.

A woman's heavy breathing.

"You're late." I said it with a smile to keep Eithne from hearing the hate on my tongue.

Eithne's breathing hitched. I could hear her hammering heart like the beat of a bodhran, no doubt sending a wealth of blood rushing south. She smelled different today, like raindrops on rose petals. If she weren't so revolting, I may have liked it. I had her pinned against the shed wall before she could give me some excuse. There wasn't time for that.

Her hips didn't feel as bony as they usually did. Or her arse. She didn't grab for me, either. The last thing I needed was for her to start showing restraint.

My mouth met her rose-scented skin. And burned.

Eithne whimpered.

The sound was too high. Too sweet. Too nervous.

I jerked back, ramming into the feckin' table, sending whatever was on top crashing to the floor.

Not Eithne. Not Eithne. Not Eithne.

Shit. Shit. Shit.

"Why have you come?" I demanded. "Who sent you?" And where the hell was Eithne? I scrubbed my mouth with my sleeve, still burning burning *burning*.

"No one sent me," clipped a high voice. The woman's posh accent held a hint of Vellana, slight but definitely there. "Next time, plan your trysts someplace with a little more light."

Accosting a woman was a capital offense. If she reported me, I'd meet the wrong end of a hangman's noose. It wouldn't matter that it had been an accident. A misunderstanding. A case of being in the wrong place at the wrong time. How many times had I heard those excuses cried at the foot of the dais? How many times had I ignored them?

My mind screamed for me to evanesce, but the worthless hole in my chest begged me to stay. The hollowness living inside me almost never spoke. When it did, I listened.

I flicked my wrist, conjuring a ball of flame in my palm.

Heart-shaped face. Freckles across the bridge of a pert nose. Golden curls that I could imagine slipping through my fingers. Fisting. Pulling so I could taste the nectar living on the column of her throat. Magnificent chest heaving beneath a dark cloak.

Good. Pure. Unblemished.

Forbidden.

Her ice-blue eyes reflected my dumbfounded expression. And my face.

Feck it all. My glamour had slipped. No one outside Tearmann saw my true face unless I allowed it.

"Who are you?" she whispered through full lips that turned down slightly at the corners, not in a frown but a perpetual pout.

"I am whoever you want me to be." Her slave. Her puppet. Her prince. All she had to do was say the word and I could become the thing she wanted most.

Her eyes narrowed. "The only thing I want you to be is gone."

I could do that too. A flick of my wrist and I could be all the way across the feckin' country. I would've. I should've. Only the hollowness echoed for me to stay.

"I was here first." And since I was here and she was here, we may as well be here together.

"Fine. I'll go." She walked away, and I had to have a serious chat with my feet to keep from following her. I wasn't the type of man to go running after some woman, even one as beautiful as her.

"Oisin?" a grating voice hissed from outside the shed. "Are you in there?"

Eithne had the worst feckin' timing. I couldn't do what I needed with her with this gorgeous creature watching. I suppose I *could*, but I didn't want this stranger who tasted like roses getting the wrong idea—even though the "wrong idea" happened to be the truth. But it wasn't the whole truth.

The hinges on the door creaked open.

Run. Run. Run.

Stay. Stay. Stay.

I grabbed the mysterious woman's cloak and pulled her with me to the other side of a high wooden bench. "Not a word," I whispered, my lips still burning from whatever she'd used on her skin. Damn, she was beautiful. I'd known plenty of beautiful women. This one, though. This one would be a feckin' master-piece stripped bare. Curves and softness and pouty pink lips.

"Oisin?" Eithne's footsteps drew ever closer.

The soldiers. The king. I could deal with them another day. This woman? I wanted to deal with her now.

"Eithne? Where'd you go, pet?" a man called, his voice weak and gravelly. Strong Vellanian accent. He held onto the "o" in "go" a touch longer than most. *Where did you gooo, pet?* He sounded like an insufferable prick. No wonder she'd been so easily seduced.

Eithne grumbled a curse. Her boots thumped against the wood when she stomped back toward the door. Sounds of the town swelled, then faded.

"That was close," I said with a laugh, relieved and, for some reason, a little nervous. I wiped my clammy hands on my knees.

Instead of returning my conspiratorial smile, the woman got up, dusted off her skirts, and started for the door. I jumped to my feet, ramming into the feckin' bench. "You're leaving?" I didn't know why I'd asked. It was fairly feckin' obvious when she slipped out the door without another word.

The shed felt empty. The *world* felt empty.

From a crack between the wooden slats, I watched her mount a brown mare and turn toward the road leading out of town.

My fingers grazed over my lips.

I should leave and never return.

I should put her out of my mind.

And I would.

But first, I wanted to know her name.

Being in this decrepit country without a glamour felt like standing in the middle of a busy city square without a stitch of clothing on. All this feckin' rain wasn't helping, either. Was there anything worse? Death was probably worse, but once it was over, you were free. But rain? It seeped into your clothes and socks. Settled into your bones.

Don't even get me started on mud.

I hated wasting magic on creating a ward, but I hated wet socks more. And sitting in a tree waiting for the human to reach me ensured my boots remained mud-free. There was only one road in and out of Graystones, the fork just below my perch. I turned my head, listening with my good ear for the sound of hooves on wet earth.

There.

Coming this way. And fast.

I smiled. Not because I was excited about meeting the human again. What use did I have for another one of those? Still, something about her intrigued me. I traced my lips, thinking about the way they'd burned. Witch hazel? No. I'd have smelled it on her. Unless she concealed it in the rose oil she obviously used on her soft, supple skin—

A fat raindrop splatted on my forehead.

I shook away the fanciful thought, focusing on pouring more magic into my shield against the elements and on the increasing volume of the hooves, until a woman with golden hair and a billowing cloak came into view.

Just before she reached me, I sent a bolt of magic toward the horse, freezing its limbs.

The beast came to an abrupt halt, and the woman flew forward, damp curls slapping her cheeks. She looked around, presumably searching for what had spooked her horse.

She still hadn't noticed me sitting right above her. Beautiful *and* unobservant. I kicked my feet in front of me. Her head swung around, and she had to catch herself on the saddle to keep from careening headfirst into the mud and cracking her skull. *Not* a fun way to die.

I catalogued the emotions flitting across her face: Confusion. Realization. Irritation.

"You never told me your name," I said by way of greeting, cleaning a smudge from the top button on my waistcoat. How the hell had it gotten so dirty? Damned dusty shed. Next time Eithne said she wanted to meet, it'd be on my terms.

The woman's chin lifted ever so slightly. "You never asked."

Ah, yes. How rude of me. "My mouth was otherwise occupied."

Despite the layer of makeup she wore, I could see her cheeks flush a deep, dusky rose. "My name is Lady Aveen Bannon, daughter of Lord Michael Bannon."

Bannon. Bannon. Bannon. I'd heard that name somewhere. Shipping manifests, perhaps? No matter. I'd find out soon enough. *Aveen.* "Radiant beauty."

Her eyes narrowed as they dragged from my hair to the soles of my boots. "Do you say that to all the women?"

"Only the ones called Aveen. It's what your name means." Living for eternity left one filled with such useless knowledge.

"And what does Oisin mean?"

Ah, so she'd caught Eithne calling me by the false name, which meant she'd been paying attention. "Oisin means 'little deer.' But that's not my real name." She may have seen my face, but knowing my name was an entirely different story.

The horse stamped its hoof, spraying mud across the already dirty hem on Aveen's cloak. "It was a pleasure meeting you, not-Oisin," she said. "But I'm afraid I must be on my way."

The air between us sweetened. I'd have bet my boots she was lying. Before I could call her out, Aveen knocked her heels against the horse's sides, and the beast lurched forward.

Wasn't she the least bit intrigued by me? I was a feckin' prince.

Not that she would know that, but she could've gleaned that I was well off from the black waistcoat with solid gold buttons that I'd spent a fortune on. And I'd made it pretty feckin' clear that I was powerful.

Did she not find me attractive? Was that the problem? Plenty of Danú women found me handsome. Not as handsome as my brother, but who could compete with a fantasy? I couldn't even blame her dismissal on a bad glamour.

She didn't like me.

Me.

I refused to let that stand.

I evanesced to the center of the road, determined to set the world to rights and leave this irritating human thinking of me long into the night.

The horse came to another neck-breaking halt. A quiet curse punctuated Aveen's low hiss.

"Where are you off to in such a rush?" I asked.

The human had the gall to roll her eyes. "Home. It's getting late, and I don't want to miss dinner." When I caught the horse's bridle, Aveen's frown dipped into a full-on scowl. "If you'll kindly get out of my way, I'm soaked to the bone and would hate to catch a cold."

"Aren't you even a little bit curious as to who I am?" A thousand questions hung on the tip of my tongue. What was her favorite dessert? Her favorite color? Her hopes and dreams and fears? What color was her stay? Would she consider showing it to me? What sounds would she make if I snatched her off that horse and pinned her against the soggy bark on that tree over there?

"Not curious enough to miss dinner." She kicked her horse once more and galloped away, golden curls flying behind her until she disappeared around the bend.

The nerve of that obstinate human. Dismissing *me*. ME. As if I were nothing more than an inconvenience, not even worth missing dinner over. *She* was the inconvenience. I didn't have time to waste on someone so weak and pathetic and . . .

Dammit.

I'd been so distracted that I'd dropped my ward, and now my boots and clothes were splattered with mud.

That feckin' woman . . .

She'd ruined my favorite breeches.

2

THE AIR INSIDE THE CASTLE HAD BEEN TOO STIFLING TONIGHT, SO we'd shifted our chairs and settee down to the beach to drink by the light of the moon. I hadn't been thrilled when Tadhg suggested it, but Ruairi always sided with him, so I lost the vote. The beach was grand, but I'd be finding sand everywhere for the next month.

Ruairi tilted his glass toward me, moonlight glinting off the dark liquid within. "I can hit ye so hard it'll knock ye off yer feet."

We'd been debating who was the strongest of the three of us. Surprise, surprise, the pooka believed he could best me. "That's a load of bollocks." He couldn't hurt a flea. Sure, he was a big fecker, but size didn't always equal strength. I'd beaten plenty of men who were bigger than me.

"Will I prove it to ye?"

Was I going to let my brother's dog hit me in the face? *Fuck it.* Why not? It wasn't like there was anything else happening tonight. I sat my drink on the low table sitting unevenly in the sand. "Go on, then. Let's see it."

Ruairi's eyes lit up like those of a child with a new toy. "Seriously?"

I nodded and lurched to my feet, readying my stance. Ruairi

bounced up from the chair, his boots sinking as he searched for solid footing, clenching and unclenching his fists.

"What do I get if I stay on my feet?" I asked.

"Bragging rights," Tadhg said from the settee, sitting upright for the first time since he'd plonked himself down two hours earlier.

I was already the most powerful man in this castle—possibly even in Tearmann. I didn't need bragging rights. "Not good enough." I needed to think of something better. Something that would piss him rightly off. "If I win, I get to cut your hair."

Ruairi's fanged smile vanished. "Ye can feck right off."

Pooka had a thing about their hair. I remembered the dog confessing something about it a few months back, when I pretended to be passed out on the settee. It was amazing the sort of shite you could learn when people thought you were unconscious.

"Then no deal." I reached for my drink ever so slowly. It was only a matter of time before Ruairi gave in. He always took a bet. Always.

His brow furrowed as he dragged his fang over his lower lip.

Five. Four. Three. Two . . .

"Sod it. If I hit ye and ye stay upright, ye can cut my hair. But ye can't use magic."

"I won't need to."

"Waaaait!" Tadhg spilled drink from the glass he apparently forgot was still in his hands. "Ruairi should get something if he wins."

"He gets to hit me. Isn't that enough?"

Ruairi and Tadhg exchanged grins before Tadhg said, "If Ruairi wins, he gets your boots."

My boots wouldn't fit him. Not that the observation would make a bit of difference once the pair of them had come to a decision. I inhaled slowly, the oaky notes from my wine tickling my tastebuds. There was really nothing to worry about because I was not going to fall. If anything, the idea of losing my boots only provided extra incentive. "Fine." I took a sip from my glass, waiting for the warmth to spread down my throat.

Then I angled my body, braced my boots in the sand, and told Ruairi to hit me.

Ruairi's fist became a blur. Lightning exploded behind my eyes. I stumbled back and back, my arms cartwheeling. It took every bit of strength I had, but I didn't fall.

Once I'd regained my balance, I laughed so loud, it echoed off the cliffs surrounding us. Blood dripped from my undoubtedly broken nose, over my lips, down my chin, and splattered on the sand. "Did you do it yet?" I muttered.

Tadhg burst out laughing, doubling over and nearly falling off the settee. Ruairi cursed, cradling his fist in his chest.

I withdrew a handkerchief to clean my throbbing nose, then shifted a pair of sheep shears from the shed back at the castle and set them on the table between us.

Ruairi cursed and threw himself onto the chair, tugging his black hair free from its queue.

"Such a shame. It's so pretty when it's down." I picked up the shears and *snip snipped* the air, drawing out the torture.

Ruairi's massive shoulders curled as he hunched like a child about to get his tooth pulled. "Just get on with it."

I kept opening and closing the shears right behind his head, stifling a laugh every time he shrank away. "If you don't hold still, it's going to be crooked." *Joke's on you, it's going to be crooked no matter what.*

Tadhg sniggered, pouring an over-large glass of puítin and handing it to his mate. "When's the last time you got a haircut?"

"The time Bromwen thought it'd be fun to use candles in the bedroom and damn near lit me on fire."

For some reason, the mention of fire sent my mind racing back to Graystones and a woman whose skin had made my mouth burn. There was something there, like a memory I couldn't quite grasp. "Say that again."

Ruairi glanced over his shoulder, glowering at the shears. "Bromwen likes to use candles?"

"Not that. The second part."

"She damn near lit me on fire?"

My fingers grazed my lips.

When I was little, I used to visit Tadhg in the castle one week a month. Before his mother was murdered by humans, she would read us stories from this hideous pink book. The title now eluded me, but I remembered a poem inside that I'd always loved. A nonsensical one about soulmates.

Tadhg and Ruairi started chatting about the kinky witch and her love of hot wax, and all their back and forth along with the infernal sloshing of waves made it hard to concentrate. "Both of you, shut up."

Ruairi spun around in his chair, levelling a thick finger at my face. A finger he was about to lose if he didn't move it in the next two seconds. "Don't tell me to—"

All it took was a burst of magic to make the irritating pooka disappear into the bowels of the castle dungeon. I never said *when* I would cut his hair. I'd catch him when he least expected it. "Tadhg, where's that book your mam used to read us?"

He eased against the cushions and stretched his arm over the back of the settee. "Which one?"

"The pink one with the princess on the front."

"How the hell should I know?"

Useless.

I left him there, evanescing back to the castle to search his mother's rooms. Tadhg probably wouldn't be impressed with me being here, but from the dust covering every square inch, I was fairly certain he'd never find out. If I wasn't careful, I'd be a swollen, snivelling mess by the time I left. Thankfully, it only took two minutes and a handful of sneezes before I located the book inside his mother's bedside locker.

I evanesced down to the study before my eyes could swell, lit the candles with magic, and sank onto the chair behind the desk.

Flicking through the pages drummed up memories of cherries. When my aunt would tell Tadhg that she loved him, the air would taste as sweet and tart as a ripe red cherry.

I remembered going home and telling the Queen that I loved her. She'd repeated the words back to me as any dutiful mother should, and yet the lie had tasted like ash.

I shook away the thought, focusing on the task at hand. In the center of the book, I found what I'd been searching for: a dog-eared page more worn than all the others.

Her lips are made of fire.
Her touch is made of flame.
I've never even met her
And yet I know her name.

She burns me from the inside out.
Still, I need her all the same.
She is the other half of me
My life, my love, my flame.

Because of a fortune I'd been told long ago, I'd wasted years researching "soulmates." From ancient lore to fairy tales in children's books, all of them said the same shite: your soulmate was your perfect match, your other half, the one you were destined to be with.

My life, my love, my flame.

I'd completely forgotten about this book because it hadn't been relevant. Until now. Could Aveen be the one I'd been "destined" to meet? No. Maybe? *No.* But if she was . . .

What was I thinking? It couldn't be her. Surely fate wouldn't curse me with a human soulmate. What hope would Aveen have of surviving what was to come? The woman was weak. Powerless. I needed someone strong. Someone who could defeat the Queen and save me. Another witch, or at the very least, a fae. Not a feckin' human.

I dragged my thumb across the poem's first line.

Her lips are made of fire.

I closed the book and shifted it into my room for safekeeping.

There was one way to know for certain.

I just needed to convince Aveen to kiss me.

According to some drunks at a pub in Graystones, Lord Michael Bannon owned the old O'Shaughnessy place on the coast.

I evanesced to the far side of a pine forest, where a long drive connected with the road. The stone manor hadn't changed much since the last time I was here, although there was a lot more red ivy climbing the walls, and the dark pitched roof had a few shingles missing.

From what I remembered, the family's quarters were located around the back. I crossed through the barren garden, stumbling upon a horse tied near the fountain. It didn't look like the one Aveen had ridden earlier. Why had someone tied the thing back here instead of leaving it in the stables?

The moment I rounded the untrimmed laurel hedges, I had my answer.

A man clung to the trellis at a back window. Aveen waited in the room above, her curls unbound and a little disheveled.

Aveen had a lover.

The realization felt like being punched by Ruairi all over again.

How was I supposed to convince her to give me the time of day if she loved someone else? She couldn't love someone else, though. Your soulmate was meant to love you and you alone.

I'd loved someone else, hadn't I? I'd loved her, and that love had cost Leesha her life.

I evanesced as close as I dared, hiding behind a tree far too thin to conceal me completely, but it was the best place to overhear their whispered conversation.

The man adjusted his grip on the windowsill, reaching for Aveen. "I care for your sister—" he said, his accent clipped and crisp. Definitely high-born. Likely Airren peerage, which made sense since Aveen was a member of the upper-class as well.

And he'd come here for Aveen's sister.

Relief fell like a misty rain, cooling my ire. Shouldn't he be at the sister's window, then?

Aveen told him it was time to go. When he protested, she threatened to scream. I wouldn't mind seeing how Lord Bannon dealt with the whinge bag. Maybe he'd have him clapped in irons and hauled down to the jail. Or maybe he'd shove the bastard off the trellis, and he'd accidentally break his neck.

When the man tried to grab Aveen's hand, she jerked back and started counting.

"No one will ever love you once they meet the miserable woman beneath all those false smiles and feigned manners," he said. "You think you know me, but I know you too—"

The window slammed shut. When she didn't lock the latch at the top, a smile tugged at my lips.

The man cursed as he descended the trellis. I shifted his horse to our paddock so he'd have to walk wherever he was headed in the dead of night. He could use a good long think about speaking to Aveen like that. I may not have had the capacity for love, but even I knew that wasn't how to win over a woman. Human men at that age were such eejits.

Aveen remained silhouetted in the window, her head slowly lifting until it appeared as though she were staring straight at me. Part of me wanted to step out of the shadows and into the soft yellow light to see what would happen.

Would she smile? Would she scream? Would she lock the window and pull the curtains tight?

I didn't give her the chance to do any of those things, remaining hidden as I called forth my magic.

Evanescing somewhere you'd never been could be tricky. You only had a split second before landing to make sure nothing—and no one—was in your way. From this angle, I could see the top of a canopy bed. When I evanesced, I ended up on the opposite side, between the bed and a closet.

The left side of the quilt had been tugged down, and the pillow above had a telltale dent.

Aveen slept on the left side of her bed.

The fact that I always slept on the right side didn't mean anything. It was a coincidence, plain and simple. Still, when I sank onto the right side, my smile grew. "Lover's quarrel?" I said.

Aveen whirled, clutching her chest when she saw me on her bed. The shadows of her legs danced beneath the modest shift she wore. Somehow, the high collar made the garment seem even more indecent as her chest rose and fell in the most delicious way. "How did *you* get in here?" she gasped.

"I evanesced."

"Evanesced?"

Ignorant human. With a flick of my wrist and a bit of magic, I appeared by the window. Aveen leapt out of her skin, stumbling into her chair with a quiet curse.

"Evanesced," I repeated. "I had planned on taking the trellis, you see, but it was otherwise occupied. You really should start locking your door. There's no telling who'll pop in."

I caught her slight wince as she rubbed her backside. If she wanted some help, I'd be more than willing to take the pain away, so long as she didn't mind my hands lingering.

"What good would that do?" she asked.

I shook away the errant thought, focusing on her question.

In truth, locking the windows and doors wouldn't do much if one of us truly wanted to enter. But if she was locked up tight, whoever evanesced beyond the door would be in breach of the law, subject to the dire consequences. Consequences I'd gladly administer.

But I didn't tell her that because it was irrelevant. "You'd be surprised."

A small figurine of a little girl in a blue dress sat on the corner of her dressing table next to a tiny porcelain bunny. She had a bottle of rose oil as well. The stuff smelled heavenly, without a hint of witch hazel.

When she asked me my name, I couldn't help but grin. It was about damned time she showed some feckin' interest. "Oisin, Colin, Ciaran, Cian, Liam, Fionn, Dara, Shay. Take your pick or call me whatever you like." I made my way over to her chair. A bit worn around the arms, like she spent a lot of time sitting there. I sat down but immediately stood again. The thing needed new springs. "Makes no difference to me," I muttered. She could call me Lady Marissa for all I cared. So long as she never learned my real name. If my mother found out what I was up to, she'd have both our heads.

"Whatever your name is, you cannot be here. You need to leave."

"First, I need a favor." *Oh!* Would you look at that. Aveen had a jewelry box painted with little pink roses. How fitting. None of the jewels inside looked too fine, most of them appeared to have faux gemstones. She did have one or two decent pieces that looked old enough. Family heirlooms, most likely.

"What sort of favor?" she asked with obvious reluctance.

Being direct was the best course of action. Still, to be so forward with a maiden could send her into hysterics. To think, someone like *me* would be requesting something so "scandalous" from a "proper" lady like *her*.

"Are you going to tell me or not?" she demanded. "It's late, and I want to go to bed."

I'd be more than up for that. The two of us tangled in those white sheets. Bodies intertwined. Waking the whole house with the sound of her headboard slamming against the wall.

"Alone," Aveen insisted through clenched teeth.

"What's the matter? Do you not find me attractive?"

"No. I don't."

Her lies tasted like the honeysuckle candy Eava used to make when we were children. Fragrant spring. Warm sun. Buzzing bees. I eased closer, savoring the roses on Aveen's skin. "Liar."

Her beautiful throat bobbed when she swallowed. "Get out of my room, or so help me, I will scream."

"But if you scream, you'll wake your poor sister."

A deep flush crept up her neck. Her sister was her weakness. *Foolish human.* Weaknesses were to be avoided at all costs. If you were stupid enough to have one, you kept it hidden.

She licked her lips, leaving them glistening in the firelight. "Tell me your favor."

"I would like you to kiss me."

Aveen stumbled back, nearly colliding with the chair a second time. "Absolutely not."

"You don't have to look so appalled. It's not like I'm asking for a feckin' ride. It's a kiss." She should've been the one begging *me*. She was nothing. No one.

"Why?"

"That is none of your concern." The less she knew about the hold she may have on me, the better.

A small wrinkle appeared between her light eyebrows. "If I agree, you must swear to go away and leave my sister and I alone forever."

If she was my soulmate, there wasn't a hope of that happening. We'd be bound together by fate. No distance, not even death, could truly separate us. "I swear on my mother's life that I will leave her alone."

She agreed too quickly to allow my actual promise to sink in. *Foolish and naïve. Feckin' brilliant.* The Queen was going to eat her alive.

Aveen closed her eyes, pursed her lips, and leaned forward.

Hold on. Had she never been kissed before? She was at least nineteen or twenty. She must've stolen a kiss or two by now. How innocent was she?

Her eyes snapped open. "Well? What are you waiting for?"

I was waiting for her to appear less like a woman about to go to her death. "You look miserable." She should *want* to kiss me. I certainly wanted to kiss her. Just the thought of feeling those soft, supple lips beneath mine made me hard. Was I wrong about our connection?

"Then tell me how I should look so that I may be rid of you. Should I smile? Should I swoon?" Her hand flew to her forehead, and she fainted dramatically onto the settee like an actress in a play. "I have it now. I should flutter my lashes and be grateful that someone so handsome would ask me for a kiss."

"So you do think I'm handsome," I teased.

Her soft blue eyes narrowed. "I think you're irritating."

"Does that mean you're going to kiss me or not?"

Her feet stomped across the wooden floor, closing the distance between us until her lips met mine.

I'd been struck my cannon fire.

I'd fallen face-first into a bed of hot coals.

I'd been burned at the stake.

I'd lived and died for centuries, but never in my life had I felt a fire like this.

I swore I felt my absent heart beat for the first time since the Queen had stolen it from me.

"Shit. *Shit.*" *No no no.* "I finally found you."

Her lips are made of fire,

Her touch is made of flame . . .

My soulmate was a feckin' human.

3

Waves crashed far below, a never-ending cycle, patiently chipping away at the impenetrable cliffs. Did they ever grow weary of their task? Did they ever wish for stillness and silence? A respite?

I stopped on the rocky path, clutching my knees, my breaths sawing in and out.

I ran to stay fit.

I ran to stay sane.

I ran to keep memories at bay.

And I ran to work off the heaping portion of venison Eava had made last night. And the two slices of apple crumble I'd managed to steal before Tadhg commandeered the rest.

The shadows living within me stirred, uncoiling and slithering through my veins, leaving me chilled despite the sun beating on my brow. Some were a result of the black magic used to keep me alive despite my lack of a heart; others were the result of me attempting dark, ancient spells to release myself from this prison.

Darkness bred darkness.

If you were to cut me open, even my soul would be black. Assuming I still had one.

I shifted into a dry set of clothes right before an unforgiving tug like a leash around my throat robbed me of my breath. I sank into the shadows and let the Queen send me wherever she willed, which happened to be along the bank of the inky black river separating the Black Forest from Tearmann's lush green landscape. The moment I arrived, the heaviness of a tost settled over my skin, thankfully keeping out most of the stench from across the water.

The Queen may have been a few inches shorter, but somehow, she managed to look down at me where I stood. My black eyes reflected in her glossy black crown.

"You know better than to keep me waiting," she said, her red lips flattening into a thin line.

"My apologies." No sense giving her an excuse she didn't want.

"I haven't seen or heard from you in almost a month."

"I've been kept busy."

"What of the Vellanian troops?"

I gritted my teeth, determined to keep from telling her anything about my work. How'd she know I'd been inquiring after the troops in the first place? She never left the Forest, and we had barely any staff at the castle. Every time I'd discussed the topic with my brother, I'd used a tost.

The pressure around my throat returned; shadows coaxed the words from my lips. "Two ships arrived between this week and the last," I gritted out, "one to the port in Burnsley and the other to Windwick, filled to the brim with soldiers."

"Weapons?"

"No, flowers."

Her hand struck me with a burst of blinding speed. My cheekbone made a cracking sound beneath the force of the blow. "Don't test me, boy. Are they iron?"

I bobbed my head, the movement making my face ache. Not that she noticed with the way she'd started pacing between the river and where I stood, leaving a trail of blackened grass in her wake. The many curled brown leaves scattered on the ground seemed to know better than to stick to the hem of her feathered skirt.

"What is your brother doing about it?" she demanded.

"What he always does."

"So nothing, then," she muttered, coming to a halt in front of me. "This responsibility falls to you. Have you spoken to Muireann about getting the merrow involved?"

How did she know about—Feckin' fish. No feckin' loyalty. "It's not my place."

"If your brother will not do what is necessary, then you must step up and rule in his stead. Let the people see you for the leader you are."

The people? To them, I was the son of a monster. A soulless murderer.

They weren't wrong.

"Speak to Muireann," the Queen went on. "Ask what it would take for them to sink the ships. If you don't," she said with a smile, "then I will make you."

I had nothing against seeing every last Vellanian ship sent to the bottom of the ocean, except, "The treaty forbids—"

"The treaty is worthless now that they are mounting an attack against us."

It did appear as though an attack was imminent, but to what end? Our land was a pittance compared to theirs. Unlike our ancestors, we had no army to use against them. According to the treaty, we weren't even allowed to train one because our ability to wield magic already gave us an "unfair advantage."

I was missing something. And I feckin' hated it.

"Let me see the ledgers." The Queen smacked my arm when I didn't jump at her command. "The ledgers, boy!"

I shifted the books filled with names of the most recently executed Danú and handed it to her.

She dragged a blackened nail down each account. Names, alleged crimes, sentences. "Are they all false accusations?"

"Most, but not all. Ailbe got too sloppy, and Brian got too drunk." Two out of fourteen in the last two weeks had been guilty. All fourteen had been executed.

She flicked through the rest of the pages. "And the false witnesses?"

"Taken care of."

A small smile pulled at the edge of her lips, infinitely more terrifying than her frown. "Excellent." She shoved the ledger into my chest, forcing my hands to take it. "I'm finished with you now." With a flick of her wrist, the tost disbanded, and the cold, dead air from the Forest punched me in the lungs.

When she evanesced, the only lingering sign of her presence was the patch of blackened grass. I gasped carrion-laced air until the pain in my face dissipated.

Someday, I would be strong enough to destroy her.

Someday, but not this day.

Back at the castle, I took a detour to the fountain, sinking onto the low stone edge to splash my fingers against the chilly water. A few wispy clouds drifted across the sky as I waited. And waited. And feckin' waited.

I was on the verge of giving up when a mass of dark hair appeared, followed by a narrow face and dark, lashless eyes.

The pale blue skin of the merrow's face darkened where it reached her curling lips. "Hello, Wicked Prince. Here to play in the daylight, are ye?" The gills behind her ear opened and closed with each rasping breath. Her bare breasts rose and fell, the left one marked by my blade years ago.

Magic swelled in my palm. I sent it spinning into the air with a flick of my wrist, creating a soundproof barrier so the grogoch hunched in the garden didn't overhear us.

"I'm here to talk sinking ships."

Muireann's smile grew. "And whose ships would we be sinkin'?"

"I think you already know."

Muireann lifted herself out of the water on thin arms, perching far enough away to keep the water dripping down her greenish-blue tail from getting onto my breeches. "Ye know the rules."

"And if the Queen wishes you to bend them?"

Her gaze dropped to my breeches, and her sharpened black teeth gleamed with her own grin. "I suppose I could be persuaded to speak to my father."

Muireann's father ruled the seas off both Airren and Tear-mann's coasts. I'd met him once—a hideous man with a snout and hair and teeth the color of seaweed. Was it any wonder the female merrow preferred dalliances with land-dwelling creatures?

"And to persuade you?" I asked, even though the thought of Muireann's cold hands on my body didn't stir me as it usually did.

"A swim is all."

I kicked off my boots, removed my waistcoat and shirt, and fell backward into the freezing water.

Negotiations with Muireann had taken longer than expected. By the time I made it to the kitchens, Tadhg was already on his stool, hunched over a plate piled with enough food to feed an entire family.

Eava waved at me from where she stoked the fire. A plate of roast pork appeared on the table in front of my empty stool.

Tadhg's gaze swept from my damp hair to my fresh breeches. "I doubt he's hungry, Eava. He just had fish for dinner."

Eava smacked him in the back of the head before giving me a disappointed frown. "What're ye thinkin', leadin' that poor woman on when you've no more interest in her than this one does a steak?" She gestured to where my brother sat rubbing his skull.

"Muireann and I have an arrangement," I said.

Eava grumbled something that sounded an awful lot like,

"Arrangement, my arse," before returning to the ovens to remove our dessert for the evening. Strawberry-rhubarb pie.

I nudged Tadhg's shoulder. "Where's your pet?" Ruairi must've been around here somewhere. He claimed to have a house of his own, but I wasn't convinced considering he spent just about every waking moment in mine.

"Swiftfell."

"And you didn't join him?"

Tadhg shrugged and laid into his vegetables. A responsible decision for once. I would've been impressed if he didn't smell like he'd slept in a puddle of puitín. No, my brother was probably just too hungover to leave the castle for another binge session.

We ate in silence except for Eava's tuneless humming and the occasional scrape of cutlery. Once our plates were clear, Eava scooped out two generous portions of still-steaming strawberry-rhubarb pie, topping both with a glop of fresh cream.

"He got more than I did," Tadhg whined, gesturing toward the plate Eava set in front of me.

I licked my dinner fork clean and stabbed a bite. "That's because Eava loves me more than she loves you."

Eava shifted a spoon and cut into the flaky crust for a nibble herself. "I love ye both the same, which is why yer slices are exactly the same."

"What do you call that?" Tadhg pointed to the extra crunchy bits at the corner of my plate with his fork.

"Love," I said with a smirk, scooping them up and stuffing them into my mouth before he could shift them to his own plate.

Tadhg's hand shot out, stealing what was left of my slice and stuffing it between his lips.

I knocked him on his arse, choking him so he couldn't swallow. I'd been looking forward to dessert all feckin' day, and he'd stolen it from me. In Tearmann, theft could be considered a capital crime. *Time for you to die, big brother.*

He smiled the entire time, his teeth stained red with berries.

A spoon clattered to the ground near his head. Eava braced her hands on the edge of the high table, gripping until her knuckles paled.

I loosened my hold on Tadhg. "Eava?"

Her black eyes turned milky white.

"Eava, is everything—"

"She's lookin' fer ye," Eava whispered in a haunting voice, her head slowly turning toward me.

Who? The Queen? If that witch wanted me, she'd have drawn me to her, and no amount of magic could break that bond.

Tadhg smacked my hands away.

Eava's mouth lifted on the right side in a mocking smile as she unlatched her hands, her head cocking to the left like a demented pigeon. *"Pity the girl from Graystones who loved a heartless prince. For the only way to save him—"*

Her eyes rolled back in her head, and she slumped to the ground. I jumped off my brother, catching the old witch before her skull cracked on the hard stone floor.

Tadhg punched my shoulder. "What did you do now?"

"Nothing." Unless you counted abandoning Eithne and assaulting Aveen. Neither of those women loved me. Perhaps it was a coincidence? Oh, who was I kidding? A feckin' coincidence?

Graystones. Heartless prince.

I gave Eava's weathered cheek a gentle pat. "Eava? Eava, wake up."

Her eyes burst open, black and fixed on me. "She's lookin' fer ye."

"Who? Eava, I don't know —"

"She's the one. The one ye've been lookin' for."

Find your soul's one true mate
For she will save you from your fate . . .

Aveen. It must be Aveen.

Pity the girl from Graystones who loved a heartless prince.
For the only way to save him . . .

"Go. Find the woman." Tadhg took Eava from me, cradling her in his lap. Her eyes had fallen closed again, but her breathing appeared steady. I could count on one finger the number of people I genuinely liked, and if anything happened to Eava—

"I said go!" Tadhg growled.

I stumbled to my feet, racing to the kitchen's back door, up the stairs, and out into the sunny garden. Oscar and his companion were planting something. They didn't bother waving as they used to when I was a boy, and neither did Muireann when I sprinted through the courtyard. The moment I breached the wards, I evanesced to the abandoned shed in Graystones.

From between a gap in the door, I could see dark clouds blowing in off the sea and hear waves battering the creaking hulls of ships tethered in the port.

A flurry of blue skirts and golden curls raced up the hill toward a black carriage with an old man hunched at the top, struggling to keep his cap on despite the whipping wind.

Aveen.

She's lookin' fer ye.

Aveen threw herself into the carriage; the door banged behind her. The driver's whip cracked like thunder, and the horses lurched forward, starting for the road out of town.

I evanesced into the bobbling carriage, landing on the seat next to Aveen.

She gasped, throwing herself back against the plush cushion. "Rían?"

Ice settled in my bones. Not only did she know my true face, she knew my true feckin' name. "I see you learned my name," I ground out. "Who gave it to you?"

The carriage bounced and jerked, flying up the road like a banshee escaped from the underworld.

"Why does it matter?"

"I need to know who to kill."

The obstinate woman refused to tell me. Just what I needed today. More shite.

"I can think of a few delightful ways to change your mind." I could chain her up back in the shed and have her on her knees begging for mercy before the storm subsided.

"You said you'd leave me be. You promised."

"Did I?" *Humans. Never listening.* "I recall swearing on my mother's life to stay away from your sister. Not from you. But I should probably warn you that I despise my mother," I added, leaning close enough to smell the rose oil on her flaw-less skin. "Now, let's try this again. Who gave you my name?"

"I'm . . . not . . . telling . . . you."

Who was she protecting? If a human knew my name, Eava's spell wouldn't have picked up on it. It had to have been a witch. Why would Aveen care what happened to one of us? "All right, then." I shifted my ceremonial dagger, its cold weight familiar in my hand. "A different question. Why were you inquiring after me?"

She bit her lip, as if that would keep her secrets inside if I decided to pry them out.

"This was a gift from my father," I said, giving her a good, long look at my dagger. "I like to keep it very sharp. Can you imagine what it would do to your throat?" I pressed the tip against my finger, drawing a single drop of blood.

Aveen had a lovely throat, long and smooth, smelling of sweet, sweet roses.

"Killing humans is illegal," she whispered.

Killing *humans.*

Killing any living being should have been illegal, but it wasn't. Not in this forsaken place. The humans could kill us again and again as long as they had a "good reason." Lucky for me, I was above Airren law. Instead of saying any of that, I let the silence speak for me.

Her lips pursed as she seemed to come to a decision. "I cannot get you out of my head," she said in a quiet whisper.

I searched the air for the lie, tasting only truth. Knowing I plagued her thoughts made me a little less murderous. "What did you plan on doing with the information you gleaned?"

"Nothing. I just wanted to know who you were. I swear it."

I inhaled her words deeply. Another truth that made me send the dagger away.

Her hair reminded me of the golden thread used in my favorite waistcoat. I couldn't stop my hand from reaching for one silky curl to wrap around my finger. How glorious it would be to grab the whole feckin' lot, drag her head back, and devour every inch of skin along that lovely, lovely throat. My chest tightened, making it difficult to focus on the task at hand. "I'm afraid I must beg another favor."

Her tongue nipped out to wet soft pink lips. The way she'd felt beneath my mouth would forever live in my memory. "Are you going to stab me if I don't kiss you?" She made it sound as if the idea of kissing me was the worst in the whole entire world.

Women had fallen at my feet. Begged to come to my bed. And this human thought she was better than me? "I don't want a feckin' kiss. I want you to break my curse."

Find your soul's one true mate
For she will save you from your fate

I wasn't sure how, but this weak human was meant to save me from the most powerful witch in Airren. If I'd had any doubt before, now I knew for certain.

For the only way to save him . . .

Aveen snorted. "Very funny."

She thought the notion of me being cursed was funny, did

she? Only the strongest witches who practiced black magic had the power to curse. All it took was one look at a witch's eyes to know if darkness lurked. Their magic became tainted. Very few on this island had resisted the call of dark power.

My brother had sunk into darkness, searching for a way to break Fiadh's curse, and I'd fallen prey to its call in my quest for vengeance.

Aveen returned my stare, her eyes slowly widening. "I don't know the first thing about curses—or how to break them. You'll have to find someone else."

If I could just pick a random person, then this feckin' curse would've been broken centuries ago. It had to be her. Neither of us had any choice in the matter. "I don't want anyone else. It has to be you."

"Let me guess," she sneered. "If I refuse, you'll slit my throat."

I could, but then I'd be damning myself to a hopeless future. Not that I'd ever held out much hope for escaping my mother's curse in the first place. No, death wouldn't convince someone like Aveen to help me defeat the Queen. I needed to find a different motivation.

What motivated a good person? Good things. Foolish things like love and loyalty.

I couldn't help the smile spreading across my lips. "If you refuse, I'll ask your sister."

Aveen's breathing hitched as she clutched the edge of the cushion. "What do I have to do?"

Destroy the Phantom Queen.

Best get her on my side before telling her that part. "All in good time, my dear. All in good time. First, we must discuss the terms of our bargain."

"I break your curse, you leave my sister and me alone for all of eternity."

If she intended to succeed and manage to come out with her heart and life intact, I should probably give her more than just my absence as an incentive. "I'll do you one better. If you agree to help me, then in addition to your demands, I will grant you one wish." What would a woman like this—high-born, wealthy, beautiful—want? "Perhaps you'd like a new dress. Or a new horse. How about some diamonds?" A diamond necklace to wear around her beautiful throat. "You women still love diamonds, don't you?"

"I don't want any of those things," she insisted.

No, no. That would be too easy. Someone like her would probably have dresses and diamonds in droves. "What do you want?" I found myself holding my breath, awaiting her response. *What do you want, Aveen?*

"I . . . I don't know."

A woman who didn't know what she wanted was a dangerous thing. "I suggest you figure it out by the time I return."

Her hands fidgeted with the edge of the cushion. "When will that be?"

I evanesced to the forest outside, using a simple spell to leave my words behind to slip into her mind like a promise. "*Whenever I feel like it.*"

Back at the castle, Tadhg had eaten all the pie and fecked off somewhere, probably to join Ruairi or find his own bottle and bed to warm. Eava was still in the kitchen, drying dishes from dinner.

"If Tadhg didn't wash those, he's dead." Eava cooked, we cleaned. Those were the rules. If he'd left her to do it all, I'd have his head.

She set the plate onto the counter with the others. "Don't ye be worryin' about these dishes. Tell me about yer woman."

"She's not my woman."

Her brow furrowed as she turned to fully face me. "Yer the only heartless prince I know."

"Could be metaphorical."

Eava shook her head. "Ye know as well as I do that she's the one."

I knew. I felt it in my bones. Had tasted it on her lips. Aveen was the one. "There was more to the prediction. What was it?"

Eava's eyes shuttered. "I'm sorry, my boy, but I didn't get any more than that before the darkness took me. Whoever gave her yer name must be a powerful witch indeed to keep me out."

If I learned the rest of the prediction, maybe I would find out how to save myself.

4

According to my records, two witches lived in the town of Graystones itself. I planned on starting there and working my way out until I found the person responsible for telling Aveen my name. My first stop was a tiny apartment above the cobbler's shop. I knocked, feeling no wards. Not that a smart witch would use a ward on this side of the wall, where humans could feel something amiss. When no one answered, I tried the door, finding it unlocked. A prickle of unease crept up my spine.

The stale air inside reeked of cat piss; broken glass glittered across the worn floorboards. Drawers from the sideboard and dresser in the bedroom had been torn out and emptied across the floor. Either she'd left in a hurry, or the place had been raided.

Instead of waiting around to see if the old witch known as Molls returned, I left the apartment via a creaky back staircase and started for the square.

Women in fine gowns strolled between buildings on the arms of their men. A couple of them occupied an iron bench near the church, chatting about slippers. A horde of men were already drinking in the pub. Sailors loaded cargo onto ships docked in the port. I passed them all without a second glance on my way to the seamstress's shop.

Three women, one older than the others—the mother, perhaps—were just leaving as I arrived. When I heard no one else inside, I opened the door. Meranda and I had never been friends —I didn't have any of those—but we'd tolerated one another through the years, hadn't we? I didn't want to believe she would've betrayed me.

If she had . . .

The bell on the door jingled when I shoved the barrier aside.

The place was a mess, with bits and bobs everywhere. No rhyme or reason to the room whatsoever. The dresses were fair enough, and the cloth on bolts felt fine. Was that Vellanian lace? That shite cost a fortune. And cotton from Iodale. The colors were much more vibrant than their Airren or Vellanian counter-parts. *Fae* silk. No feckin' way. If I had to kill her, I'd be taking the silk with me.

"Good afternoon, sir. What brings you in—" The red-headed witch froze on the other side of the counter, her face white as snow. "Are ye outta yer feckin' head? What're ye doin' here?"

Glamours were a tricky thing. Not everyone could use them— and not everyone who used them was any good—but the one thing no one could hide: the eyes.

Even with an exceptional glamour, it was nearly impossible to fool those who knew me.

I tugged a blue ribbon free from its spool, smiling when Meranda cursed again. "I heard a rumor that someone in Gray-stones has been using my name."

"Well, it wasn't me." She snatched the ribbon out of my hand. "I wouldn't call the devil down upon myself even if someone had an iron blade to my gullet."

Truth. Not Meranda, then. It must've been the other witch. "Have you seen Molls?"

"Arrested—day before last."

I glanced at the jail's rooftop across the courtyard through Meranda's windows. I'd have to pay her a visit, now, wouldn't I? I thanked the witch for her time and went back out into the gray day.

When two women with their arms locked together stopped to gawk at me, I pretended not to notice.

"Who is *that?*" the shorter one with mousy blond hair asked. Her skirts billowed twice as wide as the other one's. Must've been wearing a hoop beneath. Those wretched things had gone out of fashion decades ago.

The other one swatted her friend with the fan dangling from her wrist. "Don't waste your time, Nettie. He's probably just another suitor from some far-off town asking for directions to the Bannon estate."

"She can't marry them all, Sienna."

A suitor to the Bannon estate? Maybe they were calling on Aveen's sister. I should probably check, just in case. "Pardon me, ladies," I said with a tip of my head, "but you wouldn't, by chance, know where the Bannons live, would you?"

The taller of the two nudged the other with her elbow, giving her an "I told you so" glare. "Of course, milord." She bobbed a curtsy. The silly hat pinned to her hair flipped forward before falling back into place when she righted herself. "Lady Aveen's father lives just outside of town. Take a right at the fork, and it's the first large estate you come across. Tall, white gates on either side of the drive. You can't miss it."

Not the sister, then. Aveen. On the hunt for a husband, was she? Not on my time. She could marry whichever pillock she wanted once she'd saved me. Assuming the Queen didn't kill her first.

I thanked the women for their time and started for the road leading out of town, giving the jail a final glance as I passed. The old witch wasn't going anywhere, but if I didn't get over to the Bannon estate, my savior might be.

Two black carriages had been parked in the Bannons' driveway, their drivers chatting to one another. I evanesced closer, to a wide glass door leading to what appeared to be a parlor, listening intently to a fat man with a high-pitched voice telling Aveen how beautiful she looked today. Was he here on behalf of his son or nephew? Some matches used to be made like that, with the couple never meeting before their wedding. But if this man's son looked anything like him, Aveen would be smart to run far and fast.

The man withdrew a handkerchief from his breast pocket to dab at his sweaty forehead. It wasn't even warm out. If anything, there was still a winter nip to the air. Aveen sat there with her hands folded in her lap, smiling demurely, the picture of subservience. Where was the spark I'd seen the other night when she'd kissed me? The defiance. The fire.

The man reached for her hand, and it took everything within me to keep from strangling him with his own cravat. "My dearest Aveen, would you do me the great honor of entertaining a match with me?"

A match with *him*? The fat oaf would squish the poor woman if he took her to bed. She couldn't honestly be considering such a thing. It was preposterous.

"I've two thousand a year, an estate almost as fine as this one. My first wife—rest her soul—seemed very content there." He dug through his stretched waistcoat pocket, a hideous thing the color of aubergines that made his already pallid complexion worse. "I've brought you a token of my affections." He held out a large enough diamond ring. From the sound of it, he'd only just met the woman. She was fair, to be sure, but a proposal on the first day? That screamed desperation.

"I appreciate your proposal," Aveen said, refusing to take the proffered ring. "You've certainly given me a lot to think about, but I think you should hold onto that until I've made my final decision. Thank you for coming all the way from Burnsley to see me."

"I would travel the entire island for a woman as fine as you, Lady Aveen."

What a wanker.

She murmured a polite reply. There was some shuffling, a quiet curse—probably the man trying to squeeze himself through the door—and then a different voice announced the next suitor, a weasel of a man named Sir Henry Withel.

A smile curled my lips. I knew exactly how to get some time alone with Aveen.

A servant led me into a cavernous foyer with gleaming marble floors. Old fashioned floral drapes hung in the bay windows, but they appeared in good nick. "May I take your coat, master—?"

"*Sir* Edward DeWarn, His Majesty's Ambassador from Vellana," I said in a strong Vellanian accent that had the man snapping to attention. "And no," I added, looking down my glamoured nose at him. Those clammy hands wouldn't be coming anywhere near a coat that cost more than his yearly wages.

A slender, dark-haired woman appeared at the top of the stairs in a lacy lavender dress. Must be the sister. Definitely younger than Aveen. Starker. She may have smiled, but I spared her no more than a passing glance on my way to the parlor.

"Sir Edward DeWarn. His Majesty's Ambassador from Vellana," the servant announced from the door. There were flowers everywhere.

Dammit. I should've brought flowers.

Ah, well. No sense dwelling on it now. It wasn't as if I could shift the things with the servant watching. Besides, I wasn't actually courting the woman. I was only here to keep my soulmate from ending up with someone else before she could save me. I wasn't sure how she was meant to save me yet, but she couldn't very well do it if she had some eejit of a husband plowing her morning, noon, and night, now, could she?

Aveen twisted on the settee, her curls glistening in the evening sun, eyes and smile warm and welcoming as she considered me.

The buttons at the top of my shirt felt too tight. I couldn't feckin' breathe.

She's not looking at you, I reminded myself. She was admiring a glamoured man with dark, curly hair, no scar across his straight nose, and no emptiness hidden inside his chest.

If she'd seen me, she would've run straight out the glass doors.

I had to swallow twice to rid myself of the lump in my throat. "Good evening, Lady Aveen," I said in "Sir Edward's" voice. "I hate calling this late, but I was anxious to meet the woman who has become the talk of the town."

Her welcoming smile turned brittle as she gestured for me to join her on the settee. "And what is the town saying about me?"

"Only that the most beautiful woman on the East Coast is in want of a husband."

For some reason, the compliment wiped the smile from her face completely. "And are you in the market for a wife, Ambassador?"

"No. I'm not." Could you imagine? Me marrying a feckin' human. My mother would have her skewered by dinnertime.

One eyebrow arched. "So you've come to see me as if I'm some sort of exhibit at the zoo?"

The animals she'd been entertaining belonged at a zoo. The last one had looked exactly like a ferret. Still, there was no sense in letting her know how invested I was in her marital pursuits. At least not yet. "Something like that."

Oh, cakes. I plucked one from the tiered tray and took a bite. Nothing like Eava's, but tasty enough. At least Tadhg wasn't here to steal them from me.

"Now that you've seen me, you can be on your way," she said.

As if I'd leave now that I'd gone through the trouble of creating an entirely new persona for myself. Edward was a bit of a prick, so he ignored her statement entirely. "Why is your father so anxious to marry you off?" Was she a drain on his finances? A shrieking shrew? An annoying whinge? For some reason, I couldn't see it. None of the normal human attributes seemed to apply to Aveen.

Her chin lifted. "I am nearly twenty-one. It is time for me to marry."

I'd bet my cufflinks she had no desire to wed. For some reason, that knowledge left me smiling. Not that she could do much to deny a match if her father pressed. Even the high-born women in this country were little more than chattel to be sold to the highest bidder.

Aveen took my feckin' cake with a smirk playing on her lips. "My apologies, these are for suitors only."

I stole it back, eating half of it in one go so she wouldn't take it from me again. "I'm intrigued. What sort of trouble would your husband be acquiring?"

"No trouble at all. I would be the perfect wife. Placid and complàcent and completely happy."

Lie after lie after lie. I barely knew Aveen and already it was obvious that *placid* and *complacent* didn't begin to describe the woman sitting next to me. You know what did describe her? "Contrary."

She sat back, her mouth gaping. "Excuse me?"

"You're contrary, I see." I pulled a serviette from beside the tray of cakes, dabbing at my mouth in case any crumbs lingered. "And stubborn, no doubt. Are there any other shortcomings in your character that I should know about?"

She wanted to take the bait. I could see it in the way her eyes narrowed and the curve of her jaw pulsed as her teeth ground together. "Thank you for calling, but I'm afraid I must retire."

Come on, woman. Fight with me. Let me see how hard you bite. "Rigid too." I bet I could loosen her up. Ten minutes and I'd have her in a puddle on the floor, writhing beneath me. Begging. Shuddering.

Her icy blue eyes ignited. Cheeks flushed. Glorious chest heaved. *There she is.*

She shoved her hand in my face, lifting her fingers as she counted my faults one by one. "Arrogant. Vain. Irritating. Are there any other shortcomings in your character I should know about?"

I bit back a smile. Not five minutes in her company and she had me pegged. "Apathetic. Callous. Cynical. Devious. Hypocritical. Impatient. Possessive. There are quite a few more, but those are the ones I hear most often."

I was almost certain I caught a hint of a smile playing around her lips. "At least you're honest."

"That's debatable. But enough about me. Have you come up with that wish?"

Her mouth fell open. *"Rían?"*

My groin tightened at her breathless tone. If she kept that up, I'd be the one on the floor begging. "I'd prefer if you call me ambassador for the time being," I said with a wink, forcing the enticing images of what I could do to her from my mind. "Makes it less confusing for any eavesdroppers who may be listening at the door." Like the dour servant whispering with Aveen's sister about me. Good to know I'd piqued her interest. Could come in handy in the future.

The cushion next to me dipped as Aveen edged closer. She reached for me, scouring my face with her fingertips, leaving tiny sparks in her wake. Nothing compared to the fire I'd felt the other day. Then again, there was an entire glamour keeping her from me.

Still, I couldn't move. Couldn't breathe.

I barely managed to keep the glamour in place, desperately wanting to let it drop so that her fire could burn straight through and make me feel something.

"How are you able to change your form?" she whispered.

That damned lump returned to my throat, refusing to be swallowed. "I have my father Midir to thank for that." *And nothing else.*

She kept touching me, my control slipping until only a fraying thread remained.

"May I have my face back?"

She jumped as if I'd shouted, bolting to the other side of the settee to collect a blue book from the marble-topped table. She flipped through the pages, her finger dragging down the words and lips moving as she read.

"Now, back to that wish," I said with a smile that didn't belong to me. "Edward" was the sort to smile fully, showing off all his pearly white teeth. He had a very strict dental regimen.

"I haven't decided on one yet," she said.

How hard was it to come up with a wish? All she had to do was think of something she wanted, and I would find a way to give it to her. Everyone wanted *something*.

"I've given you a week."

She gestured toward the vases of flowers surrounding us. "I've been a little busy."

"Don't tell me you're actually considering marrying any of the pillocks who've called. The last man practically pissed himself when he kissed your hand goodbye." I glamoured myself to look like the weasel, right down to his thin, hooked nose. Imagining her with someone like him turned my insides. "Now, I'm not a woman, but I'm fairly certain that is not an attractive quality in a husband."

"At least none of them threatened me with a knife," she shot back.

She couldn't still be upset about that, could she? I'd barely threatened her at all. I shifted back into the ambassador. *More cake? Don't mind if I do.* "It was just a little knife. And I only showed it to you because you were being contrary."

"So it's my fault you threatened to slit my throat, is it?"

She did have a lovely throat. Especially when she blushed. "Did I threaten you?" I asked around a bite. "I distinctly remember asking if you could imagine what it would do to your throat, not saying I had any plans to do it."

Her gaze fell to my lips. "It was implied."

"Implications don't hold up in court, my dear." The cake left behind a greasy residue on my fingers. If I didn't clean them, I could stain my clothes. Edward and I both had an aversion to stains. I dragged a serviette from the coffee table to clean my hands. When I sat back, I found her still staring at my mouth. "If you want to kiss me again, all you have to do is ask."

She shook her head, as if breaking out of a trance, wide blue eyes flying to mine. "I'd rather see your dagger."

This woman. She was funny. Pity my mother was bound to destroy her. "That can be arranged."

Aveen shifted closer, her hands falling to my shoulders as she lifted to her knees and leaned forward until I could taste the sweetness of her breath. "Rían?"

What was it about the way she said my name? "Yes, Aveen?"

Chills slid down my spine when her fingertips grazed the hair by my ears. "Get out of my house."

She thought she could tease me? *Foolish human.* Two could play that game. I slipped a hand to the back of her neck, beneath her curls, my lips skimming her thrumming pulse. "I'll be back."

I evanesced to the garden, remaining close enough to hear Aveen let out an indignant sound.

The sister came in a moment later, asking what Aveen was doing, and she told some lie about a hair pin that left my lips curling into a smile. A smile I quickly squashed.

I didn't want to like the human, let alone care for her.

I could handle attraction. Get it out of my system.

Caring?

Far too dangerous.

A vulnerability I couldn't afford.

5

I FOUND MY BROTHER BENT OVER THE DESK IN THE STUDY, HIS head in his hands and a telltale bottle of puítin open at his elbow. He didn't bother looking up when I crossed the threshold.

"What do I need to know?" I asked, sinking onto the edge of the desk so that he had to acknowledge my presence and plugging the decanter to keep the smell of that rot from giving me a headache first thing in the morning.

Tadhg slid a sheet of parchment toward me. "The usual. Another trial in some shite town on the east coast."

"Which shite town would that be?" All the towns in Airren were shite if you asked me.

"See for yourself."

I collected the missive, scanning the scrawled words for a location. *Graystones.* Two Danú were to be tried, one of whom happened to be Molls Gardner.

"With the trial today, there'll likely be executions set for tomorrow or the next day," Tadhg went on. "Seeing as Ruairi is already in Guaire, he can just swing by—"

"Ruairi is useless. I'll go."

For the first time since I'd come in, Tadhg raised his head. His bloodshot green eyes swirled with shadows. The ledger of the lives he'd claimed with his curse sat at his elbow. I'd bet my new waist-coat that if I checked the storeroom where he kept the bodies, there'd be one more than there was yesterday.

"Why would you volunteer? You never volunteer to do anything," he said.

That wasn't entirely true. I'd volunteered to murder him on more than one occasion. "I need to visit my source," I told him. "This way, I can kill two birds or whatever shite they're saying nowadays."

He grabbed the decanter, popped the top, and lifted it to his lips. His throat bobbed as he drank. After he slammed it back onto the desk, he used his shirtsleeve to clean the drops from his mouth. "Are you ever going to tell me who it is?"

"Not a feckin' hope." If my brother knew half the shite I did, there'd be no hope of him keeping it to himself. Even if he did have the best of intentions—and he most assuredly did *not*—his truth curse was a liability. The less people knew, the better for everyone involved. Meaning me. The better for me.

"Swing by Guaire first. Bring Ruairi with you."

"Why on earth would I want that animal tagging along?"

"Because as much as you like to think otherwise, you can't be everywhere at once. He needs to learn what to do."

"And what's that?" I picked up the letter opener on his desk. Drew the blade along my fingertip.

"You think I don't hear the whispers that witnesses have gone 'missing' in Airren? Witnesses at all the trials you've attended."

"Could be a coincidence," I said with a shrug.

"You and I both know it's not."

Why, oh why couldn't my brother have been drunk already? He was far less meddlesome when he was drunk. "That mutt doesn't have it in him to do what needs done. I will go on my own." Ruairi was as soft as they came. It was a wonder he could shift into anything besides a fluffy bunny.

"You *will* bring Ruairi." Tadhg sounded exactly like our father when he used that sort of commanding tone. Which made me hate him even more.

Unfortunately, Tadhg ruled this forsaken country—when he felt like it—so I would do what was requested of me like a good little foot soldier.

"Go on, then." Tadhg gestured to the door. "Let me know what happens when you get back."

I found my brother's mate in an alley outside a Danú pub. The second I arrived, Ruairi's nose lifted, wrinkled, and his narrowed golden eyes landed on mine.

"Well, isn't this convenient?" I drawled. "You're sitting on your arse doing nothing, and I'm in the need of a dog for the day."

His lips tugged into a grin, revealing his elongated canines. "As much as it warms my heart that ye'd like my company, I'm afraid I'm going to have to disappoint."

"I bet that's what you say to all the ladies."

He snorted into his pint of amber.

"Unfortunately for us both," I said with a sigh, "your prince has ordered me to bring you to Graystones. So you can either come of your own free will, or I can make you."

Beneath his dark beard, his jaw pulsed. He lifted his pint and finished it in two swallows before grabbing his coat and rising to his feet. Since his arse always seemed to be parked on my settee, it was easy to forget how big he was.

I hated that I had to look up at him.

And from his sharp-toothed grin, the big bastard knew it.

When I held out my hand, his nose wrinkled like he'd just stepped in shite.

"I know how to get there on my own," he said.

"Yes, but I don't have time to waste trying to find you once we arrive. Just take my feckin' hand."

Although he grumbled about it like a child, he took my hand

long enough for me to bring us to the edge of town, right behind the sign welcoming us to Graystones.

I glamoured myself into someone the old eejits in the court-house would respect. A "stately" gentleman with a bulbous nose, thin lips, and the same paunch most of the old men in this town sported. Ruairi just stood there with his hands in his feckin' pockets. "What are you waiting for? Hurry up and shift."

His golden eyes narrowed. "Shift into what?"

"A horse, obviously."

"Fer what?"

"I can't be seen just strolling into town, now, can I?"

His inky hair slipped over his shoulders when he shook his head, reminding me that I still had yet to cut it. "Not a hope, lad."

"Stop being a pain in the arse. You let Tadhg ride on you all the time."

"That's different. I like Tadhg."

"A fine man needs a fine horse. Since there are none present, you will have to do."

Ruairi looked so indignant, it made me laugh. His hands balled into fists at his sides, but instead of hitting me like he so obviously wanted to, he took a deep breath, exhaled a curse, and shifted into a massive black stallion with a beautiful leather saddle ready and waiting. The stitching was impeccable—not that I'd be telling him that.

I caught the horn and slipped my foot into the stirrup, but when I went to lift myself, the bastard moved, leaving me flat on my ass in the feckin' dirt. "Do that again, and I will end you."

Ruairi snorted.

I caught his bridle, tugging his head toward me. "And keep your gob shut so no one sees those disgusting fangs of yours."

We met no other riders as we descended toward the town of gray cobbled streets, gray buildings, and gray skies. Once we hit the mercantile, I tied Ruairi to a post, my smile growing wider the longer he glared. It wasn't my fault he'd shifted into a horse and couldn't turn back into a human with all these people around.

Oh, wait. It was.

"You wait here like a good little mule." I gave his coarse head a pat. "I'll be back eventually."

He tried to nip at me, but I was quicker.

The way he stamped his hooves left me laughing all the way to the town hall that doubled as a courthouse. I couldn't remember being in Graystones for a trial in the last hundred years.

There were Danú here, but they were more careful than those living in other parts of Airren. This town's strong ties to Vellana and distance from Tearmann made it a dangerous place for us to reside.

The hall was full to the brim with humans come to see the spectacle. I managed to get a seat toward the front, between a youngish man with pockmarked skin and a woman in a hideous white wig that belonged in the last century. All their chatter died the moment a side door swung open and a man with three wobbly chins in a powdered wig and black robes entered, cutting through the aisle to a desk at the very front. A man I recognized: Lady Eithne's husband.

A moment later, three guards in red livery led a white-haired woman into the room. Her veiny hands had been bound together with iron chains that scraped and dragged along beside her bare feet. Wicked red marks encircled her wrists where the iron had branded her paper-thin skin.

The guards brought her to a lone stool left in a gap between the crowd and desk, forcing her to sit. She hunched forward and started rocking back and forth, the legs on the stool creaking with the motion.

"State your name for the record," Lady Eithne's ancient husband chortled, his necks swinging like a turkey's warbler.

After a moment, the witch responded. "Molls Gardner."

"You have been accused of witchcraft. How do you plead?"

"*Pity the girl from Graystones who loved a heartless Prince,*" Molls replied in a dry, crackling voice.

I gripped the end of the bench when her milky eyes found me.

"For the only way to save him——"

"Order! I will have order!" The gavel banged, cutting off her final words. The witch started humming, lost to whatever darkness plagued her mind, the chains banging against the floorboards each time she rocked.

One of the soldiers slammed the hilt of his sword against her temple. Blood oozed from the wound. Molls fell silent.

What comes next? I almost shouted.

"How do you plead?" O'Meara demanded a second time.

The gavel flew from his hand, straight through a window, leaving the humans sitting beneath running like rats to avoid the shards of glass raining down. With the iron chains, the witch should've been rendered powerless.

Her only response was another haunting cackle.

"You are hereby found guilty of practicing witchcraft. At noon tomorrow, you will be brought to the gallows and hung by the neck until dead." O'Meara went to swing his gavel, seeming to realize too late that it was gone. Instead, he slammed his fist against the desk.

The guards hauled her out of the room, passing two more guards bringing in the second prisoner, a trembling grogoch with red hair sprouting through the holes in his breeches and thread-bare shirt. He hobbled forward, falling right as he reached the stool.

Not one feckin' human made any attempt to help him.

I ground my teeth together until my jaw ached. Every single human in this feckin' room looked down their noses at the grogoch as if he were nothing more than an inconvenience.

"State your name for the record," O'Meara clipped.

"Charlie O'Shea," the grogoch replied.

"You are charged with theft of a woman's purse. How do you plead?"

"Not guilty, sir. A kind woman gave me that purse——"

The women in the room gasped and held their hands over

JENNY HICKMAN

their mouths as they whispered to one another. The men scowled, exchanging frowns and shaking their heads in disbelief.

None of them would've been able to taste the truth in those words.

Whatever about the witch; she'd been foolish enough to use magic in plain sight. But this man hadn't done what they'd accused him of. I'd stake my life on it.

O'Meara banged his fist against the desk. "I would like to call the first witness, my wife, Lady Eithne O'Meara."

The doors opened, and Eithne swept in wearing a mauve day gown with scalloped edges. There was no way she knew who I was, yet my stomach sank, and I sent a little extra magic into my glamour.

Tight curls swung back and forth at her temples in time with the clicking of her heels against the wooden floorboards. She went to a chair to the right of the desk, giving her husband a demure smile.

"Lady Eithne," her husband began, "if you could please recount the harrowing events of this man's crime."

Alleged crime, you gobshite. *Alleged.*

"Last week, I was in town minding my own business, and that man"—Eithne's voice wobbled, and false tears filled her eyes as she pointed a manicured nail at Charlie—"demanded I give him my purse. I was so afraid of what he might do to me that I handed it over."

What he might do to her? The poor man reached her shoulder, his back was so hunched he could barely stand, and he had one feckin' leg. What did she honestly think *he* would do to *her*?

"Are there any other witnesses who can corroborate this story?" Lord O'Meara asked.

Two men stood from their seats at my back. I'd seen them before. They worked for the magistrate. Wasn't that feckin' handy?

"We heard Lady Eithne's screams and came as quickly as we could," the tallest one lied, squeezing a flat cap between his hands.

66

"Saw the purse in the bastard's bucket where he sat on the church steps."

If Charlie had stolen the purse, why would he take it, sit on a step, and put it in a feckin' bucket? Was I honestly the only person in here with a brain?

I cleared my throat loudly enough for the entire room to hear before easing to my feet. "If I may?"

Lord O'Meara's narrowed gaze swung toward me. "And who might you be?"

"Sir William Worthington." *Your worst feckin' nightmare.*

Although Lord O'Meara raised his bushy white eyebrows, he nodded as if he'd known who I was all along. "Oh, yes, yes. Sir William. My apologies. Go on."

"I find it hard to believe that after—" I looked pointedly at Eithne. "I'm sorry, I've already forgotten your name."

"Lady Eithne."

"Right, right. Lady Edwina. As I was saying, I find it hard to believe that a villain who had stolen someone's purse would then put said purse in a bucket and proceed to sit on the steps of a building in the center of the town."

"It's Eithne. And I . . . I wounded him," Eithne claimed. "He tried to accost me, but I found the strength somewhere deep inside and knocked him down. He hurt himself and wasn't able to run."

"He hardly looks able to run whether he's been knocked down or not," I said, gesturing to Charlie's single leg.

Charlie gave me a hesitant smile.

Eithne's face burned red as the crowd began to murmur.

Lord O'Meara demanded silence, his fist acting as his gavel one more. When the room quieted, his attention returned to me. "Thank you for your input, Sir William. You have certainly given this court a lot to think about."

I bowed my head, sinking back to the unforgiving wooden chair.

O'Meara flicked through a stack of pages from his desk drawer far too quickly to actually be reading them. Not two minutes later, he set them aside and clasped his hands together, sitting back in his chair to make room for his swollen stomach. "In light of the evidence presented, I have found the grogoch guilty of theft. As he is Danú, he is subject to the harshest penalty and will join the witch at the gallows tomorrow."

The grogoch. He couldn't even say Charlie's feckin' name.

I couldn't do a thing besides sit there and watch an innocent man be led away—not dragged like the witch, but hobbling, head bowed as if he'd done something shameful.

I shoved my way out of the hall, hatred swelling in my chest. It took everything I had to keep darkness from invading my eyes, giving away what I was.

Ruairi wasn't where I'd left him. I searched the street, finding the bastard tucked between two buildings, munching on a scone.

When he saw me, he pushed himself off the wall. "How'd it go?"

I couldn't even respond. The nerve of those feckin' humans. I should've killed every last one of them.

Ruairi took another bite of scone. A large chunk dropped out of his mouth, tumbling toward his brown boots. "That well, eh?"

I glowered across the square toward the jail. "I have a few stops to make before I return. You can go back without me."

I glamoured myself to look like one of the guards walking toward the corner pub. Without knowing his voice, I'd have to improvise. Before Ruairi could protest, I started for the jail.

The man standing guard at the jail's entrance bobbed his head when I approached. "I thought ye were goin' fer a pint."

"Forgot something," I mumbled in a gravelly voice.

The young lad unhooked the heavy ring of keys from his belt and unlocked the door. Damp, dank air closed over me as I stepped into a narrow hallway. Most jails were built the same, with guard's offices and quarters at the entrance and the cells toward the back. One way in, one way out, to minimize the chance of escape. I continued down the hall until I stumbled upon another guard digging at his grimy nails with a penknife.

All it took was a little magic to leave him unconscious on the floor.

Behind the bars of the first cell, I found Charlie curled in the corner, staring toward gray clouds drifting past the window's iron bars.

"Charlie?"

He turned, and I dropped my glamour long enough for him to see my face.

He scrambled back against the wall, rambling and shaking his head. "I didn't do what they claim. I swear it. I'd never——"

"I know." He was to die for existing. "What happened? Why did you have her purse?"

He gave a humorless chuckle. "It doesn't matter now, does it? My fate is sealed, and I'll not let anyone else be dragged down with me." He went back to looking out the window.

Fair enough. If he wanted to take this secret to his grave, I'd let him. I shifted a draught Eava made for such occasions, something that should help take away any lingering fear. "Here." I set the vial between the bars next to a scrap of moldy bread. "Take this at dawn."

Charlie didn't turn back around.

"*Oh, Rían,*" a raspy voice called from down the hall.

The witch couldn't see me from her cell. How did she know who I was? I stepped around the wall to find her clutching her knees in the far corner, her white hair and white eyes stark against the shadows.

"You're looking well, Molls."

Her head fell back, and her throaty cackle echoed around the empty cell. "I've always heard ye were a wicked thing." Once she'd recovered, she crawled forward, her chains clanging on the stone floor. "Ye have questions fer me."

"Mmmm . . . I don't think I do."

"That heart of yers may be gone, but ye've felt it beat. It's beatin' fer *her*."

"I don't know what you're on about."

She jabbed a knobby finger at my face. "He lies! Shall I offer ye a lie as well?"

Would it be so bad to admit the truth if she told me how Aveen was meant to save me? She was dying tomorrow, after all. Who could she tell? "I've felt it," I confessed.

Her chapped lips pulled into a grin, revealing a mouth full of rotten teeth. "Pity the girl from Graystones who loved a heartless prince. For the only way to save him was at her own expense."

I'd wondered how Aveen might save me from this curse the Queen had me under.

I'd assumed she wouldn't survive.

But now I knew for certain.

To save me, Aveen *needed* to die.

6

GRAY MIST SETTLED LIKE A CARPET OVER AN UNNATURALLY STILL sea. I watched it burn away with the sunrise from a bench in town, until the square filled with humans coming to watch the spectacle. Slurs and words of hate spewed from the ones closest to the jail and along the path to the gallows as guards led Molls and Charlie to their deaths. The ancient witch died with a cackle cut off by the snap of her neck. Part of me had hoped Charlie would be first. Not that it really mattered when the result would be the same.

They'd both be swinging from ropes soon enough, and I'd have about ten minutes before their life force returned to the earth. Charlie wasn't very powerful, but Molls was, and that power could be what tipped the scales in my favor when I finally took on the Queen.

Charlie struggled to climb the wooden stool while the executioner fitted the coarse rope around his gullet. From the back of the crowd, I heard a woman shouting for them to stop. The humans next to me whirled toward the plea, but I kept my gaze on the way Charlie's eyes softened toward whoever she was. A sister? A daughter? A friend? A lover?

"Stop!" the woman shouted again.

I could have sworn Charlie smiled.

I turned to catch a glimpse of the person attempting to save him. When I saw Aveen weaving between spectators toward the wooden platform, my jaw dropped. What sort of fool interfered with executions? Did she honestly think she could stop this?

The executioner knocked the lever forward, opening the trap door beneath Charlie's single leg.

Crack.

Dead.

Guards in red livery left their post at the front of the dais, headed straight for Aveen. Before I could make a conscious decision, I was shoving everyone aside on my way to the foolish human, grabbing her, and dragging her away.

She thrashed and kicked in a pitiful effort to free herself. "No! Please! Please!" she cried. The orange hair of my glamour reflected in her wild, tear-filled eyes. "Let me go! They need to stop—"

"Shut up," I growled, doing my best not to squeeze the life out of her. I had better things to do than save this foolish human from getting herself killed. If I didn't get back to the bodies, their life forces would be gone, and all of this would've been a colossal waste of time. I towed her to the closest alley, making sure no one followed. Thankfully, the guards seemed to have decided that fighting the crowd was too much effort. "Have you lost your feckin' mind?" I snarled. "Interfering with executions is treason."

If she were one of us, she'd have been hauled right up to the dais without so much as a trial and hung with the others.

Hold on . . .

For the only way to save him was at her own expense.

Maybe I should've let them take her. Ah, well. Too late now.

Her beautiful eyes widened. "Rían?"

I clamped a hand over her gaping mouth. "*Quiet.* Do not use my name." There was no telling who was in that feckin' crowd.

When she nodded, I dropped my hand.

"They killed him," she cried, tears streaming down her flushed cheeks. "They killed an innocent man."

"Charlie was caught with a stolen purse. There were witnesses." Witnesses I would be taking care of as soon as I finished here. After the trial yesterday, I'd followed them to the pub, then to their houses, which were conveniently located at the edge of the O'Meara estate.

Her curls slipped over her shoulders when she shook her head. "You don't get it. He didn't steal it. I did."

Truth.

Feckin' hell . . . The person Charlie had been trying to protect was Aveen.

I created a tost so no one could hear us. "Tell me exactly what happened." If this was her fault, then I'd be the one taking her life. For some reason, the idea of exacting justice didn't delight me as much as it usually did.

She inhaled a shaky breath and swiped at her tears with the back of a trembling hand. "I asked Eithne about you, and she said awful things and made me so bloody angry. So, I-I . . . I blackmailed her."

Hold on. This innocent human had blackmailed someone? I had to admit, I was sort of impressed.

"I took her purse and gave it to the grogoch—to Charlie," she went on, her voice breaking. "I thought he could use the coins and . . . *Oh god.* I'm going to be sick." She jerked away, bracing her hands on the plaster wall and heaving onto the ground. The smell of sick nearly left my own breakfast on the stones next to hers.

I shifted a handkerchief, doing my best not to breathe through my nose as I ordered her to take it and go home. The truth wouldn't help Charlie now.

"I c-can't," she said. "I have to collect Keelynn's dress."

"Tell me where it is, and I will collect it for you."

She didn't answer, just pressed a cheek to the gritty wall and closed her eyes. I didn't have time for this. I needed to get back to the gallows and then head over to the O'Meara estate. "Is it at Meranda's?"

"I don't want your help."

She may not have wanted my help, but she was going to get it. "Don't make me threaten you." How the hell was she going to get home if she could barely stand? She needed a lift. I disbanded the tost and shifted Ruairi from where I'd left him this morning. The brute appeared in the alley, still in his horse form, which saved me a headache.

I caught Aveen's hand and led her toward Ruairi. "Get out of here before you get sick all over my boots."

She resisted like usual, muttering about her coachman.

I told her I'd handle it. What was one more thing added to my never-ending list? I lifted the infernal woman onto the saddle and told the pooka where to take her. There wasn't much time. I had to get back to the gallows now.

Ruairi took off, Aveen clutching his reins for dear life.

I sprinted from the alley straight to the dais, dodging the humans who lingered. A murder of crows had already gathered on the wooden beam where the bodies swung. I went to Molls first, but when I caught her cold foot, there was nothing there to syphon. Biting back a curse, I tried the grogoch. Nothing.

That feckin' human had cost me dearly.

Darkness swelled with each step I took up the cobbled street. Witches were cunning and rarely caught. Molls' power could've been mine. My trembling hands flexed at my sides. It should've been mine, but now it was gone.

Hadn't I learned my lesson about letting emotion get the better of me?

I should've let the woman suffer the consequences for her actions.

A hunched man with white whiskers and a weathered face waited on the bench at the front of the carriage, parked in the same spot it had been on the night Aveen had learned my name. When I approached, he looked up from the ham sandwich clutched between his dirty hands.

"Lady Aveen asked me to give ye a message," I said in the weak, whimpering voice I'd settled on for this character—Mr. Paul

McLoughlin, a farmer from down the coast. "She said that she will meet ye back at her father's estate."

The driver set his sandwich aside and climbed down from his perch with surprising agility for a man of such advanced years. "And why should I believe ye, stranger?"

"Don't. I could care less. Wait here all night if ye want. Either way, she won't be comin'."

I went to turn, but the old man caught my arm in an iron grip, yanking me back around. "What've ye done with milady? If ye've harmed her, I swear—" His blue eyes bounced between mine, suddenly widening. "*You.*" He jerked back, scrubbing a hand down his faded overcoat.

He couldn't know who I was.

Except, from the way his face paled, I had a sinking feeling that he did.

I lunged, but before I could grab him by the throat, the old man, the carriage, and horses all vanished, leaving me standing alone in the alley with a dumbstruck expression.

Who the hell was Aveen's coachman?

As soon as I collected her sister's dress, I would have to find out.

A warm breeze fluttered the curtains on the other side of the manor home's open windows as I passed. Not that I could feel it with this glamour choking the life out of me. It felt too restrictive, like squeezing into a pair of new breeches after eating too much dessert. But if I wanted this to work, I needed to look like one of the pock-marked teens watering horses and mucking stalls.

I headed for a large stable with at least ten stalls. Only four of them held horses. Surely an estate of this size should have more?

A boy came bounding out, ramming head-first into my chest.

He cursed, rubbing at his skull. "Can I help ye?" he asked

through a wince, still scrubbing his mousy brown hair. The same color as my glamour.

"I was sent 'ere fer work," I said, mimicking his thick country accent. He sounded as if he'd been raised in a barn. Fitting, considering his current occupation. "Is there a man I can speak to?"

"They're not hirin'."

"Didn't ask if they were, now, did I?" *Insolent little whelp.* I could have him speared with a pitchfork by his next feckin' blink.

"The man yer lookin' fer is called Padraig," the other boy called from the stall. "He's out with milady."

"Does he live nearby?"

The boy nodded to the far side of the stable. "First cottage down that way."

I thanked him and started down the trail, holding my glamour until I reached a shite little cottage. Finally able to stretch to my full height, I checked the door. Locked, of course. He was Danú. He'd know the rules. I strolled around the back to wait in a garden overgrown with weeds.

"Your secret is safe with me," a familiar feminine voice whispered from within.

Aveen had come to the cottage as well. What a coincidence. I assumed that meant she knew who her coachman was. I couldn't remember anyone powerful enough to be worth noting living around here. How long had this Padraig fellow been in Graystones? Maybe he'd come from one of the other islands.

"I know it is, milady," the coachman said. "Will ye trust me with yers?"

I stepped closer, pressing my ear to the back wall.

Aveen said my name, then the old man shushed her.

Next thing I knew, everything went silent. The bastard must've created a feckin' tost. I couldn't hear a blasted word either of them said about me. How much did this Padraig know? He'd warn her against me, of that much I was sure. Would Aveen listen? What if he told her about the Queen? About my heart?

Very few people knew about the second, but this man was a mystery to me, and there was no telling how much he knew.

After what felt like forever, I finally heard Aveen thank Padraig for whatever he'd said and offer to repay him. The front door opened and closed. Aveen's skirts and curls flew behind her as she ran for the house. I caught the handle and dragged it open again before Padraig could lock it up tight and waste more of my time.

The old man fell back, catching himself on the edge of a shite chair that belonged in a fire. Come to think of it, the entire place should've been burned.

"You and I need to have a little chat, Padraig."

He flicked his wrist, but I'd already warded the place against evanescing in *or* out, so he was stuck until he told me what I needed to know.

The old man spat at my boots. "Be gone, devil."

"That's not very hospitable, now, is it?" I shifted my own chair so I didn't have to sit on either of these . . . *things*. "I know you've been chatting to your mistress about me."

His eyes began to glow an icy blue. The firm set of his whiskered jaw told me he had no desire to answer. And that just wasn't going to work for me. "You aren't on my list of people to kill today, but if you don't start talking, I'll add you."

His jaw unlocked. "I told her to stay clear of ye."

I inhaled nice and slow, watching the emotions play on his face. Fear, yes. But mostly anger. "And what did Aveen say to that?"

"*Lady* Aveen, to ye."

"Ah, yes. Lady Aveen. My apologies. Wouldn't want to disrespect a member of the Airren peerage, now, would I?"

"She is a good human. Leave her be, I beg of ye."

Even the best humans fell from grace to dally with the darkness on occasion. "I'm afraid I can't do that." If fate had wanted someone else to die to save me, she could've chosen someone else. She hadn't, though. Aveen was the key to my freedom, and I wasn't about to let that key slip through my fingers.

Aveen may have been good, but I wasn't.

"You will speak of this to no one, or *Lady* Aveen's—and Lady Keelynn's—deaths will be on your head." Padraig took my proffered hand without hesitation.

Speaking of death. I had to pay two men a visit.

This oak hall table was nice. I could do with a new hall table in the townhouse "Edward" had rented on a whim during his stay in Graystones. Had it been a waste of money? Probably. But now that dear old Padraig knew of my involvement with his employer, I needed to keep a careful eye on the situation until fate decided it was time for my human to die.

The men bleeding out on the floor groaned.

"Could you keep it down? Wouldn't want to disturb the neighbors." Why couldn't people die with dignity? You didn't hear me moaning every time I got my throat slit for breaking a law, did you? No. Because I was a feckin' man, not a whingey child.

What other furniture did they have in here? I climbed up the skinny staircase to the first floor. Nothing worth salvaging, although the one-bedroom suite seemed in good nick. I tore off the quilt and sheets before shifting the bed, two lockers, and an armoire into the main bedroom at the townhouse. Not that I planned on sleeping there very often. But if anyone called, I couldn't have them asking why the place was completely empty.

Back downstairs, one of the men who had testified at Charlie's trial had finally fallen silent. The other one was gone. I followed the trail of blood smeared across the tiles into the kitchen. He wasn't gone-gone. He was only trying to slide himself on broken, bleeding limbs toward the back door.

I squatted down to look into his pain-glazed eyes. "Escaping, are you? How's that working out?" I shifted my dagger and stabbed him in the heart.

He flopped around like a salmon on the shore for about ten seconds.

Oh, salmon. That sounded brilliant for dinner. I'd have to ask Eava to make some with that lovely cream sauce. Too late for today. Maybe tomorrow.

I called a flame to my palm, lighting the walls and wooden table and chairs and kitchen presses on fire. On my way out, I found a decent looking pair of candlesticks. Real silver, too. It'd be such a waste having them melt away with the bodies. I shifted them and the hall table to the townhouse. Once the flames licked at the hideous mustard-colored drapes in the sitting room, I evanesced back to the castle to change out of my blood-splattered shirt.

Another one for the bin. No matter. I had the ones Meranda had ordered for me ready and waiting. The moment I set foot inside the castle, I could hear Ruairi bellowing from the study.

"If ye don't have a chat with yer little brother, then I will."

I strolled to the doorway to lean against the frame, counting the seconds before he realized I was here.

"And I swear I'll take his—" Ruairi spun around, golden eyes wide and nostrils flaring.

"Don't let me interrupt," I said. "You'll take my what? Go on, now. I'd love to hear this. Actually, wait." I shifted a sprig of grapes from the kitchens. "*Now* you may continue." I plucked one from the stem and popped it into my mouth with a smile.

"You're a bastard. You know that?" Ruairi growled.

"That is common knowledge, yes." Dear old dad had had dalliances with both the Queen and her sister. Just so happened he'd gotten Tadhg's mother pregnant first and married her. Not that I could blame the man. Bronagh had been a saint compared to the Queen.

Tadhg clutched his head between his hands. "Will the two of you stop roaring and tell me what happened?"

Ruairi jabbed a thick finger toward my face. "He shifted me, then used me as a feckin' pack horse to carry some human."

Another grape crunched between my teeth. "I fail to see the problem."

"Hold on. Did you just say he shifted you?" Tadhg's head swung toward me, his eyes narrowed. "You *shifted* him?"

I only smiled.

"How are you so powerful?"

I tossed a grape into the air and caught it in my mouth. The trick was knowing you had more time than you thought. Rushing led to failure. "One always appears powerful amidst great weakness."

Tadhg looked ready to blow his stack. Ruairi stalked forward, fangs on full display. Tadhg held up a hand, and the pooka stopped like a good little pup. I sniggered to myself.

"Ruairi is a person, not your own personal transportation," Tadhg insisted. "Shift him again, and you'll suffer the consequences."

"And those would be?" Hungover Tadhg wouldn't hurt a flea. What was I saying? Sober Tadhg couldn't hurt me either. Sure, he could kill me. But he'd have to get the jump on me first, and when I came back, I'd be owed retribution. And I knew how to make death last a long, long time.

My brother's green eyes flared. "Don't test me."

"Ohhh, someone's in a mood." I shifted a bottle of puítin from the drinks cart. "Here. This'll make you feel better."

I set it on the desk in front of him. Tadhg didn't bother picking it up.

I clapped my hands. One more order of business, and I'd be finished for the day. "Right. If that's all, I'll be heading off. Ruairi"—I gave the beast a mock-salute—"lovely as always to see you. Do us a favor, tonight: be sure to piss outside."

"One feckin' time!" he snarled. Again, Tadhg held him back.

I ran upstairs for a shirt, changed, washed the blood from my hands, and headed back out into the courtyard. Muireann called my name from the edge of the fountain, where she was catching the last of the sun's rays before it dipped below the high stone walls. I gave a dismissive wave, having absolutely no desire whatsoever to speak with her.

Once clear of the wards, I evanesced to the farthest edge of Tearmann, to a cottage built on the southernmost tip. You could see Airren's west coast jutting out in the distance. Glittering merrow danced beneath the waves.

I eased open the rusted gate, traipsed across black earth that rivaled the Forest, and rapped on the door with a knuckle.

"Come in," a haunting voice called from within.

I opened the door but didn't bother crossing the threshold. Wouldn't want the sink of death clinging to my clean shirt. "Ned! It's been ages."

A chuckle lifted from the shadows. "Who do ye need me to kill?"

7

EAVA APPEARED IN MY BEDROOM, HUMMING AWAY TO HERSELF LIKE she always did in the kitchens.

I had to grip the towel around my waist to keep from flashing the old witch. "Dammit, Eava. You could've knocked."

She waved a dismissive hand and pottered on over to the desk. "Nothin' I haven't seen before."

"Just because you changed my feckin' nappy when I was a child, doesn't mean I'm comfortable with you seeing me in the nip now."

She set shears and a razor on the desk. "As if I have any interest in seeing yer little doo-da."

"It's not lit—Never mind." I threw on my new breeches, fastening them as quickly as I could so the old witch didn't get an eyeful of my not-little manhood. When I turned back around, she was waiting behind my chair with her arms crossed.

My arse barely touched the seat before she grabbed either side of my head and forced my face this way and that like I'd seen Oscar do with the horse I'd acquired from Robert.

"What's the occasion, my boy?" she asked.

"Why does there need to be an occasion for a haircut?"

"Here." She shifted a plate of tarts onto the desk. "This'll help ye get outta yer piss-poor mood."

"I'm not in a—"

The witch stuffed a tart into my mouth, getting crumbs all over my new breeches. Maybe I was in a mood, but that was only because my mother had me kill three humans in the middle of the feckin' night, and I was wrecked.

"Just a bit off the sides?" She tugged at my ears like she wanted to rip them clean off.

"Have I offended you, Eava?"

"No more than usual," she said on a laugh, collecting the shears and starting to cut. Which reminded me, I still needed to give Ruairi a good trimming. I glanced over at the razor. Maybe I'd shave his hair clean off. He'd probably go into hiding for months. Wouldn't that be brilliant?

Ten minutes was all it took—and thank goodness for that. My neck couldn't take much more pulling and dragging.

Eava propped her fists onto her hips, giving me a good once-over before nodding her approval. "You look very smart indeed, Little Rían."

First my doo-da, now that feckin' nickname. "How many times do I have to tell you not to call me that?" I dragged the towel from my neck, using magic to clean the hair from the floor and send it to the bin.

When I stood, she caught me in a strong embrace, her wrinkled cheek pressed to the scar across my chest. "Ye could be a thousand years old and ye'd still be my little blue-eyed boy."

"I hate hugs."

Her hold on me tightened. "No ye don't." She drew back after a moment, keeping a hold on my arms. "Are ye gonna tell me why yer goin' through all this trouble fer a woman?"

"This has nothing to do with a woman."

The corners of her lips lifted. "I know a smitten man when I see one."

"I am far from smitten." Actually, I wasn't sure why I was

going through all this trouble in the first place. Yes, I would meet Aveen at her sister's birthday ball tonight, but it wasn't as if she would see me without my glamour.

The door burst open, and Tadgh strolled in. "What do I smell?"

The plate of tarts vanished. "I don't know what yer on about," Eava said with a wink before disappearing as well.

Instead of leaving, Tadhg collapsed onto my bed with a groan. "Why aren't you ready yet? We're going to be late."

"I wasn't aware bawdy houses took reservations."

He snorted.

I went to my armoire of shirts and selected a crisp new one to pair with my black waistcoat. Tadhg lounged across my mattress. Although he didn't currently have a bottle in his hand, from the song he was singing, he was clearly well on his way to getting steamed.

The waistcoat was too . . . boring. Sir Edward would surely wear something flashier. I flicked through the hangers, exchanging the waistcoat in my hand for a different one.

"This one's better, isn't it?" I said more to myself than him. My brother was the last person I'd ask for fashion advice. Look at him now, in a pair of dark green trousers, a half-tucked white-ish shirt with the buttons opened at his scarred throat, and a pair of black braces. If I were to describe his style in one word: tragic.

Tadhg's bloodshot eyes narrowed from where he laid upside down on my bed, his dark hair hanging loose. "You're messing, right? That's the same waistcoat you had a moment ago."

"It is clearly different."

"Bollocks."

"This one has silver thread." I pointed down to the delicate stitching Meranda had added as an embellishment. A new favorite. "The other had black."

Tadhg groaned and flopped over. "Just close your eyes and pick one. You always look exactly the same. Black or blue. Like a feckin' bruise."

I'd give him a bruise in a minute if he didn't stop snorting to himself like he was the funniest man in existence. "Not all of us are content to sit around covered in shite."

If the Queen caught wind of me looking like him—missing buttons, stained collar, holes in his trousers—she'd have my head. Literally. I had a reputation to uphold: the face of justice.

How do you expect to garner any respect if you look as though you just crawled out of a barn? You are a prince. You need to look like one.

When I was a child, I'd once come home from Tadhg's with dirt on my sleeve and ended up naked for a week. If I couldn't take care of my clothes, she'd said, then I didn't deserve to wear them. It had been the dead of winter. She'd stripped my bed of its quilts and refused to let me light a fire.

I'd nearly died from pneumonia.

Not that the Queen had cared. If I wasn't strong enough to survive a little cold air, I didn't deserve to live. I never came home dirty again—unlike my brother, who couldn't seem to stay clean.

"Your clothes are going to be on you for exactly ten minutes," Tadhg muttered. "Who cares what you're wearing?"

It was far too early to arrive to the Bannons', and I couldn't use the "because I hate you" excuse for not joining him tonight—I'd used that one last week. The last thing I wanted was for Tadhg to get suspicious and start asking questions.

I'd give him three minutes before he was swept away by the finest women money could buy. Whores weren't interested in kisses, so he shouldn't kill anyone tonight. And if he did, he could take care of the body himself.

On the outskirts of Swiftfell sat a "reputable" establishment that catered to "our kind." Meaning most of the whores were Danú as well, likely forced into this life against their will. Faeries whose wings had been stolen. Fae who'd fallen prey to gambling debts that could never be paid. They smiled, but there was a lifelessness in their eyes I knew all too well.

They may have had hearts, but they were as dead inside as me.

Women swarmed Tadhg the moment he crossed the threshold, a wave of cloying air crashing in their wake. All Ruairi had to do was flash his fangs, and a handful veered in his direction.

I turned my back on the mele when two started for me, then glowered at them until they slithered off toward a pooka and leprechaun drinking at a gaming table near the back.

I joined the men, needing to keep myself occupied until I could leave for Graystones.

A pair of slender arms slipped around my neck; soft, warm hands made their way to my chest. "Anything ye want?" The woman was pretty enough, but her blond hair looked coarse and dry as straw.

"The largest glass of whiskey you have." Being in this place sober turned my stomach. I shifted a coin and pressed it into the woman's outstretched palm. Her smile grew as she tucked it between breasts thrust together by a tight black corset.

I'd have one drink, then slink away into the night and get on with my business.

I shifted a second coin and left it on the edge of the gaming table. The clurichaun dealt me in. When Ruairi dropped down onto the seat next to me, I bit back a curse. A glass appeared at my elbow, filled to the brim with whiskey.

"What're ye drinkin'?" Ruairi asked.

"None of your business."

He put his nose near my drink, and I nearly tossed the lot in his face. "Smells like shite."

"Knowing you'd hate it only makes me enjoy it more."

"I'll have what he's having," he called toward the woman who had served me, slipping a gold coin onto the table next to mine. The dealer handed him cards as well.

I didn't want to be here in the first place, and I certainly didn't want to be here with Ruairi and his obnoxious feckin' smile, but there was no way in hell that I was going to back down from what was clearly a challenge.

I'd beat him out of his gold, he'd drown his sorrow in women, and *then* I'd be on my way.

His drink appeared. He lifted it to his lips and took one long sip, and then another, and another. When he slammed the glass back to the table, it was empty.

I swallowed mine in two gulps, holding his irritating gaze the entire time. The moment I set my glass next to his, he rapped his knuckle against the tabletop, and two more drinks appeared.

The blond wouldn't leave me be, climbing onto my lap, wrinkling my breeches. Running her fingers through my hair, messing it up. Leaving feckin' rouge stains on my neck that I had to clean off again and again. Eventually, I shifted a load of coins to get her to stay away—and to keep the other women circling the table like buzzards at bay as well. Worked a treat. Not for the pooka, though. He had to balance a giggling faerie on his knee as he fumbled for the only full glass in a sea of empty ones left on the table.

The dealer was nowhere to be seen, and I couldn't quite remember who had won.

I assumed it was me because I didn't really want to murder anyone just yet.

The blue-haired faerie whispered something in Ruairi's ear. Before I could order the next round, the pooka caught the woman's waist, stood, and lifted her over his shoulder like a barbarian. "I'll be right back," he announced.

"If you leave, you lose."

His eyes narrowed. "Can't lose if I forfeit."

"Quitting *is* losing." Everyone knew that.

He pressed a hard kiss to the faerie's smiling lips and said, "Doesn't feel like losing to me."

What an . . . an eejit. That's what he was. A complete and utter eejit.

Although, he was the one with a smile on his face as he carried a woman upstairs, and I'd be going back to the castle tonight alone.

Maybe I did need to kill someone.

Luckily, death was on the agenda for midnight.

I managed to haul myself upright, clutching the table to keep from splatting face-first on the manky floor. All the empty glasses rattled. I shifted my pocket watch. *Half-nine?* Far too early to be this drunk. I would need to sober up before heading over to the Bannons'.

Then again, maybe being drunk would make a night among humans more tolerable.

I glamoured myself into the ambassador before stumbling out of the bawdy house, searching this way and that on the empty street.

For some reason, I started thinking of Ruairi carrying that faerie up those stairs.

What would Aveen do if I threw her over my shoulder and carried her to bed? She'd probably curse and threaten to kill me. The thought made me smile as I called on my magic, focusing on where I needed to go.

Not that I'd ever find out what it'd be like to bring her to bed. I didn't dally with maidens. Not a hope. They always had too many expectations I'd never be willing to meet. I'd been Leesha's first, and she'd been mine, and that was one of my few memories that hadn't been tainted by darkness. Something she gave to me and I gave to her that I would never take from another.

My magic swelled, and the void that came before evanescing took hold. Even though I knew it would never happen, a vision of Aveen lying beneath me on her bed popped into my mind, and instead of arriving in the Bannons' garden as I'd planned, I ended up in the woman's bedchamber like some child who'd only just learned to evanesce.

Dresses had been piled on the bed, a mountain of blue. More draped over the chair and chaise, and still more hung askew in the open closet. As foolish as it was, I imagined her trying to find the perfect one just for me.

This place smelled like her.

I collapsed onto her bed, staring up at the canopy. What did she dream about? What did she wish for above all else?

For the only way to save him was at her own expense.

The drunken smile that had found its way to my lips vanished.

"Sir, ye cannot be up here."

I shot upright, finding a dark-haired maid clutching the white apron covering her chest. My gaze flew to the mirror in the corner. Luckily, my glamour remained in place. Would have been a shame to have to kill her.

"My apologies," I murmured, standing and straightening my waistcoat. "I've had a little too much to drink and wandered away from the party."

"No one need know if ye hurry back downstairs," she said with a wink.

"Thank you . . . ?"

"Sylvia, Yer Lordship." Although she curtsied, her dark eyes remained on me.

"Thank you, Sylvia." I gave the maid a quick bow, then went to find my poor, unfortunate soulmate.

The moment I entered the ballroom, my eyes found hers, and damn it all if I didn't smile so wide my face hurt. Instead of avoiding me as I'd been sure she'd do, she headed straight for me, dodging men who looked as if they wanted to gobble her up. Men from her world without murderous mothers. Then again, quite a few elderly women glared in Aveen's direction, so maybe I was wrong about the murderous part.

I took in the neckline of her sky-blue dress, the cameo at her throat, the swell of her breasts, the dip at her waist, and the curve of her hips on my way to a bow. "Lady Aveen, it is a pleasure seeing you again."

"Unfortunately, I cannot say the same, *Ambassador*," she clipped, chin lifting so I could see the spark of fight in her deep blue eyes.

"Is that any way for the lady of the house to speak to a distinguished guest?"

Her nose wrinkled before she lifted a gloved hand to hide it. "It is when the *distinguished* guest smells like a bawdy house."

"And how do you know what a bawdy house smells like?" I shot back.

That chin lifted a little higher. Instead of answering my question, she said, "It's a wonder you decided to show at all. You were obviously enjoying yourself elsewhere."

That was the thing. I hadn't been enjoying myself. Not until this very moment. Pathetic. That's what I was. "And have your sister think me rude? I wouldn't want to ruin her high opinion of me."

"Says the man who showed up to her party drunk."

"Drunk? Such a scathing accusation. I'm sober as a clam." Although if I was to spend my night with these humans without murdering them all, I would need another drink—or ten. My buzz from the bawdy house was already wearing off.

"Right. I'd best be off," she said, as if she didn't care either way. "Enjoy the party." Aveen twirled away, her skirts brushing against my ankles. She couldn't leave. Not yet. If I let her leave, one of these pillocks watching her like hawks was bound to swoop in and steal her away. I followed her across the ballroom, grabbing a glass of champagne from a passing servant.

When we reached the balcony doors, she stopped. "Did you need something else, or do you plan on following me all night?"

"That depends," I muttered, taking a sip of shite champagne.

"On?"

"Whether or not you tell me your wish."

Her hands balled into fists. Fists she settled on her hips. Hips that would give me something to hold onto if I bent her over the cake table and—

"I have decided that I do not want to bargain with you."

I forced my eyes back to hers. "Is that right?"

"Yes," she said with a little nod that made the curls framing her face flutter. "And I know you're not cursed."

"Am I not? Well, that's a relief." Although my empty chest would disagree.

"While I appreciate what you did for me yesterday, I did not ask for your help, so I don't feel I owe you anything in return. The only reason I'm tolerating your presence tonight is because my sister invited you. So, you can take yourself and your wish and find someone else to torment."

There were a lot of words coming out of her mouth, and I really ought to have been paying attention, but all I could focus on was the way the pink skin of her lips glistened in the candlelight. The one kiss we'd shared wouldn't be enough. It wasn't even a proper kiss. No, I needed to kiss this woman so thoroughly that those lips would be swollen.

And after I finished kissing her mouth, I'd kiss her throat. Then I'd cut her out of that pretty blue dress and kiss the rest of her as well.

"Ambassador!" Aveen scowled at me as if I'd spoken my thoughts aloud.

I hadn't, though. I was ninety-percent sure, because if I had, she would've one hundred percent slapped me. She was so pretty when she frowned like that. "I like your dress." *I'd like it better off.*

"Were you listening to me?"

A little. She'd said something about appreciating me and tolerating my presence, and she'd used the word "torment" at least once. And something about people getting the wrong idea.

A quick scan of the room told me that her fears were for naught. "No one is paying us the least bit of attention." I tilted my head so I could hear better, listening as I drank, the last sip of champagne tasting far better than the first. "They're too busy nattering about Lady Samantha's husband going off with Lord Ketter's wife"—whoever the hell they were—"and Lady Julia's baby bump, which is rather large for someone married only three months."

Aveen's eyes darted this way and that, her head inclining toward the crowd. "You can hear them from here?"

"Fae hearing. Although this one's fecked." That blow to the head had been sore before it'd killed me. The almost imperceptible ringing in my left ear drove me mad at night.

"Why? What happened to your ear?"

As if I'd talk about it with her when there were so many more delightful topics to discuss. "You look positively delectable tonight." You know what this party needed? Better drink. I shifted a flask into my back pocket, withdrawing it as though it had been there all along.

"Did you hear what I said?" she asked in the most demanding tone that, I had to admit, really did it for me.

I'd bet she'd be demanding between the sheets. "Did you hear what *I* said?" She smelled so good. Did she know how good she smelled? She probably didn't even notice it anymore. I noticed it, especially when I moved closer. "I wonder if you taste as good as you smell."

Hearing her breath catch wreaked havoc on my body. "You mustn't speak so improperly. Someone may hear you."

If that's all she was worried about, I could fix that with a flick of my wrist. I created a tost, blocking out all noise except the sound of her racing heart and uneven breathing.

"There. Now I can say whatever I want and *noooo* one can hear us." I drank a little more, just enough to add a little fire to my throat. "You're a viper tonight. Makes me want to do all sorts of *improper* things with you." I glanced over to where two humans were eating cake. What would my little viper do if I painted her naked body with icing and then licked it off? She'd still be a maiden afterwards, so *technically*, I wouldn't be breaking my rule.

"That's quite enough, Rían."

So that's a no on the icing paint. "It's Ambassador DeWarn, remember? Or Edward, if you're feeling *improper*."

All it took was another flick of my wrist for the world to rush in, filling my head with meaningless chatter and terrible music. I noticed Lady Eithne sipping wine next to her husband. I'd wasted enough of the evening flirting with Aveen. Time to focus on the real reason I was here.

"Seeing as you and I no longer have any business together, I'm off to have fun with these humans." I sent my now-empty flask away. "If you're looking for a bit of devilment, you know where to find me."

I collected another glass of champagne and stalked toward my prey.

8

Brag, brag, brag. That's all these arrogant bastards seemed to know how to do. *I have more horses. I have more tenant farmers. My coffers are overflowing with silver. Mine are filled with gold.* On and on, round and round, a relentless back and forth of one-upmanship. The tedium had nearly put me to sleep with my eyes open. The wine in my hand wasn't helping either.

Their titles were nothing more than names written on paper that would eventually be forgotten or burned when the next tyrant decided to invade and take everything they'd never earned.

I wasn't even sure they realized I was still standing here, bored to tears and trying not to make it obvious that I couldn't stop staring at Aveen. I should have been chatting to Eithne, but her husband had been glued to her side all feckin' night.

I forced my attention back to the most insufferable peacocking man of the lot: Robert. He was obviously a younger son, trying to make up for that shortcoming by besting everyone else.

My father this . . .

My father that . . .

I could boast about my father as well. But what had Robert done to prove he wasn't a useless piece of—

Shit. Why were they all looking at me? "I'm sorry," I muttered, sipping from the glass of wine I'd shifted from Tadhg's private stash. "I wasn't paying the least bit of attention to any of you."

Two of the younger men hid their laughter behind polite coughs. The eldest's face went red, and a vein in his forehead pulsed. "I asked where you hail from, Ambassador."

"Most recently, Vellana City," I said, because it was expected. For fun, I added, "But I was born near the Black Forest."

"How near?" Robert asked.

"You could see it from my house."

"Have you ever seen the Queen?" the thin man with a receding hairline next to him asked once he lifted his jaw from the floor.

"I have."

"Is it true she feeds on souls?" asked one with a thick beard.

"Life force," I corrected.

"Is there a difference?" Robert sniffed, trying to look down his nose at me even though we were the same height.

"Well, *Robert*," I drawled, lifting my glass in mock salute, "if the Queen fed on your life force, you'd die. But if she consumed your soul, you couldn't go to hell after."

With Robert choking on his indignation, I turned my attention back to Aveen, who happened to be speaking with her sister about some man named James Wallace whom Aveen found attractive.

"*Perhaps you can marry him,*" the sister said with a grating giggle.

Poor James Wallace just made it to the top of my list of who to kill at this dreadful ball.

Aveen's nose wrinkled. "*Pass.*"

The sister kept on about marriage, not seeming to notice the tension coiling in Aveen's shoulders or the way her face paled despite the layer of paint she wore.

"*Or, you already have someone in mind,*" the sister drawled.

Had she chosen a husband? What would I do about it if she had?

"*Don't be daft,*" Aveen hissed.

Even if I were next to her, there'd be no way of knowing for sure if she was lying since she hadn't given a proper answer.

Aveen's sister searched the crowd. When her gaze landed on me, she gave me a dazzling smile. *"That's it, isn't it? Could it be a mysterious man with dark hair and blue eyes so deep you could drown in them?"*

When Aveen turned, I winked at her.

She couldn't hide her ferocious blush as she caught her sister's hand, dragging her closer and turning around as if that would keep me from overhearing their conversation.

"I am not marrying Ambassador Flirt."

"Why not? Did you see his arse in those fitted breeches?"

"Keelynn!"

This night had turned out to be entertaining after all.

"Which of our fine Airren women has caught your attention?" a grating voice asked from over my shoulder.

Robert.

As much as I didn't want to chat with him, I turned and said, "I don't see how that's any of your business."

His smile tightened. "Let us speak plainly. Which one of the Bannons are you after?"

All I did was smile.

"Dammit, man. Tell me. Is it Lady Aveen or Lady Keelynn?"

All I did was sip my wine.

"They're off limits."

"Why? Do you plan on marrying them both?"

He cursed and stomped away to ask the youngest sister to dance. After some protest, she agreed, leaving Aveen all alone. *Not alone.* At least four men started for the dance floor, beady eyes trained on my soulmate.

Not today, lads. I ran to her, catching her hand and pulling her close.

"What do you think you're doing?" she asked in a breathless whisper.

It should have been plainly obvious by the way I held her and the fact that we were on the dance floor. "Ambassador Flirt and his fitted breeches are dancing with you."

I could've danced with Aveen all night. A foolish desire I had to squash. I wasn't here to flirt with her. There were other, more important matters to attend to. I sought out Lady Eithne, finding her eyes already fixed on me. She slowly rolled the rim of her glass against her lips, likely trying to be seductive.

Edward DeWarn didn't know how awful she was, so it made sense that he would respond to the question in her eyes. I swallowed the bile rising in the back of my throat as I approached. It helped knowing this would be the last time I'd ever have to speak to the vile woman.

"Lady Eithne, isn't it?" I said.

She dipped into a low curtsey. "Lovely to make your acquaintance, Ambassador."

"You know who I am?" I feigned shock. She'd been checking up on me. *Good.* That should make the next part of this plan easier. Me reeking of women's perfume certainly helped. And all the drinking I'd done should make her believe I could be easily swayed.

"I may have inquired after you," she said, looking up at me through half-lidded eyes.

From over her head, I saw Robert beeline straight for Aveen. The man had the gall to try and warn her away from me. Where'd he get off, sticking his nose in my business? He didn't see me going around the place telling every woman what I thought of him, did he?

Eithne batted her thick lashes, drawing me back to the situation at hand. I could deal with Robert later. "What would your husband think?" I asked, forcing myself to pay attention.

Eithne's giggle left my stomach lurching. "What he doesn't know," she whispered, pressing a gloved finger to her lips.

This sort of shite happened more often than not—the joys of marrying for money, wealth, and position over a genuine connection. I stepped closer to the doorway, a breeze kicking up at my back. "The gardens look lovely this evening, don't they?"

"Perfect for a moonlit stroll," Eithne agreed, offering a pointed look before sinking into the night.

I finished my drink, abandoned the glass on the closest windowsill, and started after her. *Just shy of midnight. Perfect timing.*

I caught up to her by the path, tugging her deeper and deeper into the garden until we reached a trellis of budding roses. When Eithne caught my cravat and dragged my mouth to hers, a different face flashed in my mind. Aveen was all I could smell. Aveen was all I could think of.

Kissing this woman was like trying to catch a feckin' salmon with bare hands. Wriggling and thrashing and wet.

I came up for air, trying not to make it obvious I needed to wipe my mouth and doing my best not to gag. Eithne took the opportunity to tug at my belt, but I had no intention of being caught with my cock out when Ned came by. He'd never let me live it down.

In the distance, I heard footsteps, too light to belong to Ned. When I told Eithne I would be right back, she licked her lips and told me to hurry.

I found Aveen stomping through the gravel, scowling toward the garden.

I had one job to do tonight, and if this woman didn't get her arse back into the feckin' ball, she wouldn't live to see tomorrow.

Ned knew there was to be a woman in the garden at midnight, but if he found two, I knew he'd try to take them both.

I evanesced to a bench closer to the house, removing my glamour. I didn't want to be someone else with her. For a few minutes, I just wanted to be me. "Spying is terribly rude," I said.

Aveen's skirts billowed when she whirled. I swore I could taste the anger rolling off her in waves. When she saw me, she startled, her gaze raking down my face with such intensity, it felt like flames licking my skin.

"These are my gardens," Aveen insisted. "I suggest you take your tryst someplace else."

"And I suggest you go back to the party."

She propped her fists against her hips, leaning forward until we were nose to nose. "Lady Eithne is married, you know. She has a husband right inside."

As if I cared whether the woman was married or not when she had sent an innocent man to his death. "That sounds like her problem, not mine."

"I should've known a . . . a man so lacking in morals wouldn't care about sacred vows."

"Ah, here now. If you're jealous, I'd be more than happy to show you how lacking in morals I really am once I finish out here." As soon as Eithne was dead, I could meet her in her chambers. Was there any icing left?

"I'm not jealous."

The lie tasted of honeysuckle and sugar. She *was* jealous. Over me. The realization shouldn't have sent a thrill up my spine. "Liar."

Before I could force her to return to the house, the ground beneath my boots trembled. The telltale *thump thump thump* of hooves pounded the earth.

The heavy fog of death lingering on a carrion breeze burned my nostrils.

Aveen stood there scowling as if she hadn't heard or smelled any of it. "You are the worst person I have ever—"

Ned was coming.

Ned was here.

Ned was going to find Aveen.

I evanesced, stifling Aveen's insult with my hand, dragging her against me and pulling her as far into the laurels as I could. My magic slipped free. I hoped it would be enough to conceal her from Ned. I swore I felt my heart thundering. Or maybe it was just Aveen's hammering through her body to mine.

The hooves came to an abrupt halt. Ned couldn't see us on account of him not having a head and all, but he would be able to sense we were near. Did Aveen know of the Dullahan? Had she heard the stories of the way he fed on a human's life force and consumed their very essence? The Queen did the same, but her victims needed to be newly dead.

The Dullahan needed his alive.

Ned came around the corner, his uneven footsteps lumbering and stilted, dragging his spine whip in his free hand. He really needed to get a new head. The one he held aloft like a feckin' lantern had seen better days.

Aveen whimpered, trembling against me.

"Whatever you do, do not tell him your name," I whispered. If he knew your name, he owned your soul.

Aveen's body began to relax, like she trusted me to keep her safe.

How foolish. How naïve. How . . . strange. When was the last time a human who knew who I was had found comfort in my presence? They usually ran and hid. An odd tingling began in my chest, spreading through my limbs.

Aveen relaxed a bit more, her muscles uncoiling and heartbeat slowing.

Then she slumped.

Too late I realized that it wasn't trust but Ned's magic that had made her relax. Her face was so feckin' pale, and I could barely hear her heart. I needed to go to Eithne, demand the monster take her instead, but once he'd started draining, there would be no deterring him.

"He's not here for you. Fight it." Even as I said the words, her fortune hung in the frigid air between us.

For the only way to save him was at her own expense.

Was this her fate? If I gave her up, maybe it would lead me one step closer to ending the Queen.

All I had to do was let Aveen go.

Who was I to deny destiny? I wasn't a hero. I was willing to lie, steal, and cheat to get what I wanted, and all I'd ever wanted was to be free of the Queen's control.

Let her go, the darkness inside me roared.

My arms tightened.

Let her go!

How? How could I let her go? How could I let her die for mistakes I'd made centuries ago? *She is good. She is kind. She doesn't deserve this fate.*

"Think of something else," I begged, my voice cracking. Panic like I'd only ever experienced once in my life seized my core, crushing my lungs. "Anything else. Distract yourself."

Aveen couldn't die. I couldn't let her.

"Don't go to him. Stay with me. Please. *Please.*" My freedom wasn't worth it. Wasn't worth *her*. I removed my hand from Aveen's mouth, her face ghostly pale when I turned her in my arms. *Come back to me. Please.*

She was cold and stiff as a corpse. I needed to warm her up. If only I could light a fire without being seen. *A fire. That's it.* I eased forward until my lips skimmed hers. *Please let this work. Please.* Sparks shot through my veins. I willed them toward her.

She remained cold. Unresponsive. Silent.

Please. Please. Not her. Not yet.

I kissed her harder, deeper, forcing the panic from my mind, praying there was some way to save her from this. To bring her back to me.

Aveen's eyes burst open, and the relief I felt at seeing her pupils dilate left me clutching her against me as if she had been the one to save me.

Her mouth opened, welcoming my tongue, tangling and tasting of life and light, kissing me as if this kiss were her last. Her back arched, thrusting her glorious chest against mine. My hands skimmed her ribs, the underside of her breasts, begging to move higher, to take anything she was willing to give.

Only, to be with me meant certain death.

And now I knew that I couldn't let her die.

I had to fight fate. Deny destiny.

I had to leave Aveen—and my only chance at freedom —behind.

When I ripped myself away from her, it felt as if someone had torn me in two. She'd stolen a piece of me—a piece I would never get back. Not of my heart. I didn't have one of those.

But of my soul.

Aveen whimpered when she collided with the bench. Seeing her plump lips swollen from mine was better than any of my fantasies. Instead of giving in to despair, I clung to my rage, knowing this was goodbye. "Get inside before I send you to the underworld myself," I snarled, an empty threat from an empty man.

A bloodcurdling scream pierced the night.

I turned toward the roses where I'd abandoned Eithne. By the time I twisted back around, Aveen was gone.

9

I PASSED THE HIDEOUS TAPESTRIES DOCUMENTING DANÚ history that did nothing but gather dust in the castle hallway. The only reason I hadn't ripped them down and thrown them into the fire was because seeing the Queen's ruthless face, the delight in her black eyes as she cradled the human heads she'd severed, spurred me on. Gave me purpose.

A purpose I'd abandoned in Graystones.

I made my way into the darkened family room, not bothering to light a fire.

Family room.

What about those of us without a family? Was it just a room? Who came up with the names of these places anyway?

I fell onto the sofa and shifted a bottle of faerie wine and a glass right as Tadhg strolled in.

"Abso-feckin-lutely not," I ground out.

He froze mid-stride, seeming startled to find me sitting in the darkness.

"You don't get to drink tonight," I told him. Drinking tonight meant he'd be useless tomorrow. And I didn't have it in me to do his job any longer.

"Who put the bee in your bonnet?" Tadhg dropped beside me on the cushion.

I sipped my drink, letting the question fade into the silence.

He shifted a glass and gave himself a generous pour, ignoring my scowl. If he was hungover tomorrow, Tearmann could go without a ruler, because I planned on drinking for the foreseeable future.

He sat there for the longest time, studying me, clinking his nail against the glass. "Muireann was asking for you."

"So?"

"So, you always feel better after a dip in her pond."

"I'm fine."

"Clearly." He smirked. "What're we drinking to?"

"Love."

He huffed a humorless chuckle, raising his drink toward mine. "To the one thing we need that we'll never find."

I tapped my glass against his, prepared to drown.

My mind. It was gone. *Poof.* Like a cloud. The faerie wine rotting in my gut wasn't helping either. Every time I closed my eyes, I smelled roses. Every time I opened them, I found myself searching the darkness for golden curls and a smile as rare as snow in July.

I peered across the settee to where Tadhg lounged, staring up at the ceiling. "You know fire, right?"

He angled his head slightly to look at me. "I've heard of it."

"She just . . . every time she touches me, it's like flames licking my skin." What would it be like if Aveen actually licked my skin?

"Who are we talking about?"

"No one," I muttered into my glass, the sound echoing.

"Ah, yes, of course."

I finished what was left but couldn't bring myself to pour any more. "When I kissed her . . ." I would never recover from the utter devastation of her lips. Tadhg wouldn't understand. Not when women threw themselves at him left, right, and feckin' center. And he didn't have a psychotic mother waiting in the wings to rip out their hearts.

Every day I spent away from Aveen made it a little harder to breathe. To put one foot in front of the other. To open my eyes knowing they would never again behold her smile. I'd become a simpleton, and there was no end in sight.

"If you're so smitten, then why are you still sitting beside me, drinking my liquor, nattering on and on about shite I care nothing about?" Tadhg asked.

"What am I supposed to do? Go to her?" Could you imagine? Me evanescing into her room to ask her to put aside her own safety, to give up her life for an empty shell? What could I possibly offer her besides misery and a bounty on her head?

No, no. This was better for everyone. Until I could end the Phantom Queen and her hold over me, Aveen was better off on the other side of the island.

What I needed right now was to rid myself of her.

Tadhg called after me when I stood, but I ignored him.

Crossing the uneven stone floor was like rowing a dinghy through a stormy sea. I tripped more times than I could count on my way to the front door.

"Muireann!" My shout echoed off the stone ramparts. It was night. Or morning. Hard to tell. All I knew was that, with the courtyard blessedly empty, no one could see me stumbling forward, catching myself on the edge of the fountain, or letting the glass slip from my fingers to shatter on the gravel.

I smacked the fountain's cold water, which came straight from the sea. Bubbles of air rippled the surface, and Muireann emerged like a goddess, pointed chin raised to the starless sky, droplets rolling down her blue-tinted skin, between her bare breasts.

"Need I ask why ye were callin' fer me, or shall I hazard a guess?" The salve of her siren's voice was nothing compared to the feeling of her long, thin, webbed fingers sliding up my thigh.

"You're getting my breeches wet."

She grinned, revealing two rows of razor-sharp teeth. "Isn't that the point?"

She was right. It was the point. Aveen had found me. And now all I wanted to do was get lost again. Expert fingers unfastened my belt. Popped the buttons on my breeches. Reached inside and clasped a hand over me.

I watched her the way I always did. Wouldn't put it past the fish to tear my throat out with her teeth.

"Am I the only one playing tonight?" The sweetness in her voice shifted to a grating whine.

I kissed her neck dutifully, but her skin felt like a corpse's, reminding me of the night I almost lost *her*. She tasted like salt and seaweed. And her breasts were too small. I couldn't pretend she was someone else when everything about her felt wrong. I tried shutting my eyes, but my lids had barely closed before they popped open again. I caught her wrist and threw her hand off me. It wasn't Muireann I wanted at all. Not her hands or her mouth or her body. It was someone else's. Someone I could never have.

I left the merrow ranting on the edge of the fountain and evanesced to my room, my cock still as hard as the stone wall. I only closed my eyes once I was alone. And the moment I did, I saw *her*.

Laughing as she danced. Scowling when I said something "improper." Those soft, supple lips swollen from mine. Utter perfection.

I steadied my forearm against the wall, dropping my head against the stones, wishing their coolness would douse the fire roaring in my veins as I imagined her body beneath me, both of us stripped bare.

I tugged down the front of my breeches, gripping myself in my fist.

How she would feel. The sounds she'd make. How she'd whimper and writhe. A sheet of golden curls spread across my pillow. I'd work for it.

Fuck, I'd work.

Pumping my fist hard and fast, exactly how I would take her, I imagined the screams I could tear from that lovely, lovely throat. I came like a feckin' teenager, her name on my lips where she'd never be again.

I wasn't sure what day it was or how long I'd been laying on the settee. Could be Tuesday. Could be Sunday. Hard to tell. It definitely wasn't Friday because no one was bothering us.

I heard Oscar's voice in the hallway. Then came a feminine response.

I'd spoken too soon about being left alone. For once, I thought I was drunker than Tadhg. He didn't seem to have any trouble getting up from the chair, while I, on the other hand, could barely sit up.

"Where's yer brother? I've a message fer him," the woman said.

Hold on. I knew that voice. I pulled myself upright to peer over the back of the settee. Meranda waited in the doorway, a black cloak draped over her shoulders and a hood pulled over her frizzy red hair. From inside the cloak, she withdrew a piece of paper.

"I don't want it," I told her. She could take her message and burn it for all I cared.

"I think ye do."

If I hauled my arse off the settee and this wasn't worth it, I'd have her head.

> *I must speak with you.*
> *It's urgent.*

Who the hell needed to speak to—

From the corner of my eye, I saw Meranda's scowl deepen.

It couldn't be . . . Could it?

"What does it say?" Tadhg asked, topping up his glass.

I shifted him to the oubliette and summoned a tost. "Who is this from?"

"Ye know who it's from. And I'll tell ye right now, if ye think fer a moment that I'm going to let ye plague that good woman, ye had better set yer sights on someone else. She is one of the only humans in that wretched town that I can stand. Far too fine for ye."

Aveen. The message was from Aveen.

My stomach fluttered. *Actually* fluttered, like a feckin' butterfly. What the hell was wrong with me?

"Why is she looking for me? Did she say? How did she look?" Feckin' drink had questions spilling from my tongue like some lovesick eejit. *Reign it in, lad.*

Meranda studied me for far too long before responding. "She seemed anxious. Worried. Upset."

That couldn't be right. Humans were only anxious, worried, and upset when I hung around. "Did she say anything else? Anything at all to indicate why she needed me?"

Meranda shook her head.

I shoved the note into my pocket and eliminated the tost just as my brother barreled into the room, a murderous gleam in his emerald eyes. "Try that again and see what happens to your—"

I held up a hand, too preoccupied to hear his baseless threats.

Tadhg turned to Meranda and smiled. "Tell me your message, and I'll make it worth your while."

I caught him by the collar, dragging him back. "Breathe a word of this, and your life is forfeit," I warned the witch. Tadhg couldn't know about Aveen. The thought of him turning his sights on her . . . I couldn't cope.

Meranda's lips curled into a wicked smile as her gaze bounced between the two of us. "I'd be more than willing to keep this information from your handsome brother . . . fer a price."

"Name it."

She tapped a pointed nail against her chin, still looking at

Tadhg as if she wanted to eat him alive. "A chest of gold from yer coffers should suffice," she finally said. "I've my eye on some Vellanian leather, and that shite doesn't come cheap."

"Done."

With an obnoxious giggle, she rocked forward on her toes, clapping her hands beneath her chin. I caught her hand, allowing the magic from our bargain to bind us together.

Meranda left as soon as I shifted a chest of gold to her home back in Graystones.

"Ohhhh, would you look at that," Tadhg murmured.

I glanced over at my brother to find him clutching my feckin' note. The bastard must've shifted it when I wasn't paying attention. "Give it back, or so help me . . ."

"*I must speak with you,*" he mimicked in a high voice. "*It's urgent.*" He pinched the note between his thumb and forefinger, giving it a shake. "I take it this is from 'no one' with the fiery touch? Where is Meranda living now? Graystones, isn't it?"

Bollocks. "Don't."

He gave me a wolfish grin, drumming his fingers against his cursed lips. "Could my heartless little brother be in love with a woman from Graystones? How scandalous."

"Tadhg, please. You know what the Queen will do to her."

His smile faded, and he rolled his eyes, throwing the note onto the drink-splattered coffee table, muttering that I was no fun when I was melancholy.

I sank onto the cushion and stared at the note for far too long, trying to figure out what to do. Going to her could bring certain death. But she was clearly in trouble.

Maybe I could . . .

Feck it anyway, I couldn't believe I was saying this.

Maybe I could help.

10

Two days.

That was how long it took for Tadhg to lose interest in Aveen's note. Two long, excruciating days of having to live under his intense scrutiny. Any time I stepped out of a room, Tadhg was there, smirking.

Thankfully, Ruairi showed up the second night, distracting my brother with drink and women, and I was able to slip out the kitchen door unnoticed. If Tadhg really wanted to learn my whereabouts, all he had to do was convince Eava to do some scrying, but I was confident he'd been deep enough in his cups that he wouldn't be bothered by my absence.

It wasn't as if I intended to linger at Aveen's house. I'd simply ask what she needed and decide whether to help. I evanesced to her garden, crossing the damp grass until I could see her bedroom window. Was this a bad idea? Probably. Was I going to do it anyway? Yes.

I remembered how it felt to lie on her bed, so that's where I went.

Aveen sat on her chair, head in her hands and shoulders curled, crying. Seeing her upset did strange things to my chest. "I cannot stand weepy women," I announced.

She launched upright, twisting and catching herself on the chair's arm.

"You're here," she breathed, scrubbing at tear-stained cheeks.

My throat swelled, making it hard to swallow. *Who hurt you?* "Did you miss me?"

She gave one final sniffle, rubbing her red nose against her sleeve. "Of course not."

There it was. A lie to give me hope I didn't want. "Did you just want to stare at me, or was there something *urgent* you wished to discuss?"

She shifted on her toes, catching her skirts in her fists. "I want to avail of that wish you promised."

The useless hope within me died, turning to darkness. What had I honestly thought? That she'd called on me to confess her undying devotion? No. She wanted to use me for my magic. How disappointingly human of her. "I promised you a wish in exchange for breaking a curse. Seeing as you've refused to do your part, there shall be no wish."

"Please. I need that wish."

"Why? What has changed?" Last week she'd told me to go and shite, and today she was practically begging.

"I am to be married to a man I cannot stand."

My hollow chest wrenched, my ribs collapsing into the empty cavity. From the way men had been traipsing in and out of their manor, it was painfully obvious her father was anxious to marry her off. Still, for it to happen so soon . . . And to someone she couldn't stand? Part of me rejoiced at that. I didn't know what I would've done if she had said she'd fallen in love with someone else.

"Do you want me to kill him?" Because I would. And I would relish every moment. Carve him up like a pheasant. Feed him to some bloodthirsty merrow.

"Of course not."

"Then what do you expect me to do about it?"

She came forward, seeking me out as if I were some sort of

hero come to save her. The foolish human really didn't know who she was dealing with. "I want you to convince Lord Trench to pair Robert with Keelynn."

Robert? Robert feckin' Trench? She was to marry that arrogant prick?

Maybe I'd kill him anyway.

"My magic doesn't work like that. I can curse him, or I can kill him," I explained. "If neither of those options suit, then I'm afraid this discussion is over." This was none of my affair. I really shouldn't get involved with humans and their asinine laws.

Her hand shot out, clamping around my wrist, sending flames burning through my veins. Could she feel it too? Or was this only my curse to bear?

"I am desperate," she whispered. "I would rather die than marry Robert Trench."

Those words only made the flames burn brighter as a plan began to take shape in my mind.

"You would rather die . . ."

If I did what I was thinking, what possible consequences would there be? No one had to know. Except my brother, of course. All these years of hauling away bodies and cleaning up his messes should count for *something*.

The Queen could never find out. But if my brother kissed Aveen and she died, she would be just another faceless victim of the Gancanagh. The Queen wouldn't pay her the least bit of attention. This . . . this *could* work.

"If I grant you this wish, what will you give me in return?" I asked.

"What do you want?"

You.

"A favor of my choosing," I said before anything else could come out. Wouldn't do me any good to have her realize that I was as desperate to free her from that bastard as she was to escape.

"I cannot give you a blanket favor," she said, her tone weak and weary, as if she were trying to convince herself, not me.

"That is your choice, and you are free to make it. Goodbye, Aveen." I evanesced, but not far, just down to the garden below. Close enough to hear if she changed her mind, holding my breath until I heard her call my name.

"Rían! Come back! I accept your bargain."

I returned in a flash, finding her in a heap on the floor, tears glittering in her eyes. I took her hand before she could change her mind again, tethering her life to mine, our promises like an iron chain between us. "I have a plan to give you what you desire," I said, "but for it to work, you will need to do exactly as I say. Do you understand?"

She nodded, fear and confusion in her tear-filled eyes.

"Go about your life as though nothing is amiss. Once everything is in place, I will return to give you further instructions."

I evanesced to the castle, ran through the wards, then went straight to my brother's room. The place was a sty, clothes strewn everywhere, bottles glistening in the moonlight. There was no sign of the man, so I'd have to wait until the next morning to tell him about my plan.

At sunrise, I was up and out of bed, bursting through Tadhg's door with a smile on my face. "Rise and shine, big brother." From the cloudless sky peeking between the drawn curtains, it looked as if this would be a glorious day.

"Go away," Tadhg croaked from beneath a pillow, his voice scratchy and hoarse.

"You get to help me."

He lifted the corner of the pillow to peer out at me. "Not a feckin' hope."

For once, could he just do something without being a pain in my arse? I flopped onto the bed next to him, propping my hands behind my head. With a groan, he dropped the pillow.

"How many women have you killed?" I asked, knowing he wouldn't respond but feeling the need to poke him anyway. "I have an idea! Let's count." I shifted the green leather ledger that he kept on the bedside table. "Let's see, your first victim was—"

Tadhg shot upright, snatching the book with a curse and propping himself against the headboard. He scrubbed a hand down his stubbled cheek, his red-rimmed eyes narrowed. "Tell me what you want so that I can go back to sleep."

"I need you to kill someone."

Uncertainty flashed in his bloodshot eyes. His face was so easy to read when he had drink on board. The curse was slowly driving him mad. I knew it. He knew it. Ruairi knew it. Eava knew it. None of us talked about it. "That's your area of expertise," he said.

"The people I kill don't come back." Most of them, anyway.

He scratched his head, uncovering the tips of his pointed ears —another thing he'd inherited from our father, along with his love of the fairer sex. "And in return?"

"In return, you get a warm fuzzy feeling in your useless heart for helping your favorite brother with something important."

"Not good enough." He scoured me from my head to my breeches. "I want your black cufflinks."

"Why? You don't even wear cufflinks." Most of the time, his cuffs ended up shoved over his elbows.

"Maybe I want to melt them down and make you watch."

"Those are worth a small—" I bit my tongue to keep from making this worse. "You know what? Fine. If you help me, you can have the feckin' things."

He bounced on the bed like the child he was, all giddy and full of grins. *Insufferable.*

I braced my hands against my knees, inhaling a deep breath. Once the words left my lips, I couldn't take them back. What if Aveen fell madly in love with my brother the way every other woman seemed to? I'd been getting screwed over by fate for two hundred and thirty years. Fate owed me something good.

Out of darkness shines a light . . .

Aveen was the only light I could see.

This *would* work . . . *if* I convinced my brother not to pursue her.

If I said she was my friend, he would most assuredly try something. If I told him she was my soulmate, he may still try, if only to get under my skin. If I made him believe that she wanted to be mine and mine alone, that should give me the leverage I needed to keep his filthy hands off her.

With a flick of my wrist, a tost descended over us. "I need you to curse my fiancée."

Tadhg stopped bouncing. "Did you just say your *fiancée*?"

"That's what I said, yes."

"Since when are you getting married?"

"My relationship is none of your concern. However, her father has ordered her to marry a miserable human, and we need a way for her to bow out of the engagement while saving face."

His eyes bulged. "Your fiancée is *human*?"

I glared at him.

"And she's willing to bear a year in the underworld," he said slowly, as if the words weren't registering, "to be with *you*?" A slow smile hooked the corners of his cursed lips. "And you need *me* to kiss her."

"I need you to *curse* her and *kill* her," I corrected. Unfortunately, he had to use his vile mouth to do it.

He threw a hand behind his head and settled back down against the pillows, splaying his free hand over his bare stomach. "What's your lady love's name?"

I gritted my jaw.

"Come now. I'll need her name for this." He rapped his knuckle against the ledger.

"Her name is Aveen."

"Aveen." Hearing her name on his lips made me want to rip out his throat. "You know, I've always loved that name. Right, so. Let's pay Aveen a visit, shall we?"

"I need to speak with her first. I'll let you know when we need you."

"You want me to kiss a woman I've never met?" Tadhg clicked his tongue. "What sort of man do you think I am?"

In the end, I couldn't dissuade Tadhg from accompanying me. The best I could do was to negotiate for ten minutes alone to speak with Aveen before he stepped into the picture.

I spent the afternoon going over my speech. Too many details at this stage could do more harm than good. She needed short, sweet, and to the point. When I couldn't see her in the parlor and didn't find her in her bedroom, I ventured into the hallway.

The soft kiss of slippers swept up the stairs, growing louder and louder. I ducked into one of the bay windows, peering out to find my "fiancée" stalking down the hall toward her room.

Having already wasted most of my allotted time searching for her, when I grabbed Aveen and dragged her into the alcove with me, I skipped the formalities.

The woman squealed, but when her gaze met mine, she fell silent.

"Listen carefully, there isn't much time." I dragged the ring that I'd picked out just for her from my pocket. Stupid, really, considering all of this was a sham. But if it hadn't been a sham, would she like the ring or hate it? I should've gone with a diamond, but the sapphire spoke to me. Not that it mattered either way. It wasn't like she would be wearing the thing for any length of time.

"Put this on," I instructed, feeling strange when she accepted the ring without balking. Until she put it on the wrong feckin' hand.

"Not that finger." I flicked my wrist, shifting the ring to the proper finger, the one that meant she belonged to me. "Now pretend to be madly in love with me."

Her eyes flew back to mine. "W-what?"

Did she have to sound so feckin' confused? Was it that far-fetched for her to imagine herself caring about me beyond wanting to use me? "Pretend you love me," I repeated. "Oh, and we're engaged," I added, although the ring on her left hand should've been a dead giveaway. But she was a human, and they were known to be slow.

"You cannot be serious."

"Deathly serious," I said on a laugh, the darkest parts of me buzzing with anticipation over how she'd react when I told her my brilliant plan. The hallway was clear, so I tugged her toward the bedroom, where my brother would arrive any moment. The door had barely closed before I had her pinned against the closet, the softness of her body feeling like heaven against me.

"I'm going to kiss you now," I said, a thrill tingling down my spine. "Try your best to play along." Our mouths met, and though I'd only planned for it to be a short kiss, the taste of her consumed me until it became all I craved. Aveen clung to me as if she felt it too, as if she couldn't get enough.

My brother's voice doused my desire. "I do hope I'm not interrupting."

Aveen stiffened, her mouth falling open as she peered over my shoulder at Tadhg as if he were the most beautiful thing she'd ever seen. Not for the first time, I cursed his feckin' "curse."

"You must be Aveen," Tadhg said before evanescing closer, his smile widening to a grin. She wouldn't be staring at him if I knocked his teeth out, now, would she?

My brother reached for her hand, kissing her knuckles and lingering like a leech. "It is truly an honor to meet the woman who has bewitched my brother. Although, Rían has been quite stingy with details. Tell me, how did the two of you meet?"

He'd pawed her enough. And the whole finger down the palm trick? He'd stolen that from me. I pulled Aveen from his claws, giving him a glower that promised pain if he tried to touch her again. "We're not here to discuss that."

The fecker didn't so much as blink. "No matter. I'm sure the truth will come out eventually. It always does."

If he learned the truth—that Aveen cared for me about as much as she cared for Robert Trench—there was no doubt in my mind that he would set his sights on her to spite me. To be honest, it was no less than I deserved since I'd done it to him countless times before. Still, if he tried it with this one, I'd leave him in the dungeon chained in iron for a decade.

"What's your name?" Aveen whispered, her tongue darting out, leaving her lips glistening. Lips still swollen from mine.

"You can call me Tadhg."

She was staring at him. Of course she was. And there wasn't a damned thing I could do about it. Her gaze trailed down his body. I expected her to swoon. Instead, she asked why his clothes were in such an awful state.

Some of the tension left my shoulders. Could she truly be immune to his . . . charms?

Tadhg sank onto Aveen's chair, undoing the buttons on his waistcoat—a gift Eava had insisted I give him for his birthday a few years back. He'd ripped the top button off that very night, adding it to the pot just to give me a twitch. He'd known it cost a fortune and hadn't given a shite.

"My brother bet me that I couldn't convince anyone to share my bed if I didn't look like a prince. And I've been proving him wrong for, how long now?" He looked to me for an answer. "It must be at least a century."

"You're cursed to look like a woman's fantasy," I clipped. "Of course you won." Who could compete with that?

Tadhg's gaze swung back to Aveen. "Do I look like the man who visits your dreams, Aveen?"

I held my breath, knowing better than to hope he didn't. I could only see my infuriating brother, with his dark hair with a slight curl at the top, but women had described his features to me before, each one offering different variations. Who did he look like to Aveen? I was afraid to ask in case it was the exact opposite of me.

"I find you repulsive," she said.

I knew she was lying. Still, it made my heart swell a little that she seemed to be resisting him—for the time being, anyway.

Tadhg knew it too. "You're a terrible liar. Perhaps my brother can give you some lessons."

I kicked over the bastard's chair. What'd he do? He laughed about it like a madman. "Ah, ah, Little Rían. Wouldn't want your dark side showing, now, would you?"

Magic hummed in my veins. *I'll show you my dark side.*

Aveen cleared her throat. "I hate to interrupt, but I'm trying to figure out how Tadhg is supposed to help in my—in *our* situation."

"You didn't tell her?" Tadhg asked from the floor. He tsked me as he rolled to his feet and replaced the chair in its spot by the fireplace. "Dearest Aveen. My chivalrous brother wants me to kill you."

11

I watched the color drain from Aveen's face as if she were dead already.

When we got home, I was going to make Tadgh suffer.

Aveen pressed a hand to her forehead and reached for the bedpost, presumably to steady herself. "I'm sorry, my brain is all muddled. I thought you said Rían wants you to kill me."

"Why must you always be so feckin' awful?" I growled, doing my damnedest not to kill him then and there and ruin Aveen's fancy curtains with his blood. "Aveen, look at me." I caught her shoulders, forcing her to look at me instead of the bastard sneering by the window. "If my brother kills you, you can come back."

Her beautiful eyes widened, and she began shaking her head, making her curls tremble. "Humans cannot return from the dead. That's impossible."

"I assure you that it is quite possible. His lips are cursed, you see. All you need is to kiss him, die, and then come back. Your father cannot expect you to marry Robert if you're dead, and your family can save face."

She glanced past me to where Tadgh stood, her brow pinched and lips pursed. "You're the Gancanagh, aren't you?"

"At your eternal service," he said with a bow, like an eejit. "Although I'd prefer if you call me Tadhg. Less formal. Less dreadful."

Love talker sounded a helluva lot better than what people called me.

Aveen stood there for the longest time, staring at nothing. My brother fell onto the chaise with a bounce, toying with the curtains like a child who couldn't sit still.

After what felt like forever, she heaved a heavy sigh. "I don't know if I can do it."

I'd gone through all of this trouble—asked my feckin' brother for help—and she didn't know if she could do it? What was the issue? Did she truly want to tie herself to Robert Trench? The thought made my gut twist. "It's the only way for us to be together," I said, gathering her hair from her face. "Is our love not worth the sacrifice?"

Tadhg snorted like this was all some sort of joke. Like he didn't give a toss either way.

As Aveen stared up at me, her eyes softened, and the hard lines of her frown eased. I knew better than to believe any of it had to do with me, but a foolish part of me let myself believe, for just a moment, that this wasn't an elaborate ruse.

"Love is worth the sacrifice," she said. "I'll do it."

"You're sure? You'd really die to be with me?" This was for Tadhg's benefit and no one else's. Still, I needed to hear her answer. To taste the lie and remind myself that no part of this was real for her.

"Yes. This is what I want."

I tasted truth but couldn't tell if it was the first or last part that lingered on my tongue.

I kissed her. I couldn't help it.

And then I set aside foolishness and focused on the task at hand.

"Right. Yes. Right." I paced the floor, running through scenarios and potential consequences once more. "We should do this straightaway. The quicker you die, the quicker you'll be back." The thought of losing her for a year made my empty chest ache. *Get off it, you eejit. You can't lose what was never yours to begin with.*

Tadhg stood and straightened his stained breeches. "What's the matter? Afraid she'll change her mind if you don't rush her into it?"

Of course I was afraid. This was a mediocre plan at best.

"I'm not going to change my mind," Aveen vowed, wrapping her fingers around my arm. "But I would like a little time to say goodbye."

"You cannot tell anyone of our plans." I took her hand, staring into her eyes, hoping she would understand the importance of this secret. If word of our relationship—even though it was false—reached the Queen, there was no telling how she would punish us both.

"I promise," she said with obvious reluctance.

Those words were all I needed to cast a binding spell. Now, even if she tried to speak of our bargain, she wouldn't be able to unless I released her—which I would never do.

Tadhg evanesced and reached for one of Aveen's curls, no doubt knowing exactly how much it would piss me off. "Don't worry, Aveen. I'll make your death a pleasurable experience for both of us."

The hell he would. I grabbed his collar, this close to strangling him. "Go find someone to seduce."

"Why find my own when you're letting me borrow one of yours?" Tadhg thought it'd be a good idea to wink at her.

I tightened my grip, twisting until the veins in his forehead bulged. "Don't make me kill you."

"You know," Tadhg choked, "for someone who wants my help, you really should be nicer to me." He flicked my hand until I released him. "Aveen." He kissed her wrist this time, murmuring, "Until we meet again." Then he evanesced before I could drive my fist into his cursed face.

I watched Aveen, wanting to ask so many questions, waiting to see how she would react to meeting the Gananagh himself. She remained expressionless, dumbfounded, no doubt, by his beauty.

"So, your brother is interesting."

"I'm surprised you didn't fall at his feet," I muttered, dropping onto her bed with a groan. "You did well. I think he was properly convinced." Hell, I'd been convinced she felt something for me, and I knew the truth.

The mattress shifted when she sat next to me. "Why the ruse? He seemed more than willing to help."

"Only because I told him we were desperately in love." And if I hadn't, he would've been trying to help himself beneath her skirts.

Her head whipped toward me. "You didn't mention Keelynn, did you?"

"If you want to keep me from your sister, I assumed you'd want to keep the feckin' Gancanagh from her as well."

When she lay down beside me, I found myself longing to reach for her hand. What was it about this woman that made me so feckin' soft? I needed to kill someone.

"Do you think it will hurt?" she asked, her eyes fixed on the canopy above us.

I opened my mouth to lie, but the words died on my lips. I couldn't lie. Not about this. In this, Aveen deserved the truth. I rolled onto my side, facing her, allowing myself to bask in the intimacy of this moment for a breath. "Yes. But coming back will be worse."

"How much worse?" she whispered.

"It's not as bad as being hanged but considerably more painful than getting decapitated." As gruesome as it was, decapitation was relatively painless for the one whose head was being lopped off. "Think being burned at the stake but without the godawful smell of singed hair and melting flesh."

Her hand flew to her slender throat. "Are you serious?"

Of course I was serious. This was death, something you were only meant to experience once. Something you were never meant to come back from. It was hardly a walk in the feckin' park. "Any other questions?"

"How do you know? Have you died before?"

I'd been killed more times than I could count. Most recently, some fool in the north thought it'd be a good idea to poison my wine. I'd made sure he died a nasty death. "I've been hanged, stabbed, pushed off a castle roof, drowned in a river, drowned in the sea, impaled by a lance, met with an executioner's ax, shot with an arrow, cut down by an iron sword, and poisoned. My mother struck me with an iron bar once." Right upside my head, and my hearing hadn't been right since. "And my brother's favorite way to kill me is to slit my throat." I untied my cravat to show her the thick layer of scars hidden beneath.

I was a true immortal. Death couldn't keep me, but that didn't mean I wasn't destined to meet her time and again.

Aveen gaped at me for the longest time. When her jaw finally closed, she asked about my mother. How the hell had we gone from speaking of death to the subject of my feckin' mother? Was it possible that Aveen knew who she was? No. Surely not. She wouldn't be within arm's reach of me if she knew.

"It doesn't matter," I said. It wasn't like the two would ever meet.

"Why won't you tell me?" she pressed.

"Because it's none of your damned business." I shoved off the bed. This was a business arrangement, pure and simple. The less she knew about me, the better.

"You're asking me to trust you with my life. I think the least you could do is show me a little trust in return."

"You expect me to trust you? A feckin' human? Not a hope." If she knew how much power she held over me in this deal, she'd surely turn me in and request a better one. My mother would catch wind of this hair-brained plot and make Aveen suffer before dying a death from which she could never return. I glared at where Aveen twisted my ring around her finger, raging at myself for being such a sentimental fool. "That's mine." I gestured to the ring. "As soon as you're dead, I'm taking it back."

She huffed as she pulled the band from her finger. "You can have it back now if you wish. Here. Take it and go away." She threw it at me, but I wasn't expecting it, and the blasted thing fell to the floor.

"Fine. I will." I'd go away and leave her to her fate. Let her marry Robert Trench for all I cared. I hoped he made her feckin' miserable and that her *precious* sister never spoke to her again. I shoved the blasted thing into my pocket.

"Fine."

"Fine." My magic swelled the moment I called it forth. But when I flicked my wrist to evanesce, nothing happened. *What the hell?*

"Why isn't it working?" Aveen demanded.

"I don't feckin' know." I'd been evanescing since I was ten years old. This should've been child's play. Unless someone had warded the—*Tadhg*.

She stomped toward me with more demands, this time to fix it.

"If I don't know what's wrong, I don't know how to fix it, now, do I?" I tried again and again. How strong were these feckin' wards? Would I be able to leave the house at all?

When someone knocked on the door, Aveen's panicked gaze swung to mine. "You have to disappear," she hissed. "If anyone catches you in my bedroom, my life is over."

"At least then we wouldn't need my brother," I muttered.

"Rian!" She kicked me in the feckin' shin.

"Ow! All right, all right." Where the hell was I going to hide? The curtains weren't long enough to cover my boots, and I'd surely be seen behind the chaise and chair.

"Just climb out the window."

"I'm not climbing out the feckin' window." I could snag my new breeches on the trellis. Besides, there was a good chance my dear brother had warded the place so that I couldn't pass through at all. And if that were the case, I wasn't getting caught red-handed with my arse half out the window.

The person in the hallway knocked again.

Aveen shoved me toward the bed. "Fine. Get under the bed."

What was I? An old sock? "Is it clean? If there's dust, I'll sneeze." So many people cleaned around beds but not underneath them, making it a breeding ground for dust.

"Get in the closet and stay quiet," she hissed, giving me another shove.

"Aveen?" The husky feminine voice sounded familiar. *Her sister.* "Are you in there?"

"Just a moment. I'm . . . um . . . indisposed."

Aveen shoved me again.

I ended up curled into the bottom of the closet with my legs tucked under my chin, which wouldn't have been an issue if my thigh hadn't started to cramp. The dresses on either side of me smelled like a rose garden.

My nose started to tingle.

Shit.

I was going to—"*Aaaachoo!*"

I shifted a handkerchief to wipe my nose. How feckin' mortifying. Maybe no one heard me.

"Is there someone in there with you?" Aveen's sister asked.

"It's . . . um . . . Sylvia," Aveen lied. "She's helping me decide which dress to wear tomorrow."

"Really? I just saw Sylvia on the stairs not five minutes ago, carrying a vase of flowers to the parlor."

"I . . . Um . . ."

I'd have to teach that human a thing or two about lying if she hoped to get away with this ruse of ours.

I had to fix this.

I needed to become someone else. Someone the sister didn't know. Someone new to town. Someone like . . .

I shifted the closest dress, throwing on a glamour to make it fit. There wasn't time to check myself before I evanesced out of the closet and popped my head around the corner to wave at the two women speaking in hushed tones.

"This must be Keelynn," I said in a snooty Vellanian accent I'd once heard in Gaul. "I have heard so much about you. Aveen talks of nothing else."

"That's right." The sister looked down her nose at me. "Who are you?"

Rude. "Lady Marissa DeWarn, of course. Don't tell me Aveen has kept me a secret! You little minx." I whapped Aveen a bit too hard. *You're a lady. Be ladylike. Dainty. Simpering.* "Aveen and I met a few weeks ago at the market. She has been such a dote, helping me settle into life here in Graystones. It's so different from Vellana. Dreadfully dreary and mundane. I could die of boredom."

"You're from Vellana?" the sister asked.

I nodded. "My brother is the ambassador, perhaps you remember him?"

Aveen just stared at me as if I had turned myself into a dragon. If she didn't get it together, she was going to blow this for both of us.

"Oh, Edward. Yes. I met him." The sister's frown deepened. "It's so strange I haven't met you, though. He never mentioned a sister."

"That's because he's wretched." I swatted her shoulder like a dainty, dainty girl. Lady Marissa wouldn't hurt a fly. "Thinks women should stay cooped up in the house, spending their time pushing needles and thread through bits of fabric and banging keys on the dreadful pianoforte." Lady Marissa was a progressive woman ahead of her time, after all.

The sister's giggle made my head hurt. "If he believes that, then perhaps he is wretched. Are you staying for dinner, Lady Marissa?"

Oh! Dinner. What a lovely idea. "Yes."

Aveen said, "No," at the same time, of course. This was the

most fun I'd had in ages. I wasn't about to let it end just because she had a sour look on her face.

"I'll, um, leave the two of you to sort that out," said the sister. "You should stay for dinner, though. Aveen never has friends over. I was beginning to think I was her only friend."

The moment the door closed, I bounced to the mirror to check myself out. Damn, I made a good-looking woman. The black hair really suited my eye color. I should wear it more often.

"What the hell do you think you're doing? *Lady Marissa?*" Aveen choked.

"Have you seen the layer of dust at the back of your closet? You should fire your maid." My breasts were too small, weren't they?

"So, you have enough magic to turn yourself into a woman, and yet you cannot vanish?"

"It was a good thing too. Otherwise, that would've been dreadfully awkward." I twisted to check out my arse. "Does this dress make me look fat?"

"Rían!"

"All right. You don't need to yell." And certainly not in my good feckin' ear. I'd be deaf as a post if she kept roaring like that. "I'm standing right here. I do not know why my magic is acting up. It has never done this. It is quite embarrassing. But you have to admit, I do make quite a stunning woman." I pulled out the front of my dress to make sure I got the nipples right. People always forgot about the nipples.

She smacked me. "Don't do that."

"Why not? They're mine, aren't they? Not as nice as yours, though. Should I make them larger?"

"You can do whatever you want after you take one of my cloaks and leave out the front door."

"Leave? My dear, why on earth would I leave when I've been invited to my fiancée's house for dinner?"

12

"YOU WILL BE ON YOUR BEST BEHAVIOR," AVEEN WARNED WHEN we reached the top of the stairs, all frowns and narrowed eyes. Flickering candlelight from the wall sconces reflected off the checkered tiles. The large chandelier, however, remained unlit.

"That's no fun," I grumbled, smoothing a wrinkle at my waist.

"Exactly. Dinner will be no fun whatsoever, so you should probably just leave."

"And let your sister think me rude? Really, Aveen. Where are your manners?"

She stomped forward two steps, then stopped again. "If you do not behave, I swear I will . . ."

Yes. Go on. Tell me what you'll do to me.

"I will make it hurt," she finished.

A thrill bolted down my spine. *I bet you would.*

I danced down the stairs, through the entryway, and into an overlarge dining room decorated like some medieval castle. Brass candelabras on the walls, warding off darkness. Vases of flowers interspersed between antiques that were little more than dust collectors. Dour portraits like a bunch of flabby-faced voyeurs glaring down at us.

Lord Bannon bowed low over my hand, the thinning hair on

his crown glinting in the candlelight. "Lady Marissa, a true pleasure to meet my daughter's dear friend. She speaks highly of you."

Did she, now? Considering I didn't exist an hour ago, I found that quite amusing. "I apologize for dropping in unannounced," I said with a demure smile. Lady Marissa could be demure when she felt like it.

"Nonsense." He squeezed my fingers before letting them go. "You are quite welcome to our home any time."

I sat right next to him, ignoring the glare from my beautiful fiancée. The wine, poured by servants, was a decent vintage but a bit sweet for my liking. Not that it would stop me from drinking. Lady Marissa did love her wine, after all.

The braised pork belly served after a course of soup, however, was excellent.

Lord Bannon cut a thin slice, stuffing it between his lips. "So, Lady Marissa, how are you finding life in Graystones?"

I didn't miss the way his eyes raked over me. As if Lady Marissa would ever stoop to rutting with her best friend's father. She may have been uncouth, but she had far too much class for that.

"It is quite dreadful, isn't it? Life here is so tedious and backwards. Can you imagine, the menfolk are so archaic that they believe a woman's only worth is her ability to marry a wealthy man? Poppycock. But I can tell you are different, Lord Bannon. You are a modern man. Very forward thinking."

The human's shoulders lifted as he puffed up his chest at my lie. "It is kind of you to notice."

Aveen grumbled into her wine.

"Keelynn was telling me you moved here from Vellana." He traded his utensils for his glass. "It must be taxing for someone who is used to the splendor of a fine city to relocate to such a humble town. Nevertheless, we have our hidden gems."

Graystones was a shite town without sunlight or color. The people who lived here were tolerable at best. If the whole place were to go down in flames, Aveen would be the only human worth saving. Probably not the type of remark Lady Marissa would make in such fine company though. "Speaking of gems, your home is quite lovely." It wasn't. All the garish decorations made me think of someone desperate to be noticed, searching for meaningless compliments over his fine collection of silver candlesticks. "Is it an ancestral seat for the Bannons?" I asked, even though I knew the answer.

This house and the surrounding estates originally belonged to a rebel who had fought on our side in the war against the invading Vellanian tyrants. His descendants kept up the estate until seventeen years ago.

"This house was a gift from the king himself, for service," he confirmed. "The previous owners met an untimely demise. His Majesty needed a man with strong ties to Vellana to live here, lest the property fall into the hands of those who sympathized with the monsters."

He thought us monsters, did he? I'd show him a monster. "Is that right?"

"I'm afraid Lord Middleton was caught communicating with one of the things claiming to be their leader and hanged for treason."

Monsters *and* things. *How eloquent.* I spun my glass slowly, considering his fate. I could choke him with my magic, make it look like an accident. That would solve everyone's problem, now, wouldn't it? Aveen and her sister could sell the estate and buy something more manageable. And Aveen could default on that betrothal contract. Keelynn would be able to marry Robert the Terrible, and everyone would live happily ever after.

Aveen started nattering about the wine. I tuned her out. "Treason, you say? How scandalous." Would she mourn her tyrant father? Or would she dance on his grave as I had with mine?

"If you ask me, the lot of them should be exterminated like the rats they are. *Magic*," Lord Bannon spat. "Unnatural. An abomination. A blight on this once-great island."

I'd been born with magic in my veins, just as he'd been born with his greasy hair. It didn't get any more natural than that. As far as abominations were concerned, the only abomination I could see was the pairing of his paisley waistcoat with that brown belt.

Aveen muttered something about the weather.

The sister gave Lord Bannon's hand a squeeze right as the bastard was about to spew more hate. If he wanted to talk about a blight on this island, we should've been talking about the humans.

The Danú had lived in peace for centuries before humans showed up on their little wooden boats, staking a claim where they had none. They brought war and disease, killed and tortured anyone who opposed them. *They* were the monsters.

Aveen smacked the table, knocking things over. "I believe a lighter topic would be more appropriate dinner conversation. We wouldn't want such dark stories to make our guest uncomfortable, now, would we?"

"There's no need to change topics on my behalf," I said. "I've always been fascinated by the macabre. The bloodier, the better." As a matter of fact, Lady Marissa preferred it. Who wanted to talk about the weather when you could have a chat about murder?

The wine bottle slowly tipped toward the tablecloth, spilling like blood across the white fabric. Aveen's icy blue eyes had gone glazed and glassy. How much had she had to drink?

"No, no. Aveen is right. I wouldn't want to offend your delicate sensibilities, Lady Marissa," her ignorant father agreed.

I'd cut off his *delicate sensibilities* in a minute if he didn't stop glaring at Aveen.

"I bought a batch of tulip bulbs this week," Aveen announced, stilling the murderous thoughts swirling through my mind. "I'll be planting them in a new raised bed along the southern wall once the men finish the stonework. They'll look a bit sparse this year, but by next summer, it'll be full of color. I'll need help weeding, of course, but I'm sure Sean won't mind the extra work considering I've taken up residence in the main gardens."

She spoke with such passion . . . about *dirt*.

Fascinating.

I planted as well. Seeds of doubt. Roots of destruction. "I didn't realize you were so invested in bringing life to the world."

Aveen's cheeks flushed. "I wouldn't call throwing a few bulbs in the ground 'bringing life.'"

"What would you call it?" I asked, genuinely curious.

"A hobby."

"Hobby?" the sister scoffed. "More like an obsession. Aveen loves gardening. I think it's the only place she is truly happy."

If she loved gardens, then she should see the ones at the castle. Oscar worked tirelessly to maintain them. All the old grogochs were good for was growing shite. "We have gardens that bloom year-round."

"At the townhouse?" Keelynn asked.

I'd completely forgotten that I'd told the sister about the town-house. "Not in the townhouse. Back in . . ." Where was I from again? "In Vellana."

"Lady Marissa and her brother are renting a townhouse near the modiste," Keelynn said to Lord Bannon.

"Just until something larger and more permanent becomes available," I added.

The clock chimed, saving me from having to expand on the living situation. Lord Bannon tossed his serviette beside his empty glass and stood. "Would you look at the time? Lady Marissa, your company has been a delight. I do hope to see more of you in the future."

"I'm sure you will. Your daughter and I have grown quite close over the last few weeks. I cannot imagine life here without her," I said . . . and meant it. I couldn't imagine life anywhere without her. It all seemed so pointless.

"You're not leaving, are you?" Aveen's sister asked. "You should stay. There's plenty of space."

Aveen rocketed to her feet, squeezing my fingers hard enough to crack my feckin' knuckles. "He—I mean *she* cannot stay. There's that thing you have to do in the morning. Remember?"

Aveen's sister caught my other hand. "Oh, but she must. It is far too late to bring her back into Graystones. You know the roads aren't safe at night."

"Your lovely sister has a point," I said. "I hear wicked creatures prowl these forests from dusk until dawn."

Rage flared in Aveen's eyes.

"It isn't as dangerous as all that," Lord Bannon countered. "But I must agree with Keelynn. You should stay here tonight. Stay as long as you'd like."

"Why thank you, Lord Bannon." I threw in a curtsey like a good little lady. "You are most kind."

"Come, Marissa," the sister said. Aveen's grip loosened just enough for Keelynn to tug me into the wide hall leading to the grand staircase. "I'll show you up to the spare room." Our skirts brushed as we crossed to the staircase and climbed toward the bedrooms.

Aveen came hurtling behind us, slipping and falling straight into me. I caught her before she could topple headfirst down the stairs.

"Marissa will need something to sleep in, and your night dresses will be far too slim," she announced loudly enough to wake the feckin' dead.

Aveen's sister gave her a worried look before shrugging and saying goodnight. Then off she went, gliding away. I didn't pay attention to which room she entered. All that mattered was that Aveen was leading me to her bedroom.

I had no objections to sharing a room with her, but "ladies" who were "good" and "kind" didn't share beds with men like me. I held my breath, waiting to hear what sleeping arrangements she would suggest.

"This has gone on long enough," she said. "You need to go away. Now."

A better man would've done just that.

But I wasn't a better man, and I wanted to see how the night played out. Tadhg wouldn't be able to keep the ward there much longer. I could probably find a way to break through, but that would require too much magic I didn't feel like wasting.

I flicked my wrist for show. "Looks like you're stuck with me a little while longer. Could you imagine what would happen if it never came back and I had to stay here forever?"

Her glassy eyes narrowed. "I can't think of anything worse."

"She's feisty when she's drunk. I like it." The more bite, the better. *Make me hurt, beautiful.*

When she tried to settle her fists on her hips, they slipped right off, and she stumbled forward. "I'm not drunk."

Liar, liar, skirts on fire. "I've known my share of drunk women, and you, my dear, are sozzled." I gave her upturned nose a flick, loving the way she hissed in a breath. Knowing she hated it made me want to do it again. "Now, if the drunk lady would kindly show me to the spare room, I would like to get out of this feckin' corset." It wasn't uncomfortable per se, but it did keep my lungs from expanding fully.

"You're not staying in the spare room. You can stay here."

Hell yes. We could get up to all sorts of mischief together once she sobered up.

"I'll take the spare room," she finished.

Dammit.

"But you must promise not to leave this chamber," she added as an afterthought.

I laced my smile with just enough sarcasm to imply that I had no intention of doing just that. "I promise."

"I mean it, Rían. You must swear on your own life that you will not set foot out of this room."

My smile widened. I couldn't help it, could I? She looked so pretty when she was irritated. "I swear."

Aveen launched the pillow at my face, then stomped over to the armoire to retrieve two night dresses. As if I'd waste magic by holding this glamour in my sleep. She demanded I change into the dress and sleep on the floor.

What did she think I was, a feckin' dog? The Queen would relinquish her hold on the Forest before I slept on a feckin' floor. "I'm not sleeping on a floor when there's a perfectly good bed right there."

"You're not sleeping with me."

"*Not drunk, my arse.*" Had she forgotten the plan already? "You're sleeping in the spare bedroom, remember?"

"It is clear that I cannot trust you to stay on your own. I will stay here all night and guard you." She offered me the shift, as if I'd be caught dead sleeping in it.

When I didn't take it, she threw the thing at me. I threw it right back. "I don't need a guard. Show me to the spare room, and I will be gone by morning."

"I don't trust you!"

I dropped my glamour, letting her see the rage that lurked beneath my skin.

She'd sought *me* out, not the other way around. *She* needed *my* help, not the other way around. I'd survived centuries without her —without anyone. When she was nothing more than dust, I would still be here. "Then let's call this whole thing off."

"Fine. What do I need you for, anyway? I will simply ask Meranda to get a message to your brother and bargain with him instead."

That was the wrong feckin' thing to say, human. If she thought I'd let her bargain with Tadhg, then she had another thing coming. "I'm sure Tadhg would be more than happy to oblige. Although I can't help but wonder what poor Padraig would say if he learned you were off bargaining with the Gancanagh." At the mention of her coachman, Aveen stiffened. "Speaking of Padraig, wouldn't it be a pity if someone were to tell the Airren authorities that your beloved coachman has been using an illegal glamour for the last three decades?" They'd string him up faster than you could say the word "boo."

"You wouldn't," she gasped.

I was no hero. I'd lie, steal, and kill to get what I wanted. "Would I not?"

With the seeds of doubt taking root, I asked again for directions to the spare room.

"You're not sleeping there. You're sleeping here."

She stomped behind the screen, presumably to change. I removed my waistcoat, draping it and my cravat over the edge of the chair so they didn't wrinkle. She'd probably have a fit if I took off my shirt—not that a layer of clothing made this any more *proper*. It killed me to think of how wrinkly I'd be when I awoke, but I set aside my discomfort and climbed beneath the covers in my clothes. The things I did for this woman.

She emerged in a white shift, collected a blanket from the top of the closet and the pillow she'd thrown earlier, and went straight to the chaise, settling in like it was the most comfortable bed in the whole feckin' estate.

"Are you seriously going to stay there all night?" The contrary woman ignored me. "Aveen, you are being ridiculous."

Yes, she fit. But if she rolled over in her sleep, she'd end up falling on the hard floor. I went right over, scooped her up, and tossed her on her side of the bed.

"I cannot share a bed with you!" she screeched.

"Don't worry. You're about as appealing as a raw turnip when you squeal like that." Not to say I wouldn't eat a raw turnip, but it was hardly my favorite vegetable.

She drew the covers all the way up to her stubborn chin. "If you touch me, I'll kill you."

An entirely idle threat. Even if she did kill me, I'd only come back. "What have I done to make you believe I would force myself on you?"

"In the shed, you—"

"Stopped the moment I realized you weren't Eithne."

"In the garden, you—"

"Saved you from being the Dullahan's next meal? I'm not a

good man by any means, but there are lines even I will not cross."
Like touching a woman who clearly had no interest in me.
"Tonight, I swear on pain of death that I will not lay a hand on
you. Unless you beg me to," I added, just in case sober Aveen
changed her mind.

"Like that would ever happen. I'm not even attracted to you."

I inhaled deeply, the lie tasting sweeter than a spoonful of
sugar. "I love it when you lie."

"It's not a lie. You're a disgusting troll."

"So you're not the least bit tempted to kiss me?"

"Not the least."

So many sweet, sweet lies.

"Then it's safe for me to assume that you have no desire for
me to slip you out of that shift and taste every inch of you."

Her breathing hitched. Her blush looked all the more delicate
against the coverlet. "You shouldn't say things like that to me."

Yes or no, Aveen. I couldn't find a lie in a response like that.
"Does it make you uncomfortable?"

"Yes," she breathed.

I tasted the bitterness of truth. Except, there was something in
her eyes. A hunger that hadn't been there before. "Do you like it?"
I pressed.

"N-no."

The lie left my blackened soul singing. "Oh, my dear. You
have no idea how bad a liar you are. It's quite endearing."

"I'm not lying."

"I can taste the lies when they fall from your lips. They're
sweet, like honeysuckle. A good liar sticks as close to the truth as
possible. A great liar mixes the two. You don't bother. You say
what you believe you're supposed to say in order to make others
happy or save face. It's fascinating."

Her frown only deepened.

"Ah, here now. There's no need to get cross."

"I'm not cross."

I bit back my smile. I couldn't help it.

She gave my shoulder a good wallop.

I didn't bother hiding my laughter. "Careful now, human. Striking a prince has dire consequences."

What'd she do? She hit me again.

"Do it again and see what happens."

When she hit me a third time, I launched upright, sending her scurrying back like she could bury herself in the mattress to escape. My magic wrapped around her wrists like manacles, lifting her arms above her head. Her chest rose and fell in irritation. She looked so delectable that way, stretched beneath me. I sent another tendril of magic across her hips, pinning her in place.

The things I could do to her.

The pleasure I could make her feel.

I settled my hands on either side of her head, lowering myself so I could see my face reflected in her blown-out pupils. She smelled of rose petals and rage, a heady combination I could have drowned in for eternity.

"You said you wouldn't touch me," she rasped. "You swore on pain of death."

That beautiful throat bobbed when she swallowed. I dragged my nose down her soft skin, breathing her in. "Ah, but I like pain and enjoy death. And I swore not to lay a *hand* on you." And my hands were behaving. "What you fail to realize, human, is that I do not need my hands to make you come undone. I could use my mouth." To taste her would be heaven. I allowed myself one kiss, feeling her pulse spike beneath my lips. "My teeth. My tongue." Oh, the things I could do with my tongue. "My cock." I gave in to the urge to grind myself against her leg, hearing her breath catch. Her eyes hooded with desire. "My magic." I could sit across the room and make her come harder than she'd ever dreamed with my magic alone. "I'd let you choose, Aveen. Choose how I unravel you." One or two or all at once. I'd give her everything I had. All she had to do was say the word.

"I hate you."

Her truth stole my desire.

"First honest thing you've said all night." I forced a chuckle, retreating to my side of the bed, releasing the bonds holding her in place. She hated me—and who could blame her?

"You are the worst person I've ever met."

"Another truth. Very good. Does violent Aveen have any more confessions?"

She stole the coverlet, leaving me without so much as a corner.

"Ah, here now, sullen Aveen is no fun. Bring back the violent one."

She kicked me.

And I liked it.

13

"Witnesses are important," I told my brother. Otherwise, who's to say what happened? It would be best to curse Aveen on a night when people saw her so there could be no denying that she was gone. Did Aveen realize she could never return to Graystones? Eventually she could invite her sister to visit her wherever she ended up, but for a long time, she would need to be alone.

All to make her spoiled sister happy.

Waste of time if you asked me. If Robert loved the sister, he would've refused a match with Aveen. Spineless. That's what he was. And yet Aveen seemed content to let her sister go off with him because they were "in love."

Fools, the lot of them.

Not that I was complaining. The thought of her marrying that pretentious prick, of him laying a hand on her . . .

"I'm sorry, are you wanting a response?" Tadhg drawled from the settee. "Usually, you just tell me what to do and expect me to do it."

Speaking of useless fools . . . "Go back to your bottle." I don't know why I bothered coming into the family room. It wasn't as if Tadhg was actually useful.

"What about the ball?" he said before I reached the door.

I stilled. "What ball?"

"Don't humans celebrate impending nuptials by throwing some lavish party? I seem to remember that being a custom ages ago. Maybe it still is."

Huh. He may have had a good idea for once.

If we did this at a ball, I would need to make sure my darling brother didn't set one foot inside. Unleashing the Gancanagh on a roomful of women was a problem in and of itself that I had no time for. And I already knew Aveen would balk at the thought of him anywhere near her precious sister. If they met in the garden, though. That could work.

How was she feeling after last night? I'd bet she was hungover. The idea of her being in a foul mood made me far happier than it should've. "Right, so. I'm off."

"To see your lady love?" Tadhg drawled, his voice oozing sarcasm.

"What's wrong, brother? Jealous?"

"Of you?" He laughed but didn't deny it. Was that because his truth curse kept him honest or because he didn't think my question deserved a response? Not that it mattered either way. "Once your *soulmate* learns the truth about you, I've no doubt she'll leave you just like everyone else."

The truth behind his words cut me to the core. Still, I'd spent far too long establishing an air of unaffected irritation to lose my composure now. "Enjoy your day alone. Try not to kill anyone."

This would only be a quick trip to Graystones to tell Aveen the plan, not to visit or ask if she'd dreamed of me or if she wished things had gone further between us. Certainly not.

Like before, I evanesced to the trees just beyond the Bannon estate. But unlike the last time, I could hear a familiar voice grumbling—not from the house but from deeper in the garden.

I couldn't take the chance of someone else seeing my face, and the ambassador had no real reason to call on Aveen now that she was engaged to someone else. There was one person who had every right to be seen with her, though. I felt my lips curl into a smile and turned myself into her fiancé.

When she saw me, the smile on her face melted. Damn, she was dirty. How she could stand that shite all over her hands was beyond me.

"Good morning, Robert," Aveen clipped, going right back to what she'd been doing before I arrived, transferring what looked like onions from a canvas sack to the dirt.

I tried to recall the annoying timbre of his voice, the way he clipped his consonants and held himself as if he had a post shoved up his arse. "From this day forward, I expect you to greet me with a kiss. I am your fiancé, after all." *Nailed it.*

Aveen stabbed the dirt with her little shovel. "I'd rather kiss a goat."

The shovel clattered to the ground, and her hand flew to her lips. Wide eyes locked with mine. I wanted to trace the blush painting her skin all the way down to the square neckline on a dress far too fine to be covered in filth.

"Kiss a goat?" Had she ever seen a goat up close? Those things had crazy eyes and smelled like they'd rolled in shite. It took far too much magic, but I glamoured myself into one of the smelly beasts for the fun of it.

Aveen snagged her shovel from the ground, wielding it like a weapon as she waved it at me. "Change back. Now."

I couldn't hold it very long, anyway, letting all the glamours fall until it was just she and I and her weapon. "*Ohhhh* look who's back. Violent Aveen. If you're going to stab me with your tiny shovel, would you mind cleaning it first? This is a new shirt." Came all the way from the continent. Made of the softest cotton. I should've bought an entire trunk of them.

Aveen launched a hunk of mud right at my face. I barely had time to evade it. This was my favorite feckin' shirt! Had she forgotten who I was? The terror I could inflict on her—on her family? "I could turn you into ash, you know," I ground out.

Air tickled my unglamoured cheek, rustling the hair escaping her ribbon.

Aveen's breathing caught, her chest rising and falling in an uneven rhythm. "If you turned me to ash, then the breeze could blow me against your precious, clean shirt." She twisted and painted my sleeves with muck.

My shirt. My favorite shirt. Ruined because of this feckin' woman standing in front of me laughing like a maniac. I made a pained noise entirely unbecoming of a terrifying prince, one that would've made my brother piss himself with laughter. I shifted a handful of mud, my stomach lurching as it oozed between my fingers, and smeared it across her beautiful face.

"There. Now we're even." I flicked my wrist, trading the ruined shirt for one that didn't feel nearly as comfortable. Although I removed the mud from my hand with magic, I could still feel it coating my skin. The moment I returned to the castle, I'd be shifting another bath.

Aveen ruined my waistcoat with yet more mud. "*Now* we're even."

Even? Could the woman not count? She'd gotten me twice, and I'd only retaliated once. Not to worry. My gaze landed on a mound of dirt next to the canvas bag of onions. I kicked it at her. Dirtying my boots was worth the indignant screech tearing from her throat. Then she stomped in a puddle like a feckin' child, and I could feel the mud all the way through my breeches. I shifted an entirely new outfit, sending the other ruined garments into their designated laundry baskets. Aveen filled her hand with earth and dumped it on my head.

Cursing, I ripped at the buttons, hoping to salvage this one shirt before the dirt crumbling against my scalp ruined it as well. No feckin' good. Another one for the laundry.

I shifted another.

The madwoman attacked me with foul smelling muck overflowing with bits of rotten fruit and veg. I tried to shift more clothes from my armoire, but nothing came. They couldn't all be dirty, could they? *Dammit.*

Enough was enough. I refused to waste any more magic on this shite. "That's it. You're finished." I stalked toward her. Aveen made a pitiful attempt to escape. I loved seeing the fear in her eyes as she fell back toward the high hedges, holding up her hands in defense. I dropped down, wrapped my arms around her legs, and lifted her over my shoulder.

"Put me down this instant!" she shrieked, squirming and wriggling in my grasp.

"If you wanted to get me undressed, all you had to do was say 'please.' You didn't have to ruin my feckin' clothes."

Did she give up? No. She wiped her disgusting hands all over my back.

"*Shit.* Stop that! I don't have any more clean shirts." The laundress would undoubtedly have left a few on the drying rack, but they'd be wrinkled as all hell, and I'd rather be covered in dirt than look like a beggar who couldn't afford a bit of starch.

She bucked again, forcing me to hold her tighter. Feel the backs of her thighs. Imagine parting them.

"The fancy prince doesn't own more than four shirts?" she taunted with a husky laugh. "Poor fancy prince. You really are cursed. The curse of four shirts. Lucky for you, I know how to break it. See, there's a place in town where you can buy such things."

"I have more than four feckin' shirts, you wretched human. But the others aren't pressed." Before my destination registered, I had carried her through the pines edging the coast, the air smelling like salt and seaweed.

She punched me in the feckin' back. "Heaven forbid someone sees you in a wrinkled shirt."

"Do it again and see what happens," I warned.

This time, she had the good sense to keep her fist to herself.

I kept going until I reached a gray pebbled beach stretching toward an angry sea.

"Put me down," she said, her words laced with panic. "I mean it. This isn't funny anymore. Put me down. I'll not go in the sea. I won't."

She'd go wherever I wanted her to go. The water seeping into my boots would freeze the bollocks off me, but she'd started this, and I was damn well going to finish it. My body shrank away from the waves, but still I continued. "Next time you'll think twice about covering me in shite, now, won't you?"

"If you put me in that water, I'll—"

I dropped her into the sea, then slipped beneath the surface myself, letting the salty waves beat me clean. I emerged to the sound of her screeching, hair plastered to her head. So beautifully indignant.

"There. Don't you feel better now that you're clean?" I splashed her.

Aveen jumped at me. I braced for impact, ready to take the hit but entirely unprepared for her mouth to land on mine. Her arms wrapped around my neck, dragging me closer but not nearly close enough. I caught her glorious ass, lifting her legs around my waist, fighting to keep my feet steady as she began to rock against me.

I didn't close my eyes. Didn't want to miss the way drops of water clung to her dark lashes where they met her pink cheeks.

I caught fire, and not even the icy waters of the Airren sea could cool the flames in my blood.

"Why is it like this with you?" she murmured against my lips.

It was too dangerous to do this here, where anyone could see, anyone could hear. But I couldn't focus on a tost with her moving like that. "Stop talking."

"Rían—"

"For the love of all this is holy, shut your beautiful mouth and—"

Something glinted in my peripherals. A flash of iridescent scales. I dropped her so quickly, she vanished beneath the water. Merrow rarely traveled alone. Where there was one, more would follow.

Aveen came up sputtering. "What the hell was—"

"*Quiet.*" I threw Aveen behind me, counting at least three separate flashes beneath the water.

"What is it?" she asked, clutching the back of my shirt.

"Merrow."

"Merrow don't live in our sea."

I caught the closest one using magic, lifting her straight from the waves before she could get any closer. "Then what is this?" The merrow's bulbous eyes bulged when I choked her. She thought she could spy on me and get away with it? "I'm in no mood to play today. Tell your friends to return to the depths, or I'll boil the feckin' ocean and feed you to my mother for dinner."

I sent the bitch and the rest of her friends swimming for their lives.

Aveen's hand began to tremble where she held my shirt. I said nothing, unsure whether all of them were gone. What if they'd been sent by the Queen? I was a fool for bringing her here. For thinking anywhere on this island was safe from the Queen's influence. She rarely left the Forest, but she had plenty of eyes in Airren, waiting to feed her information for her own nefarious purposes.

Aveen waded toward the shore. I followed, keeping my eyes on the water, not the way the soaked skirts clung to her hips and curves.

All right. I looked. I looked long and hard, because I may have been a monster, but I was also a man, and Aveen was my own personal fantasy come to life. "Get out of that dress before you die from the cold," I said.

"And wear what?" she snapped.

I shifted one of the dresses from the back of Aveen's closet where I'd hidden last night.

She didn't bother to thank me. Not that I'd expected thanks after putting her in jeopardy like that.

Trembling like a leaf in a gale wasn't very intimidating, so I shifted a fire bigger than the woman trying unsuccessfully to unbutton the top of her dress.

"Hurry it on. I have places to be." Let any lingering ears hear how terribly I spoke to her. Let them lose interest in watching us.

"T-then go. I d-d-don't want your h-help."

"Will I take back the dress and leave you in that then?" Or I could offer to cut her out of all of it and warm her naked body with mine. Wouldn't the merrow have a feckin' field day with that?

When Aveen demanded I turn around, I traded my damp clothes for dry ones, shifting the first shirt Aveen had ruined.

She cursed and stomped her foot in the stones. I could hear her teeth chattering over the crackling fire. What was taking so long? I glanced over my shoulder to find her still struggling with the first feckin' button.

With a bit of magic, the seams split right open.

Even after she changed, she'd still be freezing. I shifted a blue cloak lined with fur that I'd purchased on a whim the other day. Speaking of—when Aveen awoke, she'd need clothes, wouldn't she? I couldn't very well leave her off somewhere without anything to wear.

"I'll have you know that was my favorite gardening dress," she told me, as if I cared.

"And I'll have you know this was my favorite shirt." And now it was well and truly ruined.

"All you have to do is wash it."

Even clean, there was no hope of removing the stains she'd left there. "Are you asking me to go for another swim?"

"Shove off."

I bit back my smirk. So much fighting spirit in such a small package.

Now that the lust-filled fog had left my brain, I managed a tost to keep nosy feckers from learning my business. "I spoke to my brother this morning. He'll meet you in the garden on the night of your betrothal ball."

She asked me why, as I knew she would, and I explained my

reasons. But when she asked me how long she'd be gone, I found myself hedging. I added a piece of wood to the fire, watching the flames swallow it. "It'll feel like you just closed your eyes."

"That's not an answer. Tell me."

"I can't."

"Yes, you can."

"No, I mean I physically can't. It's part of my brother's curse. But I can tell you this." I held up a single finger.

Her brows pinched. "What's that?"

It was a feckin' finger, obviously.

"One?" she said slowly.

I nodded.

"One day?"

If only. I shook my head.

"One week? One month? One *year*?"

A year and a day, to be exact—same as all curses. But close enough, so I clapped.

Pebbles flew toward the fire when Aveen shot to her feet. "I'm going to be dead for a bloody year? Are you mad?"

"A lifetime of misery, a year of death, or destitution for your family. Those are your choices, are they not?"

Her brows pinched and lips pursed. "How do you know about my family's . . . financial difficulties?"

"I make it a point to learn all that I can about those who wish to bargain with me." It wasn't that hard to see. The roof was in desperate need of repair, there were barely any horses in the stable, the staff was woefully small, and Aveen did all her own gardening. The last bit wasn't necessarily an indication, but I didn't think for a second that a proud man like Lord Bannon wouldn't take issue with his daughter playing around in dirt if he didn't need her to help maintain the estate.

She fell back to the stones with a huff. "Who will you torment while I'm gone?"

"Probably some orphan. Or a heartbroken widow. Or a crippled old man."

She threw a stone at me. "You are awful."

"I know." More awful than she could ever imagine.

"Will you be there when I wake?"

I watched the sea, searching for merrow. Today had been a close call. Only time would tell if news of my recklessness would reach the Queen.

For the only way to save him . . .

"No. But I will ensure you are kept somewhere safe. And then you can put all this nastiness behind you and live out the rest of your short human life playing in dirt."

That's what she would have. A short life. Only a spark in the endless night, gone far too soon. I cursed fate again. Why hadn't I been given an immortal soulmate instead of one that would barely exist?

"Until you come to collect your favor," she said.

I had no intention of collecting that favor. After she died, our dealings would be through. "Right. Until then."

She closed her eyes, sighing and turning her face toward the clouds above us. I swore a ray of sunlight split through just for her.

"A cottage by the sea with a garden. That's what I would've wished for," she whispered. "A place of my own where I could live as I chose without anyone telling me what to do. What to wear. Who to marry."

"If you could have anything in the world, you'd want a shack and some flowers?" How easy it must be to want such a simple, unobtrusive existence. Something so attainable. "Humans are so disappointing." She had so much fire in her, so much fight, and yet she wanted to hide away in a cottage all by herself. I understood the sentiment, really, I did. Some days I wished for the same. To be left alone. But this island would fall to ruin if I gave in to those desires. Heaven only knew what would happen to Tearmann in my absence. Tadhg had greatness in him as well, but he drowned it more often than not.

Another stone hit my back. I glanced over my shoulder to find

Aveen scowling. "All right, almighty prince. What would you wish for?"

You.

I told her what I used to wish before I knew it would cost this human her life. "Someone took something precious from me long ago. If I could have anything in the world, I would make her pay for it with her life."

14

My stomach buzzed as if I'd swallowed a hive of bees. If I didn't know better, I'd say I was nervous, which made no feckin' sense. What did I have to be nervous about? It wasn't as if I was the one dying tomorrow.

Aveen fidgeted at her dressing table, watching the flames dance in the fireplace, licking the stones. What if she backed out? She couldn't marry that eejit. I wouldn't be responsible for the consequences if she did. He'd be dead before she walked down the aisle. I could poison him, make it look like an accident. Eava probably had something handy. But then Aveen's sister wouldn't be able to marry him.

The sister.

She was the real problem.

For some reason, Aveen cared enough for her sister to go through with this. And she hadn't given any indication that she was considering any alternatives.

"What do you want to do?" I asked. If I had to sit here all night, I'd end up thinking of all the things that could go wrong tomorrow. Best distract ourselves.

"Tell Keelynn the truth," Aveen replied.

That wasn't happening. I may have trusted Aveen, but the

same could not be said for the sister. That one was a featherhead, and this bargain toed a dangerous line. "Give me something else."

She sighed toward the fire.

"What do you want to do?" I asked again.

"Tell Keelynn the truth."

When I asked a third time and she gave me the same answer, I wanted to rip out my hair. "And since you can't do that, you'd rather . . . Go on, now. Don't be shy. Surely there is something you want to do before my brother kills you."

Aveen groaned. "I just want to get this over with."

We had one night left together, and she wanted to *get it over with?*

I was going to give her a good feckin' night whether she liked it or not, and she'd always remember me for it. Probably dream of me every night for at least a decade after she returned. That's the kind of night I wanted her to have. Because this wasn't just her last night. It was mine as well.

And I refused to sit in this depressing room having to keep quiet in case Aveen's awful family came barging in. We needed to eat, have a few drinks, maybe even steal a few kisses.

"Do you like tarts?" I asked. What was I saying? Of course she liked tarts. Everyone liked tarts. Fate wouldn't have gifted me with a soulmate who didn't.

"What are you on about?"

I sprang to my feet, closing the distance between us. "You know, fruity little pastries sprinkled with sugar." I decorated an imaginary tart in my hand, then offered it to her. "Do you like them?"

"If this an attempt to distract me from my misery, can you not? I want to wallow." She didn't take the tart, instead brushing past me on her way to the bed.

Wouldn't *that* be a glorious way to spend our last night together? "Just answer the feckin' question, miserable Aveen." My least favorite Aveen of the lot.

"I don't know. I suppose they're all right."

All right? I was about to blow her mind. "Our kitchen witch Eava makes the best cherry tarts, and I happen to know she baked a fresh batch this morning." Sure, they were meant to be shared with Tadhg and Ruairi, but I wasn't above taking them all for Aveen. I jumped onto the bed next to her. "What do you say I steal the lot, and we feast on tarts until sunrise?"

I wasn't letting her go until I had to. If I had the power to make this night last forever, I would.

She side-eyed me. "Someone like you would surely prefer widow fingers or orphan ears."

I swallowed my smile. "I save those delicacies for special occasions. I could always ask Eava to whip some up if you like?"

"I'll eat the bloody tarts, you loon."

"Brilliant." Food sorted. We'd need something to drink as well. And some plates and serviettes. I rolled to my feet, straightening my breeches from where they'd ridden up.

"You're leaving?" she asked.

"There's no need to worry your pretty little head. I'll be back."

Her eyes flashed.

I loved it when she was angry.

"When I return, I want you wearing your best dress and a smile." Because if she remained in that robe and shift, I wouldn't be able to control myself. "Do you hear me, miserable Aveen?" I gave her shoulder a flick.

"I hear you, oh magnanimous prince," she grumbled, rubbing her shoulder.

I evanesced back to Tearmann, running toward the castle gates and straight to the kitchens.

Eava startled when she saw me. "What's the gleam in yer eyes about?"

"None of your business, witch. Where are the tarts?"

She turned fully to face me, a smile on her lips. "None of your business, Little Rían."

Not now, witch. I didn't have time for this. Every moment I spent here was a moment wasted. "The tarts."

She flicked her wrist, and a single tart appeared. "Ye can have *one.*"

"I need all of them."

"Why?"

I ground my teeth together. "For *her*, all right?"

"Oh! I knew it! I feckin' knew it!" She hugged me to her chest, damn near breaking my ribs. "When'll I be meetin' her?"

"Never. Now can I have the tarts?"

"Surely, after all these years, the Queen——"

"*Tarts.*"

Eava let out a long sigh before shifting a tray of tarts. I found a decent bottle of wine in the cellar, then pulled out two solid gold plates and a tray. The witch hummed while she packed everything into one of the baskets from the corner press.

I gave her wiry gray head a kiss before popping by my room to change into one of my finest waistcoats. I needed to shift some more furniture as well.

And some flowers.

Lots and lots of flowers.

When I finally returned to Aveen's bedroom, I found her sitting at the dressing table, covering her beautiful face with makeup.

Her eyes met mine in the mirror. "Lovely," she said. "You're back."

"Uh oh. Melancholy Aveen. How can we get rid of her?"

"You can't." In her haste to reach for something at the corner of the table, she knocked a glass pot onto the floor.

Melancholy Aveen would disappear as soon as she saw the townhouse, I was sure of it. And if not, after her first bite of tart, she would definitely be gone. No one could resist Eava's tarts. "We'll see about that."

The jar of black that she'd dropped smelled like tar. "No wonder you're melancholy, smearing this shite on your face every day." I handed it back even though I felt like throwing the whole feckin' lot into the fire and letting it melt into nothing. Couldn't she see how perfect she was without it?

"You are ridiculous," she murmured.

"It's better than being melancholy."

"I'm not melancholy. I'm nervous."

"What's there to be nervous about? All you have to do is go like this—" I made a kissy face and a bunch of sloppy tongue noises. "And my brother will take care of the rest." My stomach twisted at the thought. I pushed that right back, refusing to let that bastard ruin this night. "We can practice if it'll make you feel better." We could practice all night. I longed to kiss her frowny lips almost as much as I longed for vengeance. And for someone like me, that was saying a lot.

"What if something goes wrong and I don't come back?" she whispered.

I took her hands, pulling her upright. "I swear on pain of death that you will come back."

"You lie."

"About most things, yes. But not this." *Not to you.*

She stared at me, brow furrowing and frowny lips turning down. I put my thumbs on either side of those lips and forced them into a smile. "Give me a different Aveen. This one's broken."

She bared her teeth in a grimace.

"Fake Aveen? Pass. Next."

She rammed the toe of her slipper into my feckin' shin, sending a jolt of pain straight up my leg. "*Ohhh*, violent Aveen. Welcome back, my dear. I've missed you. Grab your cloak, my little viper. We're leaving."

"Where are we going?" she asked, fastening the gold clasp at her throat.

I swept her into my arms and drew on all my magic to get us

straight to the townhouse. The way she clung to me made the resulting wooziness worth it. Besides, there would be more executions, and I'd have forever to replenish my magic.

Forever without her.

I set her down but kept a hand on her elbow until she steadied herself. Once I was sure she wouldn't fall over, I brought her from the entryway to the parlor.

Her soft gasp cut straight to the void in my chest.

I watched her gaze sweep from the window to the chandelier and the table beneath, a smile playing around her lips, tugging at the corners. She was the most stunning woman I'd ever seen. Not only that, but she made me feel things I hadn't felt in centuries. Warm. Hopeful. Alive.

"There she is," I whispered.

She looked at me as if she'd forgotten I'd been standing right here. "Who?"

"Happy Aveen." Maybe this Aveen was my favorite. Hard to tell since I'd only just met her.

"Well, if you aimed to impress, you have succeeded."

"This?" I gave one of the droopy flowers a flick. "Oh, you think I did this to impress you? I hate to disappoint, but this is what I do every other Friday. You should not feel special. Because you aren't."

She returned my grin. If I'd had my heart, it would've been pounding. "Don't lie to me. Not tonight."

"All right. I don't do this every other Friday. It's usually on Tuesdays." I flicked my wrist, shifting the golden plates, goblets of wine, and tiered stand of tarts from the kitchen onto the table. Aveen unfastened the clasp at her throat and draped her cloak over the back of the chair closest to the fire.

"A bit garish, don't you think?" she asked, indicating the plates.

"As tonight is a celebration, I thought a lowly human such as yourself should dine on gold." I pulled out her chair, waiting until she'd situated herself before taking my own. Then I plucked a tart from the stand and set it on Aveen's gold plate.

She stared down at it, sniffed, then took a bite. A low moan fell from her throat, and I felt it all the way in my groin. I grabbed my wine, hoping the next bite would be the very same. Such delicious torture.

"These have to be the best things I have ever tasted." Crumbs clung to her full lower lip as she blinked up at me, a blush creeping along her cheeks. "Aren't you having one?"

"I'd rather watch you enjoy yourself." I could drown my sorrow in tarts on Sunday.

She grabbed another, guzzling wine when she finished. Instead of taking a third, she stared longingly at the remaining tarts.

I nudged the tray closer. "Have another."

Her eyes flicked to me before falling back on the stand. "I couldn't possibly."

"Do you want it?"

"I do."

I took the one from the very top, spilling over with sticky filling, and added it to her plate. "Then take it."

"That's your motto, isn't it? If you want it, take it."

Oh, my dearest Aveen. If only she knew how wrong she was. I took a slow sip of wine, holding her gaze the entire time. "If it was, we wouldn't be sitting here eating tarts."

"No?"

Not a feckin' hope.

Aveen drew her finger around the rim of her wine glass. "What would we be doing instead?"

I'd be the one feasting, and it wouldn't be on cherry tarts. She'd asked for the truth, hadn't she? Far be it for me to deny her anything tonight. "It would involve fewer clothes and more screaming." *A lot more screaming.* "Unfortunately for me—and for you—I don't bed maidens."

Her finger stilled on the goblet. "What makes you think I'm still a maiden?"

Where did I even begin? *"It's not appropriate for a man to enter a lady's private quarters. You mustn't speak so improperly. It wouldn't be proper for me to be alone with a man who is not my husband. Getting caught with you would ruin my reputation."*

So many reactions she'd given—her social standing, her upbringing, every time she'd shot down my advances. "Shall I go on, or would it be *improper?*"

Aveen sipped her wine. "Let's say, for argument's sake, that I wasn't a maiden . . ."

I eased forward, needing to see her eyes, taste her truth. "Have you given yourself to another?"

Her ragged breathing hitched. The ferocious blush painting her cheeks told me enough, but I had to hear her say it. I held my own breath as her mouth opened and she whispered, "I have."

Bitter, beautiful truth.

What was his name? Had she loved him? Did she love him still? Why hadn't she married him? Had he been good to her? Had she liked it?

Of all the questions whirring through my mind, only one found its way to my lips. "Will I unravel you now or wait until you finish that tart?"

15

I HELD MY BREATH, UNABLE TO CONTAIN MY EXCITEMENT WHEN Aveen nudged the plate aside. Her wide eyes locked with mine, and she said, "Now, please."

I caught her by the back of her head and dragged her forward so I could kiss her with everything I was. One night may be all we would have, but one night was more than I ever thought I'd get. A gift from fate that I didn't deserve but sure as hell wouldn't be turning away.

Aveen clung to my collar, pulling me closer. I nearly came out of my skin when she climbed onto my lap and her knees fell to either side of my hips. Her passion, her desire—I never thought it possible for this woman, but they seemed to match my own.

I needed her, *craved* her to the point of madness.

One glance at the fastenings her dress was all I needed to know that I'd never have the patience to undo them all. She would look awfully good bent over the table—*No, Rían.* She deserved better.

I wanted her stripped bare so I could memorize every curve, trace every freckle, taste every glorious inch. I shifted my dagger, drawing the tip down her throat, loving the way she shivered. "Do you fear me?" I asked.

"No."

I pressed the tip down to her breast, breaking her perfect skin, marking her as mine. The cut should be enough of a deterrent for Ruairi and Tadhg—and anyone who knew me—to keep their filthy hands off her if they wanted to continue drawing breath.

"You should," I confessed, running my finger along the length of the wound, healing the broken skin before bringing my fingertip to my mouth. *Divine.* Sweet as a spoonful of sun-drenched honey. The darkness that I'd tried so hard to keep from touching her awoke at the taste.

"What are you doing?" she gasped.

"I'm only half fae," I confessed. Goosebumps followed the tip of my blade along her flawless chest. "My mother is a witch."

My words were a warning to run away, to save herself. A plea to accept me as I was. Even the darkest parts.

She didn't run. If anything, it felt as if she held me tighter.

So I cut her out of the dress, leaving only her shift, wanting her to know there was still time to change her mind. Even though it would kill me to do so, if she said the word, I would stop. "Tell me where he touched you so that I may burn his memory from your skin." I tugged down the sleeves of her shift, whispering against the heat of her bare shoulder. "Here?"

"Yes."

My tongue traced along her collarbone, following the neckline to her breasts. Breasts that fit perfectly in my hands. I swallowed my moan, knowing there was no way the man she'd been with had resisted such perfection. Still, I had to know, "Did he touch you here?"

She whimpered a response, her back arching. My magic escaped, my darkness seeking her light. By some miracle, I managed a tost. It would do neither of us any good for her to wake all of Graystones with her screams.

I forced my mouth away from her skin so I could revel in her beauty. The dip at her waist. The swell of her hips. The softness of her thighs. Even her simple white undergarments made my cock swell. When I drew those undergarments aside and slipped my fingers into her slick heat, I knew I was done for.

"Here?" I choked. Her head fell to the crook of my neck, so I couldn't see her face when she nodded. "Don't hide from me. I want you to watch." *Watch me take you apart.*

I stroked slowly with one hand, catching her curls with the other the way I'd been dreaming since the day we met, twisting the wild strands and forcing her eyes to mine. "Do you feel this?" Magic pulsed through my veins, a buzzing heat reaching all the way to my fingertips. Aveen squirmed, her eyes rolling back as her chest heaved. "I can make you burn for me the way I burn for you."

I would unravel her, thread by glorious thread. Stealing her sanity the way she'd stolen mine, until I became every wayward thought, the air she breathed. She fumbled with my breeches, finding my stiff cock with her soft hands, drawing curses from my lips as we searched for a rhythm together

"How many times did he have you?" I asked. She whimpered when my thumb found the right spot, leaving me grinning like a fool and more determined than ever to wrench that sound from her throat as many times as I could tonight. "How many times must I take you before you feel me and only me?"

"Only once," she breathed on a ragged exhale.

The lust-filled haze in my mind cleared. I released her hair and withdrew my hand, needing to make sure I'd heard her correctly. "Once?"

Worried blue eyes met mine, and she nodded.

Shit. Aveen may as well be a maiden. What if I hurt her? What if she ended up hating it? What if she ended up hating me? *It doesn't matter*, the darkness in me screamed. *Tonight is all you'll ever have. Take it. Take her. You're not the hero in this story. Bring her upstairs and ruin her.*

My hands tightened on her hips as magic collected in my fingertips—

No. I couldn't do it. Not to her. If she wanted me, I'd let her be the one to take me. She could decide how much she could handle. How hard. How fast.

I brought her hips in line with mine, urging her to rock against me. When we finally came together, I wanted her dripping with desire. She adjusted her position, gripping the chair at my back so she could move on her own. *That's it. There you go.*

I could go slow.

I could take my time.

I pressed a tender kiss to her lips, the slender column of her throat, her magnificent breasts.

"Will I stop at one?" I whispered, taking her pebbled nipple into my mouth, flicking my tongue against the rigid peak.

Her curls tickled my cheek when she shook her head. She might change her mind, but the thought of her wanting this— wanting me—made me so deliriously happy that my hollowness sang.

She reached for my waistcoat. I removed it and my shirt with a spark of magic.

"How shall I unravel you, human?" I asked, unable to wait any longer, tearing her undergarments at the seams and throwing them aside. "Tell me what you want."

I needed to hear her truth. To be certain I didn't cross any line she would regret.

She gripped my cock in her hand, stroking slowly. "This. This is what I want."

Far be it from me to deny her anything. I undid my belt, searching for any hint of reservation in her hooded eyes. "Shall I take my time?"

"Make it last," she whispered.

I managed to get my breeches down, then painted myself in her desire. "Lift those lovely hips."

She did as she was told, lifting, adjusting, sinking, melting. I fought to keep my eyes open, to remember her pain even as I found only pleasure. "There you go . . ." My darkness screamed to take control. To throw her onto the table and bury myself so deep she'd feel me in her soul.

"How does that feel?"

Her throat bobbed when she swallowed. So fragile. So delicate. "It hurts," she whispered.

I'll make it better. She needed to relax, but telling a woman to relax usually had the opposite effect. So I replaced the command with a kiss. To her neck, her collarbone, her breasts, giving her body time to adjust. As it did, I felt her taking me deeper. When I bit her breast, she clenched around me. When she shifted, my eyes rolled back in my head.

I raised my hips, urging her to meet me with hers. The moment she did, I found paradise. "I knew you'd be perfect. I feckin' knew it." The way our bodies fit. This strange heat building in my hollow chest. The smile tugging at my lips as I watched her begin to lose herself in me. No. Not in me. In *us.* Together. Connecting over and over and over again. My darkness roared to drive myself into her hard and fast, to tear a scream from her throat.

But darkness colliding with light could never hope to win.

She was good and selfless. All the things I was not. And yet, in her presence, I found myself basking in her glow.

"Help me," she begged, her legs trembling.

My biceps strained as I lifted and lowered her, forcing her to slow her pace. "Not too fast. I won't last if you go fast." And I wanted this to last forever.

"Rían . . . Please . . ."

I felt my missing heart beat. *It's beating for her.*

I caught Aveen's chin, forcing her to look at me. "Say it again."

Her brow furrowed. "Please?"

As much as I loved her begging, nothing sounded sweeter than hearing my name on her lips. "My name."

"Rían," she gasped. "Rían," she moaned. "*Rían*," she cried.

So close. So feckin' close. Our souls colliding. Melding. Forging something new. Stronger.

I closed my eyes, focused on not losing myself until I knew I'd pushed her over the edge. It was my turn to beg. "Don't stop."

She whimpered my name. The moment I felt her walls clench around me, I let go, freefalling into bliss. This human, this *woman*, was my beginning and my end. My life. My purpose. My soulmate.

"Is liomsa tú," I whispered against her pounding heart. *You are mine.* A promise. A prayer.

How could I let her go to her death tomorrow? If she left me now, I'd never recover. I'd barely been living before her. After her, I would surely die as well.

"What does that mean?" Aveen asked, chest heaving against mine.

"It means you are beautiful." I kissed her pounding heart, knowing that wherever mine was, it beat the same rhythm. "You are perfect. You are all that is right and good in this world." My candle in the night, my flame calling me home, leading me away from darkness.

Mine.

When she laughed, she clenched around me. It was all I could do to keep from moaning.

"I think you're lying."

"You'll never know, now, will you?"

She pinched my feckin' arm.

"Easy now, human."

Aveen didn't seem the least bit fazed by my scowl. She laughed in my face, raking her short nails down my skin. Finding the scar the Queen had left. "What's this?" When her finger grazed the corner of the "X," I caught her hand. "A reminder to take control while you can." *For, once lost, you may never get it back.*

Her lower lip jutted out in a delectable pout I just had to taste.

Aveen rolled her hips—by accident or on purpose, I couldn't tell. Either way, I was ready for another round—or ten. "Are you sure you want to die tomorrow?"

Her answer was to roll her hips again. And again, dragging a curse from my lips. "What if you don't go through with it?" I said.

She stilled. "You mean, marry Robert?"

How dare she say another man's name with me inside of her. I lifted my hips, reminding her that she was mine and only mine. If she said his name again, I would tear out his throat. "I mean, tell them all to fuck off." She wasn't some pawn or a payment for her father's bad debts. She deserved to make her own choices.

A plan began to formulate as I started to fuck her slowly, my thighs dripping wet from us both. "You can live here. And I could . . . come to you . . . whenever . . . you want." I'd give her everything she'd ever dreamed of. Flowers growing in every corner of this place. She'd never want for anything.

Her hand fell to my stomach. "I can't."

What a load of shite. She could do whatever she wanted. The problem was, she didn't want this. Didn't want me for more than a night. "You can. But you're choosing not to."

Her hooded eyes widened, a storm brewing in their icy depths. "That's right. I'm *choosing* not to. This isn't about me—or about you, for that matter. This is about my sister."

Her feckin' sister. Why did Aveen have to be so feckin' selfless? Would the sister do the same for her? Hardly. She seemed as selfish as they came.

"Right. My apologies for misreading the situation." I gestured to my cock, still buried deep inside her. "I thought perhaps it may be a *little* about me."

"So, what? You just want me to live in this townhouse for as long as you're interested? What sort of life would that be for me?"

As long as I was interested—couldn't she see that my need for her could never be sated? That she and I were meant to be together forever?

One look into her steely gaze, and I had my answer.

"Forget I said anything," I muttered.

She climbed off me, leaving me stiff as a post as I watched her wander around the room collecting her ruined clothes. I was so hard, it ached when I tugged up my breeches.

I could still salvage this. We had a few more hours together. "You're overreacting," I said, trying to lift the fallen mood with a liar's smile.

"Am I? Because I'm fairly certain you just asked me to be your whore."

My whore? Couldn't she see how much she meant to me? *Get off it, you eejit.* She didn't know because I hadn't told her. And I could never tell her because of what the Queen would do to her if she found out.

With a flick of my wrist, all my clothes were back on. I shifted a dressing gown I'd bought for her for when she returned from the underworld. Aveen tossed it into the feckin' fire.

"Aveen, I'm sorry I said—"

"No. No more talking." She threw her cloak around her shoulders. "Take me home."

I reached for her, my lifeline. "It was a foolish suggestion made in desperation. You don't have to leave."

"Yes, I do."

"Stay with me."

She looked me dead in the eye, without a flicker of warmth, and said, "I'm choosing not to."

I wouldn't beg. Not for her. Not for anyone. Besides, what good would it do? She'd be dead tomorrow. Gone forever. I called on my magic reserves, evanescing back into her bedroom. She let me go the moment we arrived.

I should have gone. I should have left and said good riddance. Instead, I lied and said that I was only trying to help, when I knew the only person I had been trying to help was myself.

Aveen threw the pillows aside and drew down her coverlet. "Thank you for tonight," she clipped, ignoring my plea entirely.

"That's it? That's all you have to say to me?"

"You got your ride. What more do you want?"

I want you, you beautiful, stubborn, infuriating woman. Nothing more, nothing less. Every smile, every frown. Every mood. Every inch.

Instead of saying any of that, I left.

16

WHY HADN'T I KEPT MY MOUTH SHUT?

That question—along with countless others—swam through my mind for the rest of the night and the entirety of the following day. I'd barely been able to haul myself from bed to bathe and put on clean clothes. This was what happened when you let yourself feel things. You'd think I'd know better by now considering everything that had happened in my life. But no. I had to go and let that infernal human give me hope.

Someone pounded on my door. "Are you ready yet?" Tadhg bellowed from the other side.

There was no sense delaying the inevitable. I fastened the final button on my black waistcoat and glamoured myself to look like the ambassador, doing my best to take on the air of a man entirely unaffected by what was about to happen. Robert would undoubtedly be by Aveen's side all feckin' night, looking proud as punch despite being a pathetic shit. He'd dance with her. Touch her. *Kiss* her.

You don't care.

You don't *care.*

With the lie pounding through my skull, I tore open the door, finding Tadhg in a pair of clean breeches, a shirt missing no buttons, and a dark waistcoat that looked semi-clean. The most confusing part of all was what he had tied around his neck. "You're wearing a cravat."

He shifted his weight, tucking his hands into his pockets. "So?"

"*So*, you never wear cravats." Sure, he wore them draped around his neck like a scarf or stuffed into his pocket. One time I saw him using one as a handkerchief to clean rouge stains from his lips and throat. Tonight, he'd tied it properly.

"This is a special occasion, is it not? Or would you prefer I look like a homeless beggar for your lady love?" he said with a smile that was all too innocent. Tadhg was anything but innocent. He was up to something.

If I were being honest, I would've preferred him looking like a homeless beggar. With Aveen's affection for me at an all-time low, there was nothing stopping her from considering my brother a genuine contender for her affections.

"Let's get this over with." Maybe I could find the witch who'd cursed Tadhg and ask if she could curse me as well to keep him from having to kiss my—

"Such a foul mood, brother. Nice glamour, by the way." Tadhg poked my cheek like the child he was. "Who are you supposed to be? Lord Stick-up-his-arse?"

I bit back my retort, reminding myself that, as much as I loathed him, I needed him as well. I could always kill him tomorrow.

Out beyond the wards, Tadhg offered me his hand, wiggling his fingers when I didn't immediately accept. Being so weak never seemed to bother him in the slightest. Why did he need to be powerful with me at his side? His people loved him, weak or not.

We reached my spot in the trees, walking across dewy grass to where a line of carriages had been parked. Coachmen chatted and laughed amongst themselves. Every time a horse stomped its hoof or huffed a breath, Tadhg jumped. Eventually, we reached the house, where muffled music bled through the closed doors.

Tadhg went to take the first step, until I caught the back of his shirt. "You are not following me in there," I told him. Aveen would have my head, and I didn't need him spending more time with her than necessary.

He scowled at the house, then back at me. "Where do you expect me to go?"

"Wait for her in the garden."

"Ah, here now. I just want to have a little fun. You can tell your friends I'm your cousin from up north or some shite."

"No."

"What's the matter, little brother?" He nudged my shoulder too hard, sending me back a step. "Afraid your plaything would be more interested in sharing my bed than yours?"

"She's not my plaything." She wasn't my anything.

Tadhg's eyebrows lifted.

"If you set foot inside that ballroom, I will use Ruairi for target practice."

"All right. All right. I won't go inside. Unless Aveen asks me to," he added, shoving my shoulder again when he passed.

The moment he rounded the side of the house, I started for the stairs, wiping my sweaty palms down my breeches. If I'd had a heart, I imagined it would've been pounding. I paid no mind to the couple holed up in the entryway, making my way toward the lavish ballroom. For a man with no money, Lord Bannon certainly had spared no expense in celebrating the sale of his daughter to the highest bidder.

My gaze immediately found Aveen spinning on the floor with some balding twit, smiling at him like he deserved it. *At least it's not Robert.*

Her sister sipped champagne in a chair along the wall. I needed to put the woman I wanted out of my head and focus on my mission. Aveen's sister smelled like lavender and drink. When I stopped in front of her, she looked up with wide, reddened eyes.

"What are you doing tucked away in a corner all by yourself?" I asked through a forced smile.

"All this excitement is overwhelming," she said, her words

sweetening the air. *Lie.* "It's not every day one's only sister gets engaged."

I glanced toward the dance floor only to find Aveen with some fat toad. "Which means you should be on the floor, celebrating."

"Tonight, I prefer drinking to dancing," the sister said with a haughty lift to her pointed chin.

That makes two of us.

"That's brilliant news for me," I whispered, as if it were some sort of secret confession. Women loved that sort of shite, especially the drunk ones. "I'm a terrible dancer. Would you like some company?"

She blinked in surprise, glancing around the line of empty chairs on either side of hers. "These seats are reserved, I'm afraid."

Reserved? There wasn't a single person within earshot, let alone anyone looking for a feckin' seat. "Reserved for whom?" I managed without sounding as if I wanted to murder her.

The girl held out her empty champagne flute, giving it a shake. "The next man to bring me champagne."

I bolted for the closest waiter, took two glasses, and returned with the offering, giving Aveen's sister the fullest of the lot. If I got her drunk enough, she'd retire early. From the way she swayed in her seat, it wouldn't take much. "To betrothals," I said, unable to keep the bitterness from my tone as I took the chair next to her.

Her smile tightened. "To drinking." She scowled at something over my shoulder, then drained every last drop before setting the glass on the windowsill at her back. "Do you know what? I think I *do* want to dance."

I abandoned my glass as well, standing and offering my hand like a good little distraction. "If you care not for your toes, then I would be honored to be your partner."

The woman's gloved hand slipped into mine. She stumbled when she stood, but I kept her from falling into a pair of girls wearing matching purple dresses. Aveen's sister giggled to herself the entire way.

Eventually, we made it through the gauntlet of well-dressed humans to the edge of the parquet dance floor in time for the next waltz to begin. Aveen's sister stood far too close, and her brow furrowed in concentration as she counted to herself under her breath.

"I don't care for liars," she said with a mischievous grin. When I asked what she meant, she said, "You claimed to be a terrible dancer and yet you haven't stepped on my toes once."

I gave her shin a dig with the toe of my boot. "Better?"

Her grin widened. "Much."

I supposed she wasn't the worst human I'd met, which was why I allowed our first dance to melt into a second. Robert Trench watched the two of us from beside the grand fireplace. I winked at the bastard, relishing the redness in his jaw when my hand "accidentally" slipped to my partner's hip. *Whoops.*

He could've put a stop to this madness. All the fecker had to do was refuse to marry Aveen and none of this would be happening.

Before I knew it, the hour was upon us. So much for getting my charge to go to bed. If anything, she seemed to have sobered a bit. I needed to get this one out of here so Aveen could slip away unnoticed.

"This ballroom is rather stuffy," I whispered, keeping my gaze on Robert's, "wouldn't you agree?"

"It is rather stuffy," Aveen's sister said with a coy smile.

"Perhaps there is somewhere more private where we could retire for another drink." I tugged one of her curls, wishing it was gold instead of brown.

She glanced around the ballroom, her gaze landing on the door. "Go into the hallway and wait for me."

I gave her gloved hand a kiss, then started for the hallway. Some people recognized me and waved. I nodded but didn't linger. There wasn't time for idle conversations if I wanted a chance to say goodbye to Aveen.

The moment I was alone, I poured more magic into my glamour, so I was no longer Edward but his spirited younger sister, Marissa. I ran toward the ballroom, making my way between guests nattering on about this and that, and caught Aveen by the dessert table.

Let her go. Make her stay.

"I wanted to say goodbye," I blurted, sounding like a fool.

Aveen's blue skirts glittered when she whirled. Her bored expression gave nothing away. "Goodbye," she said, as if I were some stranger.

Her gaze flicked toward the balcony, where her sister had gone bowling past.

"Aveen, last night I said something I—"

"You think I want to discuss last night?" She laughed, but there was no mirth to the hollow sound. "I never want to speak of it again. As far as I'm concerned, nothing happened."

As far as *I* was concerned, it had been the best night of my feckin' life until I went and mucked it up. "I understand better than anyone that intent does not matter. But I want you to know that it was not my intention to use you in any way. I just got caught up in the lie. It will not happen again."

Her expression hardened. "Go take care of my sister."

A woman in a hideous red dress with poofy sleeves shouted for Aveen.

The distraction gave me a chance to escape to the balcony. That was it. The last interaction we would ever have. Her final memory of me would be in a feckin' dress, begging for forgiveness. So much magic wasted, and for what? A feckin' apology? And now, she was about to go to my brother, a man cursed to embody her deepest, darkest desires, and kiss him.

I balled up my fist and slammed it into the stones, cursing fate. Cursing the Queen. Even cursing Aveen. I'd been fine before that infernal human had set foot in that feckin' shed. I'd had a goal, a purpose. And now . . .

Now it felt like nothing would ever be enough. Not defeating the Queen. Not finding my heart. None of it.

I evanesced back to one of the hallway's bay windows, shifting two glasses of champagne, almost forgetting that I needed to turn myself back into the ambassador. I'd just finished my glamour when Aveen's sister fell into the window next to me.

"I thought you'd changed your mind," I said, somehow keeping the extent of my hatred for her from tainting my words.

"Not tonight," she replied, a little breathless.

One moment, she was standing on the other side of the space, shadows concealing her features, the next, she had her arms locked around my neck, lips smashed against mine. Once I got over the shock, I managed to pull away and keep from spitting to rid myself of the taste of sour wine and champagne. Aveen had insisted her sister loved Robert. If she truly loved him, why the hell had she kissed me like that?

"You're so beautiful," I said, kissing her neck instead, swallowing the bile in my throat.

"Liar."

It wasn't a lie. Not entirely. She was nothing compared to her sister, but I could see how men would find this one attractive—when she wasn't trying to jam her tongue down their throats.

She stiffened as if I'd spoken my thoughts aloud. "I've changed my mind. I want to go back."

Oh, thank the stars. She tried shrugging me off, but my feckin' cufflink snagged on the layers of frilly lace around the top of her dress. "One minute." I angled my hand toward the moonlight in an attempt to see how exactly we were ensnared.

"What are you doing?" she shrieked, shoving my chest, making her sleeve slip down her slender shoulder.

"I said give me a damned minute." What'd the shrew do? She shoved me again. "Stop hitting me. My cufflink—"

The woman drove her elbow into my gut. I jerked, ripping her dress and catching an eyeful of her bare breast before she shrieked and covered herself. Even with my eyes bulging, I still couldn't unhook my feckin' cufflink. "I'm so sorry. I didn't mean for this to happen. I'm so—"

"Ambassador?"

Shit. Aveen's father. *Shit. Shit. Shit.*

"I've been hoping to speak with you regarding—*Keelynn?*"

I needed to get the hell out of here. To evanesce. He'd already seen me, but Edward DeWarn didn't exist.

If Aveen found out, I'd ruined her sister . . .

It doesn't matter. She already hates you.

Her sister's tears glistened in the moonlight. This was bad. So feckin' bad. "Father . . . I . . . We . . ."

"*What is the meaning of this?*" the man bellowed right in my good feckin' ear.

"It's not what it looks like, sir." Not that the truth mattered in these situations. Still, I hoped he was a reasonable man.

What was I saying? He'd forced Aveen to marry Robert Trench.

"This caught on her dress and—"

The man caught me by the collar. I swallowed every instinct telling me to make him pay for his insolence. I could kill them both. Make it look like an accident. Murder-suicide over his daughter's death.

What was wrong with me? I couldn't kill my soulmate's entire feckin' family.

"You *dare* come into my home and accost *my daughter?*" Lord Bannon snarled, spittle flying against my face.

It was some effort to keep the glamour in place and add a tremble to my voice that didn't sound murderous. "It was an accident. I swear."

Why wasn't the girl saying anything? Had she been out to trap me all along? What was the point in any of this if she didn't marry Robert?

"What good is the word of a scheming bastard who lured an innocent young woman into the shadows without a chaperone?"

"Father, please," a tiny voice came from behind him. "This is all a misunderstanding."

Finally. She speaks. "It's true, sir," I said. "A simple misunderstanding."

Lord Bannon shoved me. My spine slammed against the wall. "I misunderstand nothing," he snarled.

"My dress ripped," the sister continued. "And . . . And the ambassador was offering me his coat until I could change. That's all. Father, please. You must believe me. I'm telling the truth."

A believable lie, even if the delivery left something to be desired.

"*The truth?*" Lord Bannon cursed. "You think that matters in these situations? When people hear about this, she will be ruined. No one will want her."

No one wanted her *now*. If Robert cared for her at all, he would've agreed to marry her. Had he? No. And now, here I was, with my back literally against a feckin' wall.

If I evanesced while he held me, I'd bring him too. I needed to get him to let me go. I needed to play along. "I understand how this unfortunate situation could affect Keelynn's prospects for a husband. I am happy to make this right."

The man's fingers still gripping me loosened.

"That's madness!" Aveen's sister cried, clawing at her father's arm. "No one saw us. No one has to know."

Lord Bannon let me go, then pried her fingers free, turning toward a door beyond the window. Once we were out of sight, I'd vanish. He'd tell no one for fear of people thinking he was mad. I'd return to Tearmann and never have to see any of these awful humans ever again.

A pair of ice-blue eyes flashed in my mind. *Help her.*

I'm not the hero, I wanted to shout. *I'm not selfless or kind or good.* Hadn't I already proven that time and again? Why the hell would I even consider doing something to help a woman who wanted nothing to do with me?

I didn't want to let *her* down.

Feck it anyway. I guess I was going to get married.

I followed Aveen's father into a sizeable study. The spines on the many books displayed showed very few signs of wear and tear. Lord Bannon seemed like a man to buy books but never read them.

He sank onto the chair behind a desk and unbuttoned his waistcoat. "Sit down, Ambassador."

I remained standing, clutching the back of my chair to keep from strangling him. The bastard didn't even offer me a drink from the decanter at the corner of his desk.

"With my eldest daughter set to marry, and my own funds wrapped up in investments, I'm afraid the matter of Keelynn's dowry is a bit complicated."

Complicated, my arse. The man was as penniless as a feckin' beggar after investing in failed mines and ships that had gone to sea, never to be heard from again. "Is it, now?"

A nod.

"Then I suppose it is a blessing that I do not need her dowry," I ground out.

That made his eyebrows raise. "How much is your annual income?"

I pulled a number out of the air that seemed impressive. "Six thousand a year."

He nodded, clearly fighting a victorious smirk as he withdrew a document from the top drawer of his desk. If only the prejudiced bastard knew to whom he was about to tie his precious little girl. I didn't ask why he had a betrothal contract ready and waiting.

When I signed the papers under my false name—making them as legally binding as a wink—the man finally saw fit to unstop the decanter and fill two glasses.

The door flew open, slamming against one of the shelves. Bannon cursed when a young man in short breeches and mud-crusted boots stumbled inside, cheeks flushed and eyes wild. I recognized him from the stable the day I'd gone looking for Padraig.

"What is the meaning of this?" Bannon bellowed, his fist

cracking off the top of the table, vibrating the decanter's amber liquid.

"It's Lady Aveen, Yer Lordship. She's dead."

The garden remained silent except for Aveen's sister's incessant wailing as she clutched a dark cloak over her ripped gown. Behind her, Robert raked his fingers through his hair, his face pale as he stared down at the town physician examining Aveen's lifeless body.

Blackness stained her perfect lips, trailing down her throat. I didn't need to check to know the curse had spread to her heart.

When the sister saw Lord Bannon and I, she started for us. Robert tried to reach for her, but she tore out of his grip. Instead of going to Lord Bannon, the sister came to me. Hugged *me*. *Me*. I didn't know why the hell she thought I'd be the best man to offer her comfort, but for some reason, my arms slipped around her back.

If looks could kill, Robert would've stolen my last breath. The other guests who'd flooded the garden watched with wide eyes as Aveen's sister sobbed through my shirtsleeve. The rest of us stood in stunned silence as Aveen's father and Lord Trench tried to keep the growing crowd at bay.

"How could this happen?" Bannon murmured to the stars.

Because you let her down, you selfish bastard.

I stayed rooted in place as Lord Bannon carried Aveen's limp body into the house. Aveen's sister let me go to run after him, clutching Aveen's hand and muttering through her tears.

A tiny part of me wanted to explain to the poor woman what was happening. To ease the pain rolling off her hunched shoulders. But I'd gambled with her life enough. The truth would be too risky for all of us. Meddling in human affairs, orchestrating a murder. It all amounted to me putting my life on the line for a human. An unforgivable sin in the Queen's eyes. One she could never know I'd committed.

So many whispers lifted toward the winking stars as the tide of bodies retreated toward the house. Every one of them had a different theory. Every one of them was more interested in the gossip than in showing genuine concern for a family who had lost a daughter and a sister. For the life of a beautiful young woman stolen from this world too soon.

What had begun as a betrothal ball ended as a wake.

A heavy hand landed on my shoulder. I turned to find Robert glowering at me.

"You will leave Lady Keelynn alone," he said, squeezing hard.

I brushed him off like the annoyance he was, saying, "That will be difficult, considering she is to be my wife."

17

I WAITED BEHIND THE HUMANS WEARING ALL BLACK, WATCHING them mourn a woman they hadn't even known. As sad and depressed as they appeared, none of their emotions rivaled my own. Not only did I ache with sadness, but rage and guilt filled the void inside me as well.

Pity the girl from Graystones who loved a heartless prince,
For the only way to save him was at her own expense.

Aveen had died, hadn't she? Why was I still here, still feeling the weight of the Queen's influence like an icy fog around my shoulders? Why hadn't fate freed me?

Aveen's sister clung to my arm as if I could offer her comfort when I had none to give. When she left with her father, I promised to accompany them shortly. News of our hasty betrothal had eclipsed that of Aveen's death. As if losing a light in this world wasn't as important as a feckin' scandal.

One by one, the other mourners left, until it was only me and the man dumping dirt into the hole, grunting under the weight of the earth each time he filled his shovel. I tried shifting Aveen's body to the castle, but something blocked my magic. Of course it did. Why would this be easy when it could be a pain in the arse? When my brother appeared on the other side of the tiny gray church, I resisted the urge to groan. One more thing I didn't need to deal with.

Ah, well. Since he was here, I may as well use him.

I focused my magic once more. When nothing happened, I assumed Aveen's father had bought an iron-lined casket. Where had he gotten the funds? Those things did not come cheap.

No matter.

I stepped forward, my boots knocking bits of dirt onto the coffin at the bottom of the pit. The man digging stopped to glower at me. "Would you mind giving me a moment alone to pay my respects," I said in the ambassador's commanding tone.

"Ye can pay 'em once the hole's filled in," he grumbled, scooping another shovelful.

If I did that, I'd have to dig all the dirt right back out. "That doesn't work for me."

"I don't give a—"

Tadhg stepped from the shadows, the tips of his pointed ears peeking through his unruly dark hair. The human's bulging eyes bounced between us. I smiled, allowing darkness to leak into my eyes. Instead of running, the foolish bastard adjusted his grip on the shovel's handle and swung it at my head, getting dirt all over my feckin' shirt.

"You really shouldn't have done that." I caught him by the throat and snapped his neck. Perfectly legal considering he'd attacked me first. At least it was in Tearmann. And I abided by Tearmann law. Tadhg skipped over to my side with an impish grin.

"What are you doing here?" I asked.

"You always complain about me not helping with my bodies."

Tadhg was usually as helpful as a thorn in my boot. He had an agenda, I was sure of it. Unfortunately, I didn't have time to figure out what it was. Shifting the dirt covering the coffin took no time at all, but still the wooden box inside refused to budge.

"You want to help?" I shifted a steel crowbar and thrust it into his chest. "Get in and open it up."

When he did as I asked with no protest, I *knew* he was up to something. I evanesced next to him, my boots sinking into the squelching mud, making my stomach lurch. Filthy earthworms writhed and slugs inched along the walls of the pit. The flowers engraved on the beautiful casket left my chest caving in.

Tadhg wedged the crowbar into the gap and began prying it free while I directed far too much magic toward the latches. The wood creaked and groaned, and after a bit of effort, it popped. My brother stepped back. When I lifted the lid, I felt myself wilt.

Someone had covered the black curse with layer upon layer of makeup. Aveen looked like a painted doll. A bit more magic sorted that right out. Her freckles stood out against her pale skin. She didn't blush when my eyes traced the lines of her body. She didn't smile or curse when I lifted her into my arms.

"Throw the human inside and fill the hole," I told my brother, nodding toward the casket. It would do no good to have someone passing by and finding a body.

I never would've been able to evanesce across the country with Aveen if she were alive. Seeing as she wasn't, the trip took barely any magic at all. After bringing in hundreds of Tadhg's victims, no one paid me any attention, nodding a greeting as if I were carrying a sack of grain.

Once I crossed the wards, I evanesced straight into the tallest tower, where I'd left the coffin I'd purchased in Swiftfell for a small fortune. The box may have been decorated in gold leaf, but what it held inside was infinitely more precious.

I couldn't linger, even if I wanted to.

I needed to return to Graystones to marry Aveen's sister.

Was this really necessary? Truly? What if I didn't go through with it? No one would know. I could evanesce, never to return. Edward

DeWarn wasn't real. There would be no record of him anywhere. *Ohhh*, or I could die. Make it look like an accident. But then my glamour would slip, and the town would know Aveen's family had been associating with the Danú. A scandal worse than bankruptcy and rushed nuptials put together. I could ask Tadhg to help hold the glamour until after I was buried, but that would require him being sober—something he hadn't been since we collected Aveen.

I scrubbed at my weary eyes. How could this plan have gone so horribly wrong? It was the sister's fault. If she had just listened to me and held still, none of this would've happened.

One of the Bannons' footmen opened the door to the back room where I'd holed up to keep myself from killing every single human in the chapel. When he said it was time, I straightened my waistcoat, raked a hand through my glamoured curls, and stepped into the main sanctuary.

A handful of witnesses filled the pews.

Aveen's father looked chuffed with himself, his undoubtedly new charcoal suit impeccable.

The sister's gaze remained firmly planted on her ivory shoes peeping from beneath the ivory gown she wore. She clutched a bouquet of flowers like they could save her from this fate.

After a short welcome, the priest got right to the vows. I repeated every lie, playing my role. When he asked for a ring, I withdrew the gold band I'd purchased in town the day before and shoved the thing on her finger. She had one for me as well. A ring easily removed. If this had been a Danú ceremony, there would've been magic involved, leaving us both with black rings around our fingers only death could erase. Luckily for me, this wouldn't be legal in any court of law, Airren or Tearmann, because my name wasn't actually Edward Joseph DeWarn.

The priest cleared his throat. "I said, you may kiss the bride."

For the first time, Aveen's sister raised her eyes to mine, and I met her steely gray gaze without grimacing. Swallowing the bile in my throat, I gave her a peck on the cheek, fighting the urge to wipe the taste of lavender from my lips.

Lord Bannon caught my hand, squeezing my fingers as if the pain would do anything but make me want to call fire to my palm and burn his skin clean off. "She is my most precious girl," he said. "Take care of her."

This one was his most precious? What of his daughter who had died? Had he forgotten about Aveen already? He cared for the women in his life only as far as they could help him. I should've torn his head from his worthless body and set him alight. I may not have cared for my new wife, but I had no plans to use her in any way.

I'd never thought this about anything, but perhaps she was better off with me than with him.

After the ceremony, Lord Bannon had organized a small dinner at his estate. I couldn't help thinking of the last time I'd been in this very room, wearing a dress and falling for a woman who loved to play in dirt. I'd taken Aveen's chair as my own like a sentimental fool, wanting to be near her in any way possible.

When the dinner was done, the cake cut, and final toasts given, Aveen's sister and I returned to Graystones in Lord Bannon's carriage. Her coachman, Padraig, glared at me until he took his bench behind the horses. The woman I'd married stared out the window at the landscape whizzing past while I watched raindrops collect on the glass. We reached Graystones far too quickly, and before I knew it, I found myself standing in the town-house next to my new wife.

"That's the parlor." I gestured toward the room. "The kitchen and dining room are back there, as are the library and my study." I'd shifted some furniture from unused rooms at the castle and purchased the rest. Nothing too opulent, but serviceable and in keeping with someone who had such a prestigious occupation as Edward DeWarn.

Aveen's sister glanced toward the stairs at my back. "And upstairs?"

I started for the upper floor, wincing as her heels clopped behind me. "I've a room prepared for you at the end of the hall," I said, pointing to one of the two bedrooms on my right, the one with an attached ensuite. The maids had spent the day getting it ready, bringing linens and knickknacks along with trunks full of dresses from the estate. The two maids and new cook were the only staff in the household, graciously sent by Lord Bannon. The man likely didn't have the funds necessary to cover their wages. Still, it saved me from having to hire my own staff, and the three of them should be enough to make Keelynn's life here more than comfortable.

"Which one is your room?" she asked in a quiet voice, scanning the three other doors.

"That one." Third door at the opposite end of the hall, near a circular window overlooking the neighbor's shoddy back garden.

She stepped away from me—and my room—backing toward her own. "If it's all right with you, Ambassador, I am feeling rather tired and would like to retire."

"You are not my ward and can do whatever you'd like. Although you should probably call me Edward." Our arrangement would be strange enough without people questioning why she called me by my title.

She turned toward her room, and I escaped to mine. No curtains lined the windows, no rug to soften my heavy footsteps, and only a small armoire for a handful of my least-favorite clothes. Colorful waistcoats, breeches in deep green, navy, and maroon. Items I'd clearly purchased while drunk. Or that Tadhg had bought for me and slipped to the back of my armoire.

Falling into bed face-first, I groaned into the too-soft mattress. I'd linger for a day or two, claim to be called away for some purpose or another, and return to Tearmann. I should be able to keep that up for a few months before Tadhg grew suspicious.

And then Edward would have to die. A simple accident away from Graystones so that Aveen's sister wouldn't be suspected of foul play. Then, she'd be able to live out the rest of her life however she chose. Being a widow in Airren was nothing compared to being a man, but it would afford her some rights and allow her to inherit this house and everything in it. I'd need to set up an account in her name, leaving enough funds for her to survive. Hopefully she didn't squander it all on frivolous shite. Not that I'd be coming back to check on her.

A soft knock interrupted my musings. Before I could tell the person to leave me the hell alone, the door opened. Aveen's sister stepped in wearing a green silk robe, dark hair unbound, falling nearly to her waist.

I jerked off the bed, stumbling back toward the window. "What do you think you're doing?"

She tucked a lock of dark hair behind her ear, her pale throat bobbing when she swallowed. "It is our wedding night, is it not?"

Feck it all. She thought I would actually touch her?

What was I saying? I'd married her, hadn't I? "Neither of us wanted this," I reminded her.

"I know, but—"

"The only reason I married you was to save you from scandal. This will not be a real marriage. I'm sorry you were led to believe otherwise."

Her jaw flushed.

"Return to your rooms and rest assured that I will not be joining you."

Her gaze dropped to her bare feet, and her hair fluttered as she twisted for the door.

I sank onto the floor, scraped a hand through my hair, and shifted a bottle of wine.

With my head in my hands, I stared down at the glass of amber liquid that hadn't been empty in two days. Surrounded by books I'd never read, "borrowed" from Lord O'Meara's extensive library.

Hating the woman hiding in her room upstairs.

Hating the man who'd raised her.

Mostly, hating myself.

What did it matter? Nothing mattered. Aveen would never forgive me for what had happened. Not that she'd have a chance. I planned on leaving her somewhere safe and letting her go about her human life until it ended.

In what world did I get to keep her?

One word from the Queen, and I'd be compelled to take her life.

If I could retrieve my heart—

I swallowed that useless thought with a gulp of whiskey.

The only way that could happen was if I destroyed the Queen. To destroy her, I'd have to be in complete control. To be in control, I'd need my heart. If I got my hands on a cursed dagger, I could end her. And to do that, I'd have to end myself as well.

No plan led to victory. The future remained as bleak and hopeless as ever.

The door to the study creaked open. The dark-haired maid stiffened when she saw me, her cheeks turning pink. "Pardon the intrusion, Yer Lordship." She tapped the feather duster in her hand against her black skirts. A few curls spilled from beneath her white mop cap.

"Go about your business. Just pretend I'm not here." Why hadn't I told Keelynn I had to go today instead of tomorrow?

"I've tried," she said in a silken voice, stepping toward the desk. "But yer a hard man to ignore, Ambassador."

Her hooded eyes dropped to my unbuttoned shirt, a smile playing on her lips.

My traitorous body stirred. I wanted no part of this woman. But what I wanted had never really mattered, had it? Was I to be celibate for the rest of my days? Was I destined to be on my own for eternity? This one wanted me. Maybe that could be good enough.

18

(*One Month Later*)

AFTER A TRIAL IN DREADSHIRE—A TOWN AS PLEASANT AS ITS NAME —I decided to stay at the townhouse instead of evanescing back to Tearmann. Wouldn't want the humans to think I'd abandoned my wife, now, would I? No one greeted me at the door, which wasn't a surprise considering I hadn't given them advance notice of my arrival. The scent of roast pork wafted from the kitchens. I found my wife curled up on the settee in the parlor, a book in her lap.

When she saw me, she didn't bother rising. "You're back."

"Only for the night."

She nodded, then went back to her book.

I hadn't been sleeping right since Aveen died, and at the moment, all I wanted was to trudge upstairs and pass out. Instead, I pretended I wasn't a heartless bastard and sank down next to her. Aveen's sister seemed to be faring well, the color in her cheeks high and the dark smudges beneath her eyes that had appeared the night Aveen died had faded as well. A new piece of embroidery sat on the coffee table next to a stack of books. Every time I came in, she seemed to be reading a different one.

"You like to read," I said like a simpleton.

"Yes, Ambass—*Edward*," she corrected, her gaze still pinned on her book.

"What types of books?" I liked to read as well but had a feeling a library full of books on Airren and Tearmann law would hardly interest her.

Her eyes widened as if I'd asked if she wanted to fornicate on top of the feckin' shelf.

"Perhaps I can get a few new books for you to read while I'm gone," I explained.

"Where are you off to this time?"

I pulled a name out of thin air. "Minbury."

Her gray eyes lit with a fire I hadn't seen since the night of her birthday ball. "I could go with you. I have seen very little of Airren, and—"

"That will not be necessary."

She nodded, looking back down at her book. In a quieter voice, she said, "Stories of romance and adventure. Those are the books I most like to read."

My darling wife claimed to be too tired for dinner, retiring to her room early and leaving me to eat on my own. Halfway through my plate of pork, one of the maids opened the door to the kitchen. Something thick and heavy lodged in my chest that felt a lot like guilt.

"I overheard milady say ye were back," she said with a coy smile.

If she'd told me her name, I couldn't remember. When she came closer, I shot off my seat like someone had lit a match under my arse. I wasn't drunk enough to screw her again, so I muttered some convoluted excuse and escaped out the back door.

The best part about being in Graystones was that a certain witch who made excellent waistcoats happened to live next door.

It was well after eight, so the shop windows were dark. I pounded on the door anyway. Meranda appeared not a moment later, red hair unbound and hate burning in her eyes. "What'd I tell ye about callin' after hours?" she hissed when she dragged open the door.

"Is that any way to treat your best customer?"

"Yer waistcoats won't be finished until next week."

"I'm not here for the waistcoats."

"They why are ye here?"

An excellent question—and one I didn't know how to answer. Why had I come over? My gaze landed on a bolt of cloth the same shade of blue as Aveen's eyes. An idea sparked in my mind, and I felt my lips lift into my first genuine smile in weeks.

When Aveen returned, she would need garments, wouldn't she? And she'd need funds to live on. And a place to live. Providing her with a good life was the least I could do after what had happened with her sister. Not that I expected a few dresses to make much of a difference, but . . . I skimmed my finger along the silk, remembering the way Aveen's skin had felt beneath me. "Meranda? I'd like you to make me a dress."

I flattened the curling edge of the map spread across Tadhg's desk, pinning it down with the hourglass. The candle had long since burned itself out, leaving wax dripping onto the gold holder.

Aveen had said that she wanted a cottage by the sea, so I would get her a feckin' cottage by the sea. She'd said she wanted flowers. I'd grow so many weeds that she'd have to cut her way to the door.

My finger skimmed the map as I scanned the border of this cursed island for the perfect location.

The safest place would be along the eastern coast, as far from Tearmann and the Queen as one could get. Not that the old witch knew of her existence. But with Aveen being from the east coast, it was far too likely that she may run into someone from her old life. A risk I wasn't willing to take. Southern shores were notorious for sailors from Iodale. The last thing she needed was to be set upon by a bunch of randy pirates. That left the northern coast and western coast. Somewhere quiet. Somewhere unlikely to cause her trouble.

Somewhere like . . . Hollowshade.

How long had it been since their last execution? Must've been at least fifty years. Either the Danú had been completely run out or they hid well. I focused on the map, trying to recall some memory of the last time I'd been there. The smell of the sea, the irritating call of the gulls, the slap of waves against wooden hulls.

Hollowshade.

I pulled my favorite glamour, one of the most mundane faces I'd ever seen. Bland as dry porridge and easily forgotten. Although it killed me to do it, I also shifted some of Tadhg's shite clothes. It would do me no good to show up with a bland face in the clothes of a prince.

I evanesced to the edge of the tiny fishing village, where colorful cottages lined the sloping street like a deck of cards trailing toward the docks. Aveen would probably love it. Humans dressed in brown and black were setting up for the market on the main street. A market that consisted of four stalls. One farmer had a bunch of sheep. Another, goats. A third had a cart of potatoes, carrots, turnips, and beets.

The smell of fresh bread wafted from the bakery where a short, round man worked within.

Quaint as a feckin' painting. The perfect spot for Aveen.

Now, to find her a place to live. These cottages all seemed occupied, and there wasn't much room for a garden. I continued up the winding road outside the town, passing men on carts and dead-eyed donkeys trudging along, hauling hay.

I'd forgotten Hollowshade was close to a portal. Handy, that. Not that I had any intention of coming here myself. Still, having a portal nearby would remove the magical signature if I did decide to check up on her. Just to make sure no one had murdered her and whatnot.

The colorful village surrendered to low stacked-stone walls

separating fields of grazing sheep. After ten minutes, I came upon a cottage. Or, at least what used to be a cottage. At the moment, with the holes in the moss-covered roof, the place looked more like a dilapidated shack.

Aveen would probably love it.

I kicked the building's stone walls. They seemed sturdy enough. Nothing crumbled, anyway. The windows were shite, though, half broken, clinging by the frames. The door sagged off its rusted hinges. She wanted weeds, and there were plenty of them. It wasn't a large garden, but there should be enough room for whatever she'd want to plant. I continued walking until I reached a two-story farmhouse. An angry bull glared at me from beneath its cage-like helmet from the enclosure next to the house.

A stooped man with thinning white hair and a wiry white beard stopped shoveling hay into a trough when he saw me approach.

"Mornin'," I offered in greeting, giving him a friendly wave.

"Mornin'," he returned with a stiff nod.

"You know who owns that old heap of shite down the road?"

He shifted his stance, resting his elbow on the end of the pitchfork's handle so he could scratch at his beard. "Belonged to my ma."

"You willin' to sell it?"

"Fer what?"

"It just so happens I'm in the market for a heap of shite."

It was hard to tell with the beard, but I could've sworn the corner of his lips lifted. "Suppose I could be persuaded fer a hundred pieces of silver."

"For *that?*" I choked, gesturing toward the dilapidated old chimney barely visible over the horizon.

"Sentimental value, ya see."

Sentimental value, my arse. The bastard was fleecing me. I could just kill him and take the feckin' thing. Unfortunately, my human would take issue with that, so I dragged out my purse and counted out silver coins through gritted teeth. It wasn't as if I didn't have the money, and it wasn't as if Aveen wasn't worth every feckin' coin. I just didn't take kindly to being taken advantage of.

"There." I shoved the rest of my purse into my pocket. "Do you have the deed?" I wouldn't be leaving here without it.

The man grumbled something before disappearing into the house. The bull strode forward, its muscles straining under its hide. The bollocks on the thing. *Feckin' hell.*

He emerged with a folded-up piece of parchment and handed it over with a tobacco-stained smile. "Phil's free," he said.

"Who the hell is Phil?"

The man smirked and went back to shoveling hay.

Turned out, Phil was a one-horned goat who refused to leave the overgrown garden even though the walls surrounding it had gaps as big as me and a gaping gate. I could've killed the thing, but that seemed unnecessarily cruel, so I'd shifted it into a field down the way three times.

He always found his way back.

The garden was a tangled mess of greens and browns, with a few colorful weeds growing along the front wall. Creeping ivy clung to the back of the house, and there were some blackberry bushes growing on the one side as well.

Inside, a few blocks of turf had been piled next to the dusty fireplace. When I opened the door to the first of the two bedrooms, a feckin' mouse darted across my boot. At least I hoped it was a mouse. Dust motes spun in the shafts of muted sunlight streaming through grimy, broken windows.

Once I started sneezing, I couldn't stop. My eyes itched so feckin' bad, I wanted to tear them from my skull. I might as well burn the place if I couldn't get rid of the dust.

I knocked out every single window and left the door wide open, hoping the damp, fresh air would make it so I could breathe. Phil took this as an invitation to come right inside. The beast plonked himself down next to the fireplace, gnawing on bits of an old boot, watching me through beady eyes.

I had a little under a year to get things sorted.

I honestly wasn't sure that would be enough time.

I'd spent five days in hell and the place still wasn't any closer to being livable. Every night, I had to burn Tadgh's clothes. Not that that was painful for me by any means since all his clothes belonged in the fire.

The sun beat down on my back, and I found myself longing for the breeze that had frozen the bollocks off me every other day this week. Hiding beneath the glamour felt like an extra layer of wool over my skin, making it difficult to breathe. I'd removed the bulk of the old roof tiles. For the first time, Phil was nowhere to be found.

As far as I could tell, the trusses appeared in good condition. No spots of rot, and they didn't fall over when I kicked them. That had become my test of durability: kick it, and if it didn't crumble or wobble or disintegrate, it passed. I bent to finish the second line of tiles.

"Yer not doin' it right," called a voice from below.

I glanced over my shoulder to find the farmer who'd sold me this place leaning on the post barely holding the sagging gate.

"Mind your own business, old man."

"First storm we have, that's gonna topple like it's made of sand."

Maybe I would kill him. He was so old, no one would suspect foul play.

"You think you can do better? Here." I held out the slate tile. Let's see him climb the ladder without breaking a hip, balance on the roof without falling through, and fix the feckin' thing.

The old man picked up the ball ping hammer beside the rusted saw I'd found out back, tucked it into his belt loop, and climbed the ladder like he could have done it with his eyes closed. He spun the hammer in his hand and tacked the tile down with one *thwack*.

"Well? Are ye gonna do somethin' useful and hand me another or stand there lollygaggin'?"

I knelt and handed him another tile. And another. And another. Before long, we'd finished the front side of the roof.

"How's that?" he asked, wiping the sweat from his eyes with a handkerchief.

I hated to admit that he had saved me at least two days of work. So I didn't. Instead, I gestured to a tile at the end. "That one's crooked."

He wheezed a laugh. Phil popped his head up from the other side of the wall, rolling a load of weeds between his teeth.

"You know anything about windows?" I asked.

"I might. Feed me, and I may even be persuaded to tell ye," he added, stuffing the handkerchief back into his breast pocket.

I could go into the shack and shift food from the castle kitchens; Eava usually left a meal or two when we weren't there to eat them. But then I'd have to use magic, and I couldn't take the chance of leaving a signature behind.

"I don't have any food," I confessed.

Snorting, the man slid down the roof, descended the ladder with the ease of a man half his age, and let the hammer fall next to the other tools I'd amassed as he started for the gate. "Are ye comin' or not?" he asked without turning.

I glanced around in case I'd missed someone else. Nope. Just that disgusting goat shitting in the corner. Was I going to go with him? He seemed to know what he was doing. I'd be a fool to look help in the face and turn it down, wouldn't I?

The goat narrowed its beady black eyes at me.

I started for the road, shouting for the man to wait up.

On the walk back to his house, he finally introduced himself as Marcus. Not that I'd asked. He also made me a ham sandwich on a thick slice of bread without washing his hands, like an animal.

Marcus tore into his sandwich, bits of bread falling from his mouth. "What's yer name, boy?"

I caught a glimpse of my glamour in the window above the dry sink. Mousy brown hair, unremarkable face. Entirely forgettable. I looked like a, "John."

"I hope ye don't mind me sayin', but that place of yers is in right shite. Whoever sold it to ye must be havin' a good laugh right about now."

"*You* sold it to me."

"Gonna take a lot of work to fix it up," he muttered as if I hadn't spoken. "Not sure yer up to the task."

Not up to the feckin' task? I could shift the entire feckin' castle onto that little plot of land if I wanted to. "I am perfectly capable—"

"It's settled then." He dragged a flask from his pocket and tilted the top at me. "I'll help ye."

"I didn't ask for help."

"Didn't have to." He unscrewed the lid and took a swig.

When he offered it to me, I shook my head. I didn't want his shite liquor, just like I didn't want this shite sandwich. Still, I was a little hungry, so I took a reluctant bite. "And what do you expect in return?"

"Won't cost ye no more than supplies and a meal or two."

"Why?"

"Because if I'd bought a place in shite, I'd hope someone would take pity on me."

He pitied me, did he? I may not know how to build a feckin' shack with my bare hands, but I could disembowel him with my dagger in no time at all. Carve out his heart. Kill him a thousand different ways.

"What do ye say?" Marcus asked, tucking away his flask and smiling.

I scowled down at him. "This sandwich is dry."

19

WHAT DID YOU DO WHEN YOU HAD ALL THESE . . . *FEELINGS*
overflowing like a feckin' river in a flood and the one person you
wanted to pour yourself into was dead? Even if she wasn't stuck in
the underworld forever, she sure as hell didn't want a thing to do
with me. Especially not after all the shite with her precious sister.

Even so, I went to see Aveen as I always did after a long day in
Hollowshade. I had been neglecting my duties in Tearmann, but
didn't give a rat's arse. If the Queen wanted to punish me for it,
she could. At least then I'd be back to feeling nothing but rage. I
knew what to do with that. All this other shite swimming around
inside of me, though? I hadn't a clue.

The vat of wine I'd drunk with Marcus hadn't helped either.
That human had to be part clurichaun because I was pretty sure
he could've single-handedly drunk Tadhg, Ruairi, and I under the
table. I tried to tiptoe past the castle's fountain. Mustn't have
worked because Muireann popped her head up at the exact
moment my boot hit the first step, like she'd been waiting for me.

"Oh, Rían."

"Not interested," I muttered. Only one woman held my attention these days, and she was dead.

I caught the main door's cold handle and nearly threw my

feckin' shoulder out opening the thing. Had it always been this heavy? Tadhg appeared in the hallway out of nowhere, making me jump and ram into the hall table.

His face went as dark as a storm cloud. "Where the hell have you—"

Nope. Not today, brother. With a flick of my wrist, I shifted the pain in my ass to the oubliette. Should've done the same with the irritating merrow. They could've had a right good time down in the mud together.

All it took was one look at the stairs to know there was no way in hell I'd make it up. So I evanesced to the top of the tower, to where I'd left enough wards to keep out the Queen herself. A complete and utter waste of magic, but it helped me sleep at night knowing Aveen was as safe as I could make her.

Inside, my human slept with a serene smile on her black lips. Had she been relieved at the coming respite from life, or had Tadhg's kiss been so good that she'd died with a smile on her face? The thought churned my stomach.

Bastard. I really ought to kill him. That always made me feel better.

Although, killing him would take a lot of effort, and my limbs felt as if they were made of stone. I sank onto the floor and propped myself up against the wall. "I bought you a cottage," I said to ears that couldn't hear. "It's hideous." A smile lifted the corner of my lips. "You're going to love it."

Last week, Tadhg had come in spouting some shite about a human having a ring that could break his curse. Now he was off gallivanting with her, trying to get said ring instead of coming straight out and asking for the feckin' thing. Women had given him far more for far less.

He'd had his chance. Now it was my turn.

By my calculations, they should've arrived at the portal in Port

Fear by midday. I'd been waiting at the portal near the Forest since before eleven. I couldn't bring myself to get too close to the two-story cottage that had belonged to Leesha's father all those years ago. I remembered when Leesha suggested painting the doors and windowsills green. I hated the color—it was Tadhg's, after all—but had done it anyway because she'd asked me to help.

A woman emerged from within, and my throat tightened. She wore her red hair piled atop her head. Her clothes were simple and plain. One of Leesha's descendants, no doubt.

She wouldn't see me where I waited, but I ducked behind a tree anyway, scrubbing subconsciously at the scar on my chest. Where the hell was Tadhg and the human with the ring?

I waited another ten minutes before evanescing to the granary in Port Fear, where the portal had been since its creation centuries earlier. The porter there said no one had used the portal in weeks.

Tadhg was supposed to be here. It was Tuesday, wasn't it? Between taking care of Tadhg's duties while he was gone and working at the cottage, I'd lost all track of time.

At half past one, I'd had enough waiting around for my infernal brother and returned to the castle. It didn't take much to convince Eava to find him. She never liked it when either of us were gone for too long, and Tadhg hadn't spent the night here in what felt like ages.

It wasn't that I missed his drunk arse, but the castle had felt especially empty as of late.

Just me, the bodies, and Eava.

Even Ruairi had been absent. Not that he had a reason to come by when Tadhg wasn't here. But still. I scowled down at the map Eava had spread across the counter, the corners held in place with tins of flour and sugar.

Next to me, Eava stared into a bowl of water, her black eyes glazed white as she searched the island for my missing brother. I knew better than to interrupt, but she was taking ages, and I was starving.

I was about to grab one of the sour green apples from a basket when Eava's hand shot out, her nail pointing to a spot on the map along a small river.

She blinked down at the spot, her eyes slowly returning to their inky hue. "Here."

"You're sure?" What was he doing there when he was supposed to be in Port Fear?

"He's either there or just past."

A start, at least.

She shifted the basket of apples, sending them who-knows-where. "When ye see him, tell him he gets nothin' until he comes home."

"Does that mean I'm not to eat as well?"

She gave my cheek a pat and said, "Bring yer brother home and I'll make ye something special."

Feckin' Tadhg. Once again, his shite was getting in my way.

By the time I made it to the river, night was fast closing in. Dark clouds above warned of impending rain. No birds chirped, no squirrels scurried, likely already bedded down in anticipation of the brewing storm.

Upstream, I heard a splash and a familiar curse and found my brother having a feckin' swim, as if he hadn't a care in the world.

"What the hell is your problem?" I ground out.

Tadhg slipped, his arms cartwheeling, but there was nothing to save him from disappearing under the murky water. Well, I could've saved him using magic, but I'd wasted enough on him today. He came up cursing and scrubbing a hand down his face. Water continued to drip from the sopping brown hair plastered to his forehead. "Feckin' hell, Rían. How'd you find me?"

"How do you think?"

He seemed to consider that for a moment before smiling and shaking his head. "Since you're here, you may as well be useful and shift me some clean clothes."

He'd get clean clothes when I got answers. "Why can't you do it yourself?"

He could just use magic like the rest of us, but he'd probably wasted it all doing something foolish. "Because I spent the night with Caer and Cait, the morning murdering three humans, and the afternoon in the feckin' underworld."

That explained why he wasn't at the portal. Still, how hard would it have been to let me know so I didn't waste an entire day waiting like an eejit? "Busy, busy. I see you still haven't gotten the ring."

He leaned back to give his dark hair another scrub. "Clothes. Now."

I'd do him one better. Not only did I shift him clean breeches and a shirt, I gave him a towel as well. Anything to get him dressed and home so I could eat.

Did he thank me? Of course not. Heaven forbid Tadhg act grateful for me wasting magic on him. "Any chance you could shift me something from the kitchens as well?"

"Eava's upset you haven't been home. She's on strike." And when Eava was on strike, no one ate. And when I didn't eat, it made me more murderous than usual.

"Tell Eava I'll stop by tomorrow."

"Stop by? Tadhg, you need to come back. I've things to be doing." A shipment of floorboards for replacing the rotted ones in the spare room should be arriving to Marcus's house any day now.

"I just need a little more time."

"Give me ten minutes with the human." My dagger appeared in my hand. Three to convince her to hand over the ring and the other seven to gloat about it.

He tried to hide his horror, but I saw through the mask. "Not happening."

"You actually like her, don't you?" Did a bigger fool exist? "The woman wants your head on a feckin' platter, and *you like her*. And I thought I was bad. Why don't you set your sights on one of the countless women who actually fancy you instead of wasting your time on one who wants you dead?" He could have anyone. *ANYONE.*

"I don't—It's complicated," he amended.

"How is it complicated? Fuck her and be done with it." Move on to the next feckin' woman so I could get back to living my own life.

Tadhg snorted. "Right. Because that's what you did."

"My situation is different." The two of us were nothing alike. He deserved his curse. I didn't.

"Because you're in love? That's a load of bollocks, and we both know it. The only person you're capable of loving is yourself."

I may not have been able to love Aveen the way she deserved, but I loved her in every way I could. With a flick of my wrist and a bit of magic, a tost descended over us, drowning out the sounds of the river. "Aveen is my soulmate." Something he couldn't possibly understand.

"That's a load of—"

I jabbed his chest with the point of my dagger. If he said one word about her, I'd flay him alive. "When I touch her, there's a spark that burns brighter than the light of a thousand candles. Every fiber in my being yearns for her." Even here with him in this moment, I could feel myself being tugged back home. Not to the castle. To *her*. Aveen was my home in a way the castle and the Forest never had been. "Every day I'm forced to live without her is a feckin' nightmare. You, with your 'cursed glamour', with women falling at your feet, you wouldn't know the first thing about it because you're more incapable of love than I am."

Tadgh's face went slack, the color draining completely as his eyes widened. "*Shit.*" He just stood there, staring at the hollow trunk of a dead tree. "Keelynn's my soulmate."

"What did you say?"

"All that shite you just said. I feel it when I touch Keelynn."

Oh, shit. "Who is Keelynn?" I choked.

"Aveen's sister."

"You're fucking with me, right? You must be fucking with me." He was with Aveen's feckin' sister? No. No no no. *Dammit.* No!

Why? Why the hell did fate feel the need to screw me over again and again and again?

He shook his head slowly. "She caught us in the garden that night. She's the one who has the ring. The one who wants to kill me with that cursed dagger."

A cursed dagger . . . Surely he wasn't saying what I thought he was saying? "What dagger?" My hand spasmed, and my dagger slipped, impaling the silty sand at my boot. I grabbed Tadhg, shaking him. "Tell me what feckin' dagger."

"Small. Silver. Emerald in the hilt. Kills immortals."

I shoved him back. *Fate.* How cruel. How twisted. How feckin' perfect. My ex-wife was in possession of the one weapon I needed to defeat the Queen. I could get the dagger and the ring. Glamour myself to look like someone she trusted. But who? *Lady Marissa.* Perfect. She'd question how I found her, but I'd think of something. "This is over," I told Tadhg. "You're going straight back to the castle and leaving Keelynn to me."

"Not a feckin' hope."

For once, why couldn't he agree and keep his gob shut? "You don't understand—"

"No, *you* don't understand. I helped you with your '*soulmate*' even when I thought your plan made no feckin' sense. Now you get to help me with mine. Shift us something to eat and somewhere to stay the night," he demanded in the tone I despised—the one that reminded me that he was in charge. He was, but still. Did he have to use that feckin' tone? Tadhg grabbed the shirt I'd shifted, dragging it over his head and stuffing his arms through the sleeves. "Once I have the ring, I will be back."

He wanted a place to stay, did he? I shifted a shitty little cottage I'd seen on the way in to Hollowshade and gave the bastard not one bit of furniture. I hoped he enjoyed sleeping on a hard wooden floor with Aveen's miserable sister.

"You cannot bring her to the Forest," I told him. "You'll have to find another way to get the ring." The Queen would kill her on sight.

I glared at the silent water burbling over algae-slickened stones. He wanted something to eat? Fine. I shifted some fish into the cottage. Tadhg's "favorite."

"If you're finished poking your nose in my business," he said, "I need you to kill someone."

Finally, something I would enjoy. "Who?"

"A human, about so high"—Tadhg held his hand to his temple —"silver hair. Blackened teeth. Small scar on his stubbled chin. He killed Keelynn's coachman and—"

"Padraig?"

A nod.

I didn't care that the old man was dead, but Aveen would. Yet another reason she'd have to despise me.

"He took Keelynn's carriage," Tadhg added, dragging on the rest of his clothes and his boots.

A fat raindrop splatted on my crown. And then another. I ran a hand through my hair, giving the blackened sky a silent order to hold its infernal rain in before I ended up soaked. "You want the carriage back?"

"No. But retrieve her purse, leave it on my bed."

"Anything else, master?"

"Yes." Tadhg's eyes swirled with black, and he gave me a smile I knew all too well. "Make him pay."

I found my new best friend drinking away at a bawdy house filled with other humans. I knew I was in the right place because I found Aveen's black coach parked right outside. I knew he was the right man because he had just used the ring I'd given Keelynn on our wedding day to up the ante in a game of cards. All I needed to do was wait until he was alone, which, thankfully, didn't take too long. He used a purse I recognized as Keelynn's to pay for a pint and a brown-haired whore, hauling her by the arm up the stairs at the back of the place.

I didn't even give him time for one last ride, evanescing to their room before he could get his breeches unfastened.

The woman screeched, shrinking toward the headboard, clutching her dress to cover her breasts. It took the man a second to realize what she was trying to escape from. When he saw me sitting on the edge of the window, running my thumb along the blade of my dagger, the color drained from his face.

"I ordered a private room," he slurred, dragging his sleeve across his lips. "So if yer here to watch, ye can feck off and find yer own whore."

Instead of speaking to him, I directed my words to the woman. "I hope you don't mind, but your client and I have a little business to take care of."

"I've no business with ye," the man countered.

The woman still hadn't moved.

I let go of the darkness that lived within me, sinking beneath the cold black, loving the way it zipped through my veins, giving me access to power I rarely used. "*Leave.*"

She scrambled to her feet and stumbled toward the door. If the man noticed me summoning a tost, he didn't mention it. His face contorted, the color returning in a rush of red. "Where do ye get off sendin' away my—"

I cut off his words with my blade, sticking him in the gut and watching surprise flash in his eyes. And then I twisted the hilt, leaving him screaming. I loved it when they screamed. Power rushed through me when I tore my dagger from his gut, leaving a puddle on the floor.

When Aveen learned of her beloved coachman's passing, she'd be devastated. Knowing that, I decided to take my time.

He tried to go for the door, but I appeared in front of him, slamming my fist into his face, relishing the pain in my knuckles. Pain was something I understood. Something I'd learned to accept. Much the same as death.

The man fell to the floor and let out a gurgling groan that

sounded an awful lot like a curse. Hard to tell since his jaw was broken.

"I'd say I hope you learn your lesson about taking things that don't belong to you, but you won't have a chance."

He spat on my boot before trying to slither through the growing pool of blood toward the door. I pressed my heel to his throat, waiting for his defiant eyes to go vacant.

I loved it when they were angry. So much better than the sniveling, sniffing weasels who pleaded for mercy. Pathetic. Begging did nothing but make you look like a fool.

He clawed at my ankle, leaving bloodied fingerprints all over the shiny black leather. All it took was one twist of my heel, and he stopped fighting.

I swiped my blade across his neck to make sure he was well and truly dead.

I left him staring toward the bed, shifted some clean clothes, and went to find some dinner. Venison roasted with cloves sounded good. Or maybe some pork cooked with Bramley apples. There must be somewhere in this town to get a decent meal.

20

Between me being left to deal with ruling Tearmann, presiding over executions in Airren, Tadgh's forced marriage to Aveen's sister, and kidnapping, I couldn't remember the last time I'd gotten a full night's sleep.

Even though she couldn't hear me, I'd told Aveen all of it, as if confessing to her could absolve me of my countless sins.

All I wanted was to return to Hollowshade and get back to work on Aveen's cottage. Before the sun rose on Friday morning, Tadgh burst through the study doors. I'd threatened him to ensure he didn't miss another day of airing grievances, but those threats usually fell on deaf ears.

"You're here. And you're early," I said. "And you look like shite." But he didn't smell like drink, so I took that as a small victory. Hungover Tadgh was even more useless than drunk Tadgh.

"I need your help." He closed the distance between us in three long strides. "We're crossing the Forest."

"*We?*" Last I heard, he was all depressed because Keelynn had decided to stay with Robert. "Not yourself and Keelynn, surely."

He nodded.

And here I thought today couldn't get worse. "Are you out of your feckin' mind? The Queen will kill her." For *once*, couldn't he stick to a plan we'd agreed upon? Keelynn belonged with the humans, where she was safe. She belonged with the man she "loved."

"I've spoken with the Queen," Tadhg said, "and she has agreed to let her pass twice. Once to arrive and once to leave."

The Queen agreed to this? She hadn't let a human through in at least fifty years. "And in return?"

Tadhg kept talking as if I hadn't spoken. "I need you to ensure Keelyn's safety once she arrives in Tearmann."

My chest began to ache. "Tadhg, what did you promise her?"

His jaw worked.

"Tadhg!"

"There's no need to shout. She's only going to kill me."

There it was. The one thing I'd hoped he wouldn't say. "I always knew you were a fool, but this is utter folly. You know what she did to me. How can you put yourself in the same position?" Even if she left his heart intact, she wouldn't pass up the opportunity to consume his life force—his magic. If she managed to access the centuries of bound magic within him . . . she would be unstoppable. As it stood, my hopes of defeating her were next to none. If she consumed his life force . . . "Leave Keelynn behind. I'm begging you."

He leveled me with an even stare. "I can't."

What was it with people and their refusal to see reason? "You *can*, but you're choosing not to."

He was already at the study door when he said, "I'll aim to have her at the border before noon."

He left me staring at shadows with my hopes of ever defeating the Queen fading into nothing.

I went to the Black River, keeping to the Tearmann side of the border. It didn't take long to locate the dark-haired woman kneeling on the shore, weeping and sobbing like the world had ended.

This was all her fault.

All of this.

Tadhg's body lay in her lap, blood painting his grimy shirt. "What the hell have you done to my brother?" I ground out. He must've been stabbed at least ten times. As far as I could tell, his heart was still in his chest, which didn't give me a helluva lot of comfort, but at least it was something.

Aveen's sister blinked up at me without a hint of recognition. Not that I expected her to recognize me since I looked nothing like the man who'd married her.

"I didn't kill him," she sniffled. "I swear, it wasn't me."

"I'm not talking about killing him. What I meant was you turning the poor man into a simpering eejit who's forgotten his duty is to his *people* and not some foolish human *girl* with chronic bad luck." Maybe it wasn't fair to take my frustration out on her, but she was going to get it anyway.

"I didn't turn Tadhg into anything," she insisted.

The fool loved her, that much was clear. Why hadn't she fallen in love with him in return? He'd married her to save her life. He'd just died so she could reach Tearmann and be with her sister. He looked like her feckin' fantasy. Why didn't she love him?

If she'd loved him, she could've set him free from his curses. If he was free from his curses, he'd finally get off his arse and do something for Tearmann.

And if she loved someone as worthless and terrible as Tadhg, maybe there was some tiny hope that her sister could love me.

"Yes, you did," I countered. "And since he's been neglecting his duties to play the doting courtier, they've all fallen on my shoulders. And I do not appreciate it one bit."

"That sounds like something you need to discuss with Tadhg."

Oh, I will. Preferably with his throat on the sharp side of my dagger.

"When is Tadhg coming back?" she asked, her voice an octave higher as she stared down at his lifeless body.

Not nearly soon enough. I squatted to check his wounds, feeling a bit more at ease when I saw no X across his chest. Most were still open—what little magic had returned was fighting to repair the damage from the Queen's dagger. "Feckin' hell. How many times did she stab you?" I could've used my own magic to help him, but he didn't deserve it.

Touching him left blood and dirt on my hand. I dragged a handkerchief from my pocket, cleaning my fingers before tucking the disgusting thing into Tadhg's equally disgusting jacket pocket. "He should be back in an hour or so, depending on how much of his magic was left."

I used a stick to check the wounds again. Would he ever hurry it on? At this stage, I'd be the one meeting with his people. I hated Fridays.

I knew without asking why the Queen had stabbed him so many times. He'd probably done something to piss her off, per usual. "You'd think he'd know better than to antagonize her. But he just can't keep his gob shut." I discarded the stick over my shoulder. "Can you grab his arm there? I really don't feel like getting blood and grime all over my new shirt." And if I shifted him where he lay, he'd take half the sand on the shore with him and get it all over the castle. There was no sense making extra work for anyone.

Although she did as I'd asked, Keelynn was basically no help whatsoever. Weak as a feckin' child. My heel caught on the edge of a rock, setting me off kilter. I slipped, fell, and ripped a hole in the arse of my new breeches. I kicked the bastard who had ruined everything, cursing him till I was blue in the face.

"Don't touch him!" Keelynn shrieked.

"Look what he did! *Dammit.*" The amount of clothing I'd gone through in the last six months was criminal. "These are from the feckin' continent."

"This isn't Tadhg's fault. He's *dead*, remember?"

"Oh, my dear Keelynn, you'll soon come to find that *everything* is Tadhg's fault." *His fault or yours,* I wanted to shout. "If you'll excuse me for a moment, I need to get this irritating bastard to the castle."

I made it to the gates without getting too much shite on me. It was only a matter of time before people started lining up in preparation for today's airing of grievances. When I reached his room, I dumped him on the floor with a satisfying thump and shifted a jug of water. Not because I cared if he was thirsty when he awoke, but giving him what he needed would get his arse down to the great hall that bit faster.

Since I didn't have any clothes for Aveen's sister here, I shifted clothes from her armoire back at the townhouse in Graystones. When I returned to the edge of the Forest, I found her clutching at her chest, glowering toward the Black Forest.

"Here. Put these on." I held out the dress and shift. "The last thing I need is to be seen with a human in such a horrendous state."

That got rid of the hunch to her shoulders. "Turn around and give me some privacy," she said, raising her chin.

As if I had any desire to see the woman undressed. I glared at a knot in the nearest tree, doing my best not to shift my dagger and rid myself of this latest problem. No one had to know it was me. Except, Tadhg would know, wouldn't he? He'd undoubtedly spiral, and I'd be in the same feckin' boat I had been for the last two weeks. "Are you finished yet?"

"Yes."

"Good."

I took her old clothes, sent them straight into the fire, and told her to keep up. I could've brought her to the edge of Tearmann's forest and pointed her in the right direction, but with her track record, I didn't trust her to make it to the castle without some sort of drama unfolding. Maxwell was out gardening. Anwen was in her yard hanging laundry. I kept my head down to deter conversation. Not that anyone we met would want to speak to me. Still, there was a first time for everything.

Could this human be any slower? No wonder it took Tadhg so long to get to Tearmann. I could crawl faster than she walked.

The castle came into view, a gray monstrosity breaking the endless green. Keelynn balked when she crossed beneath the wards. I told her what they were, but she didn't comment, for which I was glad. I really didn't have the time or inclination to converse with the shrew.

Oscar met us at the door, pretending to be useful for once. "Good to see yer back, Prince Rían. There's quite a line today."

Of course there was. Why would people deal with their own shite when they could make me do it? "This is your fault, you know," I told the ignorant human following me into the castle.

"My fault?" she scoffed.

I didn't respond because I didn't like her.

She stopped to gape at the godawful tapestries, delaying me some more.

"I've told him to burn these rags time and again, but Tadhg always refuses." From the other side of the doors, I heard people grumbling. That's all the Danú did. Grumble. "I don't want you snooping around the place, so I'm going to let you come inside. But don't say a word."

Aveen's sister nodded and followed me inside.

21

Eava burst into the study, her black eyes wild. "To the gates. Quickly!"

I evanesced outside to find a crowd had gathered. Then I heard Aveen's sister from beyond the wards, her husky voice cutting through the silence. "You don't understand," she said. "I can't stop myself. Please go. Please. I'm so sorry, Tadhg. I just wanted my sister back."

The crowd let out a collective gasp. I pushed my way through, my chest tightening. I didn't need to know what was going on to know it was bad. From the way all the Danú kept behind the wards, it was clear as day. It must be the Queen. Who else would strike such fear into the hearts of these people?

"I was foolish and naïve, and I thought I had nothing left to lose," Keelynn went on.

I finally reached the front of the crowd to find Tadhg and Keelynn.

One other person stood with them. A woman, yes, but not the Queen.

Fiadh.

Shit.

Keelynn clutched a dagger with a glowing green emerald.

Shit shit shit.

My chest brushed the wards, but I knew better than to cross without a plan. I needed to keep a level head, collect all the facts so I could once again fix the mess Tadhg had made.

"This isn't your fault," Tadhg said, his voice catching. "It's mine."

Feckin' right, it was. I'd told him what Fiadh would do if she caught Keelynn. I'd *told* him. And here we were.

Fiadh cackled like the bitch she was, rocking back and forth on her toes, a crooked smile on her pale face as Keelynn advanced on Tadhg. If the human couldn't stop herself, then magic must be compelling her forward. Not Tadhg's magic, he wasn't strong enough.

Fiadh's.

Tears glistened in Tadhg' green eyes. "This will be a mercy," Tadhg said. "You'll be ending a cursed life with a cursed blade." He caressed her face. "Thank you for giving me hope."

Don't give up, you eejit! Fight back. Evanesce. Do something!

"Thank you for letting me love you," he whispered as Keelynn raised the dagger to his chest.

Tadhg's forehead dropped. "Thank you for setting me free."

I recognized the sound of a blade sinking into flesh as well as I'd know my own name. The cowards hiding behind the wards gasped when Tadhg collapsed. I raked my hands through my hair, panic seizing my throat. This couldn't be happening. This *couldn't* be happening!

Thunder boomed, echoing off the stone walls, muffling the cries from the useless Danú hiding at my back. White light left my brother's body, curling toward the bloody dagger still clenched in Keelynn's fist.

My brother was gone.

Oh god . . . Tadgh was gone.

I didn't want to do any of this without him. He drove me mad, but he also made me laugh. And sometimes he made my life a little less shite. Why hadn't he fought? Why had he given up on his people? On me?

I locked my emotions inside the cavern in my chest, focusing on the cackling witch as she gestured toward Keelynn and asked for the dagger. I shifted my own. I wouldn't rest until she no longer drew breath. She may have been an ancient witch, a true immortal. But Keelynn possessed the one weapon that could end her.

When Keelynn refused to hand over the dagger, Fiadh shrieked. "Give it to me!"

"I said *no*."

Shadow magic slithered toward Keelynn, so dark it swallowed all light. "Have you learned *nothing*, you foolish girl?" Fiadh hissed. "You can hide inside this warded castle for the rest of your pathetic life, but I will get back what is mine. I will curse your family, your children, everyone you love. I will never stop haunting you unless you *give me that dagger*."

The dagger held Tadhg's life force.

I needed to find a way to return it to him.

"Our bargain isn't through," Keelynn insisted. Fiadh's shadows curled around the human's feet like low-hanging fog, never touching but dangerously close. "I killed the Gancanagh, and now I get to resurrect my sister."

No. No no no no no no.

Aveen couldn't come back. Not yet. Not *here*.

"Go on, then. Resurrect your precious sister," Fiadh crooned.

She couldn't use that dagger on Aveen. Then Tadhg would be gone, and Aveen would be stuck here forever, and the Queen would find her and—

Keelynn walked toward me, Fiadh closing in.

Bring me the dagger. That's it. I'd get the dagger, cross the wards, evanesce, and bring my brother back. Sure, Keelynn would be dead, but who honestly cared? At this stage, it was the best we could hope for.

When Fiadh said she wasn't letting the dagger out of her sight,

I almost smiled. She wouldn't have a choice. As soon as Keelynn got close enough, I was going to take it.

"You can't get past the wards," Keelynn pointed out.

Everyone around me had taken a step back, leaving me on my own as usual. The wards were strong enough to keep out the Queen, and they would keep out this witch as well.

Fiadh pinned me with her black stare. "Then ask your *friend* to let me inside."

As if I'd be stupid enough to let that bitch in here after what she'd done to Tadhg. I may have despised the Danú, but with my brother gone, this kingdom fell on my shoulders. They were now my responsibility.

Tears streamed down Keelynn's pale cheeks. "Rían, please. I need to see Aveen."

"Have you lost your feckin' mind? You just murdered my brother, and you think I'm going to let you inside this castle? Not a hope in hell. Good luck getting out of Termann alive, you traitorous bitch." The Danú at my back murmured in agreement. She was as good as dead either way.

"Give me my sister," Keelynn demanded.

"She's my fiancée," I shot back. More than that, Aveen was my feckin' soulmate, and I refused to damn her to this fate.

Shit. Oh no. SHIT! Tell me I didn't just say that out loud.

Tell me I didn't just sign Aveen's death warrant.

"Rían, please," Keelynn begged. "I need to bring her back to end this bargain."

Until the bargain was complete, Fiadh would have control over Keelynn—and that dagger. But if Keelynn brought Aveen back with the dagger, I wouldn't have any life force to use for Tadhg.

How did I turn this around? *Could* I turn it around?

Fiadh clicked her tongue, stepping forward so I could see the same soullessness that lived in the Queen in the depths of her eyes. This woman had held her grudge for centuries. There was no hope of getting her to leave it now that she was so close to her goal of ending my brother for good. "If you don't want me to turn my sights on you, Little Rían," Fiadh said, "I suggest you give the pathetic human her sister."

She thought she could threaten *me*?

I may not be able to steal her immortality without dying too, but I could send her on a holiday to the underworld with my own dagger, then lock her in the dungeon for as long as it took to convince Keelynn to kill her for me.

But I'd watched Fiadh shift that dagger as if it were a cheap bauble. I'd never even seen the Queen do that, and she was the most powerful witch on this island. What sort of unholy power must Fiadh have possessed to be able to shift an enchanted object?

Think, Rían. Think.

Keelynn needed to fulfil the bargain. I'd have no hope of getting that dagger otherwise. With my lungs caving in, I shifted Aveen's coffin to the other side of the wards.

Fiadh muttered something, but I could barely hear with the silence roaring in my ears as I watched Keelynn bring the bloody dagger to Aveen's pale palm and cut.

Aveen sucked in a breath.

And I swore it filled my lungs as well.

Bargain complete.

Forever. She'd be stuck here forever.

Fiadh asked for the dagger once more.

Keelynn whirled, driving the dagger into Fiadh's gut. Black blood spilled on the green grass like tar.

"You scheming bitch!" Fiadh shrieked, her knees slamming to the ground as blackened life force twisted from her body.

Keelynn ran toward Tadhg, but she collapsed just out of reach.

I evanesced, stealing the dagger from Keelynn's outstretched hand.

If a true immortal used it to kill, the dagger would claim them both. But what about using it to resurrect another? Would this kill me? I glanced at where Aveen struggled in her golden coffin, knowing deep down in my worthless soul that no one would care if I was gone. But Tadhg. He was the Danú's beloved leader. He was worth the risk.

I cut his hand with the dagger and waited to die.

He sucked in a breath, and still I waited.

His eyes flew open, and I shoved him toward his gasping soulmate. "Kiss her. Quickly."

This may not work, but it was the best chance we had. Tadhg kissed Keelynn just as she drew a final shuddering breath. His curse spread down her chin to her throat, leaving her limp in his arms.

"It wasn't supposed to be her," he sobbed. "It was never supposed to be her. I was the one meant to die. Why didn't you save her?"

He just kept moaning on and on like the selfish bastard he was. Couldn't he see I'd made the best choice for everyone? "As weak and pathetic as you are, you serve a purpose." Aveen's sister, however, did not.

Aveen stumbled forward. She shouldn't have been able to walk yet, let alone steal her sister's lifeless body from Tadhg and demand answers. Answers I would give just as soon as all these useless feckers staring at us from behind the safety of the wards were gone.

"Keelynn?" Aveen patted her sister's cheek. "I'm here. I'm back. Please wake up."

Tadhg growled, "Give me back my wife."

I had to hold myself back from cutting off his feckin' hand when he grabbed her. He stole Keelynn's body and stomped toward the gates. The Danú parted for him, looking on as he carried his wife into the castle.

"Where's he taking her?" Aveen wheezed. "Tell me what's happening!"

The Danú turned back to us, intrigue in their eyes. I towed her beneath the wards by the elbow, searching the whispers for anyone mentioning my accidental confession. It seemed they were all too preoccupied by the dead witch out front.

I kept going, through the courtyard, past the fountain, to the entryway where the Queen glared down at me from the tapestry in disapproval. I could hear her now. *He was dead. The throne was yours. Fool! Why did you risk your own life to bring him back?*

"Say something," Aveen clipped.

"Don't snap at me. This isn't my fault." I was sick and feckin' tired of everyone blaming me for everything.

"I don't care whose fault it is! Tell me why your brother murdered my sister."

"Because murdering her was the only way to save her life. Now instead of being dead forever, she's only dead for a year and a day. After all the shite I've had to deal with over the last six months, I'm counting it as a win." No one else may have seen it like that, but at this stage, I had no shits left to give.

"Why is she here in the first place?"

I summoned a tost, not that it mattered now that I'd told everyone what this human was to me. "She caught you and my brother in the feckin' garden and got it into her meddlesome head that she needed to save you." As if that weak human could've done anything. I thought of the body lying outside the castle. *All right.* Perhaps she had done something. But she'd also caused far more trouble than she was worth.

"Why didn't you just tell her the truth?"

"Should I have done that before or after your father caught her on top of me?"

Aveen's eyes bulged. "No . . ."

"And your father thought himself so feckin' clever, saddling an ambassador with his youngest daughter as a wife. All he cared about was my yearly income." I'd love to go back to Graystones and give that bastard a piece of my mind—and my dagger.

"You married my *sister*?" Aveen choked, clutching the stones at her back. "But Tadhg said . . ."

"Ah, Tadhg. There's a good story. Shall I tell it to you?" I sucked in a deep breath. "I married your sister, left her in the townhouse, faked my own death so she could marry her precious *Robert*, and do you know what 'innocent young Keelynn' did? She found this island's second most vindictive witch, bargained for a cursed dagger, and set off on a hair-brained revenge mission to kill a true immortal and bring you back to life."

When I laid it out like that, it sounded like a feckin' fairy tale.

"You'll never guess who she wanted to kill." I said.

Aveen's eyes locked with mine. "She wanted to kill Tadhg."

"Now you have it." Even with a death-muddled brain, she was still a thousand times smarter than her eejit sister. "She believed she could slay the monster who murdered you. Fate, being the cruel bitch she is, though it'd be a feckin' brilliant idea for the two of them to cross paths. So he's all doe-eyed, believing that wasp is the sun, moon, and feckin' stars, marries her because they're 'soulmates,' and guess who shows up?" I threw a hand toward the door. "The witch she bargained with, holding your precious sister to her promise to slay the Gananagh. That just about catches you up to today. Any questions?"

"Why didn't you tell her the truth?" Aveen repeated.

"I have my reasons."

"Do you, now?" She stalked toward me as if she were an intimidating beast instead of someone I wanted to wrap my arms around and kiss until we were both delirious. "You have your 'reasons.' Well, that's bloody brilliant, because I was afraid all of this happened because you *lied*."

"I'm too feckin' wrecked to deal with you right now." I started for the stairs. She'd see reason come morning. And if she didn't, then so be it. No skin off my back. I needed to get rid of Fiadh's body because heaven knew Tadgh wouldn't be doing it. He probably wouldn't even be sober for at least a month. Then I wanted to take a bath, wash the dirt and blood from beneath my fingernails, and sleep.

"Don't you dare walk away from me," Aveen hissed. Quick

footsteps sounded at my back. She shoved me right into the feckin' table, knocking the roses I'd created just for her to the ground.

I whirled, rage humming in my hollow chest. "Shove me again and see what happens."

She feckin' did it. She laid her palms flat on my chest and shoved. I caught her hands with tendrils of magic, snapping them to her sides and lacing them up tight so she couldn't move.

"Let me go this instant, or so help me—"

"So help you, what?" I pressed, bathing in the fire in her eyes. "What are you going to do to me, human?"

"I hate you."

The truth. So long as she hated me, she could be safe. "Good. Come on." I'd clean the mess once I got her upstairs. Add it to the list of shite I had to do.

"I'm not going anywhere with you."

"We both need sleep, and I refuse to deal with cranky Aveen."

"I'm not sleeping here." She stomped her foot like a toddler who hadn't gotten her way.

"Would you prefer to sleep in the dungeon?"

"I would *prefer* getting my sister and bringing her back to Graystones."

"And how do you plan on doing that? The penalty for crossing the Black Forest without the Queen's permission is death, and our sea is swarming with hungry merrow. Go on. Tell me your grand escape plan."

Her mouth opened and closed.

"That's what I thought." I pointed up the stairs. "Now, you can either walk up these stairs on your own, or I can carry you. What's it going to be?"

She wriggled against the invisible bonds. Even knowing she couldn't escape, she didn't give up. The infernal woman started for the door. I caught her, threw her over my shoulder, and carried her straight up the stairs, kicking and screeching like a banshee.

I didn't put her down until we reached the third floor. I ignored her glare but couldn't ignore the way she glanced at the staircase. With her hands bound, she'd probably end up toppling over and breaking her beautiful neck. "Don't even think about it," I warned before opening the door to a guest bedroom with a white sleigh bed, white coverlet, rug, and empty fireplace. With a bolt of magic, Aveen's bonds evaporated. Another flick of my wrist lit the fire. With a third flick, I filled the armoire with the dresses I'd purchased over the last six months.

"If you need me," I said, "my room is down the——"

"I won't need you."

"Dammit, Aveen. Why can't you just believe I did what I had to do and leave it at that? You are the one who sought me out. The one who begged me to help you. This wasn't part of the plan."

"You promised to keep her from your brother. You promised to keep her safe. To keep *me* safe."

Yes, I had promised that. And I'd meant it, too. Unfortunately, I couldn't control the world and every feckin' person in it. "Your sister threw herself at *me*. She kissed *me*, and when I tried to remove myself from the situation, your father showed up like a feckin' bull. Every bone in my body screamed to evanesce, to escape and leave her to her fate, and yet I stayed. I stayed because I knew, as angry as you'd be about me marrying Keelynn, you'd never forgive me if I abandoned her.

"As for the rest of it, I cannot control my brother or your sister. They found each other through no fault of mine. And you . . ." This was the only part I was sorry about. "You were never meant to wake up in this cursed place."

I went to leave but stilled when I reached the door. "And for the record, I never touched her," I said.

She told me to get out.

She didn't care. She'd made that perfectly clear the night we'd spent together.

"Do not leave this room," I said. "Lock the door and——"

She slammed the door in my face, and I heard the scrape of the bolt sliding into place.

I stalked downstairs and shifted the broken glass and roses into the kitchen bin. When I got outside, people were still milling about. "Do you not have anywhere else to be?" I bellowed, sending them scurrying away like rats.

Fiadh's body remained beyond the wards. I called fire to my palm and held the flame to her black skirts, letting the acrid stench of fire consuming flesh wash over me. Once she was no more than ash, I shifted those ashes into an iron box. One could never be too careful.

I withdrew the cursed dagger from where I'd hidden it in my sheath, mesmerized by the emerald's unnatural green glow. Surely I should feel some semblance of happiness for being one step closer to defeating the Queen? Instead, all I felt was hollow. And not the usual hollowness that lived inside me. It was as if the void had taken hold of my soul as well.

22

"WHAT'S THIS FOR?" I KICKED THE CORNER OF THE SHED NEAR the back wall. The thing shuddered but didn't give. The same could not have been said for the shed at Aveen's cottage. But that was a problem for another day.

Oscar scratched his short red whiskers with a hairy hand. "Storage, mostly."

The problem with living in a centuries-old castle was that there was useless shite everywhere. "It's mine now. Clean it out and go to Airren for some new tools."

Oscars' wide-set brown eyes swept from my immaculately tied cravat to my shiny boots, oozing judgement. "What sort of tools?"

"Ones for gardening." This was a feckin' garden, wasn't it? "And get some flowers," I added as an afterthought.

"They'll die in a shed, sire."

"Not *actual* flowers." Why was I destined to be surrounded by useless eejits? "The seeds or whatever to make flowers."

"Ye don't make flowers. Ye grow them."

"Just get them. And clean it up."

He went back to scratching his whiskers. "What sort of flowers would ye be wantin'?"

"How the hell should I know? Just get pretty ones."

"Pretty?"

"Yes, pretty. It's really not that difficult, Oscar. Get some pretty seeds and tools and leave them in the shed."

"Bulbs would be better."

I scowled at him with every ounce of disdain I felt for the useless grogoch.

He bowed low and promised to take care of it.

"She's gone," Tadhg moaned into his glass. "I had her and then I lost her."

How the hell was I supposed to make plans with Tadhg wallowing on the settee? I'd been in the study, but he'd found me in there, so I left. The moment my arse hit the chair in here, he'd appeared right across from me. If he wanted to wallow, he should've done it alone.

"Quit your whinging," I told him. "She'll be back."

He scrubbed both hands down his face, flopping on the cushion like a dying fish. "In a feckin' year. Do you know how much I can fuck up in a year? Why didn't you just let me die?"

"You think you deserve to escape this cursed life? You think you've earned a respite?" If I had to be here, then so did he. Simple as.

Ruairi came in, the smile slipping from his face the moment his golden eyes landed on Tadhg. "What's happened? Last I heard, ye were all loved up and happy."

Tadhg buried his head in the cushion, muttering a muffled, "Rían killed her."

"You want to blame me? Fine. At some point, you're going to have to start taking responsibility for your actions." I stalked out of the room and into the kitchens, where Eava was kneading dough on the counter, flour sticking to the wrinkles in her hands.

"I hope you're making something so full of sugar that it'll rot my teeth."

She shook her head. "Mince pies for yer woman."

"First, she's not my anything. Second, she doesn't deserve food. Third, I want biscuits." I let my head fall into my hands. I didn't care that it wasn't even sunrise. I'd barely slept last night and wanted to stuff myself with sugar until I exploded.

"Ye did well yesterday," Eava said, giving my shoulder a nudge.

I snorted.

"I'm serious. Because of ye, everyone is either alive or going to be soon enough."

Tell that to the eejit drinking himself blind in the family room.

Maybe if Aveen weren't stuck here, and if I hadn't announced to the entire world that we were fake-engaged, then I could have been a little proud of the way the situation had ended. But that was not what had happened.

"It'll all work out the way it's supposed to," she assured me like the pain-in-the-arse optimist she was.

"I hate it when you're optimistic."

She snorted, tucking her hands inside a dish towel to take a pan of fresh bread from the oven and set it next to three more loaves. My mouth watered as I watched her cut one loaf and arrange the slices on a plate along with a small dish of butter and jam. Not exactly what I wanted for breakfast, but it'd do for now.

Eava handed me the dish. "Deliver this to your woman in case she's hungry."

Hold on. This was for Aveen? What about me? I plucked a piece of bread from the plate and brought it to my lips. "I've decided to let her starve."

Eava's hand shot out, smacking me upside the head. The bread in my fingers tumbled back to the plate. "Get yer arse up those stairs and be sweet to that poor girl or I'll chop ye into little pieces and bake ye into a pie."

Feckin' hell, the old witch was vicious today. I took the plate so she didn't hit me again and evanesced up the stairs. When I reached Aveen's door, I found myself hesitating. I wasn't sure why.

This was my home, wasn't it? I gave the barrier a distinctively non-hesitant knock.

"Aveen?" No answer. Maybe I should've let someone else bring it up. She'd probably rather see anyone but me. When I tried the knob, the door gave way.

I found an empty room on the other side, the bed rumpled and unmade. Aveen wouldn't have been stupid enough to sneak out of the castle. Would she? I cursed myself for not altering the wards before going to bed. I slammed the tray on the bedside table and evanesced down to the hall. I was about to start for the door when I heard Aveen's voice coming from the family room.

I rounded the corner in time to catch Tadgh chucking something at Ruairi, grumbling about liking "that shite."

Ruairi rubbed his forehead and threw whatever it was back.

My human sat next to the animal, watching with wide eyes, her face pale as milk.

"I see the children are making a mess again," I said from the doorway.

Aveen's head whipped toward me. My hollow chest pinched when her expression hardened. *This is for the best*, I reminded myself. The more she hated me, the safer she'd be.

Ruairi threw an arm across the back of the settee, damn near putting it around Aveen's shoulders. Hadn't he seen the mark I'd given her? If he put his feckin' paws on her—

I evanesced, my hands vibrating and darkness swelling. "You will back off, mutt, or I will end you."

The pooka leaned far too close to Aveen, whispering, "Spoilt little prince was never taught to share." He must've valued his life, though, because he vacated the settee in favor of the second wing-back beside Tadhg.

"Did you not hear me when I said to stay in your room?" I asked.

"I heard you perfectly well," Aveen said, looking right past me, smiling at the pooka as if he deserved her attention. What'd he do? He smiled back. And I wanted to rip his fangs out one by one.

"So, Ruairi," she said, "I know Tadhg murders women and Rían torments humans, what is it you do? Dine on children?"

"Whatever it is the lads need done," he replied.

"Ruairi is excellent at burying bodies but shite at kidnapping," Tadhg muttered.

Aveen had the good sense to look genuinely worried. We weren't her soft humans, too afraid to do what it took to keep ourselves or the Danú safe. We'd lied, stolen, cheated, killed, kidnapped, and tortured for centuries. None of us, not even "noble" Ruairi, were untouched by darkness. She'd do well to remember that.

"Do either of you know the Phantom Queen?" she pressed.

My breath caught in my throat. Why the hell would she ask about the feckin' Queen? She'd have nothing to do with that witch, I'd make damn sure of it. I took Aveen's drink right out of her hand, hauled her to her feet, and evanesced straight to the study. Wherever my absent heart was, I imagined it galloping like a herd of wild horses.

"What do you think you're doing?" I ground out.

Her chin jutted forward the way it always did when she was being obstinate—which seemed to be all the feckin' time. "I don't know what you're talking about."

Had she forgotten so easily that I could taste her lies? "Aveen."

"*Rían.*"

"In Airren, I played by your ridiculous human rules. You're in my world now. It's time to play by mine." And that included staying as far away from the Queen and the Forest as possible.

She shrugged. "If it suits."

"Not if it feckin' suits." Didn't she understand what could happen? That there were fates far worse than death? "I know you're young, but I did not think you were this childish. This world has bigger problems than your little sister taking a feckin' nap in the underworld."

She held up a finger, eyes narrowed. "One truth, Rían. That's all it would have taken."

The truth may have kept her sister from bargaining with that witch, but if there was one thing I'd learned in all my years, it was that fate had her own plans. Who's to say that the shrew would've even believed me? Maybe she would've bargained with Fiadh anyway. Maybe she would've met Tadhg somewhere else.

"I can count the number of people I trust on one feckin' hand," I said. "And your sister is not one of them. Did you ever consider how this bargain could affect me? How it could affect Tadhg? I could've said no. I could've turned you down. I should have." Heaven knows I should have left her after Ned and let her marry that twat. "Instead, I chose to help you." Like some lovesick fool. And in doing so, I'd put her in more danger than she could ever imagine.

Her hands balled into fists by her skirts. There was no doubt in my mind she would've hit me if she thought she could get away with it. "So, what? You expect me to sit around here for the next year and trust that you'll help me find a way out of this mess when it's all over?"

"Yes."

"Sorry, *Your Highness*. I have my own *plans*."

She went to turn her back on me, as if I were nothing. As if I couldn't slice her in two and turn her to dust before her body hit the floor. I caught her ankles with magic, freezing her in place. She would not leave Tearmann of her own accord. I'd make damn sure of it.

Magic coursed in my bloodstream, burning like liquid fire. "Aveen Bannon. To pay the favor you owe, you will remain in Tearmann until your sister returns from the underworld." I would find a way to get her out of this place even if I had to sell my soul to do it. "Until then, you are to live in this castle with me."

She tried to keep her hand pinned to her side, but the magic from the bargain we'd struck when I'd agreed to help her escape Robert forced her palm into mine. Magic bound us, an invisible tether.

"I will never forgive you for this," she hissed. "Never."

"I can live with that." I deserved every bit of her hatred and more.

Ruairi appeared in the doorway, ever the thorn in my side. He didn't so much as acknowledge me. No, he looked straight past and locked eyes with my mate. "Everything all right, human?"

The pooka needed to mind his own feckin' business before I plucked his eyes from his skull and impaled him on a pike. "Everything is fine, Ruairi." I said. "Go back to the parlor."

"I wasn't askin' ye."

I sent the irritating bastard to the dungeon before he could cause any more trouble. "Now that we have that nasty business out of the way, would you like to see your sister?"

23

AVEEN PEERED INTO THE COFFIN THAT HAD BEEN HER BED FOR THE last six months, a frown tugging at her full lips.

"I know you won't believe me, but I love your sister," Tadhg said, his voice tinged with enough regret to fill an ocean.

Her frown only deepened. "Lust and love are two different things."

"I am acutely aware of the difference," he muttered.

Aveen touched her sister's face lovingly, tracing the black curse along her jaw. "Is the cursed dagger the only way to bring her back before the year is up?"

"I'm afraid so," I said, knowing where this conversation was headed.

"And all I have to do is kill one of you with it?" she asked.

I had to admit, the way her eyes sparked with murderous intent made me hard.

"You can kill me," Tadhg said.

Feckin' eejit. He may have been a pain in the arse most of the time, but he had a role to play in Tearmann, same as me. If I could wake up day after day and do my job, so could he. "If I have to listen to this martyr shite for the next year, I'm going to stab myself with the feckin' thing."

Aveen's head swung toward me, her curls dancing along her collarbone. "Where's the dagger now?"

As pretty as she was when she wanted to kill me, there wasn't a hope of me telling her where I'd hidden the dagger. "That, murderous Aveen, is none of your business."

She batted those long lashes of hers, all warmth and innocence, so good at playing the role, I almost believed her. "What's the matter? Afraid I'll trade your life for Keelynn's?"

"You don't have it in you."

She stepped toward me, that gleam returning to her eyes tenfold. "Give me the dagger and we'll see."

Tadhg emerged from his wallowing long enough to laugh. "I like this one. She's vicious."

I shifted my ceremonial dagger, offering it to her. How far would she push this? *How angry are you?* "Go on, then. Stab me with it."

Her fingers wrapped around the dagger, and I remembered the way they'd wrapped around my cock. This shouldn't be doing it for me, but it was. It really was. "Like I said. You don't have it in—"

She drove the blade into my arm and smiled. "You were saying?"

She wanted to play, did she? I let her see the monster living inside me, the black stain on my soul that told everyone who saw it that I didn't lose. That I was willing to go to any lengths to get what I wanted. "You ruined my feckin' shirt."

Aveen just kept smiling.

I shoved Tadhg toward the door. "You. Out."

"And miss this? Not a feckin' hope. I must say, until this exact moment, my day has been shite. Ruairi's going to keel over when he hears—"

I sent the stubborn fecker to the oubliette.

Aveen stood her ground when I stalked toward her. "Feel better now?" I asked.

"I'd feel better if I'd stabbed you in the heart."

Good luck with that. I gathered one of the golden curls from her face, brushing my fingertips against her petal-soft skin. I'd missed this. Her fire. Her light. "Get in line, my little viper. You'll have to wait your turn."

I longed to close the gap between us. But she'd made it perfectly clear that she wanted nothing to do with me. And that was the way it needed to be. So, instead of pinning her body to the stones and making her moan so loud the walls rattled, I turned and started for the door. "Are you hungry? Because I am famished." Maybe Eava would let me eat if I brought the human to meet her.

"I suppose even hostages need to eat."

I changed my shirt into the blue one that Eava said made my eyes look pretty. "Would you prefer widow fingers or orphan ears?"

I swore she almost smiled. "Surprise me."

We descended the stairs in silence, our footsteps falling in sync. By the time we reached the ground floor, she seemed to have relaxed. Eava hummed as she always did, meaning she hadn't heard our approach. When she saw us, her black eyes sparkled the way they did every Saturday night after our proposals.

"There's my boy! Is this who I think it is?" she said as if she hadn't threatened to chop me up over not bringing Aveen breakfast only an hour ago. "Oh, she is a dote! Come closer, girl, give us a look at ye."

Seeing the two of them together did strange things to my stomach. Strange, unwelcome, warm, fuzzy things. "This is Aveen. Aveen, this stunning young woman is Eava."

"Oh, you!" Eava gave me a slap. "Deceitful wretch. Young woman, my arse."

"It's a pleasure to meet the woman responsible for the world's best cherry tarts," Aveen said.

She remembered me mentioning Eava that night. Was she remembering anything else that had happened? The way it felt when I'd been buried inside her. The way I'd left her crying out for more. I had to adjust myself to keep the women from seeing how much the memory affected me.

"I'm surprised this selfish bastard shared," Eava said, side-eyeing me. "He must be smitten with ye."

Oh, please. I was obsessed, not smitten. Being smitten implied an air of happiness. All this obsession did was make life hell for us both. "Eava's mind is going. We only keep her around out of pity."

"Careful, boy. Or the next time I make ye tarts, they'll be poisoned."

An idle threat if I ever heard one. She'd kill me outright before she'd risk her reputation as the best cook in Tearmann over a batch of poisoned tarts.

Eava gave one of the stools at the counter a pat. "Hop up there, and we'll see what we have fer brekkie."

For once, Aveen did as she was told.

"Where's yer brother?" Eava threw over her shoulder.

After dying and coming back so often in such a short space of time, his magic reserves would be empty. And the moment he had a spark, he wouldn't conserve it so that he could escape the black pit. He'd shift a bottle and drink till he was scuttered. He'd be lucky to get out of the oubliette before dinner. "Busy drinking himself into a stupor, no doubt."

"Right so. He'll be needing soakage when he's through."

Eava's answer for everything: food.

I jumped onto the stool next to Aveen, watching her watch Eava bustle around the kitchen. When she caught me, she glared. Which only made me smile more. "Besides widows and orphans, what do you like for breakfast?"

Eava laughed as she stirred whatever was inside one of the black cast iron pots. Some sort of stew, by the smell of it.

"I'll eat just about anything," Aveen said.

"I didn't ask what you'd eat. I asked what you like."

For some reason, the simple question made her brow furrow. "I like . . . um . . . poached eggs and toast."

I swung my knees toward Eava, finding her smiling down at the maybe-stew. "Did you hear that, you old bat?"

Something whizzed past my ear. A wooden spoon. "Next time, I'll hit ye square between those pretty blue eyes."

Did Aveen think my eyes were pretty? Did she notice the way this shirt made them that bit brighter? Ruairi interrupted my thoughts by pounding on the floor from his cell. If he didn't keep it down, I'd flood the entire dungeon.

Eava left toast. I shifted butter. The pooka banged again.

"What's that noise?" Aveen asked, peering beneath the table as if she'd be able to see through the floor.

"That's Ruairi." Was there ever a time the pooka didn't irritate the shite out of me? If so, I couldn't remember.

"It sounds like he's under the floor."

Toast. Sometimes that was all you needed to make the day better. "He is."

"Where?"

"Where he belongs." Actually, if it were up to me, he'd be chained and swimming in his own blood. Ah, well. There was always tomorrow.

Eava slammed a tray of food on the table. "What'd I tell ye about sendin' that poor boy to the dungeon?"

I had a sneaking suspicion she liked Ruairi the best of all of us. She certainly accepted his proposals most often. "To be fair, I did warn him." He was lucky I let him live for another day after trying to interfere with my bargain.

Aveen's toast stilled halfway to her lovely, lovely lips. "How can you punish him for coming to my aid?"

"You didn't need his aid." She didn't need anything from that filthy fleabag. He was as useful as a sieve in a rainstorm.

"Do I not? My apologies. I thought you were keeping me hostage."

"Little Rían," Eava chided. "What'd I tell ye about keepin' hostages?"

"The same thing I told you about calling me 'Little Rían.'"

After breakfast, I did the washing up. Aveen slid off her stool to help. She and Eava babbled about cooking lessons and a bunch of other shite I had no interest in. What I *was* interested in was the way Aveen's face brightened every time Eava asked her a question, and the way she laughed whenever I was an ass, like when I said I hated everything.

Which wasn't entirely off the mark.

I liked Aveen.

And Eava.

I tolerated Tadhg.

And that was about it.

"He's a tricky one, our Rían," Eava said in a conspiratorial whisper. "With him, ye need to listen with yer eyes and yer heart."

I didn't have the luxury of enjoying anything because the moment I did, the Queen would take it away.

"Time to go, human." I shoved the last dish into the press and let the door fall closed. No sense staying inside all day when there was work to be done.

Eava must've created a tost because what she whispered next remained between herself and Aveen. The human gave me a strange look. I wanted to ask but didn't bother; I assumed she'd refuse to tell me. I led her out of the kitchens, down the hallway, through the dining room, and outside into stifling, overwarm air.

Aveen stilled at the edge of the patio. "The gardens?"

"No. The dungeon." Of course it was the feckin' garden.

Aveen did not like that, stomping the whole way through the manicured hedges and muttering under her breath. Then she stilled.

I watched the surprise register on her face. The wonder. Her eyes fell closed, and her chest lifted as she inhaled the balmy, floral air.

"Do you like them?" I asked.

"They are more beautiful than I imagined."

Her confession made me smile. Everything about her made me smile. I hated it and liked it at the same time. *Feelings*. Made no feckin' sense. "Humans. So easy to impress." Would she be as impressed with my gift? There was only one way to find out. "This way."

Callum and Donal chatted next to a pooka about the fine harvest. One of the banshees waited at the gates. I waved to let her know I'd be there shortly, after I finished with my "hostage."

Muireann watched us from the fountain. I probably shouldn't have ignored her but didn't have it in me to feign interest. Around the back, Oscar and Fillion were knee-deep in vegetables, where they always seemed to be this time of day.

I brought Aveen to the far side of the castle grounds, realizing I should've probably checked in with Oscar beforehand to make sure his tasks had been completed. He didn't appear worried from where he pulled carrots from the ground, so I assumed they had been. One good thing about being feared: When you asked someone to do something, they did it.

We came to a halt next to the shed. For some reason, my nerves were at me. "Here."

Aveen's delicate eyebrows came together as she glared at my gift. "What is it?"

"It's a shed." *Clearly*.

"Why are you showing me a shed?"

"It's your shed."

"You expect me to live in a shed?"

Cursing, I stalked toward the shed, slid the bolt, and opened the door. "Just look inside." There was all sorts of shite in there. Tiny shovels. Seeds. Pots. Trays of miniature plants.

Aveen didn't smile. Not even a small one on the corner of those lips. "Why?"

I couldn't very well tell her the real reason, now, could I? So I shrugged.

"Thank you."

"Don't bother me if you need anything else. Bother Oscar." I waved at the grogoch to let him know he could live another day.

"Why are you being so nice?"

Muireann's head whipped toward us. I'd have to have a little chat with her about minding her own feckin' business. "I'm not being nice. I'm showing pity to a powerless human hostage who serves absolutely no purpose whatsoever."

Tadhg returned from the oubliette, and I found him in the study. When I casually reminded him of the executions in Gaul at half-eleven, he decided he'd rather drink. Executions today, a trial tomorrow, and no doubt more executions the day after that, which left me no time to watch over my human or finish her cottage or sit down and figure out how to fix the mess my brother and Aveen's sister had made.

Who could I leave her with?

The dog's face flickered through my mind.

I didn't exactly trust Ruairi, but Tadhg did, so perhaps he'd be good enough in a pinch. I wasted a bit of magic letting him out of the dungeon. He appeared in the doorway like a beast from hell, his expression as black as his hair.

Hair I still needed to cut.

"You bastard!" the animal roared. "I ought to rip out yer throat."

"Not now, pooka. I'm dealing with something important." I shifted my coat, going over all I needed to do before I left. I'd have to strengthen the wards and ensure Aveen couldn't leave, and then deal with the banshee.

"Where's Tadhg?" he pushed.

"Holed up with drink. Where else?" I slipped my arms into my coat, deciding which glamour to use today. "This is what happens with you fall in love. You turn into a weak, miserable shell of who you once were." I thought of the man I'd been in the wake of Leesha's death. I couldn't claim to love Aveen—I no longer had the capacity for such things. But when she'd died, I'd been almost as lost.

Better to not care at all than to care and have everything stripped away.

"And since my brother is a useless piece of shite, I have to go to Gaul," I added. "You are responsible for making sure no one kills my hostage and that she does not leave the castle grounds. If anything happens to her, you'll wish for the dungeons."

Muireann waved me over to the fountain the moment I set foot outside the castle. "Oh, Rían?"

I didn't have time for her. "What do you want?"

"Who's the human?" she said in that irritating tone she used when she was trying to be seductive that made her sound like a snake.

"One of Tadhg's women."

She arched an eyebrow. "Tadhg's, eh?"

I shifted my pocket watch. I would make it in time, but only just. "Did you need something? I'm running late."

She reached for my hand as I slipped the watch back into my waistcoat pocket. "You haven't been to see me."

"I've been busy."

"Come by tonight."

If I told her no straight out, she'd ask me why, and I didn't have time to list all the reasons I had no more use for her. "We'll see."

Once I cleared the gates, I weaved another spell into the ward's protective fabric to keep a specific human from breaching them. There was no telling who'd show up to the castle, and I didn't have time to chase after her to make sure she didn't get herself killed.

Margaret floated toward me, her white hair lifting and twisting in the air as if she were beneath the sea. "I don't like to be kept waiting," she crooned in a deceptively pleasant voice, much like a siren's.

"And I don't like dealing with my brother's shite, yet here we are."

"Have ye been to see Ned?" she asked.

That was none of her business. Besides, I didn't report to the Banshee. They reported to me. "Don't you have loved ones to warn?"

Her black eyes narrowed as she bared her pointed teeth. "We've too many deaths, ye see. Flat out, so we are. Half the Danú get no warnin' at all. Somethin' must be done."

I nodded, knowing it was the truth but having not a clue what to do about it. "I'll look into it," was all I said before evanescing to Gaul. Those were tomorrow's problems.

Today, I had life force to consume.

24

THE WEEK PASSED AS IT USUALLY DID. I HAD ONE DAY WITH AVEEN. *One.* All the rest were spent on my brother's duties. When I wasn't in the castle, I found myself daydreaming about what my human was up to. *Daydreaming.* Like a feckin' loon.

Although I barely saw her, there was something comforting about knowing she was there, playing away in her dirt, sleeping a few doors down. A spark of goodness amidst the death and destruction consuming the rest of the world. I longed to be nearer to her light, to let her cull the darkness from the deepest parts of me.

Instead, I got to spend my days watching the Danú die.

Evanescing across the island felt like a colossal waste of magic, but Tadhg's people deserved to be seen. To have someone witness their suffering. To be remembered when they were no more.

Although, if given a choice, I was probably the last person they'd want to be remembered by.

But they didn't have a choice. And neither did I.

I'd continue to haul myself to the trials and executions until I could find a way to stop them.

Not that I could do that if I had no time to breathe. Before I knew it, another Friday had come. Tadhg had promised to be present.

So I decided to spend my first—and likely *only*—day off with my hostage.

A day that would start with a cherry tart. I'd asked Eava to make them specifically for Aveen, and she'd been more than happy to oblige. Just like the flower seeds Aveen planted, I wanted to plant myself in every moment of her day. From the color of the dresses she wore to the tart on her breakfast tray. I wanted to be everywhere with her, even when I wasn't.

After the executions, I had some paperwork to finish and names to write in my ledgers. Best to get all the tedious shite out of the way in the morning so I could have a free run at the day. When I finished, I poured myself a drink, preparing to do battle with my beautiful hostage.

I found her up in the tower, chatting to her sister the way I used to chat to her. If she knew, would she smile or frown? Probably the latter.

"I miss you," Aveen said to her dead sister.

Her fondness made no sense. Keelynn had been as annoying as a burr in one's boot. She and Tadhg had that in common, I supposed. No wonder fate thought they were perfect for one another. What I wouldn't have given for an entire year without Tadhg. Just the thought left a smile playing on my lips.

"And I miss *him* too," she whispered, as if it were a secret, sordid confession.

My throat felt so tight, I could barely swallow my sip of whiskey.

Him *who*? Him me? Surely not.

But what other him could she mean? Not Ruairí. She'd been with him all week.

Had Aveen really missed *me*?

"Silly isn't, it?" she went on. I held my breath, letting each word steal a little more darkness. "You wouldn't think it was silly, though, would you? You'd think it was romantic. You'd tell me I should let him sweep me off my feet."

My smile faltered.

Heroes swept women off their feet, not villains.

"I do not sweep women off their feet," I said once a tost was in place, watching Aveen's shoulders stiffen. "I drag them down with me."

She turned slowly, her throat and neck—even the tops of her ears—blushing the sweetest shade of pink. "How much of that did you hear?"

Only the best bits. I tried to take a drink, but my smile made it nearly impossible. Aveen *had* missed me. "Did you just miss me today, or have you been pining over my absence all week?"

"Don't be ridiculous." She was trying to deny it, but the way her blush darkened as she stomped past told a different story.

I could've called her back, but there was something more enticing about the idea of facing her wrath when she walked straight into the tost's invisible wall. I stepped behind her, breathing her in. Filling my lungs with gardens and sunshine, goodness and light. "I missed you too, my little viper. Will I show you how much?"

We were so close, I could count the goosebumps riddling her arms. "That sounds like torture," she said, soft and breathless.

You have no idea. "It would be." I'd make it the most delicious, delightful, delirious experience. She didn't slap me or curse me or tell me to go to hell. My beautiful hostage turned, giving me full access to her throat, her heaving chest, her full hips.

My darkness writhed, begging for her.

Something akin to hope swelled within me.

A dangerous, addictive thing.

A dark shape moved in my peripherals. When I found the pooka scowling down at us, I let go of my human with a curse. Disbanding the tost without immediately murdering him for interrupting drained my daily allotment of patience. Aveen's gaze dropped to her slippers, her face still flushed.

"I've been shouting fer ye," Ruairi announced, his voice gruff and eyes lingering a bit too long on Aveen.

I took a drink to keep from strangling him. "We're a little busy."

"He's in an awful state," Ruairi said with a scowl.

"Does he not realize what day it is?"

"Oh, he knows. He's waitin' in the great room now."

I couldn't let the Danú see him like that. It was one thing to have them witness him on the lash at night, enjoying himself. It was another thing entirely for them to realize their crown prince was a depressed alcoholic.

Let them see him for what he truly is. That's what the Queen would say if she were standing here with us. Lucky for me, I was more than happy to disappoint her every chance I got.

I sent my drink away. The Danú wouldn't be nearly as forgiving of me if I went to hear grievances today reeking of alcohol. "Get rid of him. Tell Oscar I'll be down in a moment." I shifted a new waistcoat, my head already beginning to ache at the thought of dealing with more shite.

"What's today?" Aveen asked.

"It's Friday." My least favorite day of the feckin' week. I threw on the waistcoat, my stomach sinking even more at the thought of wasting my only day off doing anything but being with Aveen. "And on Fridays, St. Tadhg hears the quibbles and complaints of the masses. Since he has become a worthless drunk, the responsibility has once again fallen on my shoulders." In my irritation, my fingers kept slipping on the buttons, and if I couldn't get them fastened, I was going to turn into Tadhg and start ripping them clean off. "Ruling over the Danú is like minding a bunch of unruly children"

Aveen's hand stretched toward me, and every rational thought fled my brain as I watched like a simpleton as she started fastening my buttons for me. It shouldn't have turned me on. But, like every other simple thing this woman did, like smiling, breathing—even feckin' blinking—it did.

"And you don't like children?" she asked.

"Only for breakfast."

Smiling, she finished with the buttons and smoothed a hand down my waistcoat, as if she were as loath to let me go as I was to leave.

"Thank you," I whispered.

Her gaze tangled with mine, her expression so soft and inviting that I wanted to stay there forever. "Careful, now. If you keep this up, I may start thinking you have a heart."

If I had a heart, I'd give it to you.

"A trip to the dungeon would remedy that," I teased, shifting a coat and adjusting my rolled-up sleeves before tugging it on. One trip down there would sort her right out.

I needed to go, but for some reason, I couldn't force my feet to turn away from her. "Would you . . . Never mind."

"Would I what?"

"Would you like to come?"

Her eyebrows shot up. "Am I allowed? Wouldn't want to blur the lines between hostage and captor."

"You blurred those lines the moment you said you missed me."

On good days, dealing with everyone else's problems felt like a respite from my own. Today was a good day. The Danú appeared as happy about working with me as I was about working with them, but no one balked at my commands. Sitting in this throne always gave me a little thrill.

All right, maybe it was a massive thrill. I'd spent centuries draining life force from those executed in Airren, hoarding my power in hopes of one day being strong enough to defeat the Queen. But this—this title, this throne, having people come to me instead of trying to run away—*this* was true power.

And it belonged to my brother.

When Madden O'Shaughnessy stalked into the room dragging Anwen by the arm, I had a sinking feeling my day was about to take a turn.

The semi-powerful witch loved nothing more than to lord himself over those living closest to him. Just last month, he'd brought in three faeries on suspicion of collusion with the Airren authorities.

I watched Anwen stumble from the man's shove, my irritation slipping so dangerously close to rage that the air of indifference I'd spent years cultivating nearly cracked. Aveen flew off the dais, helping the woman to her feet.

Madden glared at my human. If he didn't stop, he'd be meeting the wrong end of my dagger. "What's the issue, Madden?" The sooner I got the smirking fecker out of this castle, the better.

"I caught this deceitful witch shiftin' goods from Airren. Bolts of cloth and the like."

Truth.

Shit.

"Anwen, you have been charged with theft. How do you plead?" I asked, even though I already knew the answer.

"Guilty, Prince Rían." Her voice broke. "But Maisie was sick, and little Sean needed new shoes, and with the new baby . . ." Her words stopped, as if locked in her throat. As if she knew there was no use. Because there wasn't.

Still, I followed procedure and shifted Volume II of Tearmann Law into my hands, flipping to the page regarding theft, skimming the relevant section for hope I knew wasn't there.

Aveen's hand shot out, catching my sleeve. "I need to talk to you."

Madden's eyes bulged so wide, they nearly popped out of his skull.

You fool! I wanted to shout. The room was filled with Danú just waiting for me to screw up, and here she was, requesting a chat. I tore out of her hold but followed her into the study to keep the infernal human from making even more of a scene.

The door closed behind us, and I let every ounce of my irritation seep into my voice. "How dare you order me around in front of an entire room of people. I should send you to the feckin' dungeon, human." I flicked my wrist, regaining some of my composure by the time the tost settled around us. "You cannot do that here, Aveen. Do you understand?"

She nodded.

"Good. Now say you're sorry. And cry, if you can." That should be enough to keep those nosey feckers out of my affairs. I dropped the tost and gestured for Aveen to get on with it. All she did was blink her big, beautiful eyes.

"Go on," I mouthed. We didn't have all day.

She stuttered out a terribly insincere apology that even I had trouble hearing. "Louder," I whispered.

"I'm so, so sorry. Please forgive me. It won't happen again."

Once I had the tost back in place, I told her exactly what I thought of her performance. We really needed to work on her delivery. "Now, say your piece and hurry it on."

Her gaze flicked to the door at my back for the briefest of seconds. "You cannot kill that woman."

I understood that she was good and kind and wanted me to be as well, but that just wasn't reality. "Theft of this sort is a capital offense."

"It's just cloth. Surely the law allows for extenuating circumstances."

It didn't. Most cloth had to be imported from the other islands or the continent, making it an expensive commodity. We weren't discussing petty theft. "There is no gray area in this, Aveen. I'm sorry." And I truly meant that. I was sorry I couldn't do better for her, but my hands were tied.

"Rían, please."

I felt sorry for Anwen, I really did. But she had made the decision to break the law and she deserved to suffer the consequences.

"Allowing emotions to cloud my judgement will only end in disaster. And if I do not follow the rules, then no one else will either." I unhooked her fingers from where they'd latched around my arm, hating the distance I could already feel settling between us. "You should remain here until I return."

Back in the great room, Madden's smirk had returned, and I secretly wished he'd break a law so I could break his neck. Aveen came barreling out behind me, her blue eyes already swimming with tears. I gave her a silent plea to keep her beautiful mouth shut and returned to my brother's throne, the wooden seat feeling more rigid than before.

"The law is quite clear in this matter," I began, watching the way Anwen's lower lip trembled. From the corner of my eye, I saw her children waiting at the room's entrance. I saw them but chose to ignore them.

"Anwen, you will be executed at sundown. Take this time to get your affairs in order."

Aveen's whimper before she turned and ran for the study would've broken my heart.

If I'd had one.

A handful of Danú followed the hysterical woman and her gaggle of children from the room, leaving me with only a few more cases to try. Thankfully, none of them ended in death. Normally, when I finished, I poured myself a glass of something strong and ate a load of shite. Today, I didn't feel like doing any of that.

Today, I wanted to find my human.

When I did, I couldn't believe what I heard. She was in the tower, tattling to my feckin' brother like a feckin' child. Asking him to help as if he were some sort of hero. He was literally sitting on the floor because he was too drunk to stand. And she wanted him to go over my head and *fix it*.

What'd he say? He feckin' promised to do it.

And she thanked him for it.

Heat collected in my chest, and it wasn't the normal fire that came from being near Aveen. This heat belonged to hatred and indignation. This human, who was living under our roof, eating our food, wearing clothes I'd paid for, who was alive *because of me*, had gone to *him*.

And then—*and then*—Tadhg had the gall to tell her that I didn't deserve her. Of course I didn't feckin' deserve her! No one did!

I kicked open the door, the fire flaring inside me when I saw how close the two of them stood to one another. "Now, now, brother. You know better than to meddle in my affairs." He'd shirked his duty, and I'd stepped in to cover his arse, as I always did. Aveen sidled closer to *him*, as if he could protect her from me if I decided to end them both. "And *you*. Was it not enough for you to question my authority and make me look like a fool? Now you run off to my feckin' brother and beg him to undermine me?"

Tadhg draped his arm around Aveen's shoulder as if she were a rack for his feckin' coat. "You may have played leader today, but Aveen knows who's really in charge."

My darkness dragged me under, and I did nothing to fight it. With a flick of my wrist, the weak, pathetic, man in front of me vanished, sent straight to the cliffs and shoved right off.

Aveen stumbled back. "I'm sorry," she sputtered, "but you gave me no choice."

"Do not say you had no choice when you did. You had a choice, Aveen." I was the one without control. I was the one who didn't have a feckin' choice. Not Tadhg. Not Aveen. And not Anwen. They had their hearts. They were the masters of their fate. "And so did that witch," I ground out. "She knew what she was doing was illegal. She knew and did it anyway."

"She deserves another chance."

"Does she, now? And how many chances should I give her? Two? Three? No, wait. Four. Or should I give her five? I know! Six. Six strikes and then she's beheaded. No exceptions, though, I mean it."

"This isn't a joke, Rían."

"I'm not feckin' joking! That is what I hear when you say I should make exceptions. Who do I make these exceptions for? Just certain people?" That wasn't fair, now, was it? "The ones with the most tragic backstories? Only the mothers? What about the fathers? Should the law be eradicated, and everyone be allowed to do whatever they please?"

She blinked up at me, eyes glittering with unshed tears and jaw working as if she were chewing on the bitter truth of my words.

I inhaled a slow, intentional breath in a useless attempt to shove the darkness back down where it belonged. "Months ago, my brother offered Anwen some of the castle's rations if she could not afford to sustain her family. And yet her pride kept her from asking for help. She deserves to suffer the consequences of her actions."

Aveen looked me right in the eyes and told me I was wrong. "Anwen doesn't deserve consequences," she said. "That woman deserves mercy." And then she turned her back on me and walked away.

Mercy.

A word I'd heard repeated time and again at the foot of the dais, in a crowded courtroom, at the end of a noose.

Something I'd begged for once as well.

Before I realized that, in my world, mercy didn't exist.

25

ANWEN DESERVES HER FATE.

That thought followed me down the sodden path toward a row of cottages. The Forest rose in the distance, an ominous black smudge against a periwinkle sky.

That woman deserves mercy.

Aveen's words had haunted me all feckin' day, making me question everything I knew to be true. That's how I ended up stomping toward a tiny cottage with children darting around the yard, weeping and wailing like a bunch of wet cats. From the window, I could see Anwen inside the house, holding her eldest daughter by the shoulders, telling her how to carry on without her.

What would this punishment create? More orphans unable to sustain themselves. More people breaking the law in order to survive.

That woman deserves mercy.

Why? Why did *she* deserve mercy over anyone else? Had Leesha not deserved mercy? And what about me? I traced a finger over the scar hidden beneath my shirt. Where was *my* mercy?

Anwen answered the door with tears in her eyes. When she saw me, her face paled. "'Tisn't sundown, yer highness," she blurted, scrubbing her cheeks with the sleeves of her simple dress.

One of the children toddled over, clinging to his mother's skirts. He smelled like mushy peas and powder. Did she not bathe them?

"Send them away," I told her, pointing to mushy-peas.

She looked like she wanted to protest. Hell, part of me wanted her to defy me so I'd have further reason to enact this punishment. Although her chin lifted, she turned to her eldest daughter and asked her to take the little ones outside. The baby started wailing. I created a tost to keep the screeching from rattling my brain.

"My brother offered castle rations. Why didn't you take them?" I asked. There was no sense messing about with inane chat. I needed answers. And if she knew what was good for her, she'd give them to me.

She planted her hands on her hips and scowled. "Aye, he did. But fer how long? One month? Two? What good's that with winter comin'? This was enough to get me back on my feet. One haul to set my little ones up fer life. Wouldn't buy us nothin' fine but would keep my Josie outta the bawdy house until she could find a man of her own."

I shifted uncomfortably on the stoop, my shiny boots reflecting the evening sunlight. I'd seen more than my fair share of poverty, but to be faced with letting your child sell herself in order to feed the family? *That* was what should be against the law.

"I tried workin' in Airren," Anwen went on, "but can't hold a glamour fer shite. No one bought a scarf from me, even though they were the best in the market. Sat there, day in, day out, hearing their whispers, feeling their scorn. Two stalls over, this human kept at me, wouldn't shut his fat gob. Said I should give him my scarves for a fraction of the price—not even enough to cover the cloth. I shifted the bastard's entire inventory and laughed when I did it."

"So this was about revenge?" I asked.

"This was about survival."

I understood both, but revenge was a decision. A choice.

Survival was a basic instinct.

What if this had been Aveen? What if she found herself in an impossible situation and the only way to keep her family safe and fed was to break the law? Would I have it in me to hold her accountable? As much as I wanted to say the answer was yes, I knew it was a lie.

Aveen could break every single law, and I would never lift a finger against her.

That's what happened when you loved someone. You bent rules. You broke them. You did whatever was necessary to keep them safe.

I glared down at Anwen, her tears now dry and a stubborn set to her pointed chin. "Do I have your word that you will not allow another incident like this to occur? That if you find yourself in need, you will come to the castle?"

"What good's the word of a dead woman?"

I ground my teeth until it felt like they would crack. "I want your word, Anwen."

"Then ye have it, my Prince."

I nodded. Decision made. "I am giving you a once in a lifetime opportunity to change your fate. Any laws broken henceforth will be met with the swiftest, harshest punishment."

Her hand flew to her throat, her searching eyes hopeful. "What're ye sayin'?"

"You are hereby offered a royal pardon for crimes you have committed. It will not happen a second time."

She hugged me before I could stop her. I peeled the woman off me, straightening my waistcoat. "If you need honest work, speak with Eava. You are not to enter the castle," I added, wanting to keep my brother from unwanted advances. "Knock at the back door, and she will give you something to do."

"Thank ye."

I disbanded the tost and turned toward the exit. The moment I opened the door, the girl and little one fell inside, scrambled to their feet, and raced to embrace their mother. This would likely cost me dearly when the Queen found out.

But I'd made the best decision for Tearmann, ending the cycle of poverty and punishment.

And if the Queen didn't like it, she could sod off.

I waited to return to the castle until nightfall, not wanting to speak to anyone about my decisions. Weary to my bones, I paused outside Aveen's room, wanting to ask how her day was. To tell her what I'd done.

But the fewer people who knew, the better.

So, instead of knocking, I continued to my room and changed for bed. Despite my weariness, I ended up tossing and turning for half the night. Every time I closed my eyes, I saw Aveen's face when she'd confessed to missing me. I missed her so much my bones ached with it. She was right down the hall, but she may as well have been on the other side of the island.

A woman's scream dragged me from bed.

A second scream left me stumbling into the hall.

Aveen. Aveen was screaming. I evanesced to her room, finding the wards unbroken. When she screamed again, I burst inside, finding her alone, curled on the bed, her face buried in a pillow.

"It's the middle of the feckin' night. If you don't stop roaring, you'll be sleeping in the oubliette."

That brought a scowl to her face as I knew it would. "And if you don't get out of my room, I'm going to stab you again."

Idle threats. Still, I closed the distance between us, sitting at the bottom of the bed and shifting my dagger. "Go on, then. Stab me if it'll make you feel better."

"I don't want your blood soiling my sheets."

Fair enough. Blood stained something awful. I sent the dagger back to my bedside table. "Why were you screaming? Not that I care."

She fisted her sheets, probably wishing they were my throat, despising me so much I could taste it. "That's what hostages do, isn't it? They scream."

"Hostages only scream for a short while." The covers smelled like her. Roses and soft skin. Innocence and sin. "Then they cry and beg. Will I make you cry and beg, human?" The thought alone left me itching to tug down the sleeves of her shift and taste her again.

As if she heard the direction of my wicked thoughts, she hugged her knees to her chest, holding them close, yet another barrier between us. "I was screaming because I hate you."

Lie. "No, you weren't."

"I was screaming because I am sick and tired of being held hostage by someone as evil and merciless as you."

Couldn't she see that it was I who had been taken hostage? That her unyielding hold on me made it hard to breathe? That I wouldn't escape even if I could?

Although I knew it was foolish, I summoned a tost. Tired of the games. Tired of the secrets. I wanted her to look at me the way she had the night before she died. "Am I holding you hostage?" I said. "Most of my hostages do not live in my home, eat my food, or stroll through my gardens." Most of my hostages didn't survive their first night. "I haven't even gotten around to torturing you—and that's my favorite part."

If she wanted to be a hostage for the next year, that was on her.

"In Graystones, you are dead," I reminded her. "You have no place to go and no means to support yourself. I'm not holding you hostage, Aveen. I'm giving you sanctuary."

She remained quiet for the longest time before asking why I bothered.

I sat up, turning so that I could better see her shadowed face. "You'll think I'm mad if I tell you."

"I already do." *Truth.*

Fine. Maybe I was mad. But I was mad about her. "You and I . . . We are meant for each other.

"This is that soulmate nonsense, isn't it?"

Hold on. She knew? How did she—"I'm going to kill Tadhg."

That hadn't been his secret to tell. Ah, well. Nothing I could do about it at the moment. I could kill him in the morning. "It's not nonsense," I insisted, taking her hand, forcing a connection. "Do you feel that?"

Aveen shook her head.

Without her speaking, I couldn't taste a lie, but she *must* be lying. She had to feel this too. "Don't lie to me. I know you do. I am cold and dead inside, but when you touch me, something ignites, and I burn. I burn for you just as you burn for me." And I reveled in each and every fiery second. "I know I'm not good—that I don't deserve you." Such an incredible understatement. She was goodness personified, and I was sin. "I tried to let you go. Then you sought me out, and I thought maybe fate wasn't playing some twisted game. Maybe something in my cursed life was finally going right. Maybe I wasn't meant to give you up."

She tugged free of my grasp, scrubbing her hand against the blanket, her face a mixture of emotions. Confusion. Fear. Anger.

None of the softness I longed to see. "I should've known better."

The darkness may crave the light, but light could never crave the darkness.

I stood and started for the door.

"Why did you come to my room?" Aveen asked, her voice soft as a whisper.

"Because you screamed."

Surprisingly enough, I'd slept after seeing Aveen. I tried not to think too much about why that was as I descended the stairs and swung by the kitchens for a snack. As good as the scones Eava had just baked smelled, I'd been eating too much shite lately, so I snagged an apple instead.

For the first time in what felt like forever, I had nothing to do but sit around and watch my "hostage" play in dirt. It was going to be a feckin' brilliant day. I stepped out of the castle and down the stone stairs, turning toward the patch of earth Aveen had claimed as her own. Footsteps clattered behind me. I whirled, readying for an attack, leaving me entirely unprepared for a human with blond curls throwing her arms around me.

What the hell had gotten into her? Didn't she know better than to touch me? Muireann watched us through wide, bulbous eyes. At least all she saw was my abject horror. More and more eyes fell on us each passing second. I had to do something.

I shoved Aveen away even though all I wanted was to pull her closer. "What the hell do you think you're doing?"

She stumbled back, brushing her hair from her face. "Giving you a hug?"

"A *hug*? You think just because I don't keep you locked up, that means you're allowed to touch me?"

She shook her head, hair falling forward. "I'm . . . I'm sorry."

"I don't think you are. But you will be." I didn't fight the darkness swelling within me, knowing no other way to throw these fools off my scent as I caught Aveen's arm and hauled her toward the rear of the castle.

She stumbled along behind me, but I couldn't slow my pace with Muireann sneering with obvious delight. I channeled all my contempt for the fish into my rage, throwing the door to the dungeon open with a burst of magic and lighting the torches on the other side while I was at it. The familiar smell of old stones and dried blood overwhelmed as we made our way down, down, down into the depths of the cliff beneath the castle, to where death lived.

I forced my soulmate into the closest cell, letting the door slam so everyone above would hear it for miles.

"I'm sorry. I'm sorry. I'm sorry—"

I stalked toward her, feeding off the panic and fear, stopping when her skin was so close, I could feel her warmth, her subtle sweetness consuming my senses. "I will tell you this once," I whispered. "You cannot touch me or speak to me as if I am anything but the vile bastard I am. I have no friends in this castle, in this kingdom, or in this world. If anyone learns what you mean to me, I will be forced to kill them." Her delectable mouth fell open, drawing my attention to her lips. Before I could stop myself, I eased forward, stealing a kiss. "You are my only weakness," I confessed, knowing no other way to make her understand but through the dangerous truth. "And if the world found out, it would take you away."

And I would burn everything and everyone in my path to get her back.

I'd lost love before but knew in my hollowness that nothing would compare to losing this woman in front of me. My light in this shadowed world. I would do anything for her. *Anything*.

Aveen's breath caught, emotions flitting across her face.

I dropped every mask I'd ever worn so she could see the depth of mine, which had grown and grown despite my best efforts. "If I could, I would hold you close and never let you go. I would kiss you for the entire island to see. I would take you in the middle of the feckin' courtyard."

For the only way to save him was at her own expense.

That life, the life where I got to be free, wasn't worth the price. "But this place is more dangerous than you could ever imagine. The only way to keep you safe is to leave you be." I knew that, and yet here I was, stealing every scowl and harsh word because even her contempt felt like basking in sunlight on a summer's day. "But I'm not strong enough to let you go."

She licked her lips. "Then don't."

Those two words cut through me like a scythe. *Then don't.*

Maybe it was time to stop fighting who I was and give in to my most selfish desires.

I kissed her with every ounce of fear and rage in me, letting her goodness steal it away, breathing new life into my lungs. Perhaps the reason fate had chosen this woman for me was because her heart was big enough for us both.

Aveen's mouth devoured with just as much hungry desperation as mine.

I couldn't leave this cell without having her at my mercy. It was only fair considering she had me at hers. I shackled her wrist the way she'd shackled me, body and soul, and wrapped those beautiful legs around my waist, hearing her breath catch when I pressed my hips against hers. Hardening as I moved, slow and steady. "Will I torture you, human?"

Her head fell back against the stones, eyes glazed. "Do your worst, *Your Highness*."

Oh, little viper, you can't handle my worst.

When she gave me control of her body, I took all her mouth and tongue had to give, shifting my dagger, slicing through every layer keeping her from me. "You are magnificent." My fantasy made reality. Everything I desired and more.

My lips skimmed her mouth, her throat. Teased her breasts until she whimpered. The chains rattled as I stripped her bare and fell to my knees on the stones.

For her I would kneel.

For her I would bow.

For her I would live in the feckin' dirt.

I lifted her soft, supple thighs over my shoulders, sweeping my tongue straight up her center, finding my downfall. Searching for the spot that made her moan. And when she did, her heels dug into my back, dragging me closer. My fingertips bit into her skin as I buried my face against her and worked my tongue in slow, torturous strokes until she whimpered my name.

"That's it," I whispered against her. "Cry for me. Beg for me."

Aveen cried. Trembled. Pulsed. Came undone.

I couldn't wait to have her. Once more. Forever. However and whenever she would give herself to me. I released the bonds, dragging her down with me as I always knew I would. The soreness in my knees was nothing compared to the ache in my body to unleash myself on her.

Aveen tore at the buttons on my shirt, scraping her short nails down my skin.

My hands didn't falter as I unfastened my breeches, finally free to drive my cock into her dripping heat. My eyes rolled back in my head, never wanting this to end but too weak to keep my hips from drawing back when she lifted herself, urging me deeper.

"I thought I was the one torturing you," I rasped, my head already spinning.

"And I thought I told you to do your worst."

I caught her hips, angling them upwards so I could drive deeper. Harder. Faster. "Scream for me."

Her throat strained when she did. She clung to me as I clung to her, burying myself until my vision blurred and muscles coiled. Her thighs shook where they squeezed my thrusting hips.

When she cried my name, I fell apart inside her, her own climax stealing my darkness, filling me with light and hope.

Maybe I would find another way to break this curse.

Maybe I could defeat the Queen.

Maybe I could retrieve my heart and give it to this woman who deserved nothing less than everything.

26

As I GLANCED OUT THE DINING ROOM WINDOW, WATCHING NIGHT descend upon the castle, I already couldn't wait for dinner to end. But first, I needed to feed my human so she had plenty of energy for what I had planned later.

"The wards need strengthened," I told Tadhg.

He rolled his eyes as he always did when I suggested something even remotely related to work. "No one has breached our wards in centuries. They're fine as they are."

"No one has breached them because no one has tried." Now that Aveen was stuck here, I needed to make certain that she was as safe as possible. Not that I'd be able to save her if my mother decided to take control. But so long as we kept up the ruse outside these walls, there was a chance she'd leave me be.

"If you want to waste your magic, be my guest."

His wife was upstairs locked away. He really should have been more concerned about her well-being.

The fool kept glancing at the empty chair beside Ruairi with a pathetic look on his face. When he wasn't guzzling wine, that was.

Unlike my brother, Aveen sipped her drink slowly, her dainty fingers spinning her glass when she returned it to the table. "Be careful not to drink too much," I said. Faerie wine was far stronger than anything she would've had back in Airren, and the hangovers would make her wish for death.

Her icy blue eyes flashed, sending a spark of heat straight to my groin. "I can handle myself."

I'd prefer to be the one doing the handling, but that couldn't happen if she was drunk.

Right. I'd suggested having dinner together for a reason. We had important business to discuss. Business that needed to stay between us. When I conjured a tost, the lads glanced at each other over their plates, but Aveen didn't seem to notice.

The Queen needed to die. Then Keelynn could be resurrected, fall madly in love with my eejit brother, and break his curse. Then I'd retrieve my heart, and Aveen could fall madly in love with me. And *then* Ruairi would be the only sad fecker here without prospects.

Win-win-win.

We'd need a human to stab her, though. Not *my* human. We needed a different one. One that no one would miss if he were to fail.

"You know what I think we should do?" I started, lifting my glass to my lips.

"The last time ye said that, Tadhg ended up killing—how many people?" Ruairi said, glancing toward where my brother swayed on his seat.

Tadhg smiled a sloppy smile. "Only two. But one wasn't my fault," he rushed when Aveen's mouth fell open.

That one had been due to his curse, and like I'd always said, if a woman was foolish enough to kiss him, she deserved to spend a year in the underworld.

"I don't know how I feel about my sister being married to a murderer," Aveen announced.

Tadhg threw a hand at me. "He killed seven."

"Eight, actually." But the difference was that Aveen had no desire to marry me. I wasn't foolish enough to believe her interest extended deeper than physical intimacy at this stage. If she wanted to use my body until the day she died, I'd let her. I'd take whatever she was willing to give. "And they were all my fault," I added, not bothering to hide my smile.

A bunch of drunk humans had lost the run of themselves and tried to attack me—four at once. Then their little friends got offended when I'd snapped their necks. They'd seen what I could do, and yet they'd fought me anyway.

Aveen's delectable lips pursed into a pout. "You have to stop killing people, Rían. It's wrong."

What was wrong was her being so damned far away from me and wearing all those clothes. Good thing I planned on remedying that as soon as dinner ended.

Ruairi bit his lip with his fangs while Tadhg's shoulders vibrated with laughter. A moment later, their deep cackles echoed around the room.

"I'm sorry, but have you met my brother?" Tadhg gasped, swiping at his tear-filled eyes with his dirty sleeve.

"For some reason, she insists on seeing the good in me." Heaven only knew why.

"What good?" Tadhg snorted, giving me a shove. "You're not happy unless you're murdering someone."

"I do love a good murder," I said, only half joking because Aveen did not look impressed. If I told her how many times I'd *refrained* from murdering people, she'd be proud.

My brother's green eyes sparked with mischief. "What's your favorite part? Is it the way the light fades from their eyes? Or the way they always look so surprised?"

They did look surprised. Why was that? How could a human in his right mind believe he could best us? "For me, it's the coppery tang of blood. Positively delectable. The bloodier the murder, the better. Although the shite stains something awful. Just last week I ruined my favorite waistcoat."

"Murder isn't a joke," Aveen insisted, gripping the edge of the table until her knuckles turned white.

Tadhg nodded as if he agreed, hiding his shit-eating grin behind his hand.

"Would it make you feel better to know the people I kill deserve it?" I asked.

"Mostly," Tadhg whispered.

I kicked the asshole in the shin. If Aveen didn't stop giving me that look, I was never going to get under her skirts. And I had wicked plans for her.

"Careful now, lads," Ruairi said, still smiling his obnoxious smile. "She's getting proper cross."

I didn't want her frowning. I wanted her smiling. Then again, perhaps I could use this to my advantage. "I like her when she's angry." Bedding violent Aveen lived at the top of my list of goals. It may have even been above vengeance.

Aveen's shoulders rose and fell when she inhaled a deep breath. "What were you about to suggest before all of you went off on a murder tangent?"

I couldn't very well tell her now that I knew how she felt about murder. Although, maybe if I explained who I wanted to murder, she'd no longer object.

Tadhg and Ruairi laughed, no doubt knowing exactly what I had been about to suggest.

The clock from the study struck the hour.

Ruairi slammed the wine bottle in his hand onto the table. "Shite. We almost forgot. Eava!"

"Eava! Eava!" Tadhg bellowed.

How could we forget? Poor Eava would be devastated. I joined in, a chorus of shouts echoing off the gray stones as we yelled for the old witch.

She suddenly appeared, boxing Tadgh's ears first. "What'd I tell ye about roarin' down the feckin' castle walls like a bunch of heathens?"

She insisted on pretending she didn't love it when we did this. If she'd hated it, she wouldn't have stayed on past her normal working hours every Saturday night since we began almost fifty years ago, when Tadhg was in a mood over no one ever wanting to marry him. Now he'd been handfasted twice. And I had a feeling that when Keelynn came back, she'd marry the bastard again.

Aveen's cheeks flushed as she searched our faces, no doubt thinking we were a bunch of loons.

"Never leave me, Eava," Tadhg hugged our kitchen witch. "You know I cannot live without you. Marry me."

"Get off it, ye wastrel. I'd no sooner marry ye than the man in the moon."

Even though she'd agreed to marry Tadhg last week.

I stood and took her weathered hand, grazing a kiss across her knuckles. "Marry me, Eava. I'd never love another."

"I've always had a weakness fer the wicked ones. But seeing as I've changed both yer nappies, there's only so much shite a woman can take. Isn't that right, Aveen?"

She'd agreed to marry me the week before, so I shouldn't have been surprised. Still, I fainted on the floor to let her see the extent of my devastation.

"Let's hear yer proposal, ya animal," Eava said to the mutt showing off his grin.

Ruairi stood to his massive height, lifted the witch clean off her feet, and gave her a sloppy kiss. "Ye will get neither jewels nor power from me, but I can promise plenty of sleepless nights."

Eava loved that shite, throwing her head back and laughing. "There's a good lad. If yer ever lookin' to settle down, ye know where to find me."

"Right so." He carried her laughing right out the door.

I didn't like her giving him attention. Ruairi had had a mother, a family, and so had Tadhg. Mine didn't count.

Tadhg explained our game with a laugh, leaving Aveen beaming from her chair. "She must be a saint if she deals with the lot of you day in and day out."

Eava was a saint. I didn't know how we'd function without her. She was more than a cook—she was the mother we'd never had, the mother we'd lost. I'd asked her once why she'd never married and had children of her own. She'd said her hands were full enough with three boys who'd never grow up.

Ruairi strolled back into the room, a basket hooked over his arm. "God love that witch. She'll have me fat as a fool."

My brother smacked his lips together, ever the fiend for dessert. "What'd she give you this time?"

Beneath the cloth waited a pile of pear tartlets. Aveen chose first, selecting the smallest one.

"Saturdays are my favorite days," Ruairi said with his mouth full like an animal.

As I watched my human chew her tart, I had to agree. This particular Saturday may have been the best Saturday of my life.

Tadhg ended up stuffing his face with four tarts, and Ruairi had five. Aveen and I stuck to one each.

"Are there any other traditions I should know about?" she asked, wiping her hands on her serviette.

"After dinner, we retire to the parlor to take bets."

"What do you bet on?" she asked.

"Anything and everything. Death. Life. Rain. Snails." Sex. Murder. Drink. Her hand slipped into mine as if it were the most natural thing in the world. It felt right having her there, even though I should have been pushing her away.

"Snails?" she laughed, pausing momentarily to take in the Queen's tapestry.

"We've raced them," I explained. "And frogs. And squirrels. And one time, worms, but we all ended up passing out before we saw who won."

"I won," Ruairi claimed, "but these two eejits were too mean to pay up."

"Ruairi never wins." It was probably one of the only things about the pooka that I actually liked. He lost *all* the time. And he was such an entertaining sore loser.

When we reached the family room, Ruairi grabbed more wine from the cart. Tadhg would be blind-drunk soon enough, and

267

Ruairi would end up trying to take care of him, leaving Aveen and I all by our lonesome. *Tragic.*

I shifted five glasses as Ruairi offered an invitation to Aveen as if it were his place to invite my human to the afters.

She pressed a hand to her chest, sucking in a breath. "You want me to join you?"

I wanted her to join us too, but if I offered now, it'd look like I was trying to tag along.

"Only if you want," Tadhg said over his full glass of wine before drinking half of it in three swallows.

"I do. I really do. But I don't have any money."

"Oh, we don't bet money," I said before either of the other men could butt in, shifting a cufflink from my collection. Tadhg ruined his waistcoat by ripping off a button—and a piece of my soul. Ruairi added an ancient pooka medallion to the pot. I already had a fistful of them up in my room but wouldn't mind adding one more.

Aveen glared down at the bowl, her lips pursed. Then she untied the blue ribbon from her hair. Tadhg didn't seem to notice, but Ruairi did.

She shifted, getting comfortable in her spot on the floor around the coffee table. "What's the challenge?"

Before anyone else could suggest something, I told them we were going to play snap dragon. Both men whined as I knew they would. Tadhg would be too drunk to move quickly and keep missing the fruit at the bottom of the bowl, and Ruairi's arm would be bare as a baby's arse by the time the game ended.

I shifted the bowl we needed; Tadhg got the bottle of brandy, then I added the fire.

"The lads never miss a chance to show off," Ruairi whispered in Aveen's ear, scooting a little closer until their knees brushed.

Don't murder him. Don't murder him. Don't murder him.

I extinguished the candles around us, wishing there were some way to extinguish my murderous thoughts. He wouldn't be foolish enough to make a play for her. Would he? No. I'd marked her as mine. He'd be facing certain death.

Blue flames licked at the air from inside the bowl.

When I told Aveen to go first, she balked, saying she wasn't going to do it.

I showed her how easy it was, sticking my hand right in and fishing around for a brandy-soaked raisin. Sure, there was a snap of pain, but that was part of the fun. Maybe I burnt my tongue a little as well, but wine made it all better.

Ruairi cursed, muttering about how it took a month to grow back his hair the last time we'd played.

"Then sit this one out," I muttered under my breath.

His glowing golden eyes locked with mine as he reached into the fire and withdrew a flaming almond.

Tadhg was surprisingly quick for how much he'd had to drink.

"This isn't fair," Aveen insisted, the flames reflecting in her eyes. "I'm not as fast as you are." Still, she did it, winning a raisin, then cursing when she ate it and drinking deeply afterwards.

I grabbed another raisin; Ruairi got one as well; Tadhg got an almond. Around and around we went. With everyone distracted, I shifted Aveen's ribbon from the bowl, hiding it inside my pocket. No way in hell was I going to let my brother or the mutt wear my human's ribbon. Not a feckin' hope.

My head started growing fuzzy, and I found myself smiling more than usual. Which wasn't hard considering I rarely smiled. At least, that's the way it used to be before I'd met the giggling human with hooded eyes sitting next to me.

Tadhg had gone full melancholy, whimpering about life having no meaning or some shite that none of us paid any attention to.

"How do you pick a winner?" Aveen hiccupped, then giggled again.

With the stolen ribbon in my pocket and her in my bed, I'd already won the whole feckin' thing.

"Oh, we're not finished yet." *Not by a long shot, my little viper.* I cleared the mess to save us from having it everywhere once the next round of games began. "Now we play blind man's bluff."

"In the dark?" Hers were the only eyes that didn't glow, but that didn't make them any less bright.

"Everything's more fun in the dark."

Tadhg shoved Ruairi's shoulder, sending him falling back into the settee. "Ruairi's it."

"Dammit. I'm always first."

"Stop whinging and blindfold yourself." Tadhg thrust his wrinkled cravat into Ruairi's massive hands.

Ruairi started counting, and I caught Aveen before she could run off, evanescing straight into the study. I lifted her onto the desk, nudging her knees apart with my hips. She opened her legs with a breathless gasp as I stepped between them.

"I'm pretty sure leaving the room is cheating," she giggled.

"They play their games while I play mine." And in the dungeon earlier, she'd claimed to be ready to play. Did she still feel the same, or had she changed her mind? *Only one way to find out.* I kissed my way down her bobbing throat to her breasts peeking from beneath her dress. "Stay with me tonight."

Her back arched, thrusting her chest forward. "Why would I want to do that?"

"Because if you don't, I'll fill your bedroom with mice so they can nibble your toes. Or burn the entire castle to the ground except the dungeon." Oh, yes. That'd be fun. Chained up beneath me again. Taking her hard and fast against the stones.

Her fingers laced in my hair, pushing me down to her pebbled nipples. "I suppose I don't have much of a choice, then, do I?"

"Hostages rarely do," I murmured against her breast before taking the hardened peak into my mouth and flicking it with my tongue.

"Let's go before they find us."

I didn't have to be told twice, evanescing upstairs and carrying her straight to my bed. I took my time stripping her bare, kissing every inch of newly exposed skin as I went. She helped me out of my clothes until nothing but air separated us.

She kissed me, soft and slow, as I eased into her tight heat, her heels at my back urging me to sink faster. Her tongue tangled with mine, matching each thrust of my hips.

If I could have loved, I would have loved her.

Still, I gave her everything. The shattered pieces, the blackened bits, the parts no one wanted. When I told her again that she was mine, what I really meant was that I was hers.

My hand fell between us, my thumb landing on the spot that drove her wild, drawing a moan from her lips. My hips found hers over and over again, bucking faster and faster until her cries for *more* were drowned out by whimpers.

She lifted her arms to keep her head from slamming into the headboard as I drove us both to the edge. My last thought before freefall was that maybe a heartless shell could learn to love after all.

27

I KNEW AVEEN AND EAVA HAD PLANS TO COOK THIS MORNING. I also knew that Eava would be running late. How did I know? Eava told me. She'd also asked if I could pass on the information to Aveen. I had every intention of telling her, but then I had this brilliant idea to tease her instead, so I went with the latter.

I'd glamoured myself to look like the old witch a handful of times before—mostly to mess with hungover Tadhg. One time, I got him to eat an entire custard filled with eggshells and sand. He hadn't wanted to make Eava feel bad, so he didn't comment as his teeth crunched against the extra special "ingredients". The bastard had gotten me back by taking a knife to a pair of my dress shoes.

When Aveen stepped into the kitchen, I twisted back toward the pots on the stove filled with leftovers from last night. Eava was never one to stay still for long, so I kept moving, sprinkling herbs into the pots and stirring away until my arms ached.

"Good morning, Eava," she greeted, as pretty as a picture in one of the new dresses I'd bought for her. Although I missed the way she looked in blue, the soft gray color was almost as nice. I waved her off, moving pots from burners and making myself look busy. "Morning, child. Good to see such a fine color in yer cheeks. Tearmann suits ye."

Aveen's cheeks turned as red as the dishtowel on the counter. Was she remembering the way I'd bent her over the desk in my room and made her cry for more?

"I think you may be right," she said, a smile playing around the corners of lips I'd kissed until they were swollen.

I had to force those thoughts from my mind. I may have been glamoured to look like the witch, but the body beneath still belonged to me. And the memories from this morning made me swell like I'd been stung by a feckin' wasp.

I stole one of Eava's aprons and threw it at Aveen so she didn't notice me adjusting myself beneath my skirts. "Put this on so ye don't ruin yer dress."

For once, the woman did as she was told. I helped her tie the thing at her back, loving the way the printed fabric accentuated her hips. "Now fer the blindfold," I said, shifting a strip of cloth and doing my best not to burst out laughing when her eyebrows bunched.

"Blindfold?"

I tied the cloth over her eyes, and my mind immediately conjured images of Aveen blindfolded up in my bedroom. This woman. My wanting hadn't waned after having her. If anything, my obsession had gotten worse.

I made up some shite about needing to feel the ingredients to know the right amounts, which sounded so ridiculous, I was certain she'd cop my ruse.

"You don't follow a recipe book, then?" she asked.

"My recipes live up here." I gave her temple a tap that left Aveen's brow furrowing.

Now to find some ingredients.

There wasn't much salt, so I left that be, grabbing the clay container of sugar and a tin of flour. Oh! Lard. *Brilliant.*

Aveen offered to help, but I assured her there was no need.

I set all three on the butcherblock table and told her to give me her hand. Once again, she did so without so much as a word. Part of me felt bad for breaking her trust like this, but it wasn't a large enough part to convince me to stop. Blind trust could very well be her downfall.

A cloud of white dust lifted when I thrust her hand into the flour. "Know what this is?" I asked in Eava's weathered voice.

"Flour?"

"Very good." I moved her hand to the next container. "And this?"

"Sugar."

My smile grew. "And this one?"

Her fingers sank into the lard, and the twisted look on her face nearly made me lose my composure. "That feels disgusting."

"But what is it?"

"Rían Joseph O'Cleriegh!" Eava shouted from the doorway, her face flushed and black eyes narrowed on me. "What'd I tell ye about messin' in my feckin' kitchens?"

Aveen dragged at her blindfold until it fell around her neck. The way her beautiful eyes bulged and mouth dropped open would be worth the dessert Eava would undoubtedly deny me tonight. I laughed so hard, I nearly evanesced straight into Oscar.

He gave me a doe-eyed look I'd never seen directed at me before. "Mornin'. Yer lookin' well today," he said, his cheeks turning as red as his hair.

What the hell was he on about? It wasn't until my hand brushed my skirts that I remembered I looked like Eava. Good heavens. The gardener had a crush on our feckin' cook.

When my glamour dropped, the old grogoch stumbled back. "Prince Rían . . . I . . . um . . ."

"I am looking well," I said with a smirk. "Thank you for noticing." And then I left the man blushing like a fool and started for the courtyard. There were things I could've been doing today, but I didn't feel like doing any of them. As soon as Aveen finished her cooking lesson, I was going to plague her. With the sun shining overhead and not a cloud in the sky, it felt like a sin to stay inside the wards where there was no breeze.

Maybe we could leave. Just this once. Just for today. I'd be with her—not as myself. That would never work. But I could be someone else, couldn't I? Someone no one would expect. Someone like . . . the pooka climbing the castle stairs.

I hurried through the courtyard, the idea of escaping with Aveen making my stomach do that strange fluttery thing. A strange fluttery thing that died when my gaze met Muireann's. She perched on the fountain's edge, a smile playing around her blue lips.

"Ye haven't been to see me," she called when I passed.

My steps slowed. I could've offered an excuse, but the truth was, I didn't owe her anything.

"I've missed ye," she added.

I probably should've returned the sentiment to help maintain the ruse that I cared for her. That's what the Queen would've told me to do. Which is precisely why I decided not to. "Have you heard of any more ships arriving in the east?" With my days filled with executions and nights filled with Aveen, I hadn't been to check in ages.

Her lips flattened. "We've stopped keepin' track."

"Why?"

"There's naught in it fer us anymore, now, is there?"

The merrow had their own rules and laws to follow. I wasn't her prince and couldn't order her to do anything. All I could do was persuade. And the sort of persuasion Muireann enjoyed was no longer something I was willing to provide. "Then I suppose there's no longer a reason for you to linger in my fountain, now, is there?"

Her bulbous eyes narrowed. "Ye can't kick me out. The waters belong to no man."

I dipped my fingers into the frigid liquid, watching ripples spread across the glassy surface. "I never said I would kick you out," I murmured. "You can stay as long as you'd like. Although I can imagine you'd find conditions less than favorable when I start boiling the water for my tea."

Muireann lifted herself from the ledge of the fountain, dropping into the dark water with a splash. "My father will hear of this," she hissed before sinking below the surface and disappearing out of sight.

I turned and started for where Ruairi still waited on the steps, ready to escape with my hostage.

It took until lunchtime for Aveen to emerge from the castle, her cheeks glowing and skirts peppered with flour, but seeing her smile was entirely worth the wait. The way Ruairi's fangs fit into my mouth felt so awkward, until I smiled. Maybe that's why the dog was always grinning. Because there wasn't enough room in his mouth for his teeth.

"Hostage," I said by way of greeting when Aveen stopped at my side, a basket swinging on her arm.

"Guard," she returned, smiling back, setting off a new wave of flutters, until I realized she wasn't actually smiling at me. She thought she was smiling at Ruairi.

"I have a surprise for ye," I grumbled, turning toward the gate. Did she always smile at him like that? Maybe she was still thinking of my trick this morning. She couldn't be this happy about the prospect of spending the day with a worthless pooka.

During my long wait, I'd adjusted the wards so that they would allow her through. When she reached the gates, she passed beneath without issue.

"He let me out . . ." she whispered, the breeze tangling her hair around her upturned face.

"Good hostages are rewarded," I told her.

We followed the path twisting toward the cliffs. When we reached the jagged ledge, I stopped, wanting to see her face when she saw the way the land dropped into the sea.

I hadn't found joy in much over the years, but this land, its wild beauty and rugged charm, always made me feel a little more . . . I wouldn't say hopeful or happy. At peace, maybe.

It may have been hard to imagine with the way the waves slammed against the black cliffs and sea birds screeched overhead, but here amidst the wild was where I felt most calm. And with Aveen by my side, the moment felt as near to perfect as I'd ever experienced.

I searched the landscape and horizon for witnesses, finding none. Then I dropped my glamour, just for a moment, just long enough to slip my hand around Aveen's waist. Her body went rigid as a plank, and she squealed until her gaze tangled with mine.

"Disappointed?" I asked, a little breathless and a lot happy.

"So disappointed," she murmured, catching me by the collar and stamping a kiss to my lips. The way she relaxed once she knew who I was left me grinning like a fool. "Why are you here?" she asked.

"To torture you. Why else?" As much as it killed me to do it, I recalled my glamour, settling into skin that felt like a heavy, ill-fitting coat.

A frown returned to her lips. "Why can't you be you?"

I gestured toward the merrow who'd just appeared, dancing among the waves. It wasn't likely that they would recognize me from all the way up here, but one could never be too careful.

"What'd you bring me to eat?" I asked, shifting a blanket to cover the grass so we had a place to sit.

"Something far nicer than you would have made."

There was no doubt about that. The last thing I'd cooked was Tadhg's special sand-and-eggshell-custard. "Ah, here now. I can't be good at everything." Oh! Cake. Brilliant. And Tadhg wasn't around to steal it from me. I ate the miniature deliciousness quickly all the same, vanilla and sugar kissing my tongue like a bite of heaven.

Aveen watched me with an unreadable expression.

"Revolting."

When her gaze dropped to my hands, and her brow furrowed. Before I could explain that I was obviously joking, she caught my hand and shoved back my sleeve. "What's this?" she asked, tracing the ribbon I'd worn since the day I stole it. "Is that mine?"

It wasn't always around my wrist. Sometimes I tucked it into my pocket. Other times, my boot. "I was hardly going to let Ruairi or Tadhg have it."

"Sentimental Rían." She fanned her face, pretending to faint on the blanket. "Be still my heart."

It had nothing to do with sentiment. I simply could not stand the thought of my brother or his pet having something that belonged to my human.

All right. *Maybe* I liked the idea of having something that belonged to her as well, but mostly it was about the other men.

She kept looking at me, an unreadable expression flickering across her face.

"Do you always stare at Ruairi this much?"

"I stare at him all the time," she said. "Barely get anything done when Ruairi's around."

"Sounds like I need to find you a new guard. A female one."

"What's the matter? Afraid I'll fall in love with him?"

Yes. "Love him all you want," I said instead. "The dog's a waffling eunuch."

"Stop lying."

"It's not a lie. I can show you if you want." I reached for my belt as if I'd actually be willing to show her what hid beneath.

She smacked me. "Rían!"

She squealed when I caught her like a spider in the web of my arms, holding her close, wishing this damned glamour and our clothes were gone. "Violent Aveen. My favorite."

Was this normal? The wanting. The craving. The insatiable desire to be around someone even if it was just to sit quietly by the sea and watch the waves crest in their endless task of meeting and receding from the shore. I liked to think it wasn't. There was something whimsical about the idea of just the two of us experiencing this level of affection. Not that I had much experience.

Aveen nodded her chin toward the line of trees rising along Tearmann's eastern border. "Is that the Forest over there?"

"A forest, yes. But not *the* Forest. There's a river separating the two." A river as black as the Queen's soul. "Why? Are you planning on running away from me?" My chest pinched at the thought until she shook her head, tickling my chin despite the glamour.

"Good. Because I'm not beyond actually holding you hostage." I wasn't above becoming a monster to keep her safe.

"Has the Queen ever agreed to let a human cross?"

She sounded too curious. And in Tearmann, curiosity only led to one thing: Death. "Why?" I practically shouted, the pinching in my chest twisting into something ugly. Something difficult to control.

"Calm down, it's just a question."

"Dammit, Aveen. I thought we were past this." I thought she was content here. Maybe even happy.

"I was only asking out of curiosity."

"You're curious, are you? Well, then allow me to appease your *curiosity*. Yes, the Queen has let humans in to Tearmann. As a matter of fact, she let your sister through, accepting Tadhg's life as payment for her 'death tax.' There have been humans who want to get into Tearmann so badly that they bring another human to offer as a sacrifice. Do you know what else she's done? She's let people cross back and forth, then changed her feckin' mind so that those people could never cross the Forest again." There seemed to be no rhyme or reason to it, but I was convinced the Queen's decisions were made based on inflicting maximum damage.

Aveen reached for me. "Rían—"

I shrugged her off, needing her to understand the sort of psychopath who ruled that cursed stretch of land. "And then those people were foolish and thought they could break the feckin' rules, and they ended up getting killed for it. So, no, Aveen, it's not just a 'question.' Not to me."

I'd lost my first love and my heart to the Forest. If I lost my soulmate . . . I wasn't sure I would survive.

"Who was she?" Aveen whispered.

Could I tell her? How could I not? I sighed, feeling the weight of *her* name on my tongue. "Her name was Leesha." And she was as good and kind as Aveen. And look what loving her had cost us both.

"And the Queen . . . She killed her?"

"Wanted me to do it, actually. To put my duty to my people over my useless emotions. 'Your human broke the rules and must suffer the consequences.'" For years, the Queen's mocking voice had haunted not only my dreams but every waking thought, a shadow as relentless as those waves. "When I refused, she did it for me."

"Your vengeance," Aveen murmured.

My useless, pointless vengeance.

"You have the dagger now," she went on, lacing our fingers together. *Not our fingers*. Hers and Ruairi's. "Why don't you just kill her?"

"If a true immortal cuts another using that cursed blade, the curse will claim them both." A failsafe from those ancient witches who had forged the dagger centuries earlier. True immortals were powerful enough as it was.

"A human can use it," she guessed.

"All it takes is a single cut for the curse to steal our life force. But since no human can enter the Forest without her permission . . ." I shrugged. "You see the problem." In this game, there were no winners.

"What if the Queen leaves the Forest?"

"She doesn't." And if she did, there would be a lot more to worry about than that feckin' dagger.

"But what if you convinced her to? I'm human. And we both know I have it in me to stab someone."

"You're not human," I said. "You're mine."

28

THE RUG WAS HIDEOUS. WHY ANYONE WOULD CHOOSE THAT SHADE of shite-brown was beyond me. Still, there was no sense spending an excessive amount of coin on decorating the cottage when there was no knowing when, or even if, Aveen would be able to call it home. And if she did make it here alive, that woman was liable to sweep in and change everything. Best to leave it the way it was.

"Should hold in a storm, which is about as good an indication as any that yer one won't be drowned when it rains," Marcus said, the smoke from his pipe vanishing into the salty air. The sea crashed on the horizon.

When I'd arrived this morning, I couldn't believe the progress he'd made while I was back in Tearmann. All that was left to do was straighten the hinges on the door that seemed to go crooked every other day and give the place a lick of paint.

I turned away from the house, catching a glimpse of Phil meandering by a thicket that still needed cut. I'd decided to leave the overgrown gardens to their own devices so Aveen could have more weeds to play with.

Marcus was still staring at the cottage, puffing on that pipe. I couldn't have done this without him, meaning I was in his debt. A place I never stayed for long. "Thank you," I said.

He wasn't looking at me, but his mouth twisted into a smirk around his pipestem. "That wasn't so hard, now, was it?"

Ungrateful oaf. I fought off a smile of my own. Phil seemed to have gotten stuck behind some bushes. They rattled, and he bleated. Served him right after shitting all over the lawn.

"You know where I can get a tin of paint?" I asked.

Marcus shifted on his feet, tucking his free hand into his pocket. "Might. What color would ye be wantin'?"

There was only one color I wanted painted on my human's door.

"Blue."

The apartment I'd rented in Graystones seemcd to be empty. I didn't bother checking to see if any of the furniture remained. None of it mattered anymore. So, instead of stopping, I kept my glamour in place until I reached Meranda's shop, finding her where she always seemed to be: hunched over her sewing machine at the back of the empty store.

Meranda's head snapped up when the doorbell jingled. She was on her feet a moment later, stalking between dress forms and hanging garments, closing the distance between us.

Before she could say what was clearly burning on her tongue, I told her, "You will come with me."

She scoured the empty shop over my shoulder. "Is that an official order from the throne, then? Because I do not see yer brother."

"It is a request," I said through my teeth.

Meranda crossed her arms over her chest. "Didn't sound like a request."

"Come with me, *please*."

A smile. "That's better. Where are we goin'?"

I held out my hand. When she took it without hesitation, I tried not to think too much about it. Except, why didn't she hesitate? Why wasn't she pressing me for details? She wasn't foolish enough to truly trust me, was she? Why wasn't she terrified? She should have been. Had my leniency on Anwen already reached this far? Was my reputation in tatters already?

Meranda's magic mingled with mine, allowing me to bring her all the way to the portal in Hollowshade. I wouldn't dare arrive any closer to the cottage for fear of someone finding out where I planned on hiding my human. *If* I could get her out of Tearmann.

Meranda didn't ask questions. She simply followed me down the embankment toward the sea, away from the faint orange glow of the village.

When we reached the cottage and I found the door had been painted blue, it took everything in me not to grin. The shade was perfect. Aveen would love it.

Meranda reached for the gate. A hairy head popped up from the other side of the wall, making us both jump.

"Why did you bring me here?" she asked, exchanging a scowl with the devil goat.

"I want you to ward the cottage against magic so no one can use it within or evanesce directly inside." That cottage would become a sanctuary from me and my kind. The safest place for Aveen outside of the castle.

Meranda's lips pursed. "Who lives here?"

"No one."

She glanced sidelong at me. "Ye want me to waste magic warding a cottage with no one in it?"

"That's right."

"Why can't ye do it?"

I couldn't do it for the same reason I'd renovated this place by hand: I didn't want my magical signature anywhere near this cottage or this village. Without a signature, even the best scryer wouldn't be able to find it.

But I didn't explain any of that because it was no one's business but mine.

"If ye don't give me answers, then I'll be headin' away." Meranda turned back toward the road.

I caught her arm before she could evanesce. "It's for . . . *her.*"

Meranda wasn't a complete eejit and seemed to understand my meaning. "So she's not dead, then?"

I shook my head.

She pulled out of my grasp, returning to rest her hands on the gate. This time, Phil paid us no mind. "It's a mite small, isn't it?"

It wasn't small, it was quaint. Aveen would love it. I was ninety percent sure. "If you tell anyone about this place, I will end you."

"She was my friend long before she was yer . . . whatever she is."

"She is nothing. This is the final part of a bargain we struck. Still, it would do no good to have *someone* learn of my involvement and mistake it for something more."

Meranda studied me for what felt like forever. I pinned a bored expression on my face, waiting for her to get on with it. Eventually, she turned back to the cottage and lifted her hands, twisting them and speaking in low tones as an ancient spell fell over the quiet cottage. Magic in every shade of green painted the exterior as Meranda poured more and more into her spell. It wasn't the one I would've used, but interrupting would've broken her concentration, potentially weakening the ward. When she finished, the house emitted a faint, iridescent glow. The colors would fade in no time, but for the moment, it looked as if the cottage had been encased in a soapy bubble.

Meranda sagged against the wall, gasping for breath.

"That's the best you can do?" I asked, earning a glare from the witch. "Don't give me that look. It's a simple question."

She pushed away from the stones, gathering her hair back from her face and sighing into the breeze. "If I want to get home, it is."

"Why'd you use that spell instead of Cosantóir?"

"Sciath is a more subtle cast and shouldn't draw the attention of any callers comin' by."

Aveen wouldn't be having any callers. Would she? The old man, sure. Perhaps she'd make a friend or two. I couldn't begrudge her company, now, could I? But what about other men? They'd be arriving in droves once they spied an unmarried woman. Smelly fishermen. Dirty Sailors. Even that fat baker would come sniffin' around.

"Can you make it so that only she and her sister are allowed inside?" I asked.

"That'd cause her a great deal of problems, wouldn't it? Not bein' able to invite folks in fer a cuppa."

I didn't want to cause Aveen problems, but . . . "Only women then."

Meranda scowled up at me. "Is this yer home or hers? If she wants to be keepin' out male callers, then all she has to do is tell 'em to stay away. If that's all, Yer *Highness*, then I'll be goin' back to my sewing."

"Thank you." *Look at that.* Twice in the same day. Miracles did happen.

My eyelids slowly lifted as the sun rose through the curtainless windows. As much as I would have preferred to spend all morning lying abed with Aveen, there was pain to inflict. When I'd returned to the castle last night, I'd found her drunk as a lark, laughing and giggling with my brother and his pet. I'd managed to extricate her from their dreadful company and bring her up to my chambers, where she'd proceeded to strip out of all her clothes and torture me with her curves and silky-smooth skin.

When I insisted that I wouldn't touch her when she was drunk, she'd edged closer, her legs grazing mine, putting my nerves on high alert. I'd promised to make her life hell in the morning.

And now morning had arrived.

I tickled her cheek. She swatted at me. I did it again, and she mumbled a sleepy protest.

When I flicked her beautiful nose, her eyes flew open, red-rimmed and glassy. If she thought she was miserable now, she was in for a big surprise. "Good morning," I said brightly.

"Leave me alone." She stole all the covers, leaving me as bare as the day I was born.

I flicked her nose again. "Not a feckin' hope. Wake up." One way or another, she would be out of this bed in the next five minutes, or I'd shift a bucket of water and dump it on her beautiful head.

"I don't want to," she whined, frowning as she rubbed her reddened nose.

"And I don't care." I couldn't resist one cuddle, because I'd gone soft and the idea of waking her with anything but kisses caused me physical pain. "The sun is shining, and we are going out for a long, strenuous hike. At least ten miles."

She rubbed her arse all over me.

Not a hope would I let her win this game. My cock could wait its turn. Aveen giggled as if victory was already hers, so I gave her nose one more good flick.

"Ouch! That hurts."

If she wanted to talk about pain, I'd gladly go into explicit detail of the pain she'd caused me last night. "Fair's fair. You torture me, I torture you."

She stretched her hands toward the headboard, the quilt slipping low enough to leave me reconsidering my method of torture this morning. I reached for her breast, but the knowing smirk on her lips was enough to keep me on my original path. "Out of bed hungover Aveen. There's walking to be done."

Like every other time I left the castle grounds with my human I wore a glamour. Any time my hand brushed hers, I could feel the barrier between us, and I hated it.

I never slowed my strides, not even when she fell behind. After a moment or two, she usually caught up, out of breath and cursing. And when she didn't, I grabbed her hand and hauled her along behind me.

"It's a beautiful day, isn't it? Just look at that sunrise."

Aveen stubbed her toe on a rock, swearing and stomping around like a child having a tantrum. "You are far too happy this morning."

"Torture is my second favorite thing to do."

"And the first?"

"I'll show you when we get back to the castle." The fact that I had to use Ruairi's voice to make the suggestive comment gave me a twitch.

"Where are we going?"

"Down the coast."

"Why?"

"Why not?"

"I can think of a million reasons," she groaned.

"I take back what I said about miserable Aveen. She is quite entertaining. Maybe you should remember this next time Tadhg asks you to go drinking." We all enabled him at one point or another, but she'd think twice the next time.

"He didn't ask. I offered."

"Why?"

"He's my sister's husband. I should try to get to know him."

"What's there to know? He's a miserable drunk who happened to be born first, so his arse sits on the throne."

Aveen trudged around a large boulder. "If you truly believed that, you wouldn't be following him."

I evanesced to the top, then met her on the other side with a smirk. "It's my duty to follow him." Just as it was my duty to make her life hell this morning.

She snorted. "I don't believe for a second that if you thought he wasn't what Tearmann needed, you would let him rule."

It was adorable that she believed I had a say in the matter. "I don't let Tadhg do anything. He is his own man."

"You love him."

"I tolerate him. Just as I tolerate you." I nudged her shoulder with mine.

She nudged me back, a smile playing on her lips. "You're not as scary as you think you are."

"Those I've murdered would probably disagree."

"Can't fool me."

"No?"

"Not anymore. I see through the glamours and lies to who you are deep down."

I stopped dead. "And who is that?" I asked, trying not to let my desperation show. She considered me for a moment, her head tilting. The beads of sweat along her hairline glistened in the sunlight. I found myself holding my breath. Who did this woman think I was?

Eventually, a smile tugged at her lips, and her eyes softened. "Someone worthy of love."

She didn't know the things I'd done, the things I would continue to do when necessary. She couldn't understand the depth and breadth of the hatred filling the empty cavity in my chest. Burrowing into my marrow. Tainting my soul.

I swallowed my disappointment, knowing it was only a matter of time before she realized the person she thought I was wasn't the real me. "Less talking, more walking."

She cursed and grumbled, but continued on, following me down the coast and through the hills.

It was one of the nicest days I'd ever had.

29

Aveen wasn't in her garden. I'd come straight here after the trial, hoping to find my sunshine playing in the dirt. Oscar waved to me as I approached the kitchen door. For some reason, I waved back.

I found Eava in the kitchens, and Ruairi on my seat, munching on a pile of raw vegetables. He raised his head, a carrot dangling between his fingers. "What are ye doing with yer face?"

I stamped a kiss to Eava's temple and stole a cinnamon biscuit, wondering if Aveen had put in the request. "What are you on about?"

"That thing. With yer mouth," Ruairi said, gesturing toward me with the carrot.

"Smiling?"

"That is not a smile."

I scowled.

"Oh, thank feck." Ruairi clasped his heart. "I thought it would stay like that forever."

Eava giggled from the fireplace. Not sure why. It wasn't even that funny.

I took another biscuit. "Where is my hostage?" I asked the dog.

"Hasn't come down yet. Not sure what she's doing, but she left me a note asking me to meet her here."

Strange. I'd left her shortly after breakfast, and she'd said she wanted to get some planting done today. Why would she have told Ruairi to meet her in the kitchens instead of the gardens? I checked her rooms, but they were empty. She wasn't in the tower with Keelynn either.

I checked the gardens once more, and even asked Oscar if he'd seen her. He said she'd come out around half an hour ago and met Ruairi by the fountain. Then they'd gone for a walk, same as they had every other day this week.

Only Ruairi wasn't on a walk with Aveen. He was in the feckin' kitchen.

The humid air felt too thick for my lungs. I tried to drag in a breath but couldn't. "Which way did they go?"

"Down toward the cottages."

I didn't hear another word he said, sprinting through the wards. If she had a thirty-minute head start, there was no telling how far she'd gone. My gaze met the line of trees in the distance. In thirty minutes, she could've made it to the feckin' Forest.

I evanesced to the cottages and went straight to Anwen's stoop. The moment my fist connected with the door, the barrier flew open. Anwen's eldest stood on the other side, glaring.

"Have you seen the human I keep at the castle?" I asked, not caring that I sounded like a raving lunatic.

"The pretty one with curly hair?"

"Yes."

The girl pointed toward the forest. "She went that way with the handsome lad she's courtin'."

Is that what people thought? That Aveen and Ruairi were together? Sure, why wouldn't they? I'd been taking her out every day glamoured as the beast. *It doesn't matter.* If anything, I should've been happy that the rumors were helping my ruse.

I evanesced straight to the Black River, searching for any

traces of my human on either side of the shore. I couldn't find her. No footprints. No sounds. No body . . .

Bile burned up my throat.

What if she'd already crossed? What if the Queen had taken her? What if she was gone forever? I was about to evanesce to the Queen's castle when I heard a scream that brought winter to my soul.

My boots slipped. It was impossible to pinpoint where she could be. Evanescing would be useless. So, I ran. And ran. And with each step, I prayed. Even knowing no one had ever answered my prayers, I prayed.

Through the trees, I glimpsed a flash of blue. Her shrieks of terror would haunt me until my final days. I evanesced, finding Aveen in a ball on the leaf-strewn ground, her hands bound with coarse rope, the skin beneath raw and bleeding.

I pressed a hand to her back, racking my brain for who could have done this. She rolled, punching and kicking and scratching my arms, my face.

"Aveen, stop."

She blinked and blinked, my horrified expression reflecting in her still-searching eyes, as if she couldn't see me kneeling right next to her. "I'm here."

"I can't see," she wailed. "I can't see. Help me. I can't see you."

"I'm right here." *I'm here. I'm sorry. I never should've left.* I smoothed my thumb along her tear-stained lashes, sending healing magic to remove whatever spell the fiend had used to steal her sight. When I found the person responsible . . . He would pray for death.

"Open your eyes."

Aveen blinked up at me, eyes still swimming with tears. I gathered the hair from her dirt-streaked cheeks, searching for lies of comfort that I couldn't find as I glanced over at the river and Forest beyond. She'd almost been sacrificed to the Forest, and it was all my fault. I was a fool for believing she'd be safe.

I shifted my dagger, cutting the ropes before inspecting them. Nothing special. Thick and brown, inexpensive. Could've been found in just about any tool shed.

I slipped my arms beneath Aveen, holding her trembling body against mine. Getting us both back to the gates drained far too much magic, but I did it anyway. I glowered at each and every suspect as we passed. The unfamiliar pooka cleaning his nails with a pocketknife in the stables. The grogoch transferring peaches from a cart into a basket. The two women carrying baskets of clean laundry. The leprechauns chatting next to the stairs. The merrow on the fountain's edge.

Aveen's eyes remained screwed shut, but some of the color had returned to her cheeks by the time I brought her into the parlor.

When they saw me, Tadhg and Ruairi rocketed to their feet, their expressions darkening as they took in Aveen's state.

"What happened?" Tadhg demanded, raking a hand through his hair. For once, his eyes weren't bloodshot.

"I found her tied up in the forest, shrieking like a feckin' banshee."

"They took me," Aveen whispered in a tiny voice. "They took me to the Forest."

Ruairi pressed a hand to Aveen's shoulder. "Who took ye?"

Aveen flinched as if he'd struck her. Her short nails dug into my arm, like she'd burrow into me if she could have. "He looked like you. I thought he was you. I wouldn't have gone if I'd known. If I'd seen his eyes."

"What color?" Tadhg asked.

"Black."

A glamour like that would've taken a considerable amount of magic and an intimate knowledge of the man. Someone who knew Ruairi well enough to imitate him. We were looking for a witch, I'd stake my life on it. And a powerful one at that.

A witch who practiced black magic. The Queen was strong enough, but she never used a glamour—she hoarded her magic like a dragon with gold. If she'd come for Aveen, she wouldn't have bothered with a glamour. It had to be someone else.

"You said 'they.' How many were there?" Tadgh asked.

"Two. A man and a woman."

Maybe. Maybe not. They both could've been glamoured. There could've been a third person involved in masterminding the whole plan. Hell, for all I knew, this could be an entire conspiracy.

Tadgh's gaze flicked to me before returning to Aveen. I held her a little closer, wishing I could tell her that she was safe now, but I couldn't. Even if we caught the culprits, she still wouldn't be safe. Humans were too fragile to survive in Tearmann.

When Tadgh asked if she'd crossed the river, Aveen shook her head.

We had no suspects. No evidence. Nothing.

Going to the Queen and asking for safe passage now would only draw her focus. What was I going to do?

Ruairi stepped forward. Aveen stiffened. I adjusted my hold, tucking her head beneath my chin.

"Aveen?" Ruairi said, his voice soft. "Is it all right if I come closer?"

She nodded, letting the dog sniff her. Then his eyes met mine.

He'd found something.

Tadgh clapped his mate on the back and promised they'd handle it.

I didn't want them to handle it. I wanted to be the one to deal with whoever had stolen her from me. But I needed to be there for Aveen. I couldn't leave her like this.

I brought her up to my room, not caring if I used every last drop of magic from my veins to get her where she needed to be.

"I'm sorry," she whispered.

She was sorry? Whatever the hell for? She had done nothing wrong. *Nothing*. And someone had tried to . . .

I couldn't bring myself to think of what would have happened if she'd crossed that border. So instead, I busied myself with unfastening the buttons on her ruined gown and burning the whole feckin' lot. I heard Aveen suck in a breath when she stepped into the bath I'd shifted, but I couldn't make myself turn from the flames and face my failure.

Fire licked up the stones, the silk smoldering. All the hope I'd found these past few weeks turned into a blackened mass of hopelessness.

For the only way to save him was at her own expense.

That was Aveen's fate, and there was nothing I could do about it.

Death would come for her, and when it did, I wouldn't be able to stop it.

"Are you going to speak to me?" she asked.

I knew what she needed of me. She needed me to pretend everything was going to be fine. That we had a future. That I could keep her safe.

I wasn't sure I had it in me.

"I'm sorry that I—"

"Stop apologizing for something that is not your fault."

"I should've known better," she whispered.

"No, *I* should've known better. This is my world, not yours. I never should've lifted those feckin' wards."

"Where was Ruairi?" Her voice broke on his name.

"He said you left him a note to meet him in the kitchens."

Aveen washed herself as if she could scrub away the memories of what could've happened to her. I wrapped a soft linen towel around her shivering shoulders and shifted her something comfortable to sleep in. She ignored the white cotton shift, slipping beneath my covers and curling onto her side.

I removed my boots and joined her in the bed, needing to hold her, to remind myself that she had survived this. That fate had given me more time with her. I'd hoard these moments, hoard *her* until she was ripped from my grasp.

I slipped an arm around her and buried my nose against her damp hair, breathing her in. "I got a cat for my fifth birthday," I said, desperate to take our minds off the day. "I named him Sir Fluffy Paws."

"That's a good name," she whispered, her tone devoid of emotion.

"It's a feckin' brilliant name. Think of the fluffiest thing you've ever seen, then multiply it by ten. That's how fluffy his paws were."

Dampness seeped into my shirt, her soft tears watering my soul.

"One time, I glamoured myself to look like my father. Nearly got me into a very awkward situation with Tadhg's mam."

"Tadhg's mother?"

"He's only my half-brother. Same philandering father. Different mothers."

After a beat, she asked if I could make myself look like her.

"If I did that, I'd want to touch myself all the time. I'd never get anything done."

I felt her smile against my chest. "You are ridiculous."

"Only for you."

For her, I'd be whatever she wanted. Whatever she needed. All she had to do was say the word.

Her heavy sigh tickled my throat. "Rían? I want a—"

Someone knocked on my door. Reluctantly, I let her go, sliding off the mattress and crossing to the doorway. Tadhg waited on the other side, his eyes swirling with black. "We found them," he said. "They're waiting downstairs."

Aveen and I waited in the study. I needed a moment to compose myself. To make sure I didn't burst through the door and murder everyone. This was a trial only. The executions would come later.

"It'll be all right," I said for what felt like the hundredth time, not sure which one of us I was trying to convince. I needed to get Aveen out of Tearmann, that much was clear. But how?

From the hall, I heard Muireann's voice. Aveen's shoulders stiffened, her wide, panicked eyes swinging toward me.

"You know who she is," I said, although her ghostly pale face was all the confirmation I needed. I should've boiled the feckin' fish when I'd had the chance.

"I need you to come with me." We needed undeniable proof that Muireann was responsible. Once we had it, I'd handle the rest.

"I can't."

"You are the only witness, Aveen. I need you to come with me. We will be with you the entire time." Tadhg, his dog, and I wouldn't let anything happen to her. When I took her cold hand, she didn't try to pull away. She laced our fingers together and clutched my arm with her free hand. I opened the door but kept myself between Aveen and Muireann.

Tadhg used his magic to restrain her, although she didn't try to leave. She just kept smiling. Unease prickled the hair at the back of my neck.

Ruairi escorted Madden into the great room. Once they'd crossed the threshold, I warded the room to prevent evanescing.

"Ah, Madden. Muireann. Nice of you to join us," I greeted.

Madden pointed at Muireann, his face contorting. "The bitch made me do it. She made me."

I always loved that excuse. "Made me." The Queen *made* me do things. She controlled me like a puppet on a string. The merrow may have persuaded him. Convinced him. She certainly didn't *make* him.

"Made you do what, Madden?" I asked, icy darkness collecting at my fingertips.

"Take the human to the Forest."

"Liar!" Muireann hissed.

"And which human is that?" I asked, just so there were no lingering questions when I finally ended him.

Madden pointed at my soulmate.

His fingers would be first to go.

"And how did she 'make' you, Madden?"

"She . . . I . . . You see——"

"I don't see." I shifted my dagger and caught his hand with magic, stretching it toward the wall. "I can *make* you cut off your own fingers." Look at that. Just a spark of magic, and his little finger was gone. I bathed in his screams. Delighted in his terror. "See there? That's me *making* you do something. Do you know what else I could do?"

"P-please . . ." Madden begged.

"I could do it myself." Blood sprayed as I sawed off the rest of his digits. He'd better get used to the pain because, by the time today was over, he'd be begging for death.

Madden whimpered, tears and snot dripping down the bow of his thin lips. I slammed a hand to his chin, forcing his pain-dulled black eyes to mine. "Did Muireann *make* you take my hostage? Because I find it hard to believe a strapping lad such as yourself could be so easily coerced by a rotting fish."

"No, no, Prince Rían," he cried. "She—she told me if I helped her . . . I'd be gettin' back at ye fer lettin' that bitch off without so much as a feckin' day in the dungeon."

He must have been talking about Anwen. Why the hell did he care so much about that witch?

"So, this is about *me* then," I said. "You thought it'd be a good idea to take something from *me*?" The merrow had the gall to sneer. "That was a silly thing to do, wasn't it?"

"I'm sorry——"

"Are you, now? Brilliant. I suppose I should let you go, then." Wouldn't that be kind of me? To forgive and forget. Unfortunately for the pitiful man sniveling against the wall, I wasn't the feckin' hero. "Or I could bring you downstairs."

I ignored Madden's pathetic protests, collecting his digits from the floor and tucking them into his waistcoat pocket. No sense in leaving a mess for Oscar to clean up later. "I'll see you soon."

I disbanded the ward and sent the bastard down to the dungeon.

Muireann met my level gaze with a defiant tilt to her chin. "We both know it's only a matter of time before she comes to take your plaything away. Do you really think—"

Before she could say another feckin' word, I dragged my blade across her traitorous throat. She crumpled to the ground like a rag doll. I knelt, inhaling her lifeforce before it could return to the earth. The warmth of magic swelled in my veins.

Ruairi and Tadhg had created a wall between my human and the spot where I knelt. I rose slowly, wrestling with bloodlust. I wanted to kill everyone. Every last being who drew breath. I wanted them all to die. To tear off their toenails, slice their skin with a serrated blade, roll them in salt, then melt their bones with acid.

I shifted a clean shirt, not wanting Aveen to see the blood on me. I should have stayed back in case I'd terrified her, but I was too weak to stay away. "Aveen, I'm so—"

"I do hope I'm not interrupting," a familiar voice said from the doorway.

My body froze. I should've known better. I should've let Aveen request passage the moment she came back. I should've done everything differently. But I'd been selfish, and now the Queen had found her.

I turned toward the ancient witch. The wards should've kept her out. I'd used every spell I knew, poured years' worth of magic into that protective barrier, and yet here she stood, in my sanctuary, glaring at my human.

I had to get Aveen out. I couldn't let the Queen take her the way she'd taken Leesha.

What the hell was I going to do?

30

"Hello, Mother. Lovely as always to see you," I said, knowing full-well she'd taste my lie. Her hand felt like a corpse's when I pressed my lips to her translucent skin.

The Queen pulled away, glowering down her nose at me, cursed eyes narrowed into slits. "You always were a deceitful boy." She glanced to where Tadhg and Ruairi stood, her eyebrows lifting. "What's this? Another human in Tearmann?"

She may have sounded surprised, but I had a sinking feeling this visit wasn't a coincidence. Muireann must've told the Queen. That was the only explanation that made any sense. I should've taken my time killing her. I should've sent her to the dungeon and carved her flesh in search of answers.

The color leaked from Aveen's cheeks.

I should've done a lot of things.

When Ruairi draped an arm around my human's shoulders, I did my best not to flinch. "We liked her so much," he said, "we decided to keep her."

Maybe the Queen would believe Aveen had stayed for him. To save her, I would look past his possessive hand on hers.

The Queen's head tilted ever so slightly. "When you tire of it, send it across the border."

Aveen clutched the hem of Ruairi's shirt. I wasn't even sure either of them noticed. But I did. I noticed that she clung to him in a way she could never cling to me.

Tadhg started toward us, muttering about feeding the Queen already.

"I'm always hungry," she replied. The Queen could consume every life on this island and I suspected she would still hunger for more death. Her feathered cape dragged with each step she took, following my brother into the hallway and across to the dining hall. The two of us sat on either side of her. Aveen had the good sense to sit next to Tadhg. Ruairi flanked her, leaving me all alone across the table.

I tried to think of ways to remove Aveen from this confrontation, but each one only ended with me showing the Queen how much I cared and with Aveen's heart carved from her chest.

Tadhg shifted a bottle of wine and a bottle of blood we reserved on the off-chance one of the ancient Abartach showed up. I could count the number of times the Queen had visited the castle on two fingers. Once when our father had been murdered, and today.

Tadhg was the first to speak, asking the Queen what brought her to the castle.

She gave some shite excuse about visiting me, phrasing it as a question so it wasn't a lie.

Tadgh muttered a response, none of the tension in his shoulders lingering in his congenial tone.

The Queen's gaze drifted farther down the table, to where Aveen and Ruairi sat far too close together. "I wasn't aware you let your pets sit at the table."

Ruairi seemed to take no notice of her tone, showing off his fangs when he grinned. "Seeing you is always such a delight, my Queen."

The air turned sour with the lie.

"Careful now, *boy*. I'm in need of a new steed."

"I'd give just about anyone a ride, but I'm afraid the Black

Forest wouldn't suit my sunny disposition. And I prefer the living over the dead."

The dog walked a thin line, antagonizing her like that, but if he kept her focus on him, it wouldn't be on Aveen. I almost respected him for it. Almost.

The rich, coppery tang of blood danced in the air when the Queen tilted the black bottle toward my untouched goblet. I tried to focus on everything but the tingling sensation on the back of my tongue, determined to ignore it. Aveen already knew I was the spawn of a monster. She didn't need to know how deep the depravity in me truly ran.

"Speaking of the dead," the Queen said, her tone light and airy, as if discussing the shape of a passing cloud, "I heard a pack of pooka were executed near Mistlaline."

Ruairi's head swung toward Tadhg, accusation in his narrowed golden eyes. "Is that true?"

"Anyone who chooses to live outside of Tearmann understands there is risk involved," Tadhg hedged.

"Tearmann is a pittance of what it once was," the Queen clipped. "When your father ruled, he commanded respect, controlling this island and everyone in it. The human uprising only succeeded because he showed them mercy."

That wasn't entirely true. Our father had shown mercy, but so had his army of Danú, after being forced to face off against humans they'd grown to know—even grown to love. It had been the people who had ultimately decided the island's fate. And our father, heartbroken over the loss of his wife, no longer had it in him to fight. To care. To live.

Tadhg rolled his eyes. Ruairi yawned.

The Queen's expression darkened. Until her gaze landed on the woman sitting between them. "You. Human. What is your name?"

I forced the air from my lungs in a slow, steady breath, hiding my trembling hands beneath my thighs.

"Lady Aveen Bannon, Your Majesty," Aveen replied with only a slight tremor in her voice.

I'd never been so proud.

"What brings you to Tearmann?"

Why hadn't I told her about my mother? Why hadn't I explained so that Aveen knew where I'd inherited my ability to taste lies? I was a fool. A feckin'—

"A kiss," Aveen said.

My human. My *brilliant* human. If she survived this, I was going to kiss her until neither of us could breathe.

"So, you're one of Tadhg's, then?" the Queen asked.

"I am."

Truth.

"Funny. He usually puts them back." The Queen took a long, slow sip from her glass. I swore I could see her mind working. "Why do you linger?"

"Tadhg kissed my sister as well."

The Queen laughed. *Laughed.* I could count the number of times she had genuinely laughed on one hand. "Men. Human or Danú, they're all the same, aren't they?"

Aveen nodded.

"Why did you kiss him?" the Queen pressed.

"To escape a fate worse than death." A smile. "Marriage."

"I'd forgotten how delightfully entertaining humans can be." In all my centuries, I had never heard the Queen's voice sound so . . . jovial. I didn't know whether to be terrified or relieved.

"Is this true, Tadhg?" asked the Queen.

He returned Aveen's smile, saluting my human with his glass of wine. "Every feckin' word."

All at once, the Queen's expression darkened. Her lips pressed tightly together, narrowed eyes searching. "What is your relationship with my son?"

To be fair, Aveen did a pretty damn good job feigning shock. "What do you mean?"

"I heard the two of you were engaged."

Had I really believed the Queen wouldn't have heard about my confession in the courtyard that day?

"We told Tadhg we were to convince him to kiss me. But no, we're not actually engaged. It was all a ruse."

Truth after truth after truth.

"Well, then. It appears as though this trip has been for naught. You see, I was told my useless son had smuggled his human fiancée into Tearmann and was hiding her inside this castle. Clearly, my source was mistaken."

Clearly, her source was feckin' dead. I would find out who had been the one to turn me in, and if it wasn't Muireann, the person would pay. And this time, it wouldn't be quick.

"Clearly," I said.

The Queen's nail clinked on her glass, picking up pace.

Tadhg practically slammed his wine glass down on the table. "Now that we have that cleared up, it's getting quite late. I'm sure everyone is tired."

Aveen's eyes widened, and she looked beneath the table, a blush creeping up her throat. She let out a small whimper, her shoulders moving but the rest of her frozen. It wasn't until her chair scraped across the stones that I realized what was happening. The Queen had her pinned to the feckin' chair by magic. And I couldn't do a feckin' thing about it without giving myself away.

Ruairi tried to stop her, but the Queen sent him away. Tadhg tried as well, but he disappeared a second later. The Queen's clinking came faster and faster, muffled by the pounding and shouting outside in the hallway.

Then it stopped.

My body felt as if it were vibrating as the Queen stretched a black-tipped nail toward Aveen's throat, following the delicate edge of her gown to her breast. Her lips twisted into a mocking smile. "Do you care to explain this, Rían?"

My mark. How the hell did she know about my feckin' mark?
Muireann.

Death had been too good for that feckin' traitor. I swallowed my boiling rage. "If you're asking if I fucked her, the answer is yes." The way Aveen flinched left my stomach sinking lower. Surely, she understood this was the way it had to be. That if the Queen knew I held any affection for her, she'd be as dead as that rotting fish.

The Queen unsheathed her ceremonial dagger, one I'd seen her use on countless humans. My heartbeat couldn't give me away, but I kept my breathing even, just in case.

The tip of the Queen's blade ran along Aveen's collarbone. I gripped the arms of my chair until the wood creaked.

"Are you truly so weak that you'd lift your skirts for a pretty face and a few whispered lies?" the Queen said. "You'd abandon your family and your people to live amongst us, where you are despised, all for a man who has more interest in his collection of waistcoats than he has in you."

"I tell her all the time how pathetic she is," I said, grabbing my wine glass, nearly dropping it when the Queen's dagger stopped at Aveen's heart.

"Pathetic enough to fall in love with you?"

"I'm not in love with him," Aveen said with conviction. Conviction that didn't make a blind bit of difference as the air turned syrupy sweet.

She loved me.

This beautiful, kind, good, human . . . loved *me.*

I couldn't wrap my head around it. We were meant to be together, our souls bound to collide, but love? I had never hoped for love.

And that foolish love had just sealed her fate.

"There's no need to lie to me, *girl.*" The Queen adjusted her grip on the hilt, pressing it against Aveen's skin until a drop of deep red blood oozed from the wound. Tears glistened in her eyes and all I could do was sit there and watch. Making a move against the Queen would be suicide for us both. And I knew beyond a shadow of a doubt that if I made my feelings clear, the witch wouldn't hesitate to make me rip the heart from Aveen's chest.

So I sat there like a coward and did *nothing*.

"You wouldn't be the first human he's played with," the Queen yammered on, "and you certainly won't be the last. He insists on these childish rebellions, rutting with chattel and the like. I've come to remind my son that he cannot afford such distractions from his duties."

Even knowing she wouldn't listen, I told the Queen to get out. The shadow guards closed ranks, flanking their master, as if we'd be foolish enough to attack.

"You think you can throw me out? You have no authority here." She waved her dagger at me as I knew she would. She could point it at me all she wanted as long as she left Aveen alone. "This isn't your castle. You're a lodger—a leech aligning himself with true power because you have *none*."

"You've made your point."

She cackled. "Oh, I don't think I have." She turned her blade over and slammed it into my thigh. Pain exploded from the wound. Her spell took hold, dragging away my control. Forcing me to stab myself over and over and over with her blade.

I screamed at the magical barrier keeping me hostage until my throat was raw. I'd been amassing power for centuries. I should have been able to break free. I should have been able to crack the barrier, and yet all I could do was stare as my hands did *her* bidding.

"You forget, *son*," she spat, as if the word were a curse, "that I have owned you since the day I tore the heart from your chest." She turned toward Aveen's pale face. "*This* is what you *love*." She slapped me so hard my teeth rattled. "An empty husk spelled to do my bidding whenever I choose to take control. If I wished him dead, he would cease to draw breath."

My hand spasmed, and the dagger clattered to the floor. My chest refused to expand or contract, frozen like I'd been encased in a steel shroud.

"Why?" Aveen sobbed, shaking her head, spilling golden curls over her shoulders.

Black spots swelled at the edge of my vision. The Queen's words turned muffled, as if I'd been buried in a shallow grave.

But I heard her final words clear as day.

Return to your world tonight, human, for my mercy will not extend to daylight.

The doors burst open. The Queen was gone, and yet her influence remained, gripping me in a chokehold.

"Rían?" Aveen spoke my name with such hope.

Hope was like love, for fools and simpletons.

She's made me weak.

End her.

No one could stop me.

Tadhg was feckin' useless. His pooka would be dead with one careful swipe of my blade.

She's done nothing wrong.

That wasn't entirely true, was it?

She'd fallen for my selfish lies. Believed I was some sort of white knight instead of a monster born of darkness and hate.

Don't make me hurt her. Not her. Anyone but her.

Tadhg grabbed me by the shoulders. "Look at me. *Look at me.* You have to fight her."

The pooka blocked my view of the girl.

Aveen.

Her name became my desperation. My prayer. My salvation.

Like swimming toward a lighthouse in a stormy sea, my head broke free of the surface long enough to rasp, "I release you from our bargain," before dragging me back to the depths where I belonged. Shadows swelled, filling my throat and lungs and veins until all that remained of me was a tiny voice, whispering not to hurt her.

I sent Tadhg and Ruairi flying.

"Rían . . . No . . . Please," the human begged. The weak ones always begged. The ones who still clung to the futility of hope.

Her throat bobbed as tears streamed.

I told the human to run, wanting the thrill of the chase. To catch her and paint that pretty blue dress red.

I felt the cold kiss of steel against my throat.

The last thing I saw before death took me was a pair of terrified blue eyes.

My gullet burned like the fires of hell. I was barely able to swallow back the bile threatening to rise. I couldn't move my feckin' arms. My eyes opened, but everything around me remained dark, and it took far too long for the world to come into focus. When it did, I searched for the one face I longed to see.

But Aveen wasn't there.

Just darkness, damp stones, metal bars, and a pair of glowing green eyes.

"Where is she?" I croaked, my innards ablaze.

Tadhg grimaced from where he leaned against the far wall.

"Where is she?" I demanded. "Just tell me. Please. Tell me where she is. I need to see her. Please." I needed to make sure she was all right. To explain. To apologize. To memorize her face one last time. To say goodbye. To say I was so sorry for putting her life in jeopardy. I'd known what I was doing from the moment I first touched her, and yet I'd kept going because I was a selfish bastard.

Tadhg's jaw ticked beneath his stubble. "Ruairi is keeping her safe."

Ruairi. Keeping her safe—keeping her away from me. Worming his way into her heart and into her bed, and the worst part was, I had no right to protest.

"Where?" I wouldn't go. I just wanted to know, to make sure wherever he'd taken her was the safest place, that they hadn't overlooked something obvious in their panic to get her away from the Queen.

"If you end up killing her, you'll never forgive yourself."

"I would never—"

"You almost did."

"No . . ." Even at my darkest, I never would have hurt Aveen.

"Rían, you know this is the way it has to be. She's safe now. That needs to be enough."

Enough? I could live a thousand lifetimes with Aveen and it would never be enough. I should've spent all the time I'd been given with her. Instead, I'd wasted it on a feckin' cottage and helping my brother rule this cursed territory. And for what?

Tadhg was a fool if he believed Aveen would ever be safe as long as the Queen drew breath. She may have let her go to bring me to heel, but if she ever found out where Aveen was hiding, she would use her against me in the worst way.

The Queen needed to die.

And fate had brought me the one weapon I needed to make it happen.

31

I READ THE LETTER ON THE DESK FOR WHAT FELT LIKE THE hundredth time, struggling to keep my mind from drifting. The Queen had been right. Aveen had distracted me from my goal. She'd made me believe that I didn't need vengeance. That I didn't need anything or anyone but her.

But now she was gone.

I wanted to wallow. To lie abed all day, every day, drinking myself into a stupor.

Instead, I killed.

First, Madden. I'd carved him up, removed digit after digit on his remaining hand before moving to his toes, making sure no one else had been in on Muireann's plan. I'd bathed in his screams. And when his screams gave way to begging and pleading, I laughed. Had he planned on showing Aveen mercy when he'd dragged her to the edge of that Forest? No. He had planned on feeding her to the Queen like a lamb led to slaughter.

I'd torn the flesh from his bones, leaving him in pieces on the ground. The moment he died, I'd consumed his life force, my hollowness filling with liquid fire as my power grew.

I'd found the witnesses from the pooka trials in Mistlaline and killed them in a similar fashion. A human's life force may have been a pittance compared to ours, but I'd need all the help I could get when I made my final stand against the Queen.

Today, a witch was being tried in Gaul.

No name accompanied the missive, so I wasn't sure how powerful she would be, but I'd take anything and everything. Hopefully it would be enough, because once I left, I wouldn't be coming back. The cursed dagger laid on the desk beside the missive, its emerald glowing brighter when I traced the hilt.

Tonight, I would evanesce to the Queen's castle and enter the gates for the very last time. Tonight, both of us would be no more.

Tadhg would have to figure out how to function without me. If Ruairi ever came back, he would help.

It's not your problem anymore.

I pushed to my feet and grabbed my coat from the back of the back of the chair. Eava appeared in the doorway, a tray of choco late buns in her hand. "Where are ye off to, my sweet boy?"

"A trial in Gaul," I muttered, tugging on my coat.

Eava's gaze followed the cursed dagger as I tucked it into my sheath and hid it behind me. "What would ye be needing that dagger fer?"

My teeth clenched so hard it felt like my jaw would shatter. "Do me a favor. Don't let Tadhg drink himself into a stupor tonight. He'll need to have a clear head in the morning."

"Rían—"

"Tell him I've left the ledgers in his bedside locker, next to the one he keeps."

"Rían, what's in yer head?"

I crossed the room, stopping when I reached the witch. Then stole a bun, kissed Eava on the forehead, and evanesced.

Cigar smoke and chatter filled the frigid courtroom. Human nattering on about the weather. Upcoming plans. Some recent scandal. Not one person assembled in the round room appeared the least bit concerned by the impending trial. It sounded like a night at the pub instead of a court of law, with about the same amount of justice being served. The magistrate—a shriveled man without so much as a strand of hair beneath his curly white wig—sat on a chair behind a mammoth desk, black robes concealing his withered frame.

Two soldiers in red livery entered through a side door. Same as always, dragging some poor—and likely innocent—Danú behind—

I blinked.

And blinked again.

I scrubbed my eyes with the heels of my hands, but nothing seemed to help.

Because every time I looked at the person the guards had clapped in chains, I saw Aveen.

Her luscious golden curls matted. Her dress torn, hem blackened, speckled with dark stains that looked a lot like blood.

Witch, a man behind me murmured.

She wasn't a feckin' witch. She was as human as the rest of them.

Monster, his bespectacled companion agreed with a nod that shook his jowls.

My hand fell to the dagger at my belt. I'd show him a feckin' monster.

Murderer.

There must have been some mistake.

She flinched when the magistrate slammed the gavel. The room fell silent as the soldiers forced my soulmate down onto the stool, swords drawn, aimed at her. If they so much as twitched, I'd have their heads.

"What's your name, witch?" the magistrate demanded.

Aveen's dirt-smudged chin lifted. "My name is Lady Aveen Bannon. And I am not a witch."

Leave it to her to hold on to her stubborn pride in the face of such an impossible situation. If they truly believed her to be a witch—and it wasn't looking good—then her fate was already sealed.

I cleared my throat, not knowing what the hell I was going to say, only that I had to say something. Aveen leaned forward on her stool, her gaze locking with mine. Although my expression remained impassive, beads of sweat collected along my hairline and at the back of my neck. Her eyes widened, as if she could see straight through my glamour. I checked my hands to ensure it hadn't slipped. They were still as freckled and pale as they had been when I arrived.

"Do you have something to say, emissary?" the magistrate sniffed.

I'd been to enough "trials" to understand the court's mind was made up well before anyone set foot inside the courthouse. Aveen wouldn't be walking out of this alive. There was only one way I could think to save her. And that meant giving the people what they were looking for.

Give them a witch.

"The witch's name is Brian," I said. "It delights in taking the form of loved ones who've passed in order to infiltrate their homes and rob their families blind."

Aveen let out a whimper, eyes shimmering with unshed tears. "He's lying. My name is Lady Aveen Bannon."

Trust me, I wanted to shout. Instead, I reached into my bag and used far too much magic to falsify a death certificate for Aveen. "According to this death certificate, Lady Aveen Bannon died last March."

The magistrate waved me forward, taking the false document as if he were admitting it to evidence instead of barely glancing at it and tucking the thing into a drawer to never be seen again. He never questioned how the hell I had gotten my hands on a death certificate with only a day's notice. And why would he, when my statement had solidified his argument?

"What are the charges against the witch?" I asked.

The old man looked down his nose at the documents on the desk. "Murder."

"Murder, you say?" I could imagine Aveen committing theft, perhaps, if she were desperate. But *murder*?

A nod. "The witch murdered a young man named Robert Trench."

Feckin' hell. My little viper had finally given the bastard what he deserved. I stole a glance, finding her glowering at me. "And how has it pleaded?"

"How do you plead, witch?" the magistrate grumbled in a tone that made it clear he'd rather be anywhere else but here. Just what you wanted from an "impartial" judge.

She shot to her feet, chains banging against the floor. "He tried to force himself on me! He attacked me! He slammed my head against a wall and tried to—"

Her accusations rang with truth. Not that the vicious crowd, pointing and shouting at her, noticed. A fresh wave of rage crashed over me. That this innocent woman had been assaulted, and these fools—these feckin' *monsters*—were more concerned with seeking "justice" for the man who had committed the crime.

The pounding gavel echoed through my mind as the magistrate demanded order. The stack of papers beside him fell to the ground. I caught sight of my dagger hidden beneath them, blood staining the blade and handle. How in the hell had they gotten my feckin' blade? Had Aveen stolen it before she left the castle? No. That couldn't be the case. I'd used it to carve up Madden. What the hell was going on?

"And I will have justice!" Aveen hissed. "I have a right to defend myself. I have a right to—" Soldiers caught her arms, forcing her down on the stool. I committed their faces to memory. Neither would be alive to see the sun rise.

And Robert . . . he was lucky she had killed him, because if I'd found the bastard—

"The punishment for murder is death," the magistrate

announced. "Tomorrow at dawn, you will be brought to the gallows and hung by the neck until dead."

I cleared my throat, waiting until the magistrate's narrowed eyes found me. "Yes, emissary?"

"With all due respect, hanging isn't the most effective way to execute a witch."

"And what, pray tell, is the most effective way to execute a witch?" the magistrate sighed.

"Beheading."

First, I located the witnesses from Aveen's trial. Although they hadn't given testimony, their addresses had been listed on the court documents. I left them drowning in their own blood at their dining room tables. Next came the soldiers who'd manhandled Aveen at court. They deserved a more gruesome death, but I didn't really have the time for creativity. Finally, I returned to the prison, glamoured to look like the one I'd left at the bottom of a staircase with a broken neck.

No one stopped me from entering the jail. I found a few guards playing cards in a room off the hallway, leaving only one guard on a chair across from the cells. A simple sleeping spell left him snoozing away like a cat on a sunny afternoon.

Aveen sat curled in the corner of her cell, holding her knees to her chest, staring blankly at a dish of bread. I dropped my glamour before kicking the doors. "What a mess you're in," I said, somehow managing to keep my voice steady.

Her dull eyes lifted, then fell back to the straw-covered floor. "Go away."

"Ah, here now, you're not nearly as fun when you're melancholy." I gave the guard's foot a nudge with my own. "Do you care to tell me why these eejits believe you're a witch?"

"They don't think a proper lady is capable of murdering a strong, powerful man."

What a feckin' joke. Some of the deadliest creatures I knew were women. "And how do you explain this?" I showed her my dagger, found at the scene of the murder, that I'd commandeered along with the documents.

"I can't." When she shifted her hold on her knees, I heard a faint hiss. That's when I noticed the red welts covering her wrists.

I fell to my knees. "Let me see your wrists." She held her hands toward me, and my stomach clenched. What had they done to her? "Feckin' hell . . ." I touched the edge of the manacle just to be sure—*dammit*. Made of feckin' iron.

Aveen was human, though. Iron shouldn't have left those marks on her arms.

I shifted a pair of gardening gloves I'd bought the week before but never got around to giving to her. "Take these."

She whimpered as she shoved the manacles higher, tears trailing down her smudged cheeks as the iron hissed and burned anew. "Thank you for the gloves."

"Anything else?"

"Thank you for telling them to chop off my head." The fire flashing in her eyes quickly died out.

"Hanging is a dreadful way to die," I explained. "Beheading is by far the quickest and most painless."

"Just get out."

Feckin' hell . . . She honestly thought I planned on leaving her here to die.

I stood, working and reworking the plan I'd forged during my morning murder-spree. Since I couldn't do it, I'd need someone to get Aveen out of the cell unnoticed. Where could she go? Tadhg had a few friends around here. Perhaps one of them could hide Aveen until we could get her out of the city and to the cottage—

Not *we*.

I'd be dead.

A bucket of water next to the unconscious guard caught my eye. When I stuck my finger inside, it burned like hell.

"It's witch hazel," Aveen muttered.

"How do you know?" Her human senses would've been too weak to smell the herb.

"The guard doused me with it. Felt like they'd peeled the skin from my bones."

I'd been doused in witch hazel before, and for months afterwards, I'd woken up screaming from nightmares. Not the sort of torture one could ever forget. Or forgive. "Who did?" I kicked the guard's disgusting boot. "This one?"

She nodded.

Witch hazel and iron burned. She'd gotten my dagger somehow. It felt like I was missing something obvious. Not that it would matter if I didn't get her out of this predicament.

She could escape the cell right now. The keys were just there. I could glamour her to look like one of the dead guards. Only, her face would be on wanted posters from coast to coast. She couldn't cross the Forest again, and after what had happened with Muireann, Tearmann wouldn't be safe even if she could come back in. How could I guarantee her safety in Hollowshade?

"Don't you have anywhere else to be?" she grumbled.

"I'm waiting."

"For what?"

"For you to stop feeling sorry for yourself and bargain with me."

I caught the first spark of hope since she'd seen me in the courthouse and her first smile. "What are your terms, oh great and powerful prince?" she asked.

"If I decide to use my immense power to save a weak, pathetic human such as yourself, then you must promise to never set foot in the Black Forest."

"I don't agree to those terms. Come up with something else."

There was nothing else. She could never come back. It was better for both of us.

"The moment you set foot in the Forest, the Queen will either carve your heart from your chest or she'll force me to do it.

would rather see you die tomorrow than watch you become one of her victims." An impossible truth but the truth all the same.

"Please."

I would not sway on this. Not even if the tears welling in her eyes filled this room and we both drowned. "Die tomorrow or choose to live far from me and my world. Those are my terms." When I reached for her, she hid her hand, refusing me again. "Take my hand, Aveen."

"Rían—"

"When I leave, I will not return. I'm begging you, do not let your foolish emotions get in the way. Swear to never set foot in the Forest and let me save you."

Hesitantly, she extended her hand. My fingers slipped into hers, magic binding us to our promises. "You will always be mine," I told her, wishing that it didn't have to be like this. That our ending could be a happy one.

But villains didn't get happily-ever-afters.

Those belonged to the heroes.

32

THE MOMENT I SET FOOT OUTSIDE THE JAIL, I SAW RUAIRI standing across the square, a head taller than everyone else, golden eyes fixed on me. He raked a hand through his inky hair and had the good sense to look properly worried.

He'd been responsible for Aveen's safety in Tearmann . . . and failed.

He'd been responsible for her safety in Airren . . . *and failed.*

And before this week was through, he would face my wrath.

But not here. Not in this town filled with humans going about their days as if the world was right as feckin' rain. I nodded my chin toward the Arches, taking the short amount of time it took for me to get inside to try and collect the torrent of emotion swirling within me.

There was a room at the back, walls painted as black as my mood and built with no windows. Inside, a lone couple shared pints at a table near the entrance. "Get out."

"Ye can't just kick us—"

"I said, *GET OUT!*"

The pair launched upright and scurried toward the door. It slammed closed, leaving me alone with the pooka.

"You were meant to keep her safe," I whispered, shadows collecting in my chest.

Ruairi bobbed his head once. "And I failed."

No excuse. No begging. A simple statement of fact.

"Yes. You failed." I withdrew my dagger.

Ruairi's eyes began to glow, but he held his ground. "I'm no good to you dead."

"You're no good to me alive either."

"Let me help you save her."

"What makes you think I would trust you after you've failed her time and again?"

His jaw worked beneath his short beard. "Because you have no one else."

"Tadhg—"

"Is likely drunk."

"I will find someone else." The only person I truly trusted was in prison for murder. But of all the Danú, and despite their many, *many* failings, I mistrusted Tadhg and Ruairi the least.

"We both know that's a load of bollocks," Ruairi ground out. "Just tell me what you need me to do, and I will do it."

"You want to help? Fine. Before she's executed at dawn tomorrow, they'll offer her confession. That's our window. If we miss it, she's fecked. You'll be the priest. I will get you in, but it's up to you to get her out. And if you fail—"

He braced his arms across his broad chest, nodding once. "I won't fail."

"You'll forgive me if I don't have much faith in you."

"Yer not the only one who cares for her," Ruairi said. "I will not let her down."

Back at the castle, I found my brother where he usually was at this hour: lying abed in total darkness, drunk as a feckin' lark. "Get out of bed, you sad sack of shite." I threw open the curtains, letting sunlight burst into the room.

Tadhg wailed, gathering an armful of pillows to burrow beneath. "Go away. And close those feckin' curtains."

"I said get up." Did he? No. I didn't have time for his feckin' wallowing. He could wallow tomorrow, after we saved Aveen. I stalked toward the door, where I'd left the pail of water I'd retrieved from the fountain.

"Close the feckin'—"

I yanked the pillows free and dumped the frigid water all over his haggard face.

"You have a death wish?" he snarled.

"I'd rather see you murderous than wallowing. You've had three weeks. That's long enough."

He stretched toward the liquor bottle on the bedside table. "Is it?"

No. Not today. Today, of all days, I needed him. I stole the bottle, launching it at the wall. Glass and liquor sprayed, covering the floor in glittering, wet shards. "The world is going to hell out there, and poor Tadhg is too busy feeling sorry for himself to give a shite."

"And you think pointing out the obvious is going to get me out of bed?" He flopped back onto the soaked mattress.

One way or another, this bastard was going to get his arse out of that bed. I aimed my dagger at him, but for once, I didn't want to actually kill him.

"Go ahead," he taunted, ripping open his shirt and baring his tanned chest.

"I need your help," I confessed, figuring it was worth a shot.

"Nothing you say could make me help you."

"Aveen is in prison for murder."

His mouth opened and closed; his face contorted as if he couldn't understand the words I'd spoken. "*Your* Aveen?"

I nodded.

"Feck. Right. What do . . ." He raked a hand through his sopping brown hair. "What do you need me to do?"

"Get her out of the jail."

A nod. "What's the plan?"

"The useless pooka is going to give her a change of clothes so that she can slip out of the jail unnoticed. I'll be waiting to take her place. I need you to get her from the jail to Hollowshade."

"Hollowshade?"

I nodded. "You know the cottage I bought a few months back?"

"The one in shite?"

"It's not in shite anymore." It was in less shite, anyway. "It's hers. The deed is in the bedroom beneath a loose floorboard."

Tadhg gripped both sides of his head as if trying to keep his skull from floating away. "Rían, I'm sorry—"

"I don't want to talk about any of this. Wake up, stay sober, and get her out. That's what I need from you. Not a feckin' chat or an apology."

"We'll save her."

I hope so.

I went to my room to work on my glamour. It took all evening, but eventually, I felt confident the humans wouldn't notice the differences between us. As long as they had someone to execute, they'd be content. Besides, I only needed to hold the glamour until I lost my head.

Standing in front of the mirror, looking at Aveen's reflection only made me sink lower, so I let the glamour drop. I didn't sleep; none of us did. We sat in the family room and discussed the plan and potential pitfalls until we'd worked out every single detail. Ruairi had his disguise; he was such a big fecker, I'd need to glamour him to get him through the doorway without drawing attention to himself. He'd be on his own when he tried to get out.

Confessions were usually held in the room opposite the offices. That's where he'd be waiting with Aveen's change of clothes.

Tadhg and I couldn't kill the guards, so we'd need to incapacitate or distract them long enough for me to take Aveen's place.

That was Tadhg's forte: distraction.

I stole uniforms from the two guards I'd killed, giving one to Tadhg.

The stage was set. All we needed to do was make it happen.

Gray sunlight inched over the horizon as Tadhg and I made our way in our matching uniforms to the jail. Ruairi marched between us, his shoulders hunched as if the glamour he wore didn't quite fit him. I could feel my magic spilling out of me like a sieve under a tap, but I managed to keep all three of us glamoured until Ruairi disappeared into the confessional.

Two more guards waited by the entrance to the cells, as if they were too afraid to step inside. Not that I could blame them with the guard I'd murdered last night still lying prone on the floor.

Tadhg and I pushed past the other two, drawing our swords in tandem. We used to play soldiers when we were boys. Only those swords had been made of wood, not iron.

"On your feet, witch," I snarled, gesturing toward Aveen with my blade. "Try anything and I'll run you through."

Aveen could barely stand. It took every ounce of my control to keep from helping her to her feet when her knees slammed into the unforgiving stones. One of the humans pushed past us, his companion shouting that Aveen was bound to curse us all.

"Leave off. The poor woman can't stand," the human said.

Tadhg kept his sword next to mine, pointed at Aveen, as we escorted her to the confessional chambers. Tadhg kicked the door three times, letting Ruairi know we had arrived.

"The witch is here fer her confession," he said in a terrible Vellanian accent. Seriously. We were lucky no one else noticed Tadhg had no future on the stage, that was for certain.

The door opened.

"Bring her in," the brute beneath the black robes muttered, his accent only slightly better than my brother's.

The human who had helped her eased Aveen onto one of the low benches at the front of the room.

"Leave us, my son," Ruairi said, gesturing for us to go.

Tadhg and I were the first out, checking the empty hallway for witnesses. There were plenty of soldiers *outside*, but that wasn't a problem for right now. Right now, we needed to get rid of these two eejits following us into the otherwise empty hallway.

"We can take it from here," I said.

"She's dangerous," said the second human, the fearful one. "Killed poor Walter from inside her cell while clapped in irons."

"Suit yerself. But I saw a box of buns in the office." I shifted the buns Eava had made last night. "We could grab a few before the witch comes out. No one will notice."

"I'll stay here," Tadhg said. "But get me one as well."

I followed the guards into the office, and we each snagged a bun. "I'll run this out and be right back."

"Thanks, lad," said the human who had helped Aveen, removing his helmet to take a bite. "I'm bloody starving."

By the time I came out, Tadhg was gone. I found Ruairi in the confessional and quickly changed into Aveen's dirty garments, calling the glamour I'd worked so hard on last night.

Ruairi blinked at me through wide eyes before stretching a hand toward my face. "That's feckin' mad. Ye look just like her."

"Touch me and lose your hand, dog." I shrank onto the bench, waiting for the guards to return.

"Where the hell are they?" a deep voice hissed from the other side of the door. "The captain will have their bloody heads."

The door opened, and we were down to two guards.

"Up you come," said the kinder of the two, hooking his arm beneath mine and helping me to my feet.

Ruairi followed us out, his head bowed. I stumbled a little, weeping and putting on a good show for the crowd gathered in the square. That gave Ruairi enough time to slip away, leaving me to face death on my own.

Each step felt like a victory. Each breath felt like a defeat.

Even though we had saved Aveen, she and I could never be together.

The magistrate's nonsense about laws and justice barely registered as I knelt on the dais, my skirts snagging on a twisted nail.

This would be the most excruciating pain I'd ever experienced.

And it had nothing to do with the axe coming for my—

33

AFTER SO MANY GOODBYES, YOU'D THINK I'D BE USED TO THE IDEA of losing Aveen forever. Instead of getting easier, it only got harder the more deeply I fell under her spell.

Tadhg appeared in the study, his expression wary.

Of the thousands of questions on my tongue, only one mattered. "Is she safe?"

"She is."

With a nod, I turned back toward the window, staring into the sunny day without really seeing anything. I traced the thick scar at my throat, the lingering pain nothing compared to the ache in my chest where my heart should have been.

"You need to go to her," he said.

"You know I can't do that." I was finished putting Aveen in jeopardy. Finished dragging her through the cursed mud with me.

"If you don't, then she claims she will throw herself into the sea at sunset."

"She didn't say that." Even as I denied it, I knew Tadhg could speak only truth. She wouldn't dare throw herself into the sea. Aveen was free, as safe as she could be on this island, and I'd given her everything she'd dreamed of. Had she not liked the cottage?

It must've been too small. I knew I should've gotten her something larger. She'd grown up in a feckin' mansion. To her, a "cottage" was probably a five-bedroom dormer with a conservatory.

"She did," Tadhg confirmed, his lips pressing flat. He eyed the bottle in my hand with such longing but didn't try to take it from me.

It'd do no good to have saved Aveen from certain death only to have her drown, now, would it?

Using threats to keep me at her side. As if I didn't already care for her enough. I liked to know that she had a touch of darkness in her as well.

"She sounded serious," Tadhg said. "I wouldn't delay."

If Aveen thought she could order me around, she had another thing coming. I would go, of course I would. But I'd leave it until the last minute, tear her from the waves myself if I had to.

When I did evanesce to the dry well, I kept moving at a normal pace, even when I felt like running, scanning the shore below the hill for signs of her. All I found was an orange sun setting over the horizon.

At the cottage, Aveen was still wearing the black priest's robes as she stomped through the front garden, muttering to herself.

"Throw yourself into the feckin' sea?" I said. "What sort of shite is that?"

Aveen whirled so fast, the front of her robe came untied. My eyes devoured her. The dirt on her hands. The red scars at her wrists. The lines of tears down her dirt-smudged cheeks. "It's how I respond to 'accept my bargain or die,'" she replied.

A smile tugged at my lips. One I couldn't let her see. "I'm here. What do you want?"

She went to step forward, tangled in the bottom of the robe. I lunged, catching her in my arms before she could go toppling head-first onto the ground. Phil side-eyed me as he chomped on clumps of yellowed grass.

Her face was too pale. Her lips almost as white as the shift peeking from beneath the black robes. "Dammit, Aveen. When was the last time you had food?" I'd left plenty, hadn't I? Did she not like what I'd left for her? No, no. That didn't make sense. She'd eaten the same at the castle, she must like it. The problem was that this stubborn woman had no sense of self-preservation.

I settled her on the sofa, wishing like hell I'd bought something nicer than the stained brown piece of furniture falling apart in front of the fireplace.

I organized a meal as best I could with the bits Marcus had left: bread, ham, cheese. With no coffee table, I was forced to place her plate on a rickety old chair.

When I told her to eat, she tore off a bit of bread and slipped it between her pale lips with dirty fingers.

She was in desperate need of a bath. I'd bought a tub, hadn't I? If not, we could go down to the sea. I thought of the last time we'd gone to the sea together. The way she'd felt wrapped around me, clinging to me as if I was worth her time instead of pushing me away as she should've.

"I shouldn't be here," I said to myself as much as to her. "I could spin out at any moment."

She swallowed her bite, toying with the next. "Does it happen often?"

"She leaves me alone as long as I don't break the rules." Or if he wanted me to murder someone on her behalf. But that was a conversation for never.

"We need to get back your heart."

We needed to forget about my missing heart and move on. I told Aveen she was out of her feckin' mind and started for the room full of junk that Marcus had insisted was "still good," moving shite around to free the copper tub and drag it into the living room.

Now all I had to do was fill it up.

I snagged a bucket from the back wall and went outside to the well.

Phil stepped in my path, and every time I tried to step around him, he shifted so that I couldn't. "If you don't move, I'll eat you for dinner."

I swore the thing rolled its eyes before finally lumbering away.

I filled the bucket and hauled it inside, spilling more than half of it on the way. First, I filled the kettle and lit the hob, then dumped what remained into the bottom of the tub. Over and over and over again, outside and inside, filling and dumping, the monotony of it allowing my mind to return to that courtroom. The jail cell.

It's over now. She's safe.

For tonight, maybe.

The same could not be said for tomorrow, or the day after that, or the day after that. It wasn't just the Queen we had to fear. Marcus's son had died in a fishing accident, swept out to sea and never heard from again. What if Aveen went swimming and met a rogue wave? A poisonous weaver fish? A bloodthirsty merrow?

What if she got a leak in the ceiling and tried to climb onto the roof and slipped and broke her neck? What if she came out to fetch some water and Phil the devil-goat rammed her in the arse and she fell into the well and drowned?

I knew I was reaching, but the fact remained: Aveen was human. Her life was as fragile as a glass bauble. It wasn't a matter of *if* she would die but a matter of when.

I shoved the thoughts aside, staring down at the now-full tub.

Aveen stuck her hand in, pulling it out just as quickly. "It's bloody freezing."

That's because it came straight from the well, beautiful. "That's what this is for," I said, removing the kettle from the hob. A bit of boiling water, and she'd be set.

"That tiny kettle won't make a blind bit of difference to this much water."

Sure enough, when I added the kettle, the water still felt as cold as ever. It'd take all night to heat the feckin' thing. "How the hell was I supposed to know that?"

"Haven't you ever drawn a bath before?"

"I've never needed to." Because I wasn't a feckin' peasant.

could shift a bath of my own or steal my brother's. Why the hell would I traipse in and out of the castle to fill it by hand?

"Just do your little flicky thing and warm it up."

I took great offense at her use of the term. "My little flicky thing?"

"You know." She waved her hand around. "Your flicky thing. Is it not working again?"

"My 'flicky-thing' is working just fine. I've warded this cottage against magic, so I have to do this the pathetic human way."

"Why would you do something like that?"

The same reason I did anything: To keep her safe. "Our magic leaves a lingering scent, and I never wanted the Queen to find out about you. This was where you were supposed to wake after Tadhg's curse wore off." If things had gone to plan, Aveen would've woken up here and been happy for the rest of her days.

But that hadn't happened. Her infernal sister had gotten in the way, and now look where we were. I stalked outside with the kettle. Phil jumped out from the thicket, taking ten years off my life. When I came back, I found Aveen stark naked in the freezing tub.

My groin tightened.

Her lips hooked into a smile. "Do you know if there's any soap?"

I dropped the kettle, running into the junk room for soap and snagging one of the two towels on top of a rickety shelf on the way back into the living room.

She thanked me, drops of water dripping down her forehead. Clinging to her lips.

I wanted to continue staring but forced myself away, going into the bedroom to find a dress for her to wear. I'd shifted a handful of garments, most of them plain so she wouldn't stand out amongst the other residents in Hollowshade. There were two nicer gowns, something she could wear for a festive occasion. Or if she wanted to look well for any callers she may have.

Feck it all. I hoped she became a spinster.

Aveen shouted for me, and I clambered for the door. The woman's skin had taken on a blue-ish tint from where she stood, water cascading down her body as she stared at her hands.

"Why are you roaring?" I asked.

"Look." She held out her hands toward me. At first, I didn't understand what she wanted me to see, but then I noticed the silver scars adorning her wrists. *Impossible.* The bundle in my arms fell to the wet ground. Those marks had been red and raw earlier today. I was sure of it.

"You don't think—" she started.

"I don't know." Healing that quickly should've been impossible, and yet here she was, with silver scars just like mine.

"I shifted your dagger," she rushed, our gazes tangling. "At least I think I did."

If she'd shifted the dagger, that meant—"Shit." *Shit.* Could this really be happening? Could fate finally be giving me a chance for happiness?

"Does this mean I can evanesce?" she asked.

"I don't know." If she could evanesce . . . the possibilities were endless. She could come and go as she pleased.

"Can I do the flicky thing?"

I almost smiled when she tried. Even if she could, calling on magic would be impossible inside the cottage because of the wards. "I don't know."

Her eyes widened, and she sucked in a breath. "Am I immortal?"

The dagger trapped a true immortal's life force, their magic. It made sense that since Aveen had been resurrected using Tadhg's that his magic now flowed through her veins.

But just because it made sense didn't mean it was true.

It couldn't be. It couldn't. I couldn't handle the hope that I would never have to save goodbye to this woman. "How the hell am I supposed to know?" The only way to truly test it out would be to kill her and see if she came back. And I wasn't about to try.

Immortal or not, my number-one priority was keeping Aveen

safe. Being a true immortal wouldn't stop the Queen from stealing Aveen's heart and taking control of her the way she had taken control of me.

I still needed to kill the Queen.

"The dagger," Aveen whispered.

The dagger didn't matter. None of it did.

"This is brilliant news, Aveen. Brilliant." I kissed her hairline, inhaling the scent of soap from her bath.

"No. No, it's not. Your heart—"

"You are my heart." Aveen and her light had taken root in the most hollow parts of me. As long as she drew breath, I would know happiness and hope existed.

She pulled away, sinking to the hideous rug. I sat beside her, wanting nothing more than to drag her into my lap and hold her to keep a chill from settling in my veins.

"We have to get your heart," she insisted.

I added more fuel to the fire, none of its heat penetrating beyond my skin. We couldn't get my heart. The Queen had it locked somewhere in her castle, and I refused to risk Aveen's life to save mine.

Because that was how our story ended.

To save me, she had to die.

"I understand you're scared," she said, "but—"

"You're feckin' right I'm scared. You can't imagine how scared I am. I have watched my mother tear the heart from a woman's chest and consume her life force. I've felt her claws reach into my body to rip out mine. If you're not scared senseless by the idea of entering that Forest, then you are a fool."

"We can do this."

"Immortal or not, you can't set foot in the Forest," I reminded her.

Her eyes narrowed. "Then I'll ride a horse through."

Obstinate feckin' woman.

"Or," she said slowly, "you can release me from the bargain."

"Not. A. Hope."

She dragged me forward by the collar, tracing the scars at my throat. "Look at this."

I didn't need to look to see the hideous marks.

"You died for me today, Rían," she kept on. "*You died for me.* You don't think I would do the same for you?"

It wasn't the same. Not really. I'd only died because I could come back. "Aveen, listen to me——"

"No, you listen to me. If you give up now, she wins. If you leave me, you are letting her take away your soulmate. We can end this. Once and for all."

"It's not worth it."

"That's where you're wrong." She lifted to her knees, cupping my face in her hands, rubbing my cheeks with her thumbs. "You are worth everything to me. And because I love you, I will give you a choice. You help me get back your heart, or you refuse, and I do it on my own."

How could I let her do this?

More importantly, how could I stop her?

I stood, tugging her to her feet as well. "How do you think we're going to take back my heart when you can no longer wield the cursed dagger?"

Her brow furrowed as she considered. Then, as if dawn were breaking, she smiled up at me and said, "I have a plan."

"Go on, then. Let's hear it."

"We just need to get her to leave the castle, sneak in, and take it back."

"Is that all?" I smacked my forehead with my palm. "Why didn't I think of that? Oh, wait. I remember. *Because she never leaves the feckin' castle.*"

She worried her lower lip. "She left the other day, didn't she?"

That's right. The Queen had left to bring me to heel. Was there anything else she'd be willing to leave for? The Queen was obsessed with duty and protecting the Danú. And she hated humans. Maybe we could . . . No. Maybe?

Aveen poked my ribs. "You thought of something."

"It probably won't work." I rubbed my weary eyes, almost certain this plan would end in both our deaths.

"Tell me anyway."

"If I can convince her that Tadhg wants to act against the humans, she *may* be willing to meet us at the castle. But it wouldn't be for long. An hour at most." And even then, there was no guarantee she would stay.

Aveen's eyes lit up, and she grabbed for my hand. "If we got her to come for dinner, it could be longer. Then you and Tadhg can keep her there for as long as—"

"I'm not letting you go into that castle on your own."

The corner of her lips lifted. "Don't you think your mother will be a little suspicious if you're not there for this big meeting?"

She would be suspicious, but . . .

"This will work," Aveen said. "I'll sneak in, have a look around—"

"Wherever she has it hidden, it is likely to be warded. And if it is, you won't be able to get in."

"Stay for part of the dinner, then slip away."

I *could* do that. Wait. No, I couldn't. "Theft of this magnitude is a capital crime in Tearmann."

"It's not theft if it's retrieving a stolen item and returning said item to its rightful owner. I checked," she said proudly. "If she harms either of us for it, her life is forfeit."

Could we rely on the Queen adhering to the law in such a rage? "I will need to pay the death tax. That is non-negotiable."

Her lips lift a little higher, bringing my hope with them. "I was hoping you'd offer so I wouldn't have to make things awkward by asking you to die for me again."

"I'd accept a thousand deaths before I let anyone lay a finger on you."

She clapped her hands together beneath her chin, rocking back and forth. "Do I get to stab you?"

"You sound far too excited by the prospect of murdering me.

But, no. Being stabbed takes too long and it's so messy. There are cliffs. I could just throw myself off one."

She grabbed both of my hands, squeezing hard. "Can I push you? Please?" Her lower lip popped out as she batted her lashes up at me.

"Fine," I groaned. "I will allow you to push me to my death. Happy?"

"Immensely. Now, the dagger."

If the Queen knew we had such a weapon, her tune would change.

Aveen gestured toward my belt. "Give it to me, and I will—"

"You can't. If you're immortal—"

"We don't know for sure, do we?" Aveen countered. "And there's a chance I'll survive, while you would certainly die. But there will be no need for it because this plan will go well."

I grimaced. "I wish I shared your optimism."

"I'll give you some if you'd like." With a smile, she braced her hands on my shoulders and eased her mouth to mine, brushing a kiss against my lips. "Better?"

"No. Maybe you should do it again."

Her tongue swept between my lips, dragging in slow dance. "Now?"

"Where's this optimism supposed to go?" I murmured.

"In your heart."

I caught her hips, pulling her so she straddled me. "Don't have one of those," I said, rocking her against my hard length. "Maybe I'm keeping mine someplace else."

I lost myself in Aveen's soft hair, kissed each bone in her spine, the curve of her shoulder blades. If I'd known how to pray, I would've said a prayer. Instead, I begged the heavens to keep this woman safe.

She unfastened my breeches, my stiff cock springing free to meet her greedy hands. Three strokes later, I had her on the flat of her back, pinned beneath me on the hideous rug.

We needed no words between us as I nudged against her

entrance, answering her breathless sigh. It felt as if I had been waiting for this moment my entire life.

Searching for her.

Finding her.

Filling her.

Giving every broken bit of me that remained.

Her heels dug into my back as she clutched the rug, our hips meeting and retreating. The harder I thrust, the more she moaned. I swallowed her cries, burying myself until she felt me in her soul.

"Rían . . ." Her whisper became the soft sigh of a summer rain on flower petals.

When she finally came, I followed the waves of her release with my own, careful not to crush her when my arms and legs gave out. We remained connected as she turned to me with such light and hope in her eyes that I dared to let some seep into my darkness.

"Tá mé i ngré leat," I whispered.

Her swollen lips grazed my collarbone. "What's that mean?"

"It's a promise." That if we succeeded, if my heart was returned to my chest, I would love her until the world ended.

34

I FLICKED OPEN MY POCKET WATCH FOR WHAT FELT LIKE THE
hundredth time, waiting for the clock to strike the hour, knowing
the Queen would never be late. Tadhg was to keep her occupied
until I arrived. I had considered trying to evanesce with Aveen in
tow, but using that much magic would be foolish. If I had to face
the Queen this day, I needed to be at full strength.

"Is it time?" Aveen asked, clutching and releasing her dark
skirts.

"Yes. But this is a terrible plan."

She assured me it would be fine, just as she had the other
times I'd pointed out the many potential pitfalls of retrieving my
heart. "While I appreciate your poor attempt at optimism," I said,
"we are depending on a man cursed to tell the truth lying to a
witch who can smell such things. You'll forgive me if I don't share
your confidence."

"Do you like being controlled by a heinous murderer?"

I knew she meant the Queen but couldn't pass up a chance to
tease her. "Ah, here now. I wouldn't call yourself a 'heinous
murderer.' You only killed Robert Trench."

Aveen pinched the sensitive flesh at the back of my arm, and it

336

feckin' hurt. "I'm being serious, you know. Now, give me the dagger."

Ah, the dagger. Yet another bone of contention between us. "What are the rules?" I asked, offering her the dagger despite my fears.

She rolled her eyes toward the thick quilt of clouds above us. "Surprise is key. Get close. Go for the kill."

"And?"

"And if you turn, I am to kill you before you kill me."

I released my hold on the dagger, watching her tuck the blade into a pocket sewn into her skirts, the emerald still glowing. Sometimes it glowed in her grasp, sometimes it didn't. Like it wasn't sure what to think of my human.

This is a terrible mistake.

"Are you ready?" she asked, nudging me with her shoulder.

The glossy black stones marking the Forest mocked me from where they shined, as if they were just waiting to take away someone else I cared for.

Aveen stepped forward, both her boots landing on cursed earth. "There. That wasn't so—"

Black roots coiled around her ankles like poisonous snakes. It took far too much magic to stop the first of many spells the Queen had cast to catch trespassers.

A strangled curse blew through my lips as I lifted my human onto the less-treacherous path that would lead us to the castle. "I know this is your plan, but I might take the lead for this part, if that's all right with you?"

I'd been on the path so many times, I could have walked it with my eyes closed. Death surrounded us on all sides, but so long as we remained on that path, we would be safe. We traversed though the monstrous trees, past the three boulders—the smallest of which always used to remind me of a faerie perched on a fat fish.

Over and down and then up again as we climbed closer and

closer to the sea. Crows circled, but without the Queen to see from her tower, I paid them no heed.

Aveen sucked in a breath when the Queen's castle came into view, the black stones not nearly as dark as the witch who lived within.

We reached the gates—empty, as I'd known they'd be.

"Where are the guards?" Aveen asked, scanning the barren front yard.

"She doesn't need them. No one in their right mind comes here." I wasn't sure where she kept the guards when she wasn't using them. Perhaps in the dungeons. I'd never been concerned enough to find out.

I cut my palm to unlock the gate, then crossed the wards. When Aveen tried, she remained stuck on the other side.

"The old crow is so feckin' paranoid," I grumbled, lacing my fingers with Aveen's, my blood smearing against her palm. I wasn't sure if it was the blood or our connection that let her through—not that it mattered since this was the only time she would ever set foot in this cursed place.

I brought her to the foyer, knowing it was past time I returned to the castle. "You know where you're going?"

Aveen nodded, showing me the map she'd drawn on her palm earlier when we were going over our plan one final time. I pressed a kiss to her head, begging once more for her to be safe, and then I crossed back into the Forest and evanesced back to the castle.

The Queen sat at the head of the dining room table, a pig's head with an apple in its mouth sitting on a tray next to steaming side dishes. My brother's face was decidedly green as he glared at that dead animal. I almost felt like laughing.

Until I realized he was wearing one of my waistcoats. When I'd warned my brother within an inch of his life to make sure he had on proper clothes, that hadn't been an excuse to steal mine.

"It's nice of you to finally join us," said the Queen, cutting a hin slice of pork and slipping it between her lips.

"My apologies. I was delayed longer than expected." I settled cross from my brother, closest to the exit, and grabbed my servi-tte, draping it across my lap. Eating was the last thing I felt like loing, but there was no sense calling more attention to myself han necessary.

"As I was saying," Tadhg began, reaching for his goblet of vine, "the situation in Airren is dire."

Although the Queen nodded her agreement, it was clear from he way her jaw pulsed that she had more to say on the matter. "It's nice of you to finally notice."

Tadhg's smile tightened. "The time has come for action. I'd ike to keep to the treaty, wherever possible, but am aware that)reaking it may be the only way to succeed in keeping our people afe."

"I had advised my son to work with the merrow," the Queen aid, setting her utensils aside in favor of her goblet of blood, "but t appears their alliance has been severed."

That was because Muireann had tried to sacrifice Aveen to the eckin' Forest. "We cannot interfere with Vellanian ships arriving o their own territory," I reminded them both. "Only if they cross nto ours, which they have yet to do."

"It is only a matter of time," said the Queen, her black eyes ike daggers as she glared at me.

"I agree," Tadhg said. "Which is why I believe it is time for us o meet with King Bedwyr."

The Queen's brows flicked up. "You must know I cannot do uch a thing. To leave the Forest unguarded would be a great folly, udeed. And if the humans learn you and I are both to be away rom the kingdom?" She clucked her tongue. "No, I will not be isiting the king."

Tadhg's head tilted as he considered, and then his eyes found nine. "I could send Rían."

This may have been an elaborate ruse, but I couldn't help

339

thinking what would happen if I did go to Vellana to speak with the king. Not that my position was recognized by the royals, but they wouldn't be able to deny my power. Could I convince them to work with us instead of against us so that all peoples in Airren were treated justly? Father had tried before, but previous monarchs wouldn't concede so much as a morsel.

"You could," the Queen said after a moment.

We spoke about the merits of renegotiating, of offering to host the king in Tearmann—which we realized he would never agree too—and the possibility of meeting in Airren at a neutral location. All of it boiled down to the same thing: Why would the humans give even an inch when they had everything they wanted?

The Queen started listing scenarios where the king may consider renegotiating, but all of them involved significant loss of life. *Human* lives. It wasn't that I was particularly fond of humans in general, but I was quite fond of one specific human. And I had a feeling she would object to razing villages and murdering innocent people in order to be taken seriously.

I threw my serviette onto the table next to my empty goblet. "If you'll excuse me. I could do with some fresh air."

Tadhg waved me off, and the Queen seemed to barely notice.

So far, so good.

I passed the shadow guards waiting on either side of the door and continued to the empty courtyard. Once I cleared the wards, I evanesced to the Queen's castle.

It was time to retrieve my heart.

A chill settled into my bones the moment I set foot in the Queen's chambers. I'd only been in her rooms a handful of times, and none of them had ever ended well for me. I found Aveen inside a long, narrow closet filled with ghostly shadows of children's toys.

She must've heard me, because I saw her shoulders stiffen and her hand fall to the dagger in her pocket. Wouldn't it be poetic she accidentally stabbed me with the thing when we were so close to the end?

"You nearly gave me a heart attack," she gasped, her chest heaving.

I recognized my old toys from when I was a boy. Why had the Queen kept them? She should've just thrown the things out instead of letting them collect dust. I picked up an old teddy I vaguely remembered from my fourth birthday. The hand-painted soldiers next to it had been a gift from my father one Yule. The rolling hoop, that had been from Eava. I'd stolen the set of quoits from Tadhg.

And here they were, all confiscated like contraband.

"Are all these toys yours?" Aveen asked.

All mine. All pristine. All pointless. "She never let me play with one for more than a week. When I'd get attached, she'd take it away." I'd have something just long enough to start thinking maybe she'd let me keep it, only for her to snatch away that hope again and again.

All these years later, the Queen was still stealing that hope. First with Leesha, and now with Aveen.

I set the bear down on my little white rocking horse. That's when I heard it. A low *thump thump* like the march of an army on the move. "Do you hear that?" I mouthed, stepping over a deflated leather ball to press my good ear to the wall. The sound, though muffled, grew louder. "There's something in there."

I tried to think of a spell to open the door, but if I chose the wrong one, it could trigger an alarm, bringing the Queen down on our heads.

Aveen's fingers skimmed the wall. I was about to tell her not to bother, that the Queen was far too smart to leave a key anywhere near this place, when the panel slid aside with a heavy groan. The air on the other side held the unmistakable perfume of blood.

Silver bird cages lined the shelves on either side of the long hallway as far back as I could see. Cages that held beating hearts. How would I find mine among them? I knew for a fact the spell wouldn't work if I didn't get the right one, and there wasn't time to try every single heart.

"Whose hearts are these?" Aveen asked.

"I haven't a clue." They must've belonged to her victims. But I'd seen her turn hearts to ash. Melt them in fire. Whose had she kept like sadistic trophies?

Aveen swiped a finger across the bottom of one cage, revealing a small label engraved with numbers. "Do you remember when she took your heart?"

Dates. The Queen had dated each kill. "Not exactly the kind of thing a man forgets."

The farther we walked, the further back the dates climbed, until finally we came to one day I would remember forever. November twenty-seventh. My nineteenth birthday.

Shit.

The heat from Aveen's chest warmed my back when she tried to lift onto her toes and see what I'd found. "What is it? What's wrong?"

"There are two from the same day." Which of the other poor souls I'd killed that day had she kept?

"We can take them both."

We didn't have much of a choice, did we? It wasn't as if we could linger or ask the Queen for assistance. We would take them both and cross our fingers that one of them worked. I stretched a hand toward the closest one.

"Look." Aveen pointed to the second heart, which seemed to beat faster as my fingers approached.

My fingertips grazed the bars, and the door flew open.

After all these years, I'd finally found my heart.

"Let me do it," Aveen said, as if she'd noticed my hesitation. I let her take it out, feeling a pinch in my chest as she cradled the organ against her.

"We need to put it back," she said, looking up at me through clear blue eyes.

I towed her toward the entrance, my eyes quickly adjusting to the brightening light at the end of the tunnel. "When we get back to the cottage." *Then* we could put it back.

"We do it now."

"Aveen, there isn't time—"

"Then stop wasting it and put your heart back where it belongs."

I hurried as fast as I could between the walls until we made it back to the Queen's chambers. Aveen appeared too busy staring at my heart to notice me forcing the wall back into place.

There wasn't time for this. Wasn't time for any of it.

We certainly didn't have time for an argument. But from the stubborn tilt to her chin, I knew that's where this would be headed. So instead, I ripped off my coat and opened my shirt.

My heart spasmed where she cradled it against her chest.

When I took a calming breath, the heart slowed.

I recited the spell Eava had taught me, balancing between hurrying and making sure each word was correct. With magic swelling in my palm, I breathed on my fingertips until they glowed, then traced the scar left by the Queen. It felt as if someone were holding a hot coal to my chest. Sweat beaded on my brow, my head swimming with the pain. "I can't . . . ."

Aveen scooted closer. "Can I help?"

I gave her my hand, willing my magic to pass like a conduit to her, fully expecting to find it blocked the way it normally was when doing this with a human. But there was no block. My magic passed seamlessly from me to her until her hand glowed.

"Finish it," I croaked.

She brought her burning hand to the scar, flaying me open as if she'd used the dagger.

Black magic pulsed through my veins, drawing my darkness to the surface. "My heart." I couldn't hold on much longer. If she didn't hurry, the shadows would surely take control.

Aveen collected my heart, staring down at it as if mesmerized by the way it pulsed.

"Against the cut," I wheezed.

By some miracle, I managed to whisper the two final words, completing the spell. My heart vanished from Aveen's palm, and I gasped at the wrenching pain, as if someone had pried open my ribs and stuffed me with stones.

"Did it work?" Aveen whispered.

"I don't know." Suddenly, the pain in my chest eased, and a thrumming pulse flooded my ears, as if I was back in that hall surrounded by hearts. "I . . . I think it did." Feckin' hell. It had worked! It had really worked!

"How do you feel?"

"Like shite." Like I'd been chewed up and spit out and then stomped over and over again. I checked my pulse. My stomach leapt when I felt the steady beat beneath my fingertips.

She'd done it. She'd saved me.

My human flew at me, kissing my face, my jaw, my chest.

"Can we do this later?" I asked, thoroughly interested but entirely distracted by the fact that I was still leaning against the Queen's bed.

"Right. Yes. Of course." Aveen scrubbed her tears before standing on unsteady legs. My own refused to follow. "Aren't you coming?" she threw over her shoulder.

When I tried, my legs gave out like a newborn foal's. Aveen's smile lit my soul with so much joy, I felt as if I could fly. If only my leaden limbs felt the same. She helped me to my feet, taking the bulk of my weight as we stumbled toward the door. "Princes," she muttered. "So pathetic and weak."

I'd like to see how she fared after wielding so much black magic.

We made it down the stairs and out into the barren wasteland of the Forest, through the gates without issue, and crossed all the way to the cliffside path where she would push me to my death. Delightfully, if her grin was any indication.

And then I saw the Queen.

35

STICK TO THE PLAN, I WANTED TO SHOUT. INSTEAD, I REMAINED silent. It wasn't clear how much the Queen knew or didn't know. Offering excuses could lead to incriminating ourselves. Right now, all we had to worry about was the fact that Aveen had entered the Forest without the Queen's permission. A problem easily solved the moment she pushed me off the cliff.

"You were free, and yet you returned. Why?" the Queen said. Although she glared at the two of us, she sounded genuinely baffled. It was no wonder. The witch had never been able to comprehend the depth of true love. It made you reckless and foolish. But it also made you strong and courageous.

"I love your son," Aveen said simply.

Don't get stuck chatting. Kill me already.

The Queen inhaled, lips tugging into a deep frown. "You know the penalty for crossing the Forest." Her dagger appeared, sending my heart rate spiking. If she heard, she didn't show any indication. "One life," she said.

"Rían," Aveen said without looking back. "I love you."

"I love you too, my little viper." It was the first time I'd said those words to anyone since Leesha. And now that I was whole again, completely in control, I meant them.

Aveen whirled and shoved me off the cliff.

I heard my mother's indignant shriek. My heart clattered against my ribcage as I plummeted toward the churning water far below.

I died with a smile on my face.

I awoke with a start, face-down in briny water, and managed to flip myself so I could choke out a handful of salty coughs. I stared up at the clouds, still smiling. The cliffs towered above, monstrous and jagged. Black and white birds swirled and swooped, diving into the sea and returning to their nests in the stone.

That's when I saw a dark shape rocketing toward the crashing waves.

A woman with golden curls flying and skirts billowing, doing nothing to slow her down.

Aveen.

Had the Queen pushed her? Had she fallen? Had she *jumped?* I tried to shout her name, but my voice had yet to return, so all I could do was breathe as she plummeted faster and faster. Too fast. Too far. No hope of survival. I tried to move my arms, my legs, but they were as flimsy and useless as the seaweed drifting past.

I was forced to float there and watch the woman I loved slam into the waves and disappear into the dark depths. I scanned the surface, hoping beyond hope that she would emerge unscathed, but the longer she stayed under, the more apparent it became.

Aveen was dead.

Feeling slowly returned to my limbs, and I couldn't stop myself from swimming toward the spot where I'd last seen her, even though I knew there was no hope. And then I saw her in a cresting wave, golden curls spread as if atop a watery pillow, neck at a wrong angle, blue eyes reflecting the clouds above. Clouds she couldn't see.

Merrow popped their heads from the dark expanse of sea, but

none offered any assistance. I hooked my arm across her chest, dragging her limp form toward the shore, trying my best to keep my darkest thoughts at bay.

The moment my boots sank into the sand, I brought us both to her cottage in Hollowshade and carried my love into the bedroom where we'd made love only a few hours ago. Where we'd made plans. Where we'd hoped.

I pressed the heel of my hand against my scarred chest, an unending ache spreading to my very soul.

How could we have thought we could defy fate?

Pity the girl from Graystones who loved a heartless prince.

For the only way to save him . . .

A choked sob wrenched from my throat.

I wasn't worth it. Wasn't worth *her*.

Yet for all my selfishness, all my failings, this woman had found something in me worth loving. Worth the risk. Worth this undeserved fate.

I gathered the hair from her sun-kissed cheeks, spreading it across her pillow. The shadows from the lace curtains made it look as if flowers had been tattooed on her skin.

She'd died so that I could be free. But I would never be free, because this woman owned every part of me, body and soul.

I closed my burning eyes, cursing fate. Cursing the Queen. Cursing this world.

How was it fair that someone like her, so good, so perfect, was dead, and yet someone like me, so twisted, so depraved, sat here unscathed?

How was it fair?

It wasn't. Not at all. But there was nothing I could do to change it.

That wasn't completely true, was it?

I dug through Aveen's sopping skirts, finding the hidden pocket and the dagger. The emerald hilt glowed as I adjusted my grip with trembling hands. I aimed the dagger at the point just below my ribs, angling it so that when the blade pierced my flesh, it would find my cursed heart.

Once more, I memorized the woman I loved, then I closed my eyes, took a deep breath, and—

Something soft brushed against my thigh.

When it happened again, I opened my eyes, watching Aveen's fingers twitch.

The dagger clattered to the ground.

They twitched.

Maybe it was wishful thinking, but I swore *they feckin' twitched.*

"Aveen?"

She didn't respond, but her finger twitched again, as if she could hear me.

And then I heard the sweetest song: a ragged, gurgling breath. Aveen's chest barely rose, but there was no mistaking that beautiful sound.

"You're back . . ." Tadhg's magic, his life force thrumming through her veins, had brought her back to me. "Aveen? Can you hear me?"

Her lips tugged down.

She must've been in excruciating pain. If only there were some way for me to bear it for her. But this was something she had to endure on her own.

"It's all right. I'm here. I'm here." I cradled her against me, holding steady as her whimpers mended my tattered soul. "I know it hurts. I know it does. Breathe through the pain." The sooner she accepted it, the sooner she would be through it.

Her next ragged breath felt stronger, fanning against my neck.

"Why are we here?" she croaked.

"I had to bring you somewhere safe. If she found your body . . ." The Queen would've taken her heart to replace the one she'd lost. "When I came back and saw you fall from that cliff . . ." Sunlight sparked across the dagger's cursed blade. "I thought you were gone forever."

And I'd almost just . . .

"What happened?"

She murmured that it didn't matter. Now wasn't the time to press. Now was the time to hold each other and revel in the fact that, despite overwhelming odds, we had succeeded.

"You said you loved me," she whispered.

Of course, I love you, you fool. How could I not?

"Only to enrage my mother," I said, a smile hooking my lips.

My beautiful, violent soulmate pinched me. "For once in your life, will you please tell the truth."

I smiled down at my light in this dark world and said, "The truth is, violent Aveen, my heart may beat in my chest, but it has always belonged to you."

EPILOGUE

EVERY TIME I CLOSED MY EYES, I SAW AVEEN PLUMMETING TO HER death.

Falling impossibly fast. Plunging into the waves. Never resurfacing. Swallowed by the sea.

I studied Aveen's cottage, trying to figure out how to keep the precious woman sleeping inside safe from what was coming. We may have won this battle, but I wasn't foolish enough to believe the Queen would let our victory stand.

I needed to return to the castle and inform Tadhg of what had transpired. I'd be gone an hour, maybe two. A lot could happen in two hours. Trouble had a way of finding these Bannon women. The thought of leaving her behind left my chest aching. Or it could've been the recently restored organ doing that. Did having a heart always feel this heavy?

With Tadhg's life force flowing through her veins, she couldn't die unless the Queen got her hands on that enchanted dagger. And I'd hidden it somewhere no one would find it. But there were fates far worse than death for our kind.

I ran up the lane toward the portal and evanesced to Ruairi's home in Tearmann.

The pooka answered on the third knock, his black hair matted

o the right side of his head. "Get dressed," I said. "You need to
guard Aveen."

He folded his thick arms over his chest, golden eyes flashing. "I
don't *need* to do anything."

"Please. Please. If the Queen finds her, there's no telling what
will happen. Please. I can't lose her. She'll take her from me.
Please." The pooka in front of me went blurry. What the hell was
happening with my eyes?

"Good god, man. Are you crying?" Ruairi scoffed.

Shit. "No." I swiped my traitorous eyes with a shaking hand,
my heart racing, panic climbing my throat, choking what
remained of my protest.

Ruairi gave me a strange look, then pulled the door closed
behind him. "Where is she?"

"Evanesce to the portal in Hollowshade. Go south, toward the
coast. There's a cottage there with a blue door."

I needed to get ahold of myself. Tadhg would never let me live
it down if I fell apart in front of him.

Was Aveen safe in that cottage? Would she have been better
off in the castle? No. No. I'd made the right choice. There was no
hiding her in the castle. My enemies were too close at hand. As
much as I hated it, she was safer among the humans . . . for now.

If she could learn to harness Tadhg's magic, perhaps I could
teach her to evanesce. That'd be something, wouldn't it?

There would be time for dreams in the future, but not
right now.

Now, we needed to prepare. To the best of my knowledge, the
Queen had never attacked without reason. Then again, I wasn't
sure if she'd ever been thwarted the way she had been last night.

From Ruairi's, I evanesced to the cliffs beyond the castle,
needing a moment to get ahold of myself. A dark figure stood at
the crest of the hill.

The wind tore at the skirts on her blue dress, and her red hair
lifted and danced like living flames.

Her name lived on the tip of my tongue.

It couldn't be.
She was dead.
I'd watched her die.
"Leesha?"

WHAT HAPPENS NEXT?

I know what you're thinking: Jenny! How could you do this to us?

Simply and with an evil smile, that's how.

There's *a lot* more story to tell and because I'm kind and gracious, I'm going to be giving you another full-length novel from all four POV's about what happens "next." (Although, to be honest, I'm not sure these characters are going to call me kind or gracious when they learn what I have in store).

Rest easy, dear readers, *A Cursed Love, Myths of Airren, Book III*, is well underway and, bar any major disasters, will be hitting your shelves this fall!

I can't wait for you to read the epic grand finale for Tadhg, Keelynn, Aveen, and Rían.

ACKNOWLEDGMENTS

I always thank my readers first and foremost and this time, it's no different. Although, I specifically want to thank those of you who didn't let your opinion of Rían in *A Cursed Kiss* keep you from reading *A Cursed Heart* or this book (and yes, there were many who hated him enough to let the story end with ACK).

So thank YOU, my Rían stans. While I still refuse to choose a favorite cursed prince, Rían has a special place in my heart (pun intended).

Meg, my brilliant editor and occasional comma goblin, thank you for helping me polish this book and ensure no one "arrived." You've had such a monumental influence on this world and these characters. I couldn't do this without you.

To my betas, especially my sister Megan and childhood best friend Miriam, thank you for your feedback and constant support.

To Elle, Lou, and everyone at Midnight Tide Publishing, I'm so thrilled to be part of this brilliant collective.

Finally, to Rían. You were so much fun to write. Thanks for being such a drama queen/complete dick.

ALSO BY JENNY

THE MYTHS OF AIRREN

(NA Fantasy Romance)

A Cursed Kiss

A Cursed Heart

A Cursed Love (2023)

Prince of Seduction

Prince of Deception

THE PAN TRILOGY

(YA Sci-Fi Romance with a Peter Pan Twist)

The PAN

The HOOK

The CROC

OMNIBUS EDITIONS

The Complete PAN Trilogy YA Omnibus

The PAN Trilogy (Special Edition Omnibus)

YA FANTASY ROMANCE NOVELLA

Married by Fate

CONTEMPORARY ROMANCE

(co-written with Natalie Murray)

The Quinn Sisters

Hating the Best Man (May 2023)

Loving the Worst Man (Fall 2023)

MORE BOOKS YOU'LL LOVE

If you enjoyed this story, please consider leaving a review. Then check out more books from Midnight Tide Publishing.

EMMIE & THE TUDOR KING NEW ADULT OMNIBUS

NATALIE MURRAY

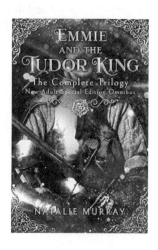

An award-winning fantasy romance with a Tudor twist This New Adult edition of the Emmie and the Tudor King trilogy contains all three books in the series with added spice for mature audiences.

Emmie and the Tudor King was an award-winning finalist in the 14th Annual National Indie Excellence Awards and has received acclaim from Foreword Reviews, InD'tale Magazine, YA Books Central, authors Brigid Kemmerer and CJ Flood, and others.

Emmie and the Tudor King

One moment, Emmie is writing her final high school history paper; the next, she's lost in 16th-century Tudor England, where she meets a dreamy but dangerous king destined for a dreadful fate.

Able to travel back to her own time but intensely drawn to the mesmeric young king and the mysterious death of his sister, Emmie finds herself solving the murder of a young princess and unraveling court secrets while trying to keep her head on her shoulders, literally.

With everything to lose, Emmie must come to face her biggest battle of all: How to cheat the path of history and keep her irresistible king, or lose him—and the greatest love she's ever known —forever.

Emmie and the Tudor Queen

True love has never been more deadly in this lush sequel to the best-selling Emmie and the Tudor King.

For an extraordinary love, Emmie Grace has given up her life in the modern world to move to the sixteenth century and marry the Tudor king she bravely saved from a dreadful fate. However, not everyone is pleased to see the glorious King Nick betrothed to the unknown and uncultured Emmie—especially the noblemen commanded to protect her.

As Emmie is drawn deeper into Nick's sumptuous and savage world—where beheadings are way more popular than time travelers—the Tudor court heads on progress across the country, and a growing rebellion against the promised queen looms.

With life and love at stake, Emmie must face the cost of changing the path of history and realize that her greatest sacrifice is yet to come.

Emmie and the Tudor Throne

What happens when your absolute happiness comes at a terrible cost to the people you love?

Contemporary College student and her sixteenth-century boyfriend, Nick Tudor, have faced unfathomable danger and made life-changing sacrifices to keep their tender love alive.

But when they learn the dreadful consequences of their decision to make a life together in the modern world, they are forced to return to Tudor England to save the throne from the invading Mary, Queen of Scots, and the lives of those they left behind.

With the Tudor king believed to be dead and no fortune or army to fight with, how will Emmie and Nick save the world from collapsing without losing everything they've worked so hard for?

The stakes have never been higher in this thrilling conclusion to the Hearts & Crowns trilogy.

Author note: Each book contains mature themes and adult content and may not be suitable for all audiences. There are also brief scenes depicting sexual assault and pregnancy loss.

Genre: New Adult, Fantasy Romance, Time Travel

START READING TODAY

COME TRUE: A BOMB ASS GENIE ROMANCE

BY BRINDI QUINN

A jaded girl.
A persistent genie.
A contest of souls.

Recent college graduate Dolly Jones has spent the last year stubbornly trying to atone for a mistake that cost her everything. She doesn't go out, she doesn't make new friends and she sure as hell doesn't treat herself to things she hasn't earned, but when her most recent thrift store purchase proves home to a hot, magical genie determined to draw out her darkest desires in exchange for a taste of her soul, Dolly's restraint, and patience, will be put to the test.

Newbie genie Velis Reilhander will do anything to beat his older half-brothers in a soul-collecting contest that will determine the next heir to their family estate, even if it means coaxing desire out of the least palatable human he's ever contracted. As a djinn from a 'polluted' bloodline, Velis knows what it's like to work twice as hard as everyone else, and he won't let anyone—not even Doll f*cking Jones—stand in the way of his birthright. He just needs t figure out her heart's greatest desire before his asshole brothe can get to her first.

COME TRUE: A BOMB-ASS GENIE ROMANCE is th romantic, fantastic second-coming-of-age story of two flawe twenty-somethings from different realms battling their inne demons, and each other, one wish at a time.

START READING NOW

ABOUT THE AUTHOR

Jenny is the founder of the PANdom and a lover of books with happily-ever-afters. A native of Oakland, Maryland, she currently resides in County Tipperary, Ireland with her husband and two children. As much as she loves writing stories, she hates writing biographies. So consider this the "filler" portion where she adds words to make the paragraph look longer.

CPSIA information can be obtained
at www.ICGtesting.com
Printed in the USA
BVHW030407140223
658390BV00004B/100

9 781953 23895